THE STREET
A Novel

Hrishikes Bhattacharya

STERLING

STERLING PUBLISHERS (P) LTD.
Regd. Office: A1/256 Safdarjung Enclave,
New Delhi-110029. CIN: U22110DL1964PTC211907
Tel: 26387070, 26386209; Fax: 91-11-26383788
E-mail: mail@sterlingpublishers.in
www.sterlingpublishers.in

The Street: A Novel
© 2018, Hrishikes Bhattacharya
PB ISBN 978 93 86245 39 7
HB ISBN 978 93 86245 40 3

All rights are reserved.
No part of this publication may be reproduced, stored in a retrieval system or transmitted, in any form or by any means, mechanical, photocopying, recording or otherwise, without prior written permission of the original publisher.

Printed in India

Printed and Published by Sterling Publishers Pvt. Ltd., Plot No. 13, Ecotech-III, Greater Noida - 201306, Uttar Pradesh, India

To

Anwesha

and

Aloke

who rekindled my latent desire to write on Street children

Your brethren you have treated with disrespect,
You have denied them their simple human rights.
You have made them stand and wait before you,
And not given them a place in your affection.
You must share with them all, their ignominy.

From your high seat you have cast them down,
With them was overthrown all your power.
There it grovels in the dust of the depressed,
If you must save yourself, descend to their depth.
You must share with them all, their ignominy.

Those you trample underfoot, drag you down,
Further backward they recede, the less you advance.
Shut off the light of knowledge from them
And a blind wall separates you from your well-being.
You must share with them all, their ignominy.

Do you not see the courier of death at your door,
ready to brand his stigma on the highest brow?
If in arrogance you shun your fellow-men and
remain withdrawn in your selfish vaunt,
then, in the ashes of vast cremation pyre,
You shall share with them all, their ignominy.

(Excerpts from the poem *Apomanito* by Rabindra Nath Tagore
translated by Kshitis Roy; it appeared in *Mainstream Annual* 1965 as *Nemesis*)

Chapter 1

It was past midnight when the rains came.

Sleepily he moved a little to his right as though to get cover under the sky; his hand touched the neck of another boy sleeping by his side. The other boy also stirred and moved a little further by sheer habit.

The day was hot as any other summer day; even in the wee hours of the morning people perspired. "Hottest of the year", he overheard the *paikar* say, for whom he worked for the day at Koley Market near Sealdah, but he did not feel much of the heat nor his friends who worked with him or for other *paikars*.

They welcomed the summer days because they felt light and free, more agile to steal away fruits and vegetables of value like apple, orange, pomegranate, grape, strawberry and onion, capsicum, beans, baby corns, mint leaves, et cetera, while unloading them from the trucks as the owner sat under a distant shade seething in the heat.

It was a repeat operation every day in the morning. The *paikars* knew the familiar faces; there would be some higgle-haggle as part of routine on wage per head and number of heads per truck. But these were settled quickly because of the competition among the *paikars* to take their wares inside the market at the earliest for display before the retailers started coming in hordes.

Generally, younger boys were not paid as they might not be able to carry the load, but they could be around to help the seniors push the baskets and bundles, though their real job was to steal select articles and quickly store them in a safe place. If per chance any of them got caught by the vendor, he was beaten up both by the vendor and his men, and also by the senior boys; the trust thus re-established, the work started again, but in the commotion and diverted attention, some more goods quickly passed hands.

After the *paikar* went inside the market the boys met at a pre-arranged place to take stock of the stolen goods, no concern shown to the beaten boys nor did they care. The goods were sorted out, put in separate jute bags, each under the charge of a senior boy who carried it away from the vicinity of the wholesale market and sold them on the pavements outside the municipal retail market at a discount.

The entire operation now over in about two hours time, all the groups went back to the Sealdah station yard, each one under a stationary station wagon and pooled together all the amount collected by each member of the group, which was shared equally among all members of the group including the younger ones irrespective of contribution made. In some groups the younger children at times got somewhat less than the seniors but these were settled before the trucks arrived; the juniors would bargain hard to settle their share which depended on the demand for their services which in turn depended on the arrival of number of trucks; if the demand was high they would claim equal share.

The members of each group having pocketed their share of earnings now dispersed and drifted away to where they even did not know; some might come back the following day, some might not.

This day had been good as more number of trucks arrived from other states who did not haggle much. He thought himself to be rich and chose to go to a country liquor pub instead of a hooch *thek* in the backyard of the railway station. He had frequented this pub before and knew some of the counter boys there. He approached one of them with a smile of recognition, paid for a pint and settled himself on a corner bench. At this time of the day there usually was not much crowd; he was the lone occupant of the bench. As soon as he opened the bottle a boy smaller than him came with an aluminium dish brimming with soaked grams and finely sliced onions. He looked at the counter boy with a broad smile and thanked him for his generosity. Relaxed, he lighted a Charminar cigarette and swallowed a small gulp of liquor followed by a handful of salads. It was blissful; he closed his eyes to savour it.

But soon he was startled by the sound of a knuckle-rap on the bench. He opened his eyes to find a boy sitting by his side with a bottle. He was annoyed but stopped short of expressing it; the boy had a charming, innocent smile, looked younger but was taller than him, and wore a multicoloured half-shirt and a wrist watch. He must have seen him somewhere before but where he could not recollect. The boy smiled once again and asked.

'What's your name?'
'What's yours?'
'Ask the Ma'am.'
'Ask the Ma'am.'
They burst out in high-pitched laughter, not uncommon in such a joint.
'Let's settle then, me, Boomba.'
'Me, Toomba.'
Again there was laughter and wide smiles. Two small palms glued together.

Taking a large gulp from the bottle Boomba said, 'I saw you this morning unloading the trucks with your gang. I'm amazed by your skill in organising the steal, quite a leader you are!'

'That's why you looked familiar; I noticed particularly the colours splashed on the shirt you are wearing.'

'This is a gift from a client who felt so good and hot after taking a swish of the drug, as to peel off the shirt from his body and throw it at me saying, "This is all yours". It's a silk shirt, must be quite costly, but it is also very conspicuous. I'll sell it off to a road-side hawker of Gariahat, but before that I want to wear it at least for a day to feel its smooth texture.'

'That's not a bad idea. Now tell me did you follow me to this joint?' Toomba was now serious.

'Yes, I was. I'll tell you why but before that let me bring two more bottles and some food, ours are nearly finished. It's all on me today.'

Boomba went to the counter, paid for the bottles and two plates of chicken kebab. When the bottles and food were placed on the counter he winked at Toomba who had his gaze fixed on Boomba all the time, now walked to the counter. They carried between them the bottles and food plates and set them on the wide bench.

After taking a gulp and putting a piece of kebab in his mouth Boomba said between munching, 'Yes, I did follow you here for a purpose.'

'I could guess as much. Now tell me why?'

Boomba took another small gulp but no kebab this time and began rather slowly.

'I told you I was impressed by your cool organising skill that comes only from a leader...'

Toomba cut him short.

'You are wrong; I'm no leader. Perhaps you don't know the kind of work we do here. Every one of us is equally competent. We just select a volunteer for the day who shall conduct the operation. Tomorrow it could be some other boy and you'd be equally impressed.'

'What a waste! Now tell me how much you earn in a day—not more than two hundred, three hundred, eh, which means...,' he began calculating slowly by the lines of his fingers for a minute or so, then exasperated in trying the arithmetic blurted out, 'Ok, five thousand for thirty days' work? Do you think...'

Toomba interjected.

'I don't work for all the thirty days of a month, I work whenever I feel like. I may not even work when I have no money.'

'Then how do you live?'

'I don't live. I enjoy. I spend my money quickly in booze and drugs with my friends. When the money is finished I inhale Dendrite—a pack of which I always carry—for half an hour; reach the pinnacle of pleasure and stay there for many hours or days I don't know. I should have been dead but I always wake up, and that's the fucking problem with life. Do you know what I feel when I wake up? I feel frustrated, more so because, I feel hungry and that's bad'.

'Very, very interesting, unlike the boys I grew up with', said Boomba and rose to buy another two pints of white liquor and some kebabs. When he settled the bottles and kebabs—this time mutton ones—and turned to Toomba he found that he was observing him intently.

'What is that?' Boomba asked.

'Well, I have already guessed you're not like me. You must've been brought under some, say a *Dada*—no, not a Dada, if it were you wouldn't have those fluffs on your cheeks; a roadside family, perhaps a *mashi*, which means you have some anchor, howsoever loose it might be, but I have no anchor nor I desire to have one.'

Boomba was surprised at Toomba's critical observation which happened to be correct. He felt he had made a right choice of leader, who though disowned leadership, could be a good friend, though a little high for him, but that's what made a leader. He knew he could no longer operate alone and needed someone to work with or under, more particularly in the new field he had just entered. And Toomba was the right person. Should he tell him now or later; surprisingly, he had not yet asked the vital question.

He turned to Toomba but he was no longer looking at him but at a distance he did not belong. He stroked Toomba's back to draw attention.

'You know, you're right. What surprises me is that you're so young, not more than two years older than me, but how keen is your observation—much better than Mashi's; well, yes, I was brought up by her and in a way I'm still under her, but I can walk out any time'.

'I guess so', Toomba was somewhat sarcastic and that enraged Boomba.

'Yes, I'll leave her; a week back I had a terrible fight with her and I haven't seen her face since then. She is a terrible woman, ugly, fat, with a terrible mouth—always trying to boss over me. I'll definitely leave her, and today itself I'll tell it on her face.'

'I guess this must be the hundredth time you'd made such a promise.'

Boomba looked at Toomba for some time, then his lips widened with a boyish smile. He put his right hand around Toomba's neck and said, 'Well, I don't know but I love that filthy woman.'

'I know'.

'Bloody hell, you know!' Boomba slapped him on the back and both burst out in an inebriated laughter.

'Let's go then and meet your ugly, filthy Mashi'.

They walked out with tipsy legs clasping each other's hand: one four and a half feet, and the other a little over five feet. Now they were real boys walking hand in hand, all precocious talks left behind.

Toomba began singing, swaying his head side ways:

'*Amay thakte de na apon monay... Amay thakte de na apon monay...*'

Boomba also joined repeating the same line: '*Amay thakte de na apon monay... Amay thakte de na apon monay...,*' none of them knew the other lines of the song.

In between singings Toomba asked in a tipsy voice, 'Can you guess why I sing this line of the song always?'

''Cause first, you don't know the other lines, and second, it speaks of your life—"Allow me to live by my wish."'

'Yes. But it is always a wishful desire that is never realised. Till this morning I was on my own; a sonofabitch descended from nowhere, and I'm now going with him—*Amay thakte de na apon monay.* Bullshit!'

Boomba gave him a mischievous smile and moved on:

'*Amay thakte de na apon monay...*

Amay thakte de na apon monay...'

It was afternoon. Footpaths and roadsides were filling up with people walking hurriedly. They often jostled with passers-by. Some just pushed them aside, some passed remarks, which they did not care except one...

As they went on signing the same line while walking, Boomba suddenly stopped by the side of the road realising that they had already reached Lansdowne-Hazra Road crossing, and now they'd have to make a choice of which turn to take. The long walk had washed off much of their inebriation but they continued to behave like two drunkards, as though by habit. As they stopped abruptly they got jostled by a six-foot burly and fell on the road. They rose quickly and looked back with curse in their eyes. But before they could utter something the young man reacted: '*Sala harami-ka-Bachha*, drunk at this age, you pair of bastards!'

What had happened next Boomba could not imagine. In a flash Toomba leaped and clasped the throat of the six-foot. They fell on the ground— Toomba on top of him beating his face mercilessly uttering a single sentence repeatedly: '*Sala,* your father's a bastard...'

By that time a small crowd had gathered round them, but none intervened, they were enjoying the sight of a four and a half feet beating a six-footer. A voice was heard from the crowd, 'Brave boy, beat him to bleed'; another voice said, "Hey big man, don't you feel ashamed taking on a small boy!' Soon others joined in chorus. Somehow the young man got himself free and stood up wiping his bruised face with a handkerchief, and looked around. He wanted to say something but the crowd would not allow nor would Toomba, who once again jumped at his throat.

Boomba was stunned at the ferocity of Toomba; so long he stood still, now coming back to his senses he thought it was time to intervene. He pushed back the crowd, caught Toomba's striking hand and said softly, 'Leave him Toomba; he got what he deserved. Let's go now.'

Toomba looked at Boomba's solemn, sincere face and said, 'Ok, let's go'. He raised his small second finger, strained it to the eyes of his adversary, uttered something through his clenched teeth and walked out holding Boomba's hand. The crowd moved back opening a passage for them, as if a hero was leaving the arena after winning a bull fight.

They crossed the road and walked some distance to enter a park named after a great man. Both felt tired: Boomba for his long walk and Toomba for release of tension. Lying face up to the sky Boomba asked, 'Do you know the man by whom the park is named?'

'No. Who was that?'

'He was a great man who fought for the freedom of our country.'

'Yes, yes, I've read about him in the school text book, but he wasn't like us, did he do anything for us?'

'Stupid! He struggled to make us free from the clutches of the *Angrez*, a great barrister he was, very rich, but left everything for the freedom struggle'.

'Ah ha, that's why we are so free, and free children like us are coming to the street every day. But look at all the houses over there. The inmates there are not as free as we are. I think your great barrister hasn't done anything for them.'

Boomba was not very sure whether Toomba was pulling his leg, but he went silent for a few moments. Bits of every day sights flashed before him; toddlers and children being pushed to the school buses every morning, some crying, some who stood obstinately to the ground were cajoled, thrashed and beaten by their parents and herded to the buses honking furiously; prison—prison van—back to the prison. He also heard the shrill cry of the children in the evening that pierced through all available pores of the concrete.

'You are probably right', Boomba said hesitantly as he at times fancied to become one of them.

'Ok. Forget it,' said Toomba with a yawn, 'but tell me how you have become such a *gyani;* who taught you all these?'

'Well it was an *Enjo* woman who once brought us to this park for a 'Sit and Draw' kind of thing.'
'Fuck the *Enjos!*'
'Fuck them all!'
The two urchins now rose nodding their heads gravely as though a great issue had finally been resolved.

They walked leisurely for some time before stopping at a roadside tea stall. Boomba ordered two large teas and sat side by side with Toomba on a bench.

Boomba turned to Toomba after taking the first sip of the tea.

'One thing that surprises me still is that you've not once asked the actual purpose of my befriending you; you've just come with me, as if we know each other for ages.'

Toomba was not looking at him, he rather looked at the tea maker or, perhaps nowhere when he answered.

'No doubt, I'm going with you to Gariahat to meet your ugly Mashi but also to make friends in the south. I like mixing with street people: good, bad, fools I don't mind; I participate in their activities: good, bad, legal, illegal, I don't care. I know though, the friendship in the street is volatile, purpose-oriented, a matter of convenience as I am to you right now. But I've also seen these selfish street dwellers coming together to fight for a common cause. I try to pick up the good traits and ignore the wrong ones according to my own criteria. You may be a devil and your purpose more devilish, I don't care.'

They resumed their walk towards Gariahat. After some time Boomba ventured.

'May I ask you something if you don't mind?'
'Go ahead.'
'All of us are abused all the time; in fact, the filthy terms we've learnt only from the civilised people, we even do not know their meaning, all *English*; some time we return the abuses back to them, that's all; we never really cared. But I've noticed when that sonofabitch at the Lansdowne crossing called you bastard you jumped at him with murder in your eyes. Why?'

"Cause I'm a bastard. I feel like killing all the bastards who call me bastard.'

They commenced walking silently. Toomba saw Boomba suddenly ran ahead and picked up something from the road side. When he came near him he found Boomba holding two beautiful tiny glass balls in one hand and a much used tennis ball in the other. Boomba said, 'Look how sparkling these glass balls are and how the patterns inside them change when you move them on your palm.' He was so amused he did not even notice when the tennis ball dropped from his other hand. Toomba picked it up, and examined it carefully;

no leakage, still good to play with. He hit the ball on the asphalt; it bounced back to his grip. He did it again and again enjoying the game immensely. Boomba got distracted by the continual thek-thok-thek-thok sounds by his side. Still playing with the marbles he observed what Toomba was doing. He told him, "I'm finished with the marbles, and I want to play the ball now; give it to me and take the marbles instead." Toomba replied without stopping the game, 'I don't care about the marbles, the ball is good to play with; I won't give it to you.'

'But I picked up the ball, not you; it's mine.' Boomba retorted angrily.

'No. You dropped it and I picked it up; it's mine now.'

'No, it's mine!' Boomba shouted and tried to catch the bouncing ball but without success as Toomba smilingly hand-dribbled the ball away from Boomba's reaches.

Frustrated, Boomba shouted again, 'Stop your dribbling and hand over the ball to me.' Toomba presently stopped bouncing the ball and replied coaxingly.

'Okay, don't fret. Let's come to an agreement: I'll give you the ball though not now, but surely before I go to sleep tonight.'

Boomba thought for a moment then asked.

'Promise.'

'Promise.'

As they resumed walking Toomba thought: the boy is still a child, amenable easily, needs a lot of growing up.

It was nearly evening when they reached Gariahat road junction. Afternoon lights began folding up the long stretches underneath the flyover as fluorescents lit up the shops adorning both sides of the roads. Toomba followed Boomba to a make-shift camp-like *jhopri*—about six feet by four, covered on all sides by tattered tarpaulin sheets, jute bags and sundry other things with a small opening at the front; one had to crawl to go inside. The stench, the putrid smell and an occasional burst of perfume from a swinging girl hurriedly taking a short cut through the stretch were all familiar.

A woman was frying something; nearby, two naked children—a boy and a girl—with rheum in their eyes were crawling to other *jhopris,* always dabbling something which they only knew ; some gave them bits of biscuits and other eatables which they immediately put inside their mouth and immediately looked back at the woman for an indulgent smile.

So, this must be Boomba's 'ugly' Mashi, Toomba smiled to himself. She wasn't ugly, rather an attractive woman: fair complexioned, buxom, a mass of hair on the head, hardly any greys; only a few hard lines on a small forehead, all sites filled with appropriate features, but all within the garb of street attire—the tattered sari which needed a wash, the blouse with holes and the pungent smell they exuded.

When they neared, Boomba said jovially, 'Hey Mashi, I'm back to your snooty *theck.*'

The woman looked up with venom in the upper eyelid and indulgence in the lower lid and burst out.

'Why come back? Are you doing me a favor? *Sala harami,* it's almost a week I haven't seen your dirty face, why show it now?' Then, her eyes darted on to his dress, 'Oh! You're also wearing a flashy shirt, looks like a monkey... though a handsome one.' She suddenly broke into a smile and said, 'Now that you have come, you may eat one or two *pakoras* I'm frying.' Simultaneously she called in the two toddlers, 'Hey, Google and Googlee, you may come back to have your *pakoras* too but you won't eat them now; these are very hot.' The kids looked back and began crawling fast.

Toomba was enjoying the scene. Besides a cursory look, the woman did not notice him in particular. A good number of boys had gathered along the stretch, some of them including a girl now thronged towards Mashi's camp, may be hearing the shouts or attracted by the aroma of fried *pakoras.*

Boomba and Toomba sat together on their haunches before Mashi. For the first time she actually noticed Toomba.

'Who is he?' she asked.

'Oh! He is Toomba, my friend.'

'Toomba, my god! That was your name a week back.'

'It's his now.'

'You two are up to some dirty tricks I guess, though I don't care as long as I get my twenty rupees per day, else I'd throw all your belongings to this *sigri.*'

'Ok, ok. Now stop shouting further, you've already gathered a crowd. Tell me how much I owe you?'

Mashi calculated: 'For seven days at rupees twenty a day, it's hundred forty plus sixty for being long away; total two hundred rupees. Give the money now before you eat *pakoras.*'

'Okay.' Boomba peeled out two hundred-rupee notes from his pile and handing them over to Mashi said, 'Now give us the *pakoras;* I promise even if they taste leather we shall eat them.'

Mashi looked at the other side of the stretch and exclaimed. 'Lo! Your bunch of nincompoops is waiting there.'

'You rail them so much they're scared to come near you,' Boomba replied diffidently.

'What'd I do? Feed them from my hand? Now without making me angrier get some dried sal leaves from inside the jhopri.'

Two kids also extended their hands out as Boomba began arranging the sal leaves. Boomba put one leaf each on their tiny hands. Seeing this Mashi cried out, 'You won't get them now, these are pretty hot, you will burn your tongues, let them cool a little.'

She put some *pakoras* on the leaf-plates of Boomba and Toomba and also filled two more plates and asked Boomba, 'Now give these to your useless friends, otherwise yours won't digest'.

As Boomba rose with the two plates Toomba looked at Mashi: he understood now why Boomba loved the woman with 'the ugly face'; she looked a mother now, the hard lines of her forehead smoothened by comeliness. Toomba felt a pang in his heart, though momentarily.

When Boomba returned they began eating the *pakoras* one by one unmindful of the children who now began crying loudly for which they got slaps from Mashi, the crying now turned to whimper. Boomba drew the kids to him and putting bits of munched *pakoras* to their mouths asked Mashi, 'Where from you got them? I hadn't seen them when I left.'

'I got them from Howrah station four days back. Bichhu, who is now a leader there, informed me over mobile phone that two kids were crawling the entire station area with an exasperated railway constable running after them. The police waited three days for a claimant to materialise, but none came. That morning they informed some NGOs but none appeared till that time. I immediately went to the house where Chameli now works, enacted some serious drama to get her out, took a taxi and went to the station. Some more drama—crying-frying—and now they are here.'

'New assets, more income, poor children,' Boomba muttered under his breath. But Mashi heard them alright. Raising the hot spud she flared up, 'What the hell I could do otherwise? You have virtually left me, Chameli might do the same any time, a few urchins who are still with me already showing signs of independence, particularly after your gang beat up Jaggu—you didn't care, no mercy—he could be my husband any time soon.' Her voice went down to remorse. Boomba tried to mollify her.

'But Mashi, you know he tried to sell some very young ones of our stretch to Ilabu gang who maim children for their *vhikari* business.'

'Why would he? He knows me, and knows that I haven't done any such things to my wards, I hate Ilabu for this and Jaggu knows that, he would never dare...'

Boomba was angry. He murmured, 'You are just a shade better than Ilabu', and then said loudly, 'I've definite information he joined Ilabu, you must've also found out the truth by now but you close your eyes for a spot of vermillion on your forehead.'

Mashi did not respond to Boomba's accusation; she became silent, her mind elsewhere, eyes turned soft. When she spoke it seemed it was coming from a distance.

'You do not as yet know what love is but some day you will. Jaggu was my anchor in this street world full of mischief and betrayals. He went to jail because of his intense love for me and that's why in my heart of heart I don't believe he joined Ilabu but I could not also ignore what the neighbours were saying. After your gang threw him out of the *mohalla* he came stealthily to me one night for reconciliation. But I shouted at him, called him names, beat him up with a splinter wood, and finally threw him out of the *jhopri*. By that time many inhabitants of this stretch woke up and rushed in with whatever they could pick up. Though lame in one leg the bastard ran like Milkha Singh. They all laughed. I also joined the laughter but... but I felt so sad after his yellow T-shirt vanished at the corner of Fern Road. All went back to their respective sleeping space, but I stood there silently straining my eyes to the corner of the road through which he vanished. Then I realised I love him still whatever it is and whatever he is.'

After Mashi's remorseful litany silence engulfed the space between them, then Boomba shrugged his shoulders and blurted out.

'Whatever it is between you I don't understand, maybe I'll when I grow up, but I promise, if I see that pig anywhere near Gariahat again I'll beat him to death'.

Mashi flared up. '*Tu sala, son of a harami*, a filthy worm of gutter, who are you to beat him? If you dare again I'll break your legs, which I should have done long back when I found you in that railway compartment. Besides, who do you think you are? You talk as if you own this place, are you a zamindar, hah? Get out of my sight right now and never dare come back!' She fumed with venom in her eyes.

By now a small crowd had gathered around them talking simultaneously, taking side, changing side, but all arguing with gusto.

Without uttering a single word Boomba pushed aside the crowd, took Toomba's hand, and walked out.

They walked silently, aimlessly.

Toomba ruminated as he walked: all the time they were at Mashi's place no one spoke to him, nor enquired who he was besides Mashi, though tangentially, but that too only once. All the street dwellers who gathered around tried to pacify both Mashi and Boomba, but none took him in even by signs. They behaved as if he did not exist, but he saw them eyeing him surreptitiously, making an estimate of him. It did not surprise him; this was the practice in their world where the boys and girls would always try to form group with likeables to put up a joint front to beat the uncertainties surrounding them, to find a little space among transient moments, and he was an uncertain character who might crack up that space. 'Fools!' he muttered to himself. Nevertheless, he enjoyed all that happened since he met Boomba. Now he nudged him with his elbow and declared like a juror.

'I think you are doomed forever, and your Mashi already a corpse, though a Tantric one that rises on occasions'.

'Yeah, I know that.'

Again they walked silently. Suddenly they heard someone shouting at the back, 'Paltu, hey Paltu...' Boomba looked back and stopped. The girl also stopped. She said amidst pants: 'Why are you leaving so soon? I heard you had a fight with Mashi but that's routine. You never sulked and left like this before, why now? I saw you there but couldn't stay back as I'd to immediately return to *baudi's* place to help her with cooking. She had given me four chapattis and some *kasha* meat. We shall eat them together, please come back.' Speaking so many words in one breath, she was now breathless.

Boomba heard her silently with a weary smile. After she finished he told her somberly.

'Go back Champi. I'd taken so much during the day I've no hunger left. Share the food with Mashi and her toddlers. I'm leaving for good.'

Boomba turned and walked briskly leaving both the girl and Toomba standing on the footpath stupefied. Toomba silently appraised the girl, nodded his head, and then walked fast to catch up with Boomba.

When he reached him he put a hand on his shoulder and remarked jocularly.

'Now I feel, besides being doomed, you are screwed up as well.'

'No!' shouted Boomba at such a high pitch the pedestrians turned to look at them, but finding nothing serious moved on.

Toomba tried to keep pace with Boomba who had now increased his pace considerably toward a definite direction; he could now guess where.

They arrived in front of a shack by the railway lines off Ballygunge station where some boys and men sat on a dimly lit grassy stretch in a semi-circle with glasses filled with grey liquid, a few aluminium plates containing minced onions and grams sautéed together with a little mustard oil scattered around them.

The boys acknowledged Boomba with drunken smiles. In a minute, a woman emerged from inside the shack and placed before them two glasses and a pair of polyethylene pouches. They tore a corner of the pouch with their teeth and poured the contents in their glasses. Boomba now pulled out a small plastic packet from his hip pocket; inside there were two *purias,* which he picked out carefully, gave one to Toomba and kept the other for him. Simultaneously they opened their packs of Charminar cigarettes; each took one out, rubbed the stick between their palms to draw out its contents on the lap half of which was thrown away, the other half now mixed with the contents of the *puria* were pushed slowly back to the hollow of the cigarette cover with a match stick. They examined their newly made cigarettes for tightness; satisfied, they lighted them with the same match stick. Taking a lungful of smoke and releasing it slowly through their nose they raised their glasses and clinked:

'Fuck them all!'

'Fuck them all!'

How many pouches they had consumed none kept a count. As the night was gaining hours, others started leaving one by one. When the last one, a boy of Boomba's height, patted his back with "carry on my friend" in a mellowed voice and left in uncertain steps, they looked around to find none besides them. Boomba thought unconsciously it was also time for them to leave. He shouted, *Baudi.* The woman appeared hurriedly with two more pouches but Boomba straightening himself said, 'No more tonight', and brought out all the money from his pocket and laid it on the grass: 'Count your money, don't cheat.' Silently she collected her due and left.

They crossed the station area and took the footpath, now strewn with sleeping mankind; people of various sizes, shapes and colours spread out in so many angles and postures as though they were dropped from helicopters, or God's chariot: dead soldiers in a battle field. The two moved carefully through them measuring space between sprawled bodies. They were drunk but their legs were not, abuses and beatings in the streets had trained them up.

Toomba brought out the ball from his pocket but stopped short of bouncing it, instead he gave it to Boomba. The stretch under the flyover and all the pavements were full. They crossed the footpath to find some space under the shades of large shops. From a distance they located a few spaces here and there, but when they came closer they saw movements under some semblance of covers with whispers and low key panting. They retreated with Boomba muttering sleepily, 'Hah! I always wonder what these *sala-salis* do under cover, may be they exchange *pisses* by pushing one another there. Whatever it is, it sure is good, and someday I'll sure learn and do it with Champi.'

Finally they found some space away from the crossing under the open sky, and fell on side by side, Boomba still clutching the ball. The last words Toomba spoke before passing into oblivion, 'This *basta* is totally fucked up.'

'Screw you', Boomba responded from afar.

Chapter 2

When Paltu (Boomba) left Chameli on Gariahat road despite her crying entreaties to come back and share the food with her, which he liked most among all things, she was dumbfounded, didn't even run after him further: that boy... that boy... she thought, must be responsible for his unusual behaviour. Wherefrom he picked him up she did not know, must be from gutter, and all her anger got directed towards him. She must do something to separate them but what and how she didn't know.

She looked as far as she could see but there was no sign of them; must've taken an alley to avoid her: "Let them go to hell, why would she bother?" she told herself leaning against the wall of a building adjoining the pavement.

A cry welled up shivering her entire being. She tried to control it by telling herself: "Why would she cry for that *harami* who could just walk out of everything they have cherished and lived for. All the sharing, all the care and compassion, all the anger, the fights and frustrations they had passed through together from their babyhood have just vanished because he has a fight with Mashi! It just can't happen; it must be that boy who has poisoned him; Paltu would soon get rid of him and come back to her." She thumped her feet on the pavement and felt happy.

Chameli did not remember how long she stood on the footpath. She was startled to her senses when she heard, 'Hey girl, like to come with me?' She saw two leering eyes licking her up and down. She fixed her gaze with that of his, spat right on his eyes and marched back to Mashi's place. She did not talk to her, nor to the toddlers who were being fed by Mashi; went inside the hut, pulled out all the food she had brought from *baudi's* place, and throwing them to dogs went to sleep at her designated place.

She was restive in her sleep, frequently changing sides and getting startled even by the smallest of sounds despite the cool atmosphere due to heavy rains past midnight.

This was unlikely of her as she was known to be a sound sleeper; too sound, as Mashi often said, to wake up even if a drum was beaten by her ears. Many a times Mashi had to throw water over her—splash after splash—to awaken her from sleep as she had to reach the *baudi's* place by seven in the morning, help her prepare breakfast for the husband and two children followed by cooking of tiffin and arranging them in appropriate boxes by 9 a.m. when the children would leave for school and the husband for the office. But this morning it was different. She woke up early with the horn of the first car moving by the road, did her ablutions and reached *baudi's* house before time.

She did not return to feed the kids during the noon, which she took upon herself since the day they came here. She searched every nook and corner of Gariahat and the adjoining areas—from Rashbehari Avenue to Ballygunge Station to Park Circus to Jadavpur—but Boomba was nowhere to be seen, nor that *harami,* his new found friend. She returned to Gariahat late in the evening, stood before Mashi and asked for hundred rupees with an edge in her voice. Mashi observed her quietly, brought in the money from inside the hut. She snatched the money from her hand and walked briskly toward Dhakuria overbridge. On reaching the approach to the bridge she took a left turn and peeped into a range of tea stalls bordering the footpath that turned hooch *theck* at night fall. She located Minu, as she knew she would, at one such *theck* and went in.

The place was dimly lit. Minu sat on the floor, leaning against a young man who had a bottle in one hand and another hand loosely hanging from her neck—the palm dangling before her breast, two empty bottles and one half-full lay before them. When she saw Chameli she exclaimed in her peculiar nasal voice, which she often claimed could just kill a man.

'Aye, Chameli, welcome to our joint.' Shoving the hand of her night's paramour she said, 'Now go and sit at the opposite corner. I'll be with my friend for some time.' The young man nodded meekly, took his bottle and quietly moved to the other side.

'Now tell me what brought you here. I know you don't drink—a goody type. Any quarrel with Mashi or that *basta* Paltu.'

'Order a bottle for me, I'll pay for it,' she said in a gruff voice.

'Ok, ok. Hey Ghana, bring a bottle here, quick.'

Chameli grabbed the bottle when it came, uncorked it and began gulping the content so fast as though to finish it in one breath. Minu snatched the bottle from her hand and said softly.

'Not that fast, take it slowly, or it will kill you.'

'I don't care'

Minu looked at her closely. Even in dim light she could see tears welling up in her eyes. She pulled her up by the hand with a 'Let's go', and told the fellow sitting opposite, 'Hey, not tonight; I'm going with my friend, pay for all the bottles', and walked out.

They walked back towards Golpark, crossed Ramakrishna Mission and entered a twilight area by its side and sat under the balcony of a dilapidated building, once owned by a Maharaja.

'Now tell me what has happened?' Minu asked.

Chameli clung to Minu and burst out crying. Minu gently rubbed her back. In between sobs Chameli uttered, 'Paltu has left me.'

'But why?'

'He fought Mashi on Jaggudada. I wasn't there at that time but came soon thereafter and learnt Paltu had just left with that *basta* of a boy. I ran and caught up with him. I entreated upon him to come back, but imagine what he said in reply, "I'm leaving for good"; he even refused to share the food which I brought from *baudi's* place. Tell me, he might be angry with Mashi but what has it to do with me, why should he leave me, as he said, for good; how could he be so cruel as to forget everything we have from babyhood?'

Chameli again started crying. Minu cradled her like a child. She realised she had developed a soft corner in her mind for the girl, the mind which she thought she had buried long back. She smiled to herself, confused though she was with this realisation. Was it good or bad to still have a softness retained in her mind without being aware of it? Why had this girl come running to *her* only? Had she ever given out any signals to her from the deep of her consciousness? Must've, she thought. In her present world to which this girl also belonged, a softness of mind was doomening, this girl had much of it, she much less. But what to do with this girl? Though she belonged to this world she had all the aspirations of the other world; she could foresee a miserable life for her. It was time she should warn her. But should she? Why not let her enjoy the bliss of joy and pangs of being born even if, for moments only.'

She lifted her face and stroked her back softly.

'Don't you worry, he'll be back.'

'You sure?' 'Yes'. 'Soon?' 'Yes.'

Chameli returned to Gariahat without the gloom she had when she left. She asked for dinner from Mashi, ate it heartily and went to sleep. But sleep eluded her this night also though for different reasons. So many things were coming to her mind like passing scenes of a movie.

Chapter 3

Chameli and Paltu's lives centred on Mashi from the day they were found abandoned in railway compartments at Sealdah station.

One of her boys while searching for valuables and bits of food articles left by passengers in their hurry to get down from the train found a girl child sleeping in a second class compartment of a long distance down train; another found a boy crying in an air-conditioned compartment. They took them to Mashi who first put aside the girl at the back to avoid the prying eyes of the police and NGOs and then took the boy on her lap as if, he was her now-found lost child. The boy who found the girl named her, Chameli after his long lost sister and the one who found the boy called him Paltu, just like that. And the names stayed with them.

Paltu was crying incessantly which could draw the attention of the police or a NGO operative in the station. Mashi moved to a side facing the wall, uncovered one of her breasts sideways and put Paltu's mouth to the nipple. He was silent for some moments, and then pushing back the breast began wailing as though from pain. Mashi observed the contorted face of the boy for some time and thought: babies cry out of frustration when they find a dry nipple, they never wail; it must be something else. She began examining the small body closely and soon located the source of pain. It was underneath the tight breech: an ulcer of the size of a one-rupee coin. She took out the breech slowly, pressed the wound with her index finger; the tiny body convulsed to a heart rending cry. A cryptic smile appeared on her face. She patted the boy, kissed him on his forehead and brought out a small bottle of coconut oil and a vial of camphor from inside a jute bag lying by her side, mixed the two together and applied the mixture slowly on the wound with puffs of air from her mouth, and began cradling the boy on her lap. The boy was soon asleep. Mashi laid him down on a rag before her.

The girl observed everything from behind. Seeing the boy putting his mouth to the nipple of Mashi's breast she also felt thirsty for breast milk and crawled out from hiding on to Mashi's lap. She opened Mashi's breasts with practised hands and sucked and sucked the nipple of both the breasts with all her breath. Mashi felt a different sensation, pressed her head to the bosom and laid back to savour it. But the girl quickly left the breasts and crawled back in frustration; the girl's frustration was her frustration too.

After recovering from the shock Mashi began planning for the utilisation of the new found assets. She knew another mashi in the station area who specialised in begging with babies. She collected toddling babies every morning from street mothers at a fixed rate of hundred rupees per day, fed them during the day and returned them in the evening. The arrangement was advantageous for both the parties: the parents who worked during the day would have their children under some protective custody, assured feeding and also some money at the end of the day—children otherwise don't earn, they only add to costs. For the beggar woman earnings increased manifold when she posed herself as an unfortunate mother of babies she could not feed. Cripple babies or those with visible wounds had a premium price.

Mashi learnt that this mashi presently had no child under her care: those she had, were now grown up and taken back by their parents. She was on the lookout for new crops.

Mashi offered her Paltu and Chameli: price settled was hundred fifty rupees for the boy and hundred for the girl.

Every morning Mashi would feed them, dress up Chameli with a colourful drawer, and apply enough coconut oil on Paltu's ulcer, which made it look more ghastly to an observer. The beggar woman would come to take them at eight in the morning.

She sat at a corner of the first landing of the staircase leading to city roads with Paltu on her lap and Chameli crawling by her side. The first things she did after putting Paltu on her lap were to take off Chameli's drawer which made her happy, and scratch Paltu's ulcer which made him cry fiercely that drew attention of the passengers many of whom would stand for a while retching at the ugly ulcer and put money in rupee notes on her proffered hand often with some small advices like visiting a doctor which the woman reciprocated by a nod; some others who were in a hurry would give coins; a section mostly composed of regular passengers would pass by with comments ranging from the capacity of the woman to produce children every six months to banning of this kind of begging by the government, while another section knowing though the falsity of the set up, give a few coins as a matter of habit.

Chameli did not at first understand the reason for Paltu's intermittent bursts of cry which happened about four-five times a day. When Chameli for the first time heard him cry she crawled to him fast, observed his contorted face but understood nothing. She kissed his forehead as Mashi did and tried to copy her lullaby, '*Sona... amar sona...*' but except for some '*Aanh... Aanh...*' nothing came out, but the wailing stopped a while, a smile though twisted appeared on his face, a tiny hand came down to his leg pointing the source of the pain. Chameli immediately knew what to do. She began blowing on the wound as much air as her tiny mouth and small lungs allowed, but she had no oil to apply on it as Mashi did. She looked around but found no such bottle of oil. Frustrated, she concentrated on blowing air, but not for long. The beggar woman shoved her out, she again came back, again shoved back which continued for some time, then she got her first slap but she was adamant, then the second slap, this time harder and more painful that made her cry. She crawled out but kept a watch on Paltu. The beggar woman now scratched Paltu's ulcer with her nails which made him cry louder than before. Chameli felt a sensation inside her mixed of anger and pity. She crawled back again to give him some relief but the woman held her back. '*Anayee... anayee...*', she tried to wriggle out of her grasp but failed. She raised her little face and looked at the woman with so much anger that could burn a mortal in the olden days of *Rishis* and Gods, but she was no *Rishi*, just a helpless child at a nook of Sealdah station where God's power never reached; she got instead a thrash from the woman that made her reel down the steps. She was caught in the middle by a young woman who carried her back to the beggar woman. Though her body was bruised, her eyes were dry; she continued her '*Anayee... anayee...*' trying to complain to her rescuer by first pointing to the ulcer on Paltu's leg and then to the beggar woman.

'What happened, what is she trying to say?' the woman asked.

'Oh-ho, this little girl of mine is so restive. I've been telling her all the time not to venture down the stairs lest she fell and hurt herself, but will she ever hear? This time I turned to apply some camphor oil on this ulcer of my son as he was crying of pain, but when I turned back she was not in her place. I had a premonition someday it'd happen, and it has happened today. But for you there could have been a fatal injury; I'm really thankful to you.' The beggar woman tried to remove dirt from Chameli's body with the edge of her sari but she turned away.

In the meantime the other woman was examining Paltu's wound closely. She now turned to the woman.

'The ulcer is bad, it's expanding. Why don't you take her to the nearby hospital where I also work as a nurse?'

'How can I go? My day's earning will be lost, how am I going to feed them?'

The woman nodded her head understandingly.

'All right, I'll bring some *purias* tomorrow, sprinkle the contents of one *puria* on the wound thrice daily, it'll be cured soon, don't worry'. The woman put a ten-rupee note on her hand, patted Paltu, caressed Chameli and left.

Chameli did not understand what the two women talked, but guessed the beggar woman must have lied because the other woman who had rescued her did not chastise her. She concluded: this beggar-woman was bad, the other woman good. She decided to complain to Mashi. But how? She could not talk like them, neither could Paltu, they could not also run away as she saw others doing it in the station area; they could not even stand on their own feet! Frustrated she began crying, tears running down her cheeks.

She refused to take the feed of cereals mixed with milk offered by the beggar woman.

She was not crying any longer. Anger had put a lid on her frustration. She had a determination now. She began observing closely how the passers-by walked: how they put forward one leg after another: that was walking; make the leg movement faster as some passengers did to catch a train: that was running. She now knew the methods, had to practise to make them perfect, and for that she must stand on her feet first. The resolution made her happy; a smile appeared on her face. Observing this the beggar woman once again offered her the feed. This time she took it.

In the evening the woman took them to Mashi, gave her two hundred fifty rupees and was about to leave when Mashi observed the bruise marks on Chameli's body.

'Hey, just a minute; what did you do to my child?'

The woman repeated the same story she told the young nurse. When she finished Chameli burst out, '*Anayee... anayee...*,' raising her small hand toward her. Mashi understood everything after scrutinizing the faces of the two. She told her in a stern voice, 'Look, this time I'm forgiving you. If it happens again I'll take them back.'

Mashi applied camphor oil first to Chameli's bruises and then to Paltu's wound, fed them, and kissing their foreheads asked them to go to sleep. Paltu was soon asleep but Chameli was not. She crawled to the back side of Mashi and attempted to stand on her feet first by resting her hands on Mashi's lower back and then on the neck. Mashi smiled, remained still as a wall while closely following her endeavour.

Chameli fell, got up, fell, got up..., quickly in first few attempts, then the gap increased and finally when she could stand still for a minute—the longest period in her first engagement; she giggled which disturbed her concentration and made her lose the balance, and she fell with a small thud. Now Mashi moved back, cradled her on her lap, wiped the perspiration from the little body and giving her a long kiss said, '*Kal abar*, now go to sleep'.

'*Ka... ka?*' Chameli's first vocabulary.

'*Hanh, ka*', Mashi smiled.

"*Ha... ka... ha... ka... ha...,*" she went to sleep murmuring her first vocabularies.

Next morning she awoke with, '*Han... ka... han... ka...*' and woke up Paltu also with these mutterings. The girl must have added one more letter in her dream, Mashi thought.

Paltu did not understand the meaning of sudden bursts of different sounds from Chameli's mouth but as she went on repeating them, he also tried, and by the time they were made ready for departure Chameli progressed to '*Hanh... kal*' and Paltu to '*Ha... ha*'.

When the woman came to collect the children both turned stiff.

'Look, how unwilling they are to go with you. I'm persuading them to go, but handle them carefully'.

She cajoled them with lot of patting and kisses and told, '*Ja* (go) with her; she won't harm you.'

'*Ja?*' Chameli responded.

'*Hanh, ja.*' Mashi smiled.

'*Hanh, ja... Hanh, ja.,*' Chameli and Paltu left with the woman moving their heads with every uttering.

The woman did not beat Chameli that day but also never allowed her to go near Paltu when he cried. Distressed, Chameli slapped the woman with her tiny hand as she did to her yesterday, but it was of no effect, she rather enjoyed the beating.

The nurse woman came with a packet in her hand. She pulled out a *puria* from inside it and told the woman.

'This is the *osud* (medicine) for the boy; sprinkle the powder on the ulcer *teen baar* (three times a day).' She demonstrated the application, caressed Paltu's cheek and left.

Chameli observed everything from a distance. She could understand the contents of the packet would cure Paltu's ulcer. When she was trying to muster the new found vocabularies, '*Os... tee... os... tee... osu... tee*', she saw the beggar woman throwing away the packet down the steps. She observed where it had fallen: four staircases away from her the packet was being bruised by moving feet of the passengers.

Since morning Chameli had been practicing standing up by using the stair wall as support; now she had to go down to collect the packet. She could crawl down, but no, she must walk down. She moved one leg at a time holding the wall and reached the edge of the stair. Now the most difficult part. Cautiously she lowered one leg on to the next stair but while doing so she lost the balance and fell back on the first stair. She sat there observing others: most of them getting down very fast jostling through the crowd, no children among them. Then she saw a thin man with white hair on his head walking down the stairs slowly. She concentrated on him till he was out of sight, and sat there for a while absorbing the techniques. With confidence thus gained she tottered down to the third step but failed to reach the fourth one; she tried twice but failed, her legs wobbled, she was exhausted. Disheartened she cried out, '*Anayee... ja anayee... ja... anayee*', which drew the attention of a man who came to her, '*Kee* (what)?'

She pointed out the packet, '*Osu... osu...*'. He picked up the packet and put it on her extended hand and then tried to make her stand holding her hands. She moved her head sideways denying help.

'*Na?*' The man asked.

'*Na*'. She pronounced the entire vocabulary all at once and stood up on her own.

The man looked at her from head to toe, turned her facing the wall, squeezed between her legs with one hand and caressed the bottom with the other; his heavy breathing dishevelled her hairs. After about a minute he released her, put a ten-rupee note on her hand and left stealthily.

After the man left Chameli turned and stood there for a while; she did not even realise she was standing on her own. She was still enjoining a sensation down there, close to but not exactly similar to peeing, and she liked it. When the feel died out she was surprised to find herself standing without any support, her both hands were full. She resolved to give the note to the beggar woman but hide the medicine packet somewhere. Looking around she noticed a crack-hole on the opposite stair wall. She tottered there, pushed the packet inside the hole, filled it with debris and slowly walked up to the beggar woman with the ten-rupee note in hand.

The woman exclaimed: 'My God! You've learnt to stand and walk too in just two days, and also earned ten rupees. Good, good,' she patted her.

Mashi was also overwhelmed when she saw Chameli tottering toward her. The woman tried to help whenever she fell but she refused with a '*Na*', got up on her own and moved forward. When she came near, Mashi drew her on the lap and showered kisses on every part of her body. Paltu also looked surprised, but congratulated her with non-stop giggles. He stopped only when Chameli kissed him back.

Chameli watched the woman leaving the station area, then tried to raise Mashi by one hand uttering, '*Osu... osu...*' and with the other indicated her to go outside. There must be something, Mashi thought and rose with Chameli. She asked one of her boys to take care of Paltu and walked outside holding her hand. This time she did not refuse.

Chameli bought out the packet from the hole and handed it to Mashi. She wiped out the dust and looked inside the packet: twenty *purias* left, one used, twenty one in all, how many times a day she did not know. Chameli observed there was no sign of joy in her face. With a feeling of dejection she asked, '*Han... na*'? Mashi saw her anxious face and replied, '*Hanh... hanh*' with an assured smile. "But how did you get it?" Chameli had no stock of vocabulary to answer. She mimed her best with hands and face and occasional, '*Aan... han... na...*' to describe the episode. Mashi could guess it must be a medicine person who gave the packet to the beggar woman and also showed its application by using one *puria*, but the beggar woman must have thrown away the packet which Chameli picked up and hid inside the hole. Mashi could not blame the beggar woman, she would also have done the same thing; after all she also wanted the ulcer to prolong, but Chameli altered all calculations. She would now insist on using the medicine: she had demonstrated to be a determined fighter, surprised everyone by jumping the stages of physical development and mental cognition, she wouldn't let it go.

Mashi had seen street children learning very fast to withstand the pressure of the street. Added to this if the motivation was love the learning became faster. She had read and seen in her earlier life how people take risk, compromise, commit crimes, make sacrifices driven by motivation of wealth acquisition, power, status, physical gratification and all that, but Chameli had proved today the motive force was highest when love was devoid of any material underlying.

Chameli's first utterances after dinner.

'*Osu, osu*'.

'*Kal*', Mashi said.

'*Na... na... .na... tee... tee...*' Chameli insisted by moving her head continuously.

'Ok, ok.'

Mashi had to take out a *puria* from the packet. Chameli snatched it from her hand, sat before Paltu and sprinkled the powder on his wound the way the nurse woman demonstrated.

'Okay, okay?' She asked Mashi.

'Ok'. Mashi smiled.

'Okay?' Chameli now turned to Paltu who just giggled in response.

Chameli insisted on medicine in the morning also but did not ask for a third application as it had to be done before that woman. Despite the beggar woman's occasional prodding the ulcer showed signs of improvement.

The nurse woman would visit them every week, examine the wound, express satisfaction with the progress and hand over another packet, which the beggar woman would throw away and Chameli would pick up stealthily, hid it in the hole to pick up after the woman had left. Soon she decided for three applications a day: one in the early morning, second before they left with the woman and the third after dinner.

In three months Chameli could run; she had also acquired a good stock of vocabulary. Paltu's progress was slow because he could not practise during the day.

Chameli was a hard taskmaster. She would wake him up early morning, make him practice standing... walking... running, and pronouncing words. The session would be repeated in the evening after dinner. The two boys who found them in the train also assisted them in their daily endeavour.

Paltu took three months to walk steadily and six months to run and communicate properly.

In two months Paltu's ulcer vanished, the scar remained.

Mashi lost the premium price but the beggar woman did not lose much; Chameli more than compensated the loss from normal begging by allowing herself to be touched by a number of people against a ten-rupee note; any one giving a note of different colour and size she would ask for '*Dosh* (ten)... dosh'.

As they grew up they began mixing with young children—some of whom were senior to them—in the station area. They observed that most of them were not as naked as they were, also learned that the thing between their legs differentiated a girl from a boy which should not be exposed to public view. They did not question, thought it was right as most observed it. Chameli began dressing up and also made Paltu do so. When the beggar woman tried to undo their drawers they put aside her hand so vehemently she dared not make further attempts. The passers who used to fondle Chameli got a similar treatment. But they invented different other ways to beg.

They learned to fight, also picked up abuses of the street without understanding their meaning. For them, it was a language to express anger. Chameli was aggressive in the use of her hands, legs and mouth, an *enfant terrible,* particularly when someone tried to harm Paltu. In contrast, Paltu was conciliatory, compromising, trying always to minimise the area of conflict, which Chameli never liked and often chastised him.

Mashi was following their development for past four years. She felt Chameli needed some taming; else someday she would get hurt badly. She had already befriended a NGO girl and had a talk with her to place Chameli at a good family nearby as domestic help. The NGO girl wanted to admit both of them to her home but Mashi refused; the girl understood and began searching for such households. They zeroed in on a family of three—husband, wife and a child living at Bowbazar, a furlong distance from Sealdah, duty hours being three in the morning and two in the evening at a monthly wage of four hundred rupees. Mashi broached the issue before Chameli who thought for a while... the money was good, duty hours not bad... but... but...

'What happens to Paltu; who'll take care of him when I'm away?' She asked.

'He would be with the boys who brought you here'.

'Yes, they're very good but... but...'

'And I shall personally see no harm comes to him, okay.' Mashi replied with a twinkling in her eyes.

'Okay.' She felt relieved.

Chameli liked the family, learnt the domestic chores and also some cooking from the wife. The child was a baby boy just about six months old. During her spare time she would play with him, teach him standing and walking as she did for Paltu. Soon they developed an affinity.

Chameli first got the idea of marriage and a happy family from this household. She would talk about the husband, wife and baby endlessly with Paltu who often felt bored but would never dare express it. Later, when they grew older and saw movies together where a boy and a girl after overcoming various hurdles ended in marriage and a happy family thereafter, Paltu got some understanding of what Chameli talked about, and gradually he also began liking the idea. When Mashi moved to Gariahat after about six years they were near adolescence, understood things better and began looking forward to a happy family of their own.

Paltu became Boomba soon thereafter.

Chapter 4

Mashi never had any milk in her breasts any time before, never got pregnant despite being married at a young age: a fallow woman, talked about in the village where she lived with her husband for four years.

One afternoon she and her husband boarded a train to Sealdah station for consulting a specialist doctor in Kolkata. When the train reached the station her husband asked her to wait in the compartment while he made a call to the doctor from a public phone booth.

Half hour passed there was no sign of him; how much time it takes to make a phone call and fix up an appointment with the doctor she didn't know; had he gone somewhere for some other purpose, got lost in the crowd; he had come to Kolkata only once before, might not be familiar with the roads here. Her anxiety increased as the time went by.

It was late in the evening when a patrolling police man noticed her and asked why she was sitting in the compartment of a train that would leave only in the early morning next day.

Seeing the policeman she felt assured and told him everything. He took her to the government railway police station where she was raped throughout the night by all the three men on night duties. In the morning she was given some food and tea. Then the same police man who located her the first time and also raped her during the night took her to a corner of the ticketing area outside the platforms and lodged her there. In a devastated state of mind and body she fell asleep soon clutching her suitcase.

She woke up in the noon to find herself amidst a sea of mankind, some going in some coming out, some standing in queues before the ticket counters, hawkers moving around, some urchins begging, children crying and mothers beating; the whole place was reverberating with different sounds and voices. She was confused. Suddenly she felt an excruciating pain down her abdomen, and all the memories of last night came back to her in a flash. But surprisingly she felt no anger, she felt hungry. Except a small breakfast at the police station, she had not had any food during the last forty eight hours, but she needed money for food. She hurriedly opened her suitcase to search for the money she had hidden between the folds of her saris without the knowledge of her husband to buy some fashionable saris and blouses after meeting with the doctor. She let a sigh of relief when she found the money, took out a few notes and knotted them securely within the upper fold of her sari. Now she looked around for some help. She noticed a young boy roaming about the place begging alms from almost everyone who came to the station.

With some efforts she drew his attention. The boy came hurriedly and hearing that he could have free food with her if he took her to a food stall nearby, he almost raised her by the hand and led her to a stall where all the young servers appeared to be known to him. With her consent the boy ordered for both. They ate hungrily in silence. Later this boy was to be her tutor and first recruit.

When they returned the boy sat by her side; he had his fill, did not feel like begging further. He called her Mashi and that pronoun had clung to her till today.

With a full stomach the pain in her abdomen was bearable but at times it shot up, though with lesser and lesser frequencies as time passed. She surmised there might not be any internal injury, only ruptures, and she didn't care. She had it before, though with her husband. After first night's premature ejaculation he made love to her again and again for next two days and nights. She could not walk properly, had difficulty in toilets but she didn't care. It was a lovely sensation that thrilled her entire being, and despite the pain she wanted more. With the policemen the thrill was absent, it wasn't also the same penis all the time but different ones with different size and thickness. She could not say she enjoyed, but all through she was moist. When the first police man—who must be the officer-in-charge to have the first right of violation—kneaded her large breasts with his thick and coarse hands she felt moist, and when he parted her legs and entered she was oozing; rest were just routines, she didn't pay any attention. She felt no pain; somewhat dazed might be not because of continuous thrusts inside her but a mental numbness that engulfed her being. She was oozing profusely, her body was enjoying but not the mind. That night she learnt between thrusts that body and mind could be separated, and that knowledge gave her the power to survive. She did not protest, rather cooperated, and that helped her earn a breakfast the following morning and many more things later.

She felt no humiliation either as she suffered the worst from her husband. She realised humiliation is a state of mind that leads to helplessness; if one is numb to any amount of humiliation, one can never be humiliated, and that's a power.

She was startled by frantic raps on her legs. It was the boy who now clung to her and exclaimed helplessly.

'Oh Mashi... Oh Mashi... Jaggudada is coming to take me away. He'd beat me for not having earned enough for the day, might also break my legs as he often threats. Please save me Mashi... please...'

Mashi observed the quivering boy and told him assuredly, 'Just sight tight, you're not going anywhere.'

She saw a young man with thick rippling muscles and a broad shoulder coming toward them in haughty steps. He stopped before them and ignoring Mashi uttered sternly.

'Hey, Chintu, just get up and come with me. I'm informed you haven't done much earning today; for long you've not got what you deserved; today I'll beat the hell out of you.'

He stretched his hand to pull up the boy. Mashi pushed his hand aside and retorted, 'He isn't going anywhere'.

Jaggu was stunned. None in the Sealdah area had ever dared raise their voice against him, and this chit of a woman, how dare she! He smirked sarcastically.

'Hey, *sali!* Who do you think you are? This is my boy, and I'm taking him with me. You dare stop me; know who I am?'

'You're just a gutter worm!'

Jaggu was spell bound. Noticing the recrimination between the most dreaded Dada of the area and the woman who had just arrived here this morning, other young urchins, probably under Jaggu, gathered around with expectation—expectation to see him down. Soon some of the returning passengers joined to observe the *tamasha*, the crowd swelled. Jaggu looked about, felt uncertain; he was being humiliated before his own boys, which might ruin his credibility, and that was the end of him. He looked at Mashi who now sat straight holding the boy's hand. In a desperate bit to save the situation he blurted out.

'But... but... you must understand this is my boy, I feed him, take care of all his needs. So I've all the rights over him.'

'From this moment he is mine. Now go back to your gutter, never dare touch him again.'

'*Achha!* You dare say these things because you feel you're protected by this crowd. That's a false belief. I'll return soon with my gang and throw you out of this area; I'd like to see who saves you then.'

Jaggu stamped the ground with his boot and left. When the crowd dispersed soon after Jaggu left, Mashi got up, took the boy by one hand and grabbing her suitcase by another entered the GRP station which was now a familiar place for her and would be so for years to come. She found her way to the cabin of the OC who looked quizzically at her and the boy by her hand; his jaws hardened expecting trouble. But Mashi disarmed him by a bewitching smile. He felt relaxed; memories of last night came back to him in a flash: she was different, not like others he had fucked so far. He took a fancy of her and asked what it was now. Mashi replied coyly.

'Sir, there is one Jaggu who threatens to dislodge me from the station area and also take away this boy whom I've taken in. I've a mind to recruit a few more but with Jaggu...'

'Ah-ha, you're already on networking, a practical woman. Good... good... go ahead.'

He rang the bell, a constable came in.

'Get that bastard Jaggu, bring him here immediately.'

When the constable left he told her, 'Go back to your place with your new found ward. Jaggu will not disturb you any time from now.'

'Thank you sir, thank you very much; you're a kind person. May we leave now?'

'Of course you can.' He arched a brow at her with a meaningful smile. She returned the smile coquettishly and left.

From that day Jaggu never threatened her, rather he tried to be friendly.

Mashi had with her about three thousand five hundred rupees that would carry her and Chintu for just about a month; she would have to establish herself in the vocation within that time. She first settled with Chintu: he would carry on his present profession; his share of earning would be sixty per hundred—double the amount he got from Jaggu, the balance she would keep for his protection.

From that day on Chintu never earned less than two hundred rupees a day. He would innovate newer ways of attracting people, convincing them to fork out more amount of alms, never less than five rupees per prey; if someone gave him less than that he would return it with such a dejected smile that the poor fellow would ultimately be poorer by five rupees.

With about eighty rupees daily the cost of food was taken care of. Thus, she could save the rest of the earnings for future contingencies. She now decided to expand her network. At the outset she decided two things: one, the railway stations and similar other places would be her abode for all time to come; and two, she would never be in high-risk activities. She did not need much; a livelihood on a daily basis, no building up for future, no savings except a small fund for giving loans to network boys—a strategic necessity.

Chintu would rise early in the morning—precisely at 4:30 a.m. with the whistle of the first train leaving the station. If Mashi was in her place he would wake her, they would walk together to the train shed, choose a bogey, check the toilets there and enter. By the time they finished almost all the stationary carriages would be teeming with inhabitants of Sealdah area.

He would start working immediately munching a few biscuits or a *roti* from yesterday's leftover and finish by 1:30 p.m.—he just needed forty-fifty targets for the day's quota. He would bring his collections to Mashi for calculations; take his full share or just a part of it keeping the rest with Mashi as his savings. But he might not always accompany her for lunch; he had his friends to lunch with at different locations, for different kind of foods, to play games of any kind and occasionally see a movie in one of the cheap cinema halls. Games included stealing whenever they found an opportunity; it was fun, the value of goods not important: a few crates of soft drinks, some boxes of bakeries, fruit baskets, a few packets of readymade garments and hosiery products: boys come cheap as loaders and unloaders, but not so always.

Chintu had introduced his friends to her: some of them worked under someone, others independent working alone or in groups. They often visited her in spare time with or without Chintu and discussed things about them, their work, the manner of spending money, the funny experiences they had in dealing with people, the beatings they had when they were caught stealing, the latest movie in the town, about the girls they are friendly with. Mashi was a good, indulgent listener and they bared their thoughts before her without any inhibitions, but rarely they spoke about their past.

Mashi had observed that these boys loved spending; earning was just a means to do that: when they had no money they would take a loan from each other or from members of other groups with promises to return, though these promises were hardly honoured, they didn't really mind. But with Dadas and mashis, it was different. They got beaten up if they failed to return by a given date double the amount they had borrowed.

Mashi was somewhat liberal, she would not go further beyond a stern look and everyday reminder, and charged only a few rupees on the loan amount. But she would give loan only on recommendation of Chintu which increased his prestige and Mashi's influence over the boys. This experience would later help her develop a full-fledged lending business.

Some nights Chintu would not return to Mashi as he feared she might not approve of his taking liquor, a puff of hashish or seeing a sex video on the smart phone of a high earning boy. He would sleep somewhere else but always near the station to hear the whistle of the first train leaving the station and wake up Mashi. He often felt she resembled his mother who chastised him for any mischief not by beating but with a stern look, though that was before she remarried a hunk who thrashed him every day, and one day drove him out of the house, his mother standing before the door frame with a miserable look.

Mashi was also not in her place all the nights. She was now OC's woman; the junior police men did not touch her any longer, though he often invited a fellow OC from another station. She learnt from them the techniques of satisfying two men simultaneously; her body relished all sex games; she had separated the lust of body from the rapture of mind. She had already transformed a lecherous smile to a desiring one.

The OCs got transferred, new OCs came but the mutual patronage continued.

Mashi learnt from Chintu that Jaggu was the most dreadful among all Dadas in Sealdah area. He had a great rapport with the police because next only to Ilabu he paid highest weekly quota to the police. Jaggus's *vikhari* business spread across many stations in the main and north section of Sealdah railways. South lines were controlled by another Dada, but income from there was not good. Jaggu picked up boys and girls found wandering at various stations; he would capture them before NGOs and police intervened, keep only those who left home on their own or were abandoned by their parents, the rest were handed over to the NGOs or police.

But he was not like Ilabu who maimed children—breaking or severing one or both legs or, hands, blinding one or both eyes et cetera—before putting them on roads. He had his factory at a large abandoned warehouse in central Kolkata by the side of a canal where he did all these and also hoarded the children. Very early morning these children were carried by rickshaw-vans and placed at different locations for begging, and brought back late evening by the same rickshaw vans.

Ilabu often fought with Jaggu over a child. He had a larger and stronger gang than Jaggu and greater rapport with the police. But Jaggu was smarter, a convincing talker who would take public on his side and get away with his prey. Both of them took care that the matter did not reach the police as none would gain in the bargain: the police would hand over the child either to a government home or to an NGO.

Besides *vikhari* business, Jaggu collected *tolas* from roadside vegetable vendors, tea stalls, food joints and *chullu thecks,* but he avoided large established stores, liquor shops and restaurants: these were the domains of political Dadas much bigger than him.

Jaggu also ran a trained gang of pickpockets and thieves operating on trains. They would jump into different compartments of a train when it was entering a platform; the more crowded the compartment the better for them. The passengers in their haste to get down from the train often became unmindful of their belongings particularly the smaller ones like mobile phone, watch, pen, purse, et cetera, which they targeted. They avoided anything of gold because despite haste people were particularly careful of gold items. If any of them got caught in the act, senior boys of Jaggu's gang would surface from nowhere and join the public in beating him—in fact beating less shouting more—and drag him to the police station wherefrom they would be released after the passengers of the train left the platform. Jaggu had connection with a network of stores who bought these stolen articles.

Mashi had learnt that some station and street boys worked independently though mostly in groups or with a network of friends. Chintu had high regard for them. He told Mashi that the Dadas and mashis would not generally tinker with them. They were so tricky, create so much ruckus, would call in so many of their network friends in minutes, so fierce in battle, and so unmindful of police torture, these Dadas and mashis had no chance to win. They avoided them, more so because influenced by their show of independence some of their wards might gather courage to leave them.

Mashi now had a clear picture before her. If she wanted to expand her network she would come in conflict with Jaggu or Ilabu or some other Dadas or mashis operating in the area, which she wanted to avoid. Ilabu, she could not do anything about, but Jaggu could be neutralised, and if handled properly could be of help to find new recruits for her.

These days Jaggu often came to her with "Hi, hello... how is your business going... no problem, eh? Just tell me if you've any I'll help you out," kinds of greetings. He wanted to be friendly, might be because of her closeness with the police, but she guessed it might be more than that. So far Mashi was polite with him but not beyond a point. She felt it was time to change her attitude.

One evening Jaggu came and started off his rogations but in between Mashi asked him to sit. Jaggu was a little surprised, and though sceptical sat before her almost obediently, and looked queerly at her. Mashi ignored the look and lifted from the floor an oil-smudged paper bag containing chicken *pakoras*. Extending the paper bag to him she said almost by way of an apology, 'I bought these from Chacha's for Chintu and myself; he loves chicken *pakora*, and me too but he'd sent a message he won't be coming this evening, so I thought I could share them with you, will you?' She ended the sentence with a pleading smile. Disarmed, Jaggu put his hand inside the packet and brought out a few pieces. For quite some time he had been harbouring a desire to know this woman, but he should proceed carefully; must start from a distance. Munching one *pakora* he asked, 'You love sharing food, isn't it?'

'Yes. I don't feel good eating alone.'

'You love Chintu; everyone here talks about it.'

'I think so.'

'And he also loves you.'

'I guess so.'

'Then how could he go here and there without asking you?'

'He is a free bird. I want him that way.'

Jaggu fell silent. He took out more *pakoras,* put one in his mouth and offered some to Mashi who picked up a few from his hand; their hands touched, Jaggu felt a quiver within, Mashi, nothing. He looked at her with glazing eyes but reacted somberly as though to overcome the emotion.

'I think you're right; you can't get love from a caged bird. But the funny thing is though I'm a free man, I don't want my wards to be free; I ruthlessly suppress even a slight expression of freedom. That's why they don't love me. But I don't care; I want it this way only.' He finished with a haughty defiance.

Mashi offered him the last *pakora* with a silent smile, read quickly the prints on the paper bag, found nothing important, transformed it to a ball and threw it at a distance which was immediately picked up by some station urchins for a game of football.

Jaggu took the *pakora* unmindfully; saw the boys waving their hands gleefully and Mashi smiling back conspiratorially. He now looked confused, dismayed, but still maintained that edge in his voice when he spoke next.

'Look, I've never thought it the way you think. I've never been loved nor do I know what love is. Whatever it is, in my profession love has no place.' He got up and left in a huff, the uneaten *pakora* still in his hand.

Mashi smiled at his departing figure. That smile followed him to the bazaar area outside the station when he discovered he was still holding the *pakora* in his hand. He smiled broadly before taking a bite of it.

News spread in the station area that Mashi had a fight with Jaggu. Smaller Dadas and other mashis came to enquire whether there really was a fight. They had also assured full support if the fight escalated. Mashi had two-syllable answer to all these: 'No. Nothing'.

Next morning Chintu asked the same question with anxiety in his voice. He had been enjoying a good time under Mashi's care, his prestige high in the group since Mashi had wrested him from the clutches of Jaggudada, it rose higher when Jaggudada himself was making courtesy calls to Mashi. All these would be lost if Mashi quarrelled with Jaggudada.

Mashi could understand Chintu's anxiety. She comforted her assuredly.

'No. We had no fight.'

'Nothing!' Chintu was doubtful.

'Yes, nothing at all.'

'But I heard from others he was so angry he stormed out of your sight.'

'Others are fools. He wasn't angry with me at all.'

'Then?'

'He was angry with himself.'

Chintu could not understand what Mashi meant; it was too much for him. He asked a final question.

'Will Jaggudada come again?'

'Of course he will.'

'Then it's all right.'

Fully satisfied Chintu ran back to his work.

Three days passed but Jaggu did not turn up. Chintu was restive. He stopped going out with his friends and stayed by her side after finishing his work. Mashi responded to all his anxious questions only with a cryptic smile. He often vented his anger against her nonchalant attitude. But in response Mashi only patted his back and smiled.

On the fourth evening Jaggu came. He had in his hand the same type of oil-stained paper packet though of larger size. He smiled as he sat on a low stool advanced by Mashi, then he saw Chintu sitting by her side and feigned his usual stern voice, '*Sala*, Mashi's *chamcha*, out from here.' Chintu cringed. He rose fast and was about to run when Jaggu said, 'Ok, ok. Don't get scared. I've a treat for you'. He pulled out a chicken cutlet from the packet and placed it in his hand. 'Now scram,' he ordered. Chintu was all smiles. He wrapped the cutlets with both hands and fled. Jaggu and Mashi broke into a smile together.

Jaggu said as he handed the packet to Mashi, '*Chacha* had informed me you also love chicken cutlet, so I...'

Mashi smiled and placed two cutlets on a paper plate and one on another with rye-sauced cucumber-onion salads and handed the first plate to Jaggu keeping the other for herself. When Jaggu broke one of his cutlets in half and was about to put it on Mashi's plate she raised her hand to stop, 'No, you eat all the two, I'll eat only one as I'm not that hungry, but you look to be so.' She gave him one of her sweetest smiles. Jaggu smiled back.

'Next time I shall bring five instead of four—one for that swine, Chintu.'

As they were eating, Jaggu's eyes frequently darted toward the cleavage between Mashi's breasts, which were more prominent now as she sat on a low stool with thighs drawn towards her torso. Jaggu felt uneasy and to overcome that he started a conversation.

'Mashi... everyone here calls you Mashi. But you must have a proper name.'

'Do you have one?' Mashi answered back with a smile.

'Yes... what... Jaggu'.

'Who gave you this name, or is it your proper name?'

'Well, yes. No', Jaggu moved his head uncertainly, and his eyes again fell on her breasts. He swore to himself, *sotto voce,* and averting his eyes forcefully explained himself.

'I could understand what you were saying. When I first came to this station I was about 4-5 years old. I didn't know what I should do next and wandered here and there. All the passengers of the train left, the platform was almost empty except a group of boys hustled together at a corner round a very tall person who appeared to be settling some disputes among them. As I advanced towards them I heard the tall man say, "Hey, stop your quarrels. Look, there's a new arrival. Let's take him". All the boys stepped toward me. I got scared but Mannudada—that was his name, wrapped me to himself and said, "Your face looks washed out; must be hungry. Let's go to a food stall, we shall eat together."

'After we finished the meal Mannudada said, "Let's now give him a name... well, Jaggu will be all right, eh?" I tried to say that I have a proper name but I was drowned by the shouts of the boys, "Jaggu... Jaggu", and the name stayed with me, though the name-giver was killed four months after that in a gun battle, and we came under Bimledada.'

Jaggu had never before spoken at such length. He felt exhausted but also relieved for having shared it with someone for the first time in his life. He was somewhat morose when he spoke again.

'You know, Mannudada was a loving and caring person like you, but Bimledada was cruel like me.'

Mashi turned the discussion back to the original theme.

'So tell me what's there in a name? It is always given by some other person to express his or hers ideas about you. Your parents gave it to you when you were born; you had no part in it. If your parents were nowhere, the person who picks you up awards a name to you. As you grow, your friends call you by some name, may not be your original name. You may get a different name from your lover or spouse. Those who hate you call you by a hateful name. The police over there ascribe you different names on different occasions. A name is always an expression of others' love, desire, hatred and convenience. Your own self has no part in it.'

'My god! I've never thought of it that way. Wherefrom have you learnt all these?'

'It's nothing great, simple observation. By being in the station for last six months I've learnt that Chintu was no Chintu before he came here and may not be so in future. It's same with all Jaggus and Mashis and many others in our world. You may feel, and often feel proud or hateful believing that to be your identity. All bullshit! A name is always a pronoun. So, why bother? Your identity rests with your own self which none can take away. Call me Mashi or by any other name I don't care'.

Jaggu was amazed. He started the discussion to distract himself from a carnal desire but how it ended! A discourse on identity he never bothered till a few minutes before, but now he had to; it had given him a new understanding of self. He surmised Mashi must be highly educated, then why was she here? He could not help ask this question. Mashi smiled but replied coolly.

'I won't answer your question directly. I'd only say that in my geography class I'd learnt how to pin point important places in the map of West Bengal. I was very good at map pointing; I could tell even with closed eyes where different places are in the map including Sealdah junction station, but I didn't know the place at all, didn't know someday I'll be here, didn't know there is a police station, didn't know how the police behave with a lost person, didn't know there are many lost people like me, didn't know there is a Chintu and a Jaggu. Life has brought me here, it teaches me all the time, no need of a text book any longer.'

Both felt the situation had become somewhat grave. To lighten it Mashi remarked with a soft laugh.

'Oh-ho! Look at our plates; we haven't eaten even half of what you've brought. Let's do justice to them.'

She picked up her quarter-eaten cutlet, Jaggu did the same. They both laughed.

Jaggu realised to his amazement that during their long discussion he had not for once looked at her cleavage. But now the urge came back. To conceal the shame from her askance look he blurted out, 'Since you do not care about a name, may I call you my darling?'

'You must be seeing a lot of movies. Next time it might be Hema Malini, I suppose.'

Chapter 5

Toomba woke up first. It was pouring now. All the water the sun had sucked mercilessly every day and night during the past one month was stolen surreptitiously by the rain-God who was now giving it back to the earth.

He looked at Boomba who though stirred now and then was still in deep sleep. He saw all the open spaces were getting empty as people ran for alternative shelters: soon rain waters would flow toward the footpaths; it was time to wake him up. He patted Boomba slowly at first, harder next. He woke up puzzled, saw Toomba first, then the waters around. Fully awake now he said, 'I know a place where we can take shelter, let's run.' When they were about to leave he said again , 'Just a minute' and waded the road now full of water, reached near Mashis' shanty which was dry as the stretch was three feet above the pavement, stood for a while and then waded back, 'Ok, let's go.'

They ran through Dover Road to its end and stood before a high-walled gate of a mental asylum. Boomba picked up a stone and began hitting the iron gate shouting, 'Hey Bhaglu... hey Bhaglu...' After about a minute a powerful torch light fell on them from an out guard room. Someone said from inside, 'Oh, Paltu Babu.' The torch light now moved toward them, a man with an umbrella on his head opened the gate and they ran to a small room, water dripping from their bodies like rain. The guard soon returned after closing the gate. Both of them had already peeled their wet shirts from their bodies and were now squeezing water out of them on the small veranda adjacent to the room. Boomba now dropped his pant which was picked up by Bhaglu to do the same. He looked at Toomba once and asked Bhaglu to give him a spare *lungi*. 'Feeling shy, eh?' the man said as he handed him a *lungi*. Boomba picked up two *gamchas* from a rope strung to both sides of the veranda, gave one to Toomba and the other for him to wipe water from their bodies. Toomba saw Bhaglu staring at Boomba's penis, now hardened due to rubbing with the *gamcha*. After they dried up Bhaglu touched Boomba's penis and exclaimed, 'Oh! I find your thing has grown quite a bit since we met last.' Boomba replied smilingly, 'But yours has already set up a tent down there.'

Bhaglu asked whether he would prepare some food for them. When both refused he said, 'Then, let's sleep the rest of the night,' and put out the light. Though it was dark, a ray of light fell on them from somewhere. Toomba saw Bhaglu snuggle to Boomba.

They woke up late in the morning. Bhaglu gave them *roti* and *bhaji* for breakfast when they returned from bathroom. After food they rose to leave when Bhaglu put a hundred-rupee note in Boomba's pocket and said, 'Come again.'

Their garments were not fully dry but they did not care.

The rains must have stopped early in the morning, not much water logging on the roads; the sky was still cloudy though sun rays glittered here and there between cracks of cloud; another downpour unlikely, the monsoon still a month away.

They purchased a pack of cigarettes each from a roadside stall. With the first puff of smoke Boomba said, 'You know, whenever I run out of money I go to Bhaglu and give him this small service. My job's over when a whitish liquid jerks out from his cock. He says it is much better than doing with his wife. I don't understand nor do I care as long he gives me hundred rupees.'

'Where to now?' Toomba asked.

Oh, yes. Now we must catch a Moulali-bound bus.'

It was office time. Busses were over packed, no space even on the stair case. As their bus came, they jumped to catch the handles on two sides of the gate and remained suspended, no support even for one leg. When the bus was about to take speed another boy jumped to catch Boomba's side of the rod. 'Hey Paltu', he muttered and quickly entered inside by pushing and pulling other passengers with practised manoeuvres.

They got down at Moulali crossing; the bus conductor did not ask for fare. They crossed the road and entered a lane that led to a jigsaw of bylanes.

As they walked Boomba said, 'You know, that boy was my mate in pick pocketing. We were trained under the same person Mashi sent me when I showed interest in it. Imagine how my first lesson began! Six-seven persons jumped on me as I entered the training site, beat me mercilessly for about half hour and just left me there after it was over, none came for help. After some time I got up on my own and limped toward what you call an office. A person now appeared and helped me go inside. He made me lie down, applied some ointment to my bruises and gave me a bottle of strong liquor to drink. The beating was repeated every day for a week. When I passed the primary test actual training began: during the next six weeks I was taught technical things like how to hold a blade between two fingers, and inside the mouth, feeling the contents of the bag or pocket of the target et cetera., and also the behavioural characteristics of the target: man with a girl or single, how he or she is holding a bag, restive or cool, anxious or nonchalant, absorbed in listening music through ear phone or, just sitting or standing erect, et cetera. You know, every posture tells you something about a person, which the boss explained meticulously. This is very important for selecting a target.'

'Weren't you ever caught?' Toomba asked.

'Oh yes, twice. First time it was a conductor who caught me clearing the hip pocket of a man; they normally don't do it, they don't even ask fare from us; we have an understanding, this one must be new, didn't know about it. Whatever, I was caught red-handed, dragged down and you know, what happened thereafter. I had two other mates inside the bus, one of them came down and started beating me with feigned violence and I cried out more in response, as we were trained to do. He lifted me up by the collar and pushed me forward as if taking me to the police station. In the meantime the other mate cleared all collections from the conductor's bag and left a permanent mark on his wrist with blade before joining the crowd. The man got the lesson, never disturbed us any time thereafter.

'Second time it was simpler. A policeman rescued me from the crowd, brought me to the nearest police outpost, waited for the crowd to disperse, applied some first aid things on my bruises, gave a small kick on my bum with, "Next time, be careful". I walked out peacefully. Why you know? Our boss feeds all the police stations in his zone with weekly packets.'

'Then, why did you leave the line?'

'You know, there's not much money in this vocation compared to risk and uncertainty. Some days, particularly during the last week of a month we may just go dry. Besides, I've to give thirty percent of my income to the boss and twenty percent to Mashi. That doesn't leave much for me. Of course, I could've joined a group specialising in mobile phones and laptops where the boys are paid a fixed monthly salary of not less than ten thousand rupees. They are trained for six months at a place called Tin Pahari in Jharkhand. As I'd the basic training I could've finished the course in three months. But you know, I cannot stay out of Kolkata for three months at a stretch. So I abandoned the idea.'

By now Toomba had become used to Boomba's pre-fixing every major statement with "You know", he smiled unconsciously.

'Why are you smiling?' Boomba asked.

'Nothing much. I guess you're changing the line not because of risk but of your lure for big money. I've a feeling this has something to do with your dream around Chameli.'

'The devil you know.' Boomba smiled sheepishly.

'Yes, people also call me by that name. But tell me why are you dragging me to this?'

'You'll be my leader and guide, together we'll earn lots of money.'

'I do not guide any one simply because no one can guide anyone except oneself, and I've already told you I'm no leader, I prefer being a devil.'

'Ok, ok, the devil of a friend then.'

'That's a better term. But I also don't want big money. I don't want a future, I suffer no dreams. I'm happy the way I'm. Then why me?'

Boomba was thoughtful. They silently traversed a bylane and stopped to smoke. Boomba spoke inhaling a lungful.

'You know, when you'd start earning big money you'd develop an inclination toward it; money has that attraction. Even if you don't need it you go on earning. It's the enjoyment of earning that matters not the money per se; it's like a pricey whisky, intoxication comes slowly, then it takes over, and it's really good.'

'Which one, money or whisky?'

'Both. You know once I stole a bottle of very good whisky from the house where Champi works but I didn't know how to take it. So I went to my Boss who taught me: take a small quantity, say one half of a quarter of a glass, fill the glass with water, put some ice cubes and sip, not gulp like what we do with pouch. You slowly go up; find gates of heaven opening before you and you enter, slowly. Oh. It's heavenly!'

'Bloody poet! You get the same feeling when you take a good drug.'

'No, no. Drug kicks you up fast, whisky takes you there slowly, you enjoy every moment of your voyage to heaven; you land there softly, no suddenness, no thud.'

'Bloody poet again! With my first earning of big money I'll buy a bottle of whisky, and we shall visit your heaven together.'

'Promise.'

'Promise.'

They stopped before the gate of a factory shed. A Bhaglu type of person sat on a stool, his eyes focused on the palm of his left hand where a mixture of raw tobacco and lime was being kneaded by the thumb of his right hand. After being satisfied with his art work he puffed out extra lime molecules from the mixture put it carefully inside his lower lip and looked up.

'What do you want at this time?' he asked recognising Boomba.

'The boss has sent for us.'

'Wait.'

He opened the gate, stepped in, again locked it from within and entered the factory through a side door. Soon he came back, opened the gate and holding the saliva inside his mouth indicated them to go in.

The place smelt of detergent powder; must be the front to hoodwink the law, Toomba thought. They entered a half-lit room. A man sat on a place which was once a couch; you couldn't see his face properly. An effeminate voice spoke.

'So, this is your friend.'

'Yes.'

'You're responsible for him.'

'Yes'.

'We'll find out about him; in the meantime he can start working from tomorrow.'

'Thank you,' Boomba said.

The man continued.

'There'll be two packets for each of you every day with addresses written on a separate sheet of paper; collect them from the gatekeeper by nine in the morning, memorise the addresses and return the paper to him. After making deliveries come back here, but not before five in the afternoon, by which time I'll get message confirming the delivery. You'll be paid five hundred rupees per delivery. If you're found good, I may increase the number of packets to a maximum of five per day. For an urgent delivery and delivery in the night the payout will be doubled.'

He now focused on Boomba.

'Do not bring another person, your quota is over. By the way, have you told him the rules?'

'Yes.'

Before leaving Toomba clasped Boomba's hand and told the man. 'Initially, we shall work for three days a week.'

'That's your choice; tell me the days'.

'Say, every alternate day'.

'Fine, no problem.'

As soon as they were out of the gate, Boomba snatched his hand from Toomba's grip and asked angrily.

'Why did you say that three days a week thing?'

'Don't move so fast; be so greedy as to jump on fire and burn. Let's see what it's all about, and then we shall raise our takes.'

'You are right. That's why I call you a leader.'

'Stupid!'

'May be, but I don't care.'

On their way back Toomba asked, 'What rules he was talking about? You haven't told me before, not that I so much care.'

'Exactly. You know, the rules are so simple I didn't think they were worthy of mention. Rule number one: you'll have to finish all normal deliveries by five in the afternoon; two, you shall not discuss it with any one; three, if we are apprehended by police we shall under no circumstance, whatever be the pressure, disclose the whereabouts of the boss or his office—disclosure means death, but if we don't succumb we shall be taken care of including a quick release and good amount of gratuity; the last rule is once you enter the trade you can't leave it except by death. You know, the fellows over there don't have any idea of street boys; for us the rules are simple—no matter how gravely the fellow said—compared to the rules of the street. Aren't they?'

'Yeah. Broadly speaking, if you think life is simple, it is simple' Toomba replied casually.

When they reached Moulali Toomba asked, 'Where's next?'

'I'm going to Mashi. She must still be very angry with me; I've got to pacify her.'

'And Chameli too.'

'The devil you are.'

'Always. But I'm not going with you. You've created the problem; you solve it, though I know it'll be resolved soon.'

* * * *

While Boomba jumped on to a running bus Toomba walked toward Sealdah station. Why to Sealdah and not Gariahat which would have made Boomba happy, he asked himself. Is it because he was trying to avoid developing any attachment toward Boomba and his 'family'? Might be; he had all along tried to avoid attachment: friendship yes, from which you can walk out any time; you might feel sorry for a while, that's all; with attachment it is different, there is permanence in it. Even when you get physically detached you feel a pang and this pang lives with you, you become attached to this pang and always revisit it, there is no escape. Love is perhaps the strongest form of attachment. He had observed this bondage between Boomba and Chameli, between Mashi and Jaggu.

He had also observed this attachment between his foster father and mother who picked him up from a dustbin near the railway station and brought him up, but he himself suffered no attachment to them. He had regards for them, was dependent on them and always felt a sense of gratitude, but developed no attachment toward them; might be it was inbuilt in him, he was not sure.

The village society also made him grow faster, precocious. He realised the childless couple reared him as an expression of love between them, not so much for the love of him, which might have come later, he had no idea.

When his foster father died of an accident while crossing the railway level crossing he observed this intense love in the grief stricken face of his foster mother; she didn't cry, didn't allow tears to wash away her love for him. The bond never snapped even when she took a man, which confused him.

He surmised it was out of necessity of feeding two mouths when the money she got as terminal benefits from her husband's office ran out. He felt perturbed and wanted to do something to lessen her burden. He got himself admitted to a school which served mid-day meal. The school was in a village far away from theirs. He still remembered the day he got admitted. The headmistress of the primary section asked; 'What's your name?'

'Jeet.'

'Father's name?'

'I'm a bastard'.

She stopped filling up the form, looked up with reddened face, but controlled herself quickly.

'Then, who gave you this name?'

'My foster father.'

'What's his name?'

'Chiranjit Dolui.'

She did not probe further; filled up the form and asked him to join the class.

On returning home he told his foster mother of his admission to school and of the mid-day meal. She smiled knowingly.

He was very attentive in the class, learnt his lessons diligently, not because he loved to study but because of the compulsion to stay in class till the mid-day meal: why not learn things in the meantime, he thought. Soon he became a darling of the class teacher who would often give him some extras over the meal quota, which made others envious.

One day a boy called him bastard... bastard... between claps, others joined the chanting till the teacher entered the class.

He marked the boy who started it, left the school early and waited in a bush by which the boy had to pass alone for a turn toward his home. When the boy was near the bush he leapt, shut his mouth with one hand and with the other dragged him behind the bush. He slapped him, kicked him, boxed him with the ferocity he never knew he had. He was not beating the boy; he was lashing out the two unknowns who brought him to this world.

There was no complaint; none in the school ever called him bastard.

The mid day-meal stopped with his completing the eighth standard. He was back to his void. He had no play mate, none would take him.

Every morning he walked to the outskirt of the village and sat before a barb-wired field where dogs of various species—from puddles to large ferocious looking dogs, were trained. The field was carved out of a large forest known as ghost forest. Villagers avoided this place. Stories abound across villages: whoever dared enter the forest was found dead next day outside the forest with a broken neck. He could not locate a ghost though he wished to find one to talk to when he sat alone under a banyan tree close to the field. During noon he would enter the forest to search for edible fruits—plenty of guavas, wild strawberries, plums, dates and wild tomato-like vegetables grew there; some he would eat directly from the tree, some sitting under among small animals running hither and thither, and some he would carry home. Occasionally he killed a few rabbits with a sharp knife he always carried.

Those nights they would have sumptuous dinner—they had not much of fish or meat after his foster father's death. After dinner they would talk—mostly she talked—which would invariably veer around her husband though dead for more than three years now. He would come back live in her eyes now glowing and glinting in the yellow light. At such times he felt he did not exist, only her husband; for him the atmosphere turned eerie. He had a confused sense of love. He felt what a deep attachment she had for her long-dead husband, she tried to recreate him out of dead ashes, how shackled she was by it, how dreamy and scary it was! He resolved he would never fall prey to it. And this continued to be the guiding principle of his life in the street despite occasional doubts: had he over reacted, over complicated a simple thing of life? But he brushed the thought aside, felt no reason to revise as it kept him in good stead in the mirage of the street.

His everyday going and sitting under the banyan tree drew attention of the men in the training field. One day he was called in. A man took him inside the tent to a room where they were having lunch. A man with a fierce face but benign eyes indicated him to a vacant chair, asked someone to serve him food, and said jocularly, 'It's lunch time for both the men and the dogs here, we also eat same thing, the meat; the only difference is they take it raw, we cooked, and of course some *rotis* to go with it, see for yourself.' He indicated a plate now placed before him with plenty of meat and *rotis*. When he began eating the man asked.

'We find you here every day. You don't go to school?'

'No. I left school at eighth standard.'

'Why?'

'We couldn't afford it.'
'Ok, no more personal questions. Tell me which dogs you like most.'
'The tallest ones you train for jumping higher and higher.'
'Ah-ha! You can also do it if you practice, you don't have to be a dog for this.'
There was laughter from all sides, he also smiled.

There was so much food; he managed to eat only half of it. He looked at his plate and turned to the man.

'I can't eat all the food; may I take the rest for my mother?'

'Of course you can.' The man asked the waiter to pack the food with some more meat put in.

While leaving he asked the man.

'May I come here and sit under the banyan tree as usual?'

'Oh sure, there is no problem.'

Next day he followed closely how a trainer coached a dog to leap from a distance to a target marked on a tree inside the field; after every successful jump the target was upped, so also the distance. The difficult part was to leap from a fixed spot without the momentum one gained from running.

He collected a broken piece of brick, marked the spots on the banyan tree and began practicing from the next day: jumping in the morning hours and knife throwing in the afternoon. One day the man came near the barbed wire and throwing a packet of white chalks to him said,

'Good progress, better than the dogs! But tell me why are you practicing knife throwing as well?'

'To kill rabbits in the forest.'

The man nodded and left.

For how many days and months he practiced he could not remember, but by the time he left the village he learnt almost everything one had to learn from dogs.

He had also learnt, not from dogs but form being alone in the vast expanse of land and forest to sit still and stand still in absolute silence, which over time became his second nature.

And the solitude made him turn inside and view the world from there which would later earn him name as street philosopher, and what he said would soon be quotable quotes among street dwellers.

That day he entered the forest, tested his knife-throwing on two rabbits one after another, they had no chance to flee. He started early for home with a happy note.

He shouldn't have, since he knew.

How could he be so oblivious of the obvious? He would curse himself forever for this indiscretion.

With two rabbits dangling from his hands, a bagful of wild fruits and vegetables in a side bag he went straight to his foster mother's room.

He shouldn't have.

The doors were ajar; he heard voices from inside. Through the opening he saw his mother locked with Vaishnav uncle, the rice mill owner of the village. He stood there glued.

He shouldn't have.

With every thrust Vaishnav uncle cried out, "Jai Radhe, Jai Krishna," which rose to a high pitch before turning a whimper as he collapsed on her body, her hands clasping his back.

He moved away slowly, unloaded the rabbits and vegetable bag on the door sill and walked out.

He shouldn't have.

He left the village, not because of what he saw—he knew it already—but he himself wanted to do it with her. Later when he masturbated behind a bush he felt miserable, and that was bad, haunting.

Toomba's reminiscence was rattled by some unusual commotion in the station area. He looked about himself: Bloody hell! Unconsciously he had walked all the way to the backyard of Sealdah station, like a dog trailing the smell of its urine, and sat himself at the same place he normally sat. Is it merely habit or something more than that? he wondered.

Presently, he rose and followed the crowd. He located a friend and asked him what had happened. 'Just heard: a girl from Triangular Park area came here to offer practical sex lessons at fifty rupees per penis. Ten enrolled. They were having it on the roof of the morgue. The girl is now dead; nobody knows when and how. All the ten boys had fled; the police have already arrived.'

A big crowd had already gathered. Toomba climbed to the roof of the morgue from the back wall, and saw a sickly girl of their age splayed on a mattress in a pool of blood down her waist, her right hand holding some currency notes.

A policeman noticed him and asked.

'Do you know this girl?'

'No sir, she doesn't belong to this place.'

'Then get lost.'

He climbed down. On his way back Toomba mused: what a novel way to earn money and what a novel way to die. Street children are really innovative! No one would claim the body; by tomorrow she would enter the cold storage under the roof she died, and later disposed of in lot. For the dead it didn't matter.

Chapter 6

Six months had passed. Jaggu had come closer to Mashi; a friend now in more than one sense. Chintu was no longer scared of him; rather they had become friends though of unequal age. He would often go out with him after he finished his day's quota, and returned very late in the night. Mashi did not bother as she was used to his nocturnal flights.

Jaggu had given him a boy who was a good thief and pickpocket trained by Jaggu himself. But the problem was he was often picked up by one NGO or the other, taken to some Home for counselling, vocational training, drawings and sundry other activities; it seemed he had great demand among them for both right and wrong reasons. In a fortnight's time he would flee from the Home but not before stealing something of value, which he would quickly sell at the Chora Bazaar nearby, board an outbound train with a broom to clean the floor of the compartment and in return ask some money from the passengers. By the time the train reached the terminal station he would have a pocket full of coins which he would sell at a premium to bus conductors who needed 'change'. He would roam about the market place to keep himself practiced—'but not much money at those god-forsaken villages', he commented when he returned to Jaggu.

When Biltu—that was the name he ascribed to himself—was working for Mashi for about a week a young girl working for a NGO met her. She had information of one of their registered inmates who fled from a Home had come back to Sealdah station and was presently working under Mashi.

Mashi reacted with an edge in her voice,

'Nobody works under me; I'm no employer.'

'Please don't get angry with me. If you know some of the platform boys here you may help me locate Debanand and get me out of a jam.'

Mashi looked at her: a thin girl, wrapped up in poverty, not more than twenty years. For a moment Mashi got softened but she immediately brushed off the emotion and answered in a casual voice.

'What is wrong with this boy?'

'Well, there is this boy, Debanand who is my find from this station. I took him to the office, got him registered and put him to a Home as we failed to elicit names of his parents, the village he has come from et cetera. He behaved well at the Home, attended all counselling sessions conducted by our experts, participated in vocational training in arts and crafts, joined enthusiastically in all educational programs and games organised by Home and sundry other activities designed by us specially for railway children. He appeared very intelligent, a quick learner and highly promising. For this reason, we allowed him some laxity like going out for a walk outside the campus. One such day he didn't return and some of our demonstration articles and cooking utensils were also found missing. We informed the police though we know they won't do much, but we've to keep our records straight.'

Mashi interjected, 'Any idea why did he flee the place; stealing cannot be the only reason, as you say he demonstrated a very good behaviour and showed interest in learning.'

'No idea. At that time we just thought he'd come back or we'd find him soon. After about a month, one of our operatives had found him at Bongaon engaged in pushing cows on to various trucks for export to Bangladesh. He was threatened a little but cajoled most to return. This time we placed him at a different Home. He reverted to his old good behaviour as if nothing had happened, but again fled, and again we got him back. This has happened four times during the past eight months. We will face problems if something happens to him because in our register and also of the Homes he was recorded as "Missing" in the Disposal column. My problem is worst as he is my recruit; I've got to find him.'

Although the girl said all these things slowly and hesitantly, she looked tired when she finished. Mashi offered her a glass of water but she brought out a bottle of mineral water from her side bag and drank half of it in one go. Mashi did not mind but she noticed the cap of the bottle which revealed that the branded bottle contained only spurious water poured into it by a group of railway children who collected used bottles from train compartments, sides of platforms, roadside et cetera, filled them with water from any nearby source, tightened the cap by a hand machine and sold them to stalls in and around Sealdah at rupees three to five depending on the size of the bottle. The girl must have picked up one such bottle while coming to the station at a discount on MRP. A smile appeared on Mashi's face which the girl mistook as an offence.

She began explaining but Mashi raised her hand and asked instead whether she would like to take some tea with her. She affirmed hurriedly. Mashi called in one of the boys and handed him a glass.

'Ask Chacha to send two teas in glasses cleaned twice with hot water, buy also four biscuits for us and two for you and tell him to add them all to my *khata*.' She patted the boy at the back and asked him to hurry up.

Mashi now looked at the girl with a disarming smile and said, 'Chacha's tea is very good; you'll like it.'

'Yes I know, I also take tea from his stall, though occasionally.'

'Is it? Then, we can be partner-in-tea. So let me tell you, your Debanand might be my Biltu; with him I've a different kind of partnership.'

'Then please hand him over to me; I'll be very grateful.'

'But what are you going to do with him? Put him to another Home? He'll again flee.'

'That's true,' the girl sounded uncertain.

'I think working within the framework of your systemised organisation you have not understood his need properly. Stealing or pick pocketing is just a vocation for him for making a living; he is so intelligent he could switch to any other vocation with ease. But that's not his need. He is a free bird, a wanderer beyond redemption.'

'But we found him tremendously enthusiastic about all the activities in every Home he stayed. He executed all his assignments so quickly we often wondered how can a boy of his age do so which we ourselves wouldn't be able to do. A wanderer would not exhibit such behaviour. I'd rather say he is a misguided child who if groomed properly could be an asset to the society.'

'No, your grooming will slaughter the life in him. You said he is a quick learner. You're right, but the society overboard—and yours is a part of it, is a stereotype, has only limited things to offer for learning which Biltu learns quickly and then gets bored and then starts hating them, and because he hates he finishes them quickly, and also most efficiently as he hates to repeat them all over again: a person is efficient when he loves a job but most efficient when he hates it. I've learnt this from Chintu, Biltu, Chottu, Kittu and other boys working with me and also a great deal from Jaggu, a big Dada here.'

The girl reacted angrily hearing the name of Jaggu.

'I know Jaggu; he treats us like enemies and he is the person who's spoiling Debanand's kind of bright boys.'

Mashi looked at the angry face of the girl and smiled cryptically before responding.

'One thing is competition. The street children are a huge market for NGOs, Dadas and mashis. They compete with each other, for you to fulfil your quota and for them to increase their entourage, for you to obtain more donations and for them to increase their earnings. You provide one kind of service and they another; you try to showcase boys like Biltu by bringing them to the mainstream of society, Jaggu dadas let them live the way they want to.'

In the meantime the teas were getting cold and biscuits waiting to be munched. Mashi picked her glass and indicated the girl to do likewise. Between sipping and munching Mashi fished out an oil smudged paper now straightened and gave it to the girl. It was originally a paper bag in which she brought fish fry from Chacha's yesterday. She was an avid reader of newspapers and books while in village; her husband would bring books from Town Library and she would collect other news papers of different publishers subscribed by their neighbours on the following day and read them during her free times from family chores. After coming to Sealdah station she had abandoned many of her earlier habits, newspaper reading was one of them. But her eyes would automatically get attracted to any printed material that came to sight. Chacha's paper bags made out of old newspapers and journals were one such source of her reading. She would throw away most of them after reading but preserved those relating to her present life. The one she had just handed to the girl must be from a journal as the thickness of the paper suggested. The girl began reading.

The world of these children is far removed from the make-believe world we live in.

The society, as it is profoundly called, mimics the goodness of belonging and suppresses all its ills by ascribing them to fate and feeling relieved by doing it. The society knows the street children exist: one section placates them as unfortunates who need help, another section feels they are a nuisance, eyesore and must be removed, a third section feels they may not belong to the society, but they live on society, hence should be brought back and be readied for the mainstream to contribute meaningfully to the society. These three sections give birth to three groups of NGOs each according to its approach to the street children. Funds flow in from here and abroad; contributors are relieved of their sins, Homes are built, scholars funded for doing research, getting a PhD and publishing papers in scholarly journals, which bring in more fund; a new source of employment and income generation is created for those belonging to the society; the marginals remain beyond margin, and as the society is unable to solve the basic problems of the society at source, marginals multiply. The issue here...

The girl turned the paper to find the continuation of the article but it was not there, the packet manufacturer did not know its other usage besides packing.

The girl re-read the portion once again, this time more slowly and then spoke.

'Well, I agree with the basic thrusts of the writer; yes we can't solve the basic problems of society which drive the children to the street but we can't wash our hands off to wait for the day when the society changes itself. We belong to the third category of the NGOs; we believe we can't just stand aside when we find a boy of Debanand's merit going astray in the dungeons of your so called free bird community. We want them to bloom, to be responsible members of the society. It is an inclusive effort. But the Jaggus and Mashis like you are blocking the effort.'

The girl developed a taunting edge in her voice while ending the sentence but Mashi ignored it and responded in a level voice.

'I also agree with the basic proposition of the writer that the society is not willing to address the ultimate causes behind the children coming to the street. When the problem surfaces it creates the NGOs to make it pliable for the society, and when you fail to do it you pass on the failure to *us*. For me I'm no different from Biltus. I don't exercise any authority over them. Biltu is partnering with me for about a week now. Where he'll be next day or what he'll do next, I do not know, nor does he; where I'll be tomorrow and what I'll do, I do not know, and no one cares. This is the concept of freedom in the street. It may be they often over fantasise it because I've also seen them falling into routines as society people do, but this is their basic philosophy which is handed down to them from one street-generation to the other. There are children like Biltu who are fiercely independent; it is more enchanting than life, and you can't give it to them because your concept of freedom and their concept of freedom are different.'

'But some of them might end up becoming gangsters if left to them, and it is our duty to prevent it.'

'Yes, some may end up forming gangs, and thus make an entry to the society through the underworld. And if the pawns are appropriately moved on the society's chess board a few of them might go overboard. Kanu, Nadim and Benga that I know of are already there and Jaggu is trying to join the league. Your society needs them, it lures the most powerful to move up, but then, they no longer belong to the street, they become you.'

The girl said almost resignedly, 'But Mashi do you think we've nothing to do? You are so informed, so clear minded, so knowledgeable about what is happening around, you yourself can counsel the boys you know, or at least Jaggu, whom I understand you know closely, to avoid treading on wrong path.'

'I don't counsel.'

Silence. The girl was confused, devastated. She sat there with head low, hands on her lap. Observing this Mashi broke the silence.

'We've discussed so many things but I suppose your problem remains unsolved.'

She woke up as though from slumber and said meekly, 'Yes, that's true.'

'I can suggest a way out.'

'Oh! Please do.'

'Let me call Biltu.' She beckoned a boy to bring Biltu.

Biltu turned stiff when he saw the girl sitting humbly by Mashi's side. Ruffling his hairs with one hand and raising his chin with the other Mashi said, 'Don't be so stiff, Biltu.'

Biltu responded rather haughtily, 'I know why auntie has come. I won't go back. If she forces me again as she did last time calling other aunties and that elephant guard, I promise I'll again run away, and this time I'll steal something big.'

Mashi said, 'Okay, okay. You don't have to go with her except for one last time, and only for a few minutes.'

'Why?'

"Cause when you first came here she provided you a shelter, and when you first disappeared from the Home stealing something she didn't pursue with the police to arrest you. And when you did it for the fourth time she also didn't lodge further complaints. Isn't she good? But for doing all these for you she herself is in trouble now and she needs your cooperation to get her out of it.'

For the first time Biltu looked at the auntie with soft eyes. Mashi put her hand around his neck and implored.

'Go with her to the NGO office for the last time and tell them your mashi who had brought you up has at last found you, she is presently staying at the station before finding a shelter. Can you articulate these things before them?'

'No problem'. Biltu was all smiles now.'

'Is that all right?' Mashi asked the girl.

'I hope so.'

'Then take him with you, complete the formalities, if you want me to sign any paper, I'll do that.'

'That may not be necessary. Biltu's statement and my corroboration will be sufficient.'

'Then go, and send him back quickly.'

From that day the girl and Mashi became friends. She would often bring her colleagues from similar such NGOs and soon Mashi's corner became a meeting place for them which enriched both.

Chapter 7

Mashi had begun liking the station life though she had not explored it fully. Now she wanted to do it firsthand. She desired to visit places where her kind of lives existed; she also needed a vocation of her own.

On her first journey she wore an inconspicuous sari with holes made on it, removed whatever trace of vermillion that existed between her braids, picked up a much used broom and boarded a local train. Immediately she started sweeping the floor of the compartment, more particularly the narrow space between the rows of seat facing each other. Often her hand touched their legs, and her chest touched the knees of the sitting passengers; occasionally the upper edge of the sari might slip which she would immediately set right but not before revealing her cleavage. When she finished sweeping and did her Namaste with a solicitous hand she found a good number of coins and small notes falling in her hand: those giving note invariably touched her hand on the pretext of preventing it from flying away by the gust of wind—they were mostly middle aged men, younger men avoided touching her hand.

She got down at every station to make a quick survey of the platform and its immediate vicinity to locate her counterparts. If she found one, she noted down the name of the station in a small note book before boarding the next compartment.

On the first day itself she met her competitor, a chit of a boy doing the same thing from the other side of the compartment. Their eyes met though from a distance; she ignored him and continued working from her side. When they met half-way she whispered to him promising a twenty percent share of her collections. The boy smiled and they became allies. They often met at platforms. The boy noticed Mashi looking around and taking notes. Puzzled he asked her about it. Mashi replied she was searching for a friend who should be in one of the stations in this line the name of which she had forgotten.

'That's not a problem at all; I know all the stations along this line, we ourselves stay in one of the stations', the boy said enthusiastically.

'I also want to make friends with families living in the stations.'

'That'll be very nice. First I'll take you to meet our parents at Dumdum station which we've left behind. Would you like to go now? The down train would be arriving soon on the opposite platform.'

'Not now. First we shall go to the terminal station of this route.'

The train whistled. Both of them ran to board the train. The boy jumped to catch the outer handle of a compartment and helped Mashi get in as the train started moving. Mashi noted that although she could run and jump, the sari was not the right attire; the boy would not be there all the time, nor did she want it. She resolved to buy a cheap *salwar-kameez* before the next journey.

When the train reached terminal station they waited for the passengers to leave and then began searching empty compartments. Mashi followed the boy who was very systematic; he knew places where passengers were likely to leave behind articles unmindfully.

Total collections included a variety of items: used and unused bottles of water, cold drinks, baby milk bottle, nappy packs, food items, books, small packs of sanitary napkins, hair clips and sundry other small items. Mashi did not have much as compared to the boy's collections which included a standard mobile phone that drew Mashi's attention: she had been thinking for some time to have one. She picked it up and was about to press a button when the boy snatched it from her hand. Mashi felt offended, but he did not explain busy as he was in opening the back side of the phone. He drew out the small SIM card and showing it to Mashi explained, 'The first thing you must do when you pick a mobile phone is to take out the SIM card and destroy it like this.' He cut it with his teeth into several pieces and throwing them on the railway lines continued, 'If you don't do that you may be located by the police, though for a small piece like this no one will lodge a complaint, still one must be careful.'

'Yes, I understand; I'll never do it next time. Now tell me what'd you do with this phone?'

'I already have one; my parents also own one each; I'm going to sell this.'

'How much do you expect?'

The boy examined the phone with critical eyes, pulled out the battery deftly, measured the dust under it, wiped out all the dust from inside the case and then shutting the cover with a click replied, 'This is about two years old; I expect to get about three hundred rupees for this.' Then he looked at Mashi and asked, 'Do you have a mobile?'

'No.'

'Then you may buy this from me; say at two hundred fifty rupees.'

'Let's settle at two hundred.'

'Ok, done.' The innocence returned to his face.

When the exchange was complete the boy said, 'You'll have to buy a SIM card. Naboda sells it at rupees eighty for hundred minutes talk time a month. He has a mobile shop outside Dumdum station; I'll take you there while returning.'

The down train would leave in two hours. They had time for lunch, but first they had to dispose of the articles collected from the train compartments. Both of them carried the articles to an open godown near the market place. A man sitting on a stool evaluated the articles and paid hundred rupees to the boy and thirty rupees to Mashi after some bickering. They returned to a station side food stall and ordered lunch separately. Before the food arrived Mashi asked. 'Are you all from a village?'

'My parents are, but we were all born at different railway stations: I at Liluah, younger brother at Diamond Harbour and the sister at Belur. You know Belur; it's a holy place, Goddess Kali lives there in person in a temple built by a great seer, Swami Vivekananda. My mother says Chumki is very lucky for being born at Belur. Everyone loves her for this.'

'Have you ever visited the temple?'

'We tried, but it was a bad experience. All of us stood in a long queue, moving slowly. Chumki was crying intermittently as she was hungry. After about an hour we reached the temple. When we were about to scale the steps a Sadhu in saffron attire appeared from nowhere and stopped us.'

"You cannot have Darshan of the Mother wearing these dirty garments and a crying child; Mother Goddess will be very angry and curse you for this. Now leave the place at once and never show up again to incur the wrath of Ma Kali."

'We left the place. My mother was angry and took it on Chumki by giving her a slap, father was down faced. After we walked for some time leaving the temple courtyard father tried to console us by saying, "The Sadhu was right. One should not try to get a Darshan of a living Goddess wearing dirty garments; it'd be a sin". I didn't understand this sin-fin, nor my younger brother who clasped my hand strongly with a resolve.'

'Next day the two of us went there. On the way we picked up two solid brick stones. It was late afternoon; we scaled the wall to the courtyard and waited in a bush near the wall. We saw saffron clad Sadhus roaming about in groups of two or three. We tried to locate the Sadhu who ill treated us but failed, all of them looked so alike! We resolved that since all of them look same all must be bad, hitting anyone should be okay. After waiting for a few minutes we saw two Sadhus coming near us discussing something. We threw the brick stones with all our might. As soon as we heard an "ankh" and saw a target falling we jumped the railing and fled.'

Mashi heard the story amusedly. Now she asked, 'Did you tell your parents about this adventure?'

'No. It was our personal vengeance.'

The lunch finished, they rose together, paid their bills and left for the station. The train was already on the down platform to leave in a few minutes. The boy entered from the front, Mashi the rear with their respective brooms. They often met on platform before changing compartment to share their experiences and also to laugh heartily on the funny behaviour of some passengers.

When the train reached Dumdum junction station they proceeded to the exit gate with brooms in sweeping posture. Once they were out they went to Naboda's shop. The boy approached the counter with Mashi in tow and addressed the man behind the counter.

'Naboda I've brought a new customer. Give her a SIM with hundred twenty minutes talk time. The man took a look at the mobile, opened the drawer and selected a SIM and a battery charger. Handing these to Mashi he said, "Hundred minutes talk time, hundred rupees, the charger goes with it," in one breath.'

Mashi paid the money, took the articles and left with the boy. They found a place nearby and the boy immediately began demonstrating how to put in the SIM card at the appropriate socket and also to take it out, as next time when she came to recharge she'd get a new SIM card. Mashi practiced it several times. When the boy was satisfied he asked her to put the back cover in place which she did. The boy now switched on the phone. When the light appeared on the screen he nodded satisfactorily. Next, Mashi learnt how to switch on the phone, make a call, receive one, save a number, turn the phone to silent mode, and finally switch it off. He also showed how to charge the battery from an electric outlet now available at most of the big stations. The first call she made was to the boy's number and the first number she saved was also his. In the coming few days Mashi would practice all these to gain full control of the apparatus.

Mashi could anticipate the next destination as the boy led her back toward the station. She noted the boy was intelligent, did things seriously and loved his family.

Adjacent to the iron railing fencing the station she saw a *jhopri* made of flattened bamboo sticks on sides and a tarpaulin sheet on top. Outside, a woman was cooking something while keeping her eyes on a child crawling the open space, a male voice from inside asking for something. The boy taking Mashi's hand went to the woman and said, 'Look Ma, I've brought in a new Mashi to meet you.'

The woman checked the progress of cooking; satisfied she lifted the pan from the *sigri* and placing it by her side lowered down the fire by pushing in and out an iron stick through a window like opening at the bottom of the *sigri* and finally shutting its lid she looked at Mashi, and offered her a low stool to sit on. The woman's eyes reflected an interplay of anxiety, suspicion and cunning but underneath there was that innocence, the urge to believe that she saw in the boy's eyes.

Mashi said with an acquainting smile, 'Your son is a very good boy and a good teacher too; he taught me so many things.'

'You're new in the line?'

'Yes.'

'Husband, children?'

'None. My husband left me at Sealdah station.'

'Ah-ha, that's very sad, very... very... sad, these men are...'

At that time they heard a coughing sound from inside the *jhopri*. 'That's my husband seeking permission to come out as if he always cares.' Without turning her head she said, 'Yes, you may come out and meet Banku's new found Mashi; shall I help you?'

'That won't be necessary; I may come out on my own,' a guttural voice came from inside.

Slowly a man emerged supported on a make-shift crutch. The woman waited for him to come nearer, and then she got up to help him sit down on a stool. He was perspiring and breathless from the exertion. Regaining his breath he said, 'So, this time he's dragged you here, often does this, such an innocent boy, but where is he now?'

'Must've gone out taking Chumki to the railway colony to visit Krishna,' the woman answered. Then turning to Mashi she said, 'Krishna is my second son who works at a railway quarter nearby. I've named all my children after a god or goddess: Banku or Bankubehari, and Krishna after Lord Krishna; Chumki's given name is Shyama after Goddess Kali. Isn't that good?'

Before Mashi could respond the husband spoke in a dismal voice.

'I never wanted Banku and Krishna to work at such a young age. They were studying in a school before I had that accident; they had to leave school to earn. Even my wife works as a washerwoman. Now, in my family everyone works except me.'

Feigning anger the woman rasped. 'Stop lamenting. An accident is an accident, why blame yourself for this? We all love you; we work so that you can take rest, as the doctor wants you to, for quick recovery. By God's grace you'd regain your health soon and start working again, and then we shall stop working.'

Mashi turned her eyes to the husband to congratulate him for having such a loving wife but stopped short of doing so when she observed the man leering at her bosom unmindful of what his wife was saying. Their eyes met and he shifted his eyes to the wife who now turned from the *sigri* and said, 'Now eat these chops I've just fried.'

The chops were good, made of a combination of different leftover vegetables: next day the taste would be different with different set of vegetables. Mashi felt nostalgic but quickly shrugged it aside, and also that leer of the man. Munching a chop she commented. 'Your chops are good, so are you; every piece smells of love for your husband and the family'. Then addressing the husband she said, 'You're fortunate to have such a loving wife and lovable children.'

'Yes', he responded with downcast eyes.

Observing this his wife complained, 'Look, again he has turned sullen. He was never like this before, he never complained. Even when he was lynched severely by village folks led by my father, he did not complain, did not hit back, he also stopped his friends from retaliation out of respect for my father except, when they tried to snatch me out. It was too much for him. He rose from the ground—a bloody spectre— and jumped on them with such a vehemence all got puzzled. With one hand he recovered me from the grasp of my father, pushed me inside our house and with the other he snatched a *lathi* from one of my father's henchmen and started hitting them with such a force that his friends who had by now joined him were also surprised. He threw away the *lathi* with a 'saala' when they fled, and fell flat on the ground. We carried him inside, blood all over his body. He was hit on the head, on his torso, legs, everywhere.'

'I suppose your father was against this marriage.' Mashi interjected.

'Yes. My father could never approve our marriage: he is a Brahmin and a *jotedar* and my husband is a *chamar* orphaned in his childhood.'

'I guessed as much. Now please go ahead.'

'Yes. I wiped his wounds with warm water, applied *keshut* leaf paste all over his body and fanned him with a palm-leaf fan. His friends thought he wouldn't survive but I knew he would. After about an hour he opened his eyes and smiled—what a beautiful smile it was!'

At this Mashi looked at her husband. He also blushed and smiled, perhaps the same smile he gave to his wife on that day. The woman also blushed at his gaze. Mashi felt that the person who leered at her minutes back and the one who was now looking at his wife with so much love were two different persons: one a body and the other a soul and the two were not in conflict now. She also thought: the police officer who fucks her might have a loving wife at home to make love with.

When the couple settled down from their love exchanges Mashi asked, 'What happened next?'

'The first sentence he spoke after gaining consciousness was that we must leave the village soon because my father would reorganise and come back, and with his present state he wouldn't be able to resist. He had difficulty in speaking but he continued, "A train would be leaving for Howrah station in about three hours. I'll be all right by then." He asked his friends to stay back and asked me to pack quickly whatever we had.

'He was very weak, couldn't walk; we carried him to the station by a hand cart, his friends helped him board the train. During the journey he was semiconscious; I could feel he had high fever. An elderly woman who sat by my side asked what had happened and where were we going. I told her he had fallen from a boulder while cutting stones in a quarry and I was taking him to Howrah General Hospital. She looked at his bruised face, touched his forehead and advised me anxiously: You'd better get down at Liluah and get him admitted to the sub-divisional hospital there. We got down at Liluah and with the help of a van-rickshaw puller took him to the hospital. For the next few months the station was my home. The station dwellers were very friendly. I was four months pregnant then. They helped me in so many ways I cannot describe.'

She stopped for a while to observe her husband who still sat with his head down. She snapped.

'Look how remorseful he is now. Can you imagine that this is the same person who during his entire stay at the hospital never cursed his fate, never lamented even afterwards when he returned from the hospital.'

'We happily set ourselves at a corner of the station where Banku was born. Our savings were running out. He took up the job of pulling van rickshaw: it has one advantage, when your legs are tired you could push the cart by hands, and his hands are more powerful than his legs. He was full of confidence.

'But we couldn't stay at that station for long. A new station master came, then a new police officer. They demanded so much money none of the station dwellers could afford. The police would often throw our things; beat us up if the ransom was not paid. We left Liluah for another station and then another like that, everywhere it was the same. Finally we arrived at this junction station. It is very large with a number of platforms; number of dwellers in and around the station was very large and organised. He continued his rickshaw pulling here too; his earnings had also increased substantially. Things began looking up. But unfortunately he fell in a ditch while giving pass to a speeding lorry and broke his legs. The station master helped him get admitted to a government hospital. The bed was free but we had to buy costly medicines. To augment our income I began working as a washerwoman for the liveries of the station employees and Krishna got a job in the residential quarter of station master. They are very kind to us and we hope to stay here longer. The hospital doctor says he will recover fully in 3-4 months. Then we shall buy a van rickshaw taking a small loan, the remaining amount we've already saved. Just imagine, the van rickshaw will be *his own!* We are also thinking of renting a small room and starting life afresh.'

'I'm sure all your dreams will be fulfilled.' Mashi smiled to both and rose to leave.

'You won't wait for the children, they'll be here soon,' the woman beseeched.

'I'm very sorry. I've got to reach my destination before it is very late in the night. Please convey my love to your children and give this hundred ten rupees to Banku as his share of my earnings.'

Entering the station Mashi boarded a Sealdah-bound train about to leave. The distance was not much, but for her it was long; she cursed herself for hearing their story, wanted to reach her corner fast. She was running away from the lure of a life that lived in the future. Life had taught her to push aside dreams and live in the present only; she had no desire to reverse the process; present is much less complicated than the future.

When she settled herself at her corner of the Sealdah station, Biltu came running.

'Jaggudada had been arrested by the police for drug smuggling. As he was hit on the leg badly during cross firing, he couldn't run. Chintu was also hit but he slipped out; the police are now looking for him everywhere.'

Chapter 8

After Chameli left, Minu reclined against the back wall of the building spreading her legs forward, brought out a cigarette and started smoking. She saw people coming in to spend a quiet late night after the liquor shops shuttered them out. Soon, all the nooks and underbellies of the building, which was once a sprawling palace, would be filled up.

Decades back everything hard, soft and liquid happened here; all the wantonness displayed in grandeur inside the plastered walls, under the chandeliers, along the carpeted floor with dancers moving from one animated courtier to another; every bit of the music composed to cause arousals that ended in soft beds of well-decorated rooms. Now also the same scenes were enacted inside the same palace, not under chandeliers, but under the open sky dimly lit by stars and dying moon, not on soft beds but on cracked marbles.

So where is history? It is all present. Why should we study history at all? These were the questions she put before her history teacher when she was studying in ninth standard.

She was Shraddha then. Some teachers of the school did not like her as she was wont to ask odd questions that embarrassed them before the class, but they could not do much because her questions were right, though answers unknown, and because she was a jewel in the eye of the headmistress who was confident she would carve out a name for the school in the Secondary Examination. She always stood first with very high scores, was consecutively a champion in several sports events of the district. None of the teachers despite their misgivings could ever think of punishing her.

That day the history teacher became very angry when she questioned the very basis of studying history. She already had misgivings about her, wanted to punish her on some pretext. Now she rasped at her.

'How audacious you are to question the veracity of the discipline of history; do you think we all have been fools?'

'No Miss. I only expressed my doubts and frustration. I've read four history books and some articles from District Library. They are written by eminent historians. I found that one could never know the absolute truth of the past through historical studies. While faces disappear, writings fade, all the talks of life die with the death of the talker, the historians try to recreate the past from inanimate objects and in doing so they give a different version of the same event, even the reconstruction of events differ. So why read history at all? To increase confusion?'

The teacher was burning inside; still she tried to hold her position before the class.

'Do you think you've become a pundit just by reading a few books? One must study history to understand the present, to get prepared to face the present when similar things happen. Didn't I tell you: history repeats itself?'

'That's a myth, Miss. If no one knows the absolute truth of what happened in the past or when the historians are so opinionated in holding their own version of the truth, the analysis of the present gets vitiated; we can't even visualise the near future by analyzing the recent past. I once thought of specialising in historical studies, now I've abandoned the idea. I'd better study the present with no hangover of the past than wasting time on studying history. I think the department of history should be wound up and history books burned.'

While the entire class was following the debate with rapt attention, and appreciating why Shraddha was the darling of the headmistress, the last sentence, which was too harsh, snapped the tolerance limit of the teacher: this precocious chit of a girl had challenged her discipline at its very base, and she did not have an answer, which infuriated her even further.

Shraddha never liked the history teacher not because of her mode of teaching but for her single mode of punishment to a delinquent student. She would call the student, make her stand before the class and squeeze her budding breasts till tears wetted her dress out of pain or shame. Shraddha had observed that during such time contours of the teacher's face changed in a peculiar way and her eyes turned glassy. The girls did not complain out of shame.

Presently she rushed toward Shraddha, caught her by the hair, dragged her before the class and began squeezing her breasts with such a savage fierceness that she shrivelled, but that was for moments only. She straightened herself quickly, looked straight at the eyes of the teacher. What she did next no one could imagine! She threw herself on her, pinned her down on the floor and straddling her began squeezing her breasts with the fierceness matching that of the teacher a few seconds before. To her amazement she found the teacher did not make any attempt to throw her off, rather she lay on the floor as if in a trance. She got puzzled, withdrew herself quickly and ran out from the school.'

Minu did not change her sitting posture while reminiscing about Shraddha, did not even move her legs. Her eyes had a distant look, not visible in the dim light. She did not notice a man approaching her stealthily. She was startled by an animated voice: 'Why sitting here alone darling; let's go inside and have fun.' Coming to her senses she drew her legs instinctively before shouting at the voice, '*Hatt sala*; don't disturb me.' But the man was persistent.

'Why play game my love? I've five hundred rupees with me, I'll give you all.'

'All?' Minu got up slowly.

'Yeah, all,' he came closer.

'Then, take all.' She hit him between his legs in a flash.

'Onk', the man uttered holding his crotch.

'Not satisfied? Want more?' she advanced.

The man ran, his hands still there.

'*Sala harami*, go and fuck your mother.' She shouted at the running figure though it was unlikely the man was in any condition to hear the invectives.

She sat back, lighted another cigarette and slowly released the smoke. She tried to follow the movement of the smoke even in semi-darkness. There was not much of a wind now; the pool of the smoke took time to break into different shapes while drifting, each shape degenerating into shapes of smaller and smaller sizes before vanishing into nothingness.

Minu was back to being Shraddha again.

She was panting from running when she entered the house. It was late noon. She saw her mother sitting with Anu uncle—a childhood friend of his father—in veranda, both were laughing, probably on some jokes. She stood before them, pulled out everything from the school bag and threw them on the courtyard one by one and finally the bag itself. With rage in her eyes she declared, 'I'm not going to school anymore', and entered her bedroom. She picked up all her study materials from the corner table—the books, maps, pencils, pens, copy books, erasers, everything—and threw them out through the widow. Anu uncle and her mother rushed in together and saw Shraddha standing at the centre of the room foaming at the mouth. Anu uncle tried to say something but Shraddha looked at him with such vehemence he retreated quickly. She did not respond to her mother's questioning, explained nothing. When she embraced Shraddha to pacify she remained stiff as a dead bone.

So many things happened so fast during that day and night, and thereafter that Shraddha jumped her adolescence and became a woman.

Father came back from factory that evening. He was not drunk, which he usually was. He looked at the mess on the courtyard and entered the house shouting for Shraddha. He had heard she had beaten a teacher of the school and for that she might be rusticated. He dragged her by the hair to the veranda and pointing at the shambles asked, 'Who did this?'

No answer.

'Why did you do this?'

No answer.

'Why did you hit your teacher?'

No answer.

'Do you know you might be rusticated for this?'

No answer.

Father lost his patience and started beating her head to toe. Mother rushed in to save but he shoved her aside with such a force she fell against the wall unconscious. With renewed rage he threw her on the floor and began kicking. She did not cry, which increased his fury. He threw her out on the courtyard still damp from the morning rains. She did not cry, made no attempt to get up, just lay there. Despite all the beatings she felt no pain, only hatred, was numb in her muscles, but fully conscious.

He went inside, came back with a bottle and glass, looked at the prostrated figure of his wife, shrugged his shoulders and opened the bottle. How long he drank she had no idea as she went into a slumber on the cool earth of the courtyard. She woke up by a shrill cry. It was her mother. She stooped on her husband's figure, now sprawled on the floor and convulsing. She cried out 'Shraddha... Shraddha... ', but in response she closed her eyes and changed side.

She heard her mother's hurried steps down the veranda and courtyard, saw her opening the gate and running out. Soon she came back in a car with Anu uncle. Together they lifted the body of her father, carried him to the rear seat of the car, mother holding his head on her lap. Shraddha soon fell asleep.

She was awakened by her mother in the morning. She was groggy and her legs slipped. Her mother cradled her to the bed. She had high fever. Mother went out and telephoned Anu uncle from a pay phone nearby. He soon came with the local doctor. The doctor examined her bruises, took the temperature and wrote a prescription. Anu uncle brought the medicines and two bagfuls of eatables and informed her mother that the fever was due to bruises and her lying on the wet ground overnight; it would cure soon with the ointments to be applied thrice a day and the antibiotic twice a day. He then carried the bags to the kitchen, mother following.

Shraddha's fever showed signs of abatement in two days but her body ached. As she alternated between unconscious and conscious she could not recollect much of what happened except the teacher punishing her... she retaliating... father beating her... Anu uncle and mother carrying her father to a car... What happened to her father? Hearing voices coming from the veranda she alighted from the bed and clomped toward the main door. As she tried to open it she slipped and fell with a thump. Mother and Anu uncle opened the door and saw her sprawled on the floor. While lifting her she felt her temperature had turned normal and exclaimed, 'Oh! The fever is gone, now come and sit with us.' She helped her sit on a chair; Anu uncle sat by her side. He held her hand, she cringed, but he did not leave her hand, rather holding it firmly implored.

'You see Shraddha, don't hold a grudge against your father anymore; he had his due already for beating you so mercilessly; he had a severe stroke that night which has rendered him immobile for quite some time; he'd feel worse if he felt you're still angry with him. I can't blame him also: he heard you'd be rusticated for beating a teacher of yours. That made him mad; he had his dreams about you, he could not tolerate those dreams shattered; after all you're his only child and he loves you very much.'

Shraddha did not say a word in reply; just looked ahead. Her mother brought breakfast on a tray and arranged the food before her.

'Now eat your breakfast fully; you'll feel stronger,' she said.

Shraddha first looked at the tray and then to the food items laid on it.

'You've never before brought breakfast on a tray, and all these items I've never eaten in my life.'

Mother took her hand in hers and said, 'It's a continental breakfast, very nutritious; your uncle has chosen them personally for you. These will help you recover faster.'

'I won't eat any of these, Besides, I'm not feeling hungry,' replied Shraddha.

'You're being obstinate. You've not eaten anything for the last three days except some milk and a few biscuits. Now please eat them or your uncle will be very hurt.'

'Who asked him to bring all these?'

'Nobody. He brought all these so you recover quickly.'

Give me my *roti* and *bhaji* on a plate, I'll recover much faster.'

Her mother now turned to Anu uncle.

'See how obstinate she is, just like his father. You remember that Sunday when you brought so many goodies for our breakfast; he didn't touch any, insisted on his *roti* and *bhaji* which I had to cook separately.'

'Forget it *baudi;* she is still very disturbed. Just think, so many things had happened to her during the past few days, and she is just a child.'

'I'm no longer a child, and I don't want your sympathy.' She rose, and this time, steadily walked back to her room.

The headmistress came in the evening. Mother welcomed her heartily, advanced her a chair in the porch and called Shraddha. When she appeared mother told her with an empathising smile, 'Your headmistress had come every day when you lay unconscious. She told me yesterday, you'd not be rusticated; she had arranged everything. Now you talk with her; I'm preparing the tea.'

The headmistress was sad, not angry with the girl she loved most. She had heard what happened that day from other girls of the class. Shraddha raised a question which was being debated among the historians all over the world. As a historian herself she was aware of it. In fact, observing her inclination she advised her to read books and articles from District Library. On that day her teacher should have welcomed the debate, called her to Teachers' room, and discussed the issues with her in more details so as to kindle her inquiring mind.

It was true, Shraddha was somewhat rash but that did not call for a corporal punishment bordering on molestation, or, was it actual molestation the students had now complained?

The school Board had decided to rusticate her outright but she somehow made them agree on a compromise formula. She thought it proper not to raise the molestation issue in that meeting as she feared it might jeopardise her objective, more so because the history teacher was the niece of the chairman of the Board.

Now she looked fully at her dear student: no doubt she was still ill but her countenance and look had changed so much she felt she was not looking at a child but a hardened mature girl. She asked her to sit pulling a chair before her and thought of softening her hardness by announcing the good news first.

'Your mother's right. It's all been arranged. After all, the school cannot spoil the future of a bright student like you. You just sign an apology-cum-appeal letter I have drafted for you and join the class from tomorrow.'

'Why should I apologise?'

'Well, the history teacher had punished you for some misdemeanours; can't she do it as a teacher? But being a pupil you cannot return back, can you?'

'Punishment and molestation aren't one and same. She molested me, I gave it back to her and she enjoyed it; it's not between a teacher and a pupil but between two women; so why an apology?'

Shraddha stated it so matter-of-factly the headmistress was amazed. Who was she talking to now, the girl of yesterdays, full of life, pranks and precociousness, or of tomorrows, somber, worldly and tough? She almost resigned to herself but still made a last try: one cannot just allow such a brilliant girl go astray.

'Do you know your obstinacy may result in your not getting admitted to a school anywhere?'

'I don't care.'

'You don't want to study?'

' No. I've thrown away all my books.'

'What are you saying? You are a pride of the school, have a bright future and you want to ruin everything just because you had a fight with the teacher?'

'I don't care.'

'What then are you going to do with your life?'

'I don't care.'

Well, thought the Headmistress resignedly, arrogance goes hand in hand with brilliance.

By the time her mother came with tea and snacks the headmistress had left.

'Where has she gone?'

'I don't know.'

Shraaddha rose and walked back to her room.

It was nearly midnight. Shraddha heard Anu uncle's car stopping before the house. The beginning she thought; no, it must have started much earlier. She changed her side and slept.

After a week Anu uncle announced: father would be released in a day or two; he had survived but lost his voice and was paralysed from the waist, which required engagement of a physiotherapist who would do the massaging and also take care of his other daily needs: 'I've already found one, he'd come eight in the morning and leave at eight in the night.'

They brought father home; an emaciated person, hands dangling by his sides. He was placed at a corner of the corridor that turned toward the bath room. A well built young man accompanied him.

Shraddha had a complex relationship with her father. He wanted a male child and always blamed her mother for begetting a female one. She ignored his accusation most of the time except occasionally during a high pitch quarrel, which might have started for some other reason, but father would invariably bring this issue to the fore, then mother would speak up, 'Getting a male child required male power which you don't have, so don't shout,' and that stopped the quarrel, father retreating downcast.

Shraddha thought her father had become weak because she was a female, not male, and deep in her mind she took his side. She resolved to prove herself better than a male, to compensate her father's weakness. (What a childish thought! She mused much later). Whenever she stood first in class or in the district as a whole or excelled in any sport generally known to be a male's domain, she would run to her father for appreciation, but she never got it; though that never dampened her spirit as she felt perhaps she was yet to achieve that level which would compensate her father's weakness.

Shraddha did not understand but Minu knew it now that her father had always regarded her as a live symbol of the failure of his manhood which no amount of her achievement could compensate; he had a rudimentary idea of biological process, not much educated he was, and he was sexually weak. And this weakness prevented him from expressing love for his daughter, which she realised while nursing her father.

'*All the lording of male beings disappears when bedroom door closes. His lordship turns a minion in six seconds,*' she mused when she became Minu.

Shraddha often sat on the cot where her father lay. He tried to raise his feeble hands to caress her with tears in his eyes, and that strained him. Soon she began taking his hands into hers to express solidarity. He wanted to say so many things but only gurgling sounds issued from his throat. Soon she learnt to distinguish between gurgles signifying love and hatred, between entreaty and anger, between sorrow and happiness, and instructed the male nurse accordingly. Her mother who lived on the other side of the corridor wall visited him thrice a day: first, when the male nurse came in the morning, next, during the lunch and last, when the male nurse left. Once she asked her husband to convince her daughter to resume school. Father held her hands and made a particular gurgle sound the meaning of which she understood; her hands stiffened within the fold of his hands, he understood.

Anu uncle's coming to their house and staying overnight was now a routine. She no longer cared.

One night she was awakened by loud gurgling sounds. She rushed to find her father's chest heaving. She began rubbing his chests, the heaving subsided and the gurgle turned a whimper. Then she heard the sounds of animated talks, the urging, the shrieks, and the panting issuing from the other side of the corridor wall. She looked back to find tears rolling down her father's eyes. She leaned on him, wiped the tears and whispered. 'Father, please don't bother; I know this is going on for quite some time, do I bother? I ignore them, you also do the same. Don't pain yourself thinking about it, just relax; the doctor says you're responding to the treatment very well, you'll recover soon, and then, she smiled conspiratorially. He also gave back a smile, and holding her hands fell asleep.

Next morning Shraddha went to the kitchen when her mother was arranging breakfast on trays. She stood before her and said calmly, 'Whatever you do with Anu uncle I don't care, but if you do it less loudly father could get some sleep; shouldn't you be a little merciful to the man who is still your husband?'

'How dare you say such things to your mother, the precocious girl, now the darling of the nincompoop father?'

She slapped her hard. Shraddha returned the slap with such a force she fell on the trays. She looked at her fallen face, picked up two apples and one banana from the fruit basket and left.

The end came on the last Sunday of the month, Minu remembered clearly.

Her father was recovering fast. His legs jerked like a child, hands becoming steadier, not much improvement though in the vocal cord. The doctor said he would get it back in two months time with the new medicines he had prescribed. Shraddha snatched the prescription from her mother's hand, as she had been doing for past three weeks, brought medicines from the factory hospital and sat by her father's side who welcomed her with a near normal smile.

For the last two weeks the male nurse had been taking leave on Sundays. During this time Shraddha took over the nursing. That Sunday she finished nursing by 8 p.m. but sat with her father for another hour before returning to her room. She was asleep as soon as she touched the bed.

It must be near midnight Shraddha woke up hearing loud, incessant gurgling sounds from the corridor. For many days now this had stopped since she counselled her father. What then? Shraddha thought as she ran to him. He stopped gurgling but his chests were heaving violently. He raised his hand pointing the corridor wall. She was surprised to hear his clear voice, 'They... you...' She looked at him, then put her ears on the corridor wall and heard, 'I shall fuck the girl one day to teach her a good lesson... I shall fuck her... I shall definitely fuck her... ' She stopped listening further and turned to her father. His body was still, heaving stopped, no movement in hands, the eyes dilated, tears still rolling down. She compressed the artery on his left wrist, no pulse; put her ear on the chest, no beat.

She closed his eyes, walked to the kitchen, picked up the foot-long rounded stone used for mashing spices, and entered her mother's room. Anu uncle was still parroting the same sentence between thrusts. She held the stone with both hands and hit on the back of his head, all her forces rushing towards her hands. She saw him rolling down, his manhood still throbbing; mother naked, fully stretched, her eyes terrified. Shraddha loosened her grip, the stone rolled toward the prostrated body of the man.

She returned to her room and began packing her things. Suddenly she heard a crashing sound from the other room. She silently entered the room, saw the man still lying prostrate in a pool of blood—might be dead, and the woman hanging from the ceiling fan by a cord, a chair below her thrown aside.

Shraddha opened the *almirah* and then the locker cabinet by taking keys from the drawer, collected all the money stacked there, stopped for a few seconds before the ornaments, decided against taking them and returned to complete the packing.

She dressed herself in ordinary garments, put most of the money within the petticoat and the rest inside the hand bag. She now entered the box room, brought out all cans of kerosene and petrol (must be for Anu uncle's car) and methodically splashed the fuel everywhere inside the house. Next, she made an inspection tour with a can in hand to spray up any unattended corner of the house. Satisfied, she soaked a ball of sari, lighted it and throwing it in her mother's room left the village.

Chapter 9

On their first day together for the new assignment Boomba and Toomba changed themselves to lowly beggar boys with soiled *gamchas* tied around their waist and reached the factory gate. They collected their packets from the gatekeeper and memorised the delivery addresses, walked to an abandoned petrol pump and brought out their mobile phones.

'Let's decide on codes.'

'I don't want to talk to you.'

'Why?' Boomba looked surprised.

'Stupid! That's our code for every delivery made. When one of us completes his quota of deliveries the code is: Ok, tell me.'

Boomba said, 'The Boss has advised that if one of us perceives apprehension, he gives two missed calls to the other who should immediately throw his mobile in a dustbin and vanish.'

That settled, they went their ways: Boomba to the north-central and Toomba to the south.

They joined together before the factory gate at 5 p.m. This time the gatekeeper stood from the stool and saluted them before opening the gate.

'*Sala harami*. He wants a fifty rupee-note from each of us when we receive our wages', Boomba said in undertone.

They saw several bundles of notes stacked on the table. The man indicated two bundles which they picked up. When they were leaving the man asked.

'Are you coming tomorrow?'

'No, day after tomorrow.'

'Ok.'

As they stopped before the gate, now open before hand, to pay ransom to the gatekeeper, a person brushed past them, the gatekeeper made a double salute to him. They could not see his face properly.

They walked separately through lanes and bylanes and reached Moulali crossing. When they were debating on which foreign liquor shop to go Toomba felt a tap on the back of his neck; must be the police, he thought and turned his head slowly to find a boy nearing youth smiling ear to ear.

'Hey, I'm Raja. I saw you coming out of the factory gate when I was making an entry; new in this line?'

'Yeah,' Boomba replied.

'How many packets a day?'

'Two each.'

'Pooh! I take seven packets a day.'

'But the Boss said one could get a maximum of five packets a day.'

'Pooh, pooh again! I told him I must get at least three thousand five hundred rupees a day; either you increase the delivery wage to seven hundred per packet or allot me seven packets a day. That worked. After all I have my expenses; I'm no kid like you.'

Before they could say anything he hailed a taxi: 'See you kids.' The taxi turned north.

'*Sala harami, chutiya,* mother fucker, boasty,' an agitated Boomba hurled his choicest abuses to the passing taxi.

Toomba placed his hand on his neck and suppressing a laugh spoke, 'Calm down, Boomba. Every person has a particular way of feeling happy. He feels happy in boasting. Let him be.'

'But why take it on us? I don't like boasties.'

'I've a feeling he'll be our friend some day. There are some who intimidate you first, then become friends; he is one of them.'

'Ok, let's see. Presently we shall buy our whisky.'

They purchased a bottle of whisky, two bottles of mineral water, cutlets with chips and four Styrofoam glasses. They had to pay fifty rupees extra for the whisky as selling liquor to minors was prohibited by the government.

'Now that the passport to your heaven is at hand, we have to decide the place of take off,' Toomba said.

'I know a place near Golpark; calm and quiet. Let's board a taxi,' Boomba said.

They arrived at the same place by the side of Ramkrishna Mission where Minu first took Chameli, and later Chameli took Boomba for a reconciliation session.

'Good place,' Toomba remarked.

'Yeah, let's find a corner.'

As they looked about a female voice called, 'Hey, Paltu. Come here.'

'It must be Minudi,' Boomba said and hurried to the place wherefrom the voice came.

Minu was at the same spot where Boomba met her first.

'It seems you've reserved this place.'

'More or less; they know I like this corner and make room for me whenever I come. Now you two can sit by my side or on that slab in front of me where I've kept my bottle.'

They preferred sitting on the slab. Minu looked at Toomba and remarked, 'This must be the guy Chameli thought had spoiled you.'

'Yes. But she likes him now.'

'Good.'

'We've come here to celebrate our first big earning. Put your bottle in the bag; we shall have whisky together,' Boomba said.

'Okay. But don't spoil the temper of whisky. If you don't know the correct measurement I can do it for you.'

'I know a little but I don't want to venture this time,' Boomba said.

Boomba opened the bottle and handed it to her. She measured a peg of whisky for each glass, poured water slowly so as not to miss the line.

'Cheers... Cheers... Cheers!'

They raised their glasses and hit each others, no clinks though issued from the polystyrene glasses. After a few sips Minu asked Toomba, 'Do you know Paltu and Chameli claim they love each other?'

'Yeah'.

'And they intend to marry. Aren't you Paltu?'

'Yes. That's why I've started earning big money.' Boomba replied.

Minu asked Boomba, 'Any idea what marriage is all about? Streets' idea of marriage is simple: married now, unmarried next, married again—all in a week's time. But I know this is not your idea though you belong to the street. You two must be going to cinemas where boy meets girl—love each other—sing songs—and then marry to live happily thereafter. Besides, Chameli has also observed a married life in the family she works now. But you borrow the idea from the world you don't belong. So, why go for it; just love and be happy, marriage complicates the matter.'

Boomba was confused: He really does not know what exactly marriage is, he even does not know what love is; people just talk about these and he has learnt by rote. No doubt he feels a deep attachment toward Champi, he wants to be with her, does not want to lose her, but so it is with Mashi; but it is something special with Champi, and what is that? He was about to speak out when Minu abruptly asked.

'Hey Paltu, do you masturbate?'

'What's that?'

'Bloody hell!' Minu touched her forehead and burst out laughing.

'Toomba suppressed his own and said, 'I suppose you are pulling his leg too much; by now he might have become lame.'

'Okay, when he graduates we shall again talk of love, marriage, et cetera. He is somewhat late as he is under Mashi, but even she won't be able to stop when it comes with a torrent.'

Minu looked at her watch and announced.

'Now you two leave; I'm expecting a friend. We shall pick up the unfinished discourse and bottle some other day.'

As they walked back Toomba found Boomba thoughtful. He smiled to himself. When they crossed Golpark Boomba asked the question he was waiting for.

'What's this masturbation she talked about?'

'What you do with Bhaglu when you do with yourself, it's masturbation.'

'That's all! But I did it about a year back. Bhaglu wanted me to do it before him for which he promised additional fifty rupees. I did it. The thing became thick and stiff but nothing came out; I only felt pain. Then Bhaglu tried it for some time, but nothing still, only the pain increased manifold. I threw off his hand and poured water on it. After some time it shrivelled and the pain subsided. I felt disgusted, snatched hundred rupees from him instead of fifty and left with a promise never to do it again.'

'I suppose you weren't ready yet: keep watching your pant every morning; the day you notice dried or semi-dried patches on it you'd know, you're ready.'

'But these are there already! I've been observing the patches for last five-six days; don't know what these are for, you see.' Boomba pointed places on his pant.

'Then, just go ahead.'

Next day, when they met before the factory gate after making deliveries, Boomba could not hold any longer.

'You know, I've done it'

'I guessed as much; now let's take payment first', Toomba said flatly.

Boomba felt hurt by Toomba's nonchalance. He did not talk when they came out of the factory gate, nor as they began walking along CIT road. Toomba now chose the frontage of a closed shop opposite Ladies Park and sat down, Boomba followed quietly.

'You must've felt offended as I didn't respond to you earlier. There are certain things in life, some achievements which you savour personally and share privately. You should not discuss such things everywhere—the whole charm is lost. Do you get me?'

'Yeah I'm stupid.'

'You aren't stupid. It's the first flush of youth that has blurred your mind; it happens with many. Now if you like you may share your grand experience.'

'You know, I did it to myself the way I did to Bhaglu, and imagine what happened, the liquid things jerked out just like Bhaglu's. I felt slight pain before jerking, but what a pleasure! I did it thrice last night. Now tell me is it what people call sex?'

'No, it's just masturbation—half sex, when you do it with a girl it's sex.'

'Which means if I ask Champi to do it to me, it's sex?'

'Stupid! When you put your thing inside her, that's sex; you'll learn it gradually.'

It was Boomba who remained silent when they met next; his face had lost all the shine, head crestfallen, which he did not raise once as they walked to the same place opposite Ladies Park. Toomba nudged him after they sat.

'What happened?'

'You know, I can never have sex with Champi.'

'What! You've already tried it with her, so fast!'

'I thought if masturbation—the half sex—is so much pleasure what a full sex would be! So I went to Champi in the evening. I didn't expect her to be alone, but she was. Mashi had gone to a circus with the toddlers. I told her all about sex and proposed to have it with her. You know what she did?'

'Must've slapped you.'

'Yes. But I persisted, cajoled her by sweet words and kisses, promised a cinema and sundry other girly things. Finally she relented, though half heartedly and lay down with her eyes closed. But I couldn't enter; her thing was not opening up. Something had gone to my head, I went mad. I searched out Mashi's coconut oil, applied it profusely on mine and hers, and after a few attempts I forced myself in. She cried out but I didn't care; I didn't even look at her face so much, didn't for a moment ask her how she felt, I was just savouring my first taste of sex. Only when it was over I looked at her fully; her face constricted, lips tight, tears rolling down her eyes, and there was blood between her legs. She said in feeble voice, "Now please go." Those three words pierced through my heart like shells. I felt cruel, ashamed of what I did to the girl I love so much. I couldn't look at her face any longer. I quietly walked out with a vow never to do it again. If sex causes so much pain in her I don't want it.

'In the morning I observed her having difficulty in walking. I wanted to apologise, but she ignored me, didn't even look at me. I know she would never forgive me but I can't live without her. I'll tell everything to Minudi; I'll ask her to beat me but find a way out of it. Let's go and find her.' Boomba looked at him with imploring eyes.

'You don't have to search for her; she's already there, by the side of the Ladies Park. Just look. It seems she is in a difficult situation; let's cross the road.'

Minu was having a fight with two guys. Boomba wanted to help but Toomba held him back: 'She is a tigress, seems to be enjoying the fight; doesn't need help.'

Presently, Minu hurled a kick between the legs of one guy. 'Onk.' One down. She advanced to the other guy with 'Mother fucker, *bahenchod, sala chutiya,*' spitting from her mouth. Suddenly a third man materialised from behind and moved stealthily with a rod in his hand. When he raised it to hit her on the head Toomba leaped, almost flew through the air and in split second hit the guy on the back of his neck. He collapsed on the pavement. Seeing this other ran. *'Sala harami,* go and fuck your mother,' Minu threw the invectives to the fleeting figure. Now she looked at the other fallen guy; surprised she turned around and saw them.

'What are you two doing here?'

'Actually, we wanted to meet you. We were sitting there discussing it.' Boomba indicated the place. 'When Toomba saw you fighting we crossed over to watch.'

'Who did this?' She pointed at the fallen guy.

'Toomba. Only he can jump like a tiger; this is the second time I saw him doing it.'

Minu looked intently at Toomba for nearly a minute, then to the fallen guy who though moaning was trying to get up. She picked up the iron rod and uttering, 'Let's destroy his manhood', began hitting him between his legs. A small crowd gathered but did not interfere: first, she looked fierce; second, they could perhaps guess why such a young girl would hit the man there only. He could not speak but raised his folded hands. Minu threw away the rod and marched out with them.

After cooling down a bit she said, 'Let's sit somewhere. These bastards have spoilt my mood. I've a half bottle of whisky I picked up from the friend I was with. Let's drink to cool down.'

'We may take a taxi and go to your old place.' Boomba ventured.

'Yeah, let's go.'

They found the spot, it was unoccupied. She poured whisky and water in glasses with a double measure for herself. Without any 'Cheers' she gulped a large quantity, shrugged her shoulders, took a minute to steady herself before speaking.

'I suppose Paltu has a problem he wants to discuss.'

'The problem's over, though a little faster that created further problems,' Toomba said after taking his sip.

'Speak up Paltu,' Minu urged.

Boomba took a sip and described everything. Minu was silent, disturbed, anger flickered in her eyes. She spoke with a rage in her voice.

'You know, what you've done? You've raped her', then turning to Toomba rasped, 'and you *gyani* what made you lead him to this? Did you also show him some blue films on your smart phone; I know quite a few of the street dwellers own smart phones.' She spitted venom.

Toomba's face fell; he could only say, 'I do not have a smart phone'. Boomba did not speak. They sat in silence.

'Oh, how I hate a rapist—I hate ...I hate, I hate them all.'

Minu began hitting the ground with her heel. After the release of the venom, her rage subsided to some extent. She took a small sip and remained silent for some time. When she spoke next, her voice was somber but not devoid of her usual sarcasm.

'You need to hear my story to understand why I hate a rapist so much and then decide whether we should kill Boomba or maim him there.

'After I burned our house with Mom hanging from a ceiling fan and her paramour dead by my hands, I boarded a train which brought me to Howrah station. My first priority was to find a place where I could hide my money. I entered a restaurant and ordered a huge breakfast, I was hungry. While eating I began thinking about alternative places where I could hide it. I zeroed in on a men's urinal where they stay a little while only, the least in a station urinal where the stench and filth drive them out faster. I found a men's urinal, entered there and closed the door from within. The stench was overbearing—a mix of urine and shit, the urinals overflowing. But that suited my purpose. I looked around and noticed a cracked ceramic tile on the floor between two urinals. I opened the tile and dug a hole with the help of a rusted iron stick lying under the basin whose original purpose was to clean the jammed water joints, but never used since the British left. The hole ready I put all the money in a plastic bag and secured it by several knots. When I was about to put the bag inside the hole I heard a loud knock on the door. "Sweeper," I declared loudly and busied myself in burying the money bag. When done, I put back the broken tile and pressed it slowly for stability. Satisfied, I opened the door and brushed past a man who leaped towards the nearest urinal holding his crotch.

'Not knowing what to do next I wandered in the station area when a policeman noticed me. He took me to the police station, made me sit on a bench for nearly two hours, and in that two hours I'd learnt many things that happen inside a police station. When they took me to the OC he looked at me intently, then decided to put me at a semi-government Home for girls.

'It was like a prison, high walled on all sides and an iron gate with a security guard on a stool. I was put in a dormitory with four other girls. I was surprised to find two girls moving about fully naked. As I was laying my things on the only empty cot I heard a girl say, "Another sacrificial goat". I turned to her and asked innocently what that meant. She said, "You'd know it tonight itself and at least three nights thereafter." Another girl added, "The secretary man—the *ashura* comes here thrice a week: Monday, Wednesday and Friday, and today is Monday."

"What? He'd beat me?"

"Worse than that."

'I looked at the two naked girls with question in my eyes. One of them replied, "It's our dress-off day; some day it'll be yours too. Look at the wall near the ceiling; there's a CCTV camera; we are seen naked by the secretary, the staff members and also by the police whom the secretary desires to entertain. All dorms have this arrangement".

'Then I heard the full story: The secretary man was the first to rape a new girl brought to this Home, then, others: staff, police and all. When there's no new girl he makes a choice by monitoring the CCTV cameras.

'The girls had no way to escape. A month back one of the girls tried to escape while being taken to Juvenile Court in a police van. She was soon apprehended by the police and brought back to Home. That night the secretary man came with three others; she was beaten and then raped the whole night by all the four, and in the morning she was dead. The matter was hushed up. She was buried under a guava tree that could be seen from this dormitory. One of them said, "The secretary is very powerful, a politico; every staff here is in league with him except, perhaps the woman cook who is kind to us but scared to open her mouth."

'The secretary did come that night, entered the dormitory, made a survey and spotted me. He pulled me up and led me to his room. Without even closing the door he made me naked, squeezed my breasts and between my legs, stripped himself and asked me to suck him. I did. He then raped me twice, once then and the next at dawn. It was painful... very painful. I clipped my teeth to hold back tears. When I left in the morning he was asleep, his snoring reverberated the walls of the room.

'My roommates didn't even have pity in their eyes. They had resigned themselves to the fate.

'I could guess from the smell where the kitchen was. I entered to find the floor scattered with vegetables and two skinned whole chicken, a buxom maternal type woman supervising two girls arranging them. When she saw me she said, "Why have you come? Today's not your day, take rest". She knew it. I replied, "I don't feel like taking rest, so I thought I may help you out. I can cut vegetables and chicken, also know some cooking." She came closer to me and lamented. "Such a little girl! Why are you in this Lanka?" I lied, "I'm paying for the sin I've committed by leaving home." Then without giving her time to probe further I said feigning greed in my voice, "I find we will have chicken today; may I cut them to pieces?" She replied with a constricted smile, "Yes, you may; the smaller one is entirely for the secretary, cut them in larger pieces; the other one is for you all, cut that into very small pieces so each one of you can have at least one piece." "How many girls stay here now?" I asked. "With you the number is twenty; you've filled up the place of the girl who died a month back." The other two girls did not join the discussion, not even looked at us, they continued their work like hypnotised morons.

'Slicing the smaller chicken was no problem—I had learnt it at home—but cutting the other one in twenty pieces was really a big challenge. But ultimately I did it. She was satisfied. I stayed in the kitchen during the entire cooking. Lunch and dinner were prepared at the same time, though not separately; a part of the same food was kept for dinner—no cooking in the afternoon, not even tea. After the cooking was over we washed the utensils and placed them at appropriate places as directed by her.

'After the lunch I heard the sound of a car leaving the Home: the secretary man was leaving after having his lunch. He'd be coming on Wednesday again, but I was not scared.

'On Wednesday morning I followed the routine in the kitchen, and in the night he followed his in the bed room. After the second act he fell asleep snoring. I waited for half hour, then rose to check the depth of his sleep; satisfied, I pulled out the kitchen cutter from under the bed, which I had stolen from the kitchen in the afternoon, and severed his penis from the base in one swipe the way I practiced separating the throat of the chicken from its body. I placed the shrivelled thing on his chest, alighted from the bed and lay on the floor.

'It took some time for the sensation to reach his brain, and when it did he woke up with a start, noticed the source of his pain and saw the severed penis on his chest. Clasping the piece within the palm of his right hand he gave out a loud distressing cry that woke up every one in the Home. The security guard came first and saw the boss now fainted lying in a pool of blood down the waist and me lying "unconscious" on the floor. He was confused, could not comprehend what had really happened, but his training led him to conclude that it was police case, and he telephoned the police.

'It was full morning when the police came with a doctor. They began surveying the scene and the doctor began examining the secretary man. I could see through my squinted eyes the doctor suppressing a smile when he opened his palm and saw what was inside. He then examined me. I continued feigning the unconscious state. He asked the police to take us immediately to the hospital. Both were taken in the same ambulance, he lying on a bench opposite me.

'I took some time to *regain* my consciousness. Soon thereafter I was subjected to a two-finger test, more humiliating than rape to confirm the fact of rape. What happened to him I didn't know but the fact that the severed penis could not be joined back I learnt only when it was shown as an exhibit before a bench of three judges of a Juvenile Court presided over by a woman. I could see she was uncomfortable but she tried to maintain a judge-like composure—a little too much may be. The police dug out my past—rustication from the school for beating a teacher and burning the house. The judge asked the police prosecutor.

"Are these supposed evidence in any way related to the alleged crime?"

"Madam I'm trying to establish that she is a habitual offender."

"Is it a fact she was raped; what does the report say? Who raped her?"

"Yes Madam, she was raped, and... err... it was perpetrated by the secretary of the Home."'

'Then Madam turned to me and asked, "I find from your school record that your name is Shraddha but you've told the police and also the hospital doctor that your name is Jabala. Why?"

"Shraddha was before I was raped; now I'm Jabala, you may also call me Jaba. Later I may label myself differently."

"People don't change their name like you do."

"Why Madam? Lord Krishna has hundred names, Arjun has ten names, and Lord Rama has as many to suit different occasions. I've just been following their examples."

The presiding judge thought it better not to proceed further on this issue as her next question suggested.

"Do you have anything to say in this matter?"

"Yes Madam. This secretary man is a habitual rapist; he rapes every girl that comes to this Home. The Home may rather be called a rape house. He had killed a girl after she was gang-raped and buried her under a guava tree. There're also CCTV cameras at every dormitory and the girls are forced to remain naked during their dress-off days. These cameras are monitored by the secretary, members of the staff and also by some police men to make a choice of girl for the night's frolic. I'd pray you order a thorough investigation."

'She was agape. The police prosecutor rose to object but she stopped him. She consulted the other judges and then declared, "I'm passing two orders: one, the accused girl be placed in a safe Home till the next hearing; two, the CID is directed to investigate the crime alleged by the girl and submit a preliminary report within the week."

'She was about to move to the next case when I raised my hand as I did in the school.

"Any question?"

"Yes madam. I do not know which Home they are going to place me this time; I've learnt no Home here is safe, though I really don't care any longer. But I promise that if any one there tries to rape me I'll surely cut his thing with balls and all that and shove them into his mouth."

She looked at me for a minute and asked the police prosecutor in a stern voice, "I hope you will take care."

'When I was being taken to a new Home in a police van several people with cameras and hand mikes swarmed in. It was the media. The police wouldn't allow me to speak but I did speak. The van could only move slowly because of the media crowd, and I gave them as many bytes as possible. I finally reached the new Home with media vans and men on motor bikes at my back and a group of women standing on the doorway to receive me. It was quite a reception!

'I later learnt the media was already after the secretary man and his Home for about a month to unearth the mystery of the missing girl.

'In the next hearing at Juvenile Court I learnt that the CID did find the remains of the missing girl under the guava tree, and also the CCTVs. The secretary man was put under hospital arrest. The judge ordered my release and asked the department to arrange a good Home if I needed one, which I refused; the PP did not object.

'When I came out from the court I was quite a hero. The media took me in and gave lot of food articles and also some money collected from amongst them. I smiled, thanked them profusely and answered all their questions. But I never allowed myself to be overwhelmed. I was an avid reader of newspapers and viewer of television at home and at school, and I knew the spotlight would soon shift from me to some other sensational story and I'd be forgotten. Their last question was what I was going to do next. "I'm going back to my village," I lied and took a bus to Howrah station, none following this time.

'I entered the Men's urinal of the station where I'd hidden the money, closed the door and dug out the plastic bag which was intact, though smeared on the outside from seeped urine. I washed the bag under the basin, put it in the food bag given by the media people and fled.'

After finishing her story Minu remained silent for some time, looking beyond. When she finally looked at them, she spoke to Boomba.

'This is part of my story; you can now understand the depth of my hatred for rapists and what I do to them? Even a slight hint of rape flares me up.'

Boomba raised his head a little to reply.

'But I didn't know.'

'Yeah, that's the difference.'

'And I love her.'

'Yeah, that's another difference, and that's why I'd ask Chameli not to cut off yours.'

All laughed for the first time since they had come here. Minu looked at their glasses and exclaimed.

'My god, your glasses are still full while mine is empty! Perhaps you've not touched it beyond the first sip. I must've spoilt your evening by my sordid tales.'

'Good spoiling though and you must also be feeling good after sharing your story for the first time.'

'Wow! This is the second time I hear you speaking since we met. I thought you were dumb who occasionally bursts out some sentences, though I agree the sentences sometimes speak the truth like the one you've just spoken,' said Minu while refilling the glasses.

'I prefer listening and observing without getting involved. I know Boomba and Chameli are doomed. I don't care but you do; in fact you're hastening their doom by being involved. I guess you want to fulfil a latent desire of yours through them, a dream of family, children and all that. You dream through them. You can't really say, "I don't care", and move on.'

Minu intently observed Toomba while he spoke. Now she said, 'You may be right. Unconsciously I have been trying to blur the distinction between the two worlds, but I can't help it now, which means I've not learnt; in my subconscious I'm still attached, though I boast otherwise. My dear Toomba you're really a *gyani*. By the way, what's your age?'

'Ask the Ma'am,' Boomba prompted.

'Yeah, ask the Ma'am,' Toomba dittoed.

'Yeah, ask the Ma'am,' Minu followed the script.

A hearty laughter followed after which Minu continued.

'I guess Toomba is my age. In four to five years I may die, probably he too, when we reach the street age. In our world we work towards dying in teens. Beyond that life is so complicated one cannot handle it, and that complicates it further. I have many mates who are married, have children, but their lives are in total mess. They can't even have a good fuck at home. They seek me out for fucking, crying and giving solace to their tormented souls:

bloody hell, me giving solace! Beyond physicals I can't give them anything. So I pretend; they go back to their homes and pretend there too. Over there it's all pretensions and they are habituated to it. Their society makes a big deal about marriage, family, children, progeny and all that shit, and anoint them with more shit: security, loyalty and a fuck on demand. No one gets any, so they pretend; the society lives on them by making them live on it. It's a facade to mask its inherent decadence. Why go for it?'

Boomba tried to understand the meaning of what Minu said but could not comprehend it fully. Exasperated he shrugged his shoulders and declared, 'Whatever it is I don't care. I love Champi, and I'll marry her, that's all.'

Minu said, 'Yes I know you two are highly attached to each other from babyhood, but whether it would grow into love, I'm not sure. If that does not happen, only attachment remains, it won't even allow you to die peacefully.'

'It might even go beyond the death of one partner. I've seen that and I'm scared of it,' Toomba added.

'And I'm scared of living in the society where Boomba intends to migrate. I earn a lot, can very well take a flat and live in the society; my paramours would be too willing to set me up with appropriate facade, but I prefer living in the street.'

Minu now smiled at Boomba rather indulgently and said, 'I'm sure all this *gyan* isn't entering Paltu's head, his heart blocking their passage. Ok, be damned, as they say, but as for me I'll make sure you two get all the money I leave behind when I die to make your life a bit easier. By the way Paltu, do you know whether Chameli has menstruated?'

'What's that?'

'Stupid fucker! You don't know what menstruation is and you think of having sex with a girl! But I'm not going to explain it to you lest you create another mess. When Chameli experiences it she might share it with you. But I warn you not to pester her about it and don't touch her before it happens. Got it?'

Boomba nodded obediently.

'Ok. Now let's finish our drinks.'

After taking a few sips Minu said, 'There is a bad news. We shall soon lose this rendezvous. Ramkrishna Mission has taken over this *khandhar*, it'll soon be a god's place.

'Fuck the god,' Boomba said

'Fuck the god.' Toomba added next.

'Fuck them all.' Minu joined.' Let's dance to that.'

'But I don't know dancing.'

'Me too.'

'Stupid! Dancing is a state of mind not of legs. Just dance.' They went on dancing till they collapsed on the grass.

Chapter 10

Mashi had a premonition it would happen someday but did not expect it so fast.

Jaggu was ambitious, wanted large money quickly, which could only be earned in the drug racket. He was on the lower echelon of the pyramid but wanted to rise fast.

He indicated it to Mashi when they met for the third time. Their first meet could have been a disaster but for her. As soon as the door closed, Jaggu pounced on her like a hungry tiger, tore open her blouse to expose her breasts and began kneading them so hard she was almost out of breath. Soon thereafter he entered but ejaculated immediately. He rolled down and lay by her side, face turned back. Mashi looked at his still body and thought: this *basta* must be visiting prostitutes at hourly rate—not much money to buy a whole night—for a wham-bam kind of sex; didn't know that a better sex existed. Possibly with Mashi he wanted to do it better, to show his prowess but failed miserably which had hurt his ego. What a stupid ego men suffer from! She smiled to herself.

Presently, she pulled his head toward her, kissed him deep in the mouth, and then placing his hands on her breasts asked, 'How much time do we have?'

'I've booked the room for the night.'

'Then let's fuck like a man and a woman, not like a boy and a girl.'

She gave him a night-full of sex he never dreamt in the best of his sex dreams.

In the second meet he started behaving like a lover and in the third, at a two-room flat he rented recently, he almost proposed while confiding to her his joining a profession that would soon make him rich. She ignored his overtures and gave all indications of her unwillingness to enter into any such commitment. But whoever has ever found a man stung by love to receive negative signals. But were all the signals negative? She delved into her mind: accepting invitation for a hotel rendezvous with alacrity, the deep long kiss—she had never kissed a man with such depth during her station life, the orgasms that shook her body and filled the mind.

Were these negative signals or just the opposite that gave ideas to Jaggu for a long-term relationship? And that led him to take big risk for big money, jump the ladder faster than his capacity. Now he was lying in a police hospital with a crippled leg waiting to be prosecuted. She felt a deep pain, a cry welling up; why? She also felt sorry for Chintu who had fled with an injured leg and was languishing somewhere, and would be captured by the police some day and prosecuted similarly, and whose association with her was longer than Jaggu's, but it was just a feeling of regret mixed with some anxiety, perhaps a material loss, which she would soon make up by other means, but with Jaggu it was a different kind of loss, one she had never felt before.

Chintu never told her he was doing drugs. She noticed though that of late he was putting increasing amount of money in deposit with her, which meant his earning had also been increasing in tandem. She should have felt happy because her earnings from custodial charges: at one rupee per hundred for a block of fifteen days, had also increased. Instead, she felt anxious for the first boy who came to work with her. He at times shared with her a small bottle of whisky, which she enjoyed, but never asked him the source of his good fortune, nor did he reveal anything. She never interfered, never gave advice, never played a mother. Jaggu also never told her about Chintu's involvement. In their world the less you know, the better; she never violated it, neither did Jaggu nor Chintu. She resolved to carry Chintu's money wherever she went and returned it to him whenever he surfaced.

Mashi's soliloquy was disturbed by a call on her newly acquired mobile phone. It was Banku. He said it was a test call and then went on expressing his anguish at not having met her before she left—they had returned just a few minutes after she left—informed that his parents were very happy with her, they wanted to know when she would visit them next and finally whether she would be coming tomorrow to work with him.

It was a relief to hear a voice outside her present domain of thinking. She said so many things to Banku in various responses but carefully avoided all talk that could be construed as building a relationship. She informed Banku in response to her last question of her resolve to work in all the major lines of both the north and south sections of Sealdah and then move to Howrah station, so it was unlikely they would meet soon. Banku said 'Okay' in a deadpan voice and switched off the phone.

On a second thought Mashi decided to visit Howrah station first. From a small handbook available from a vendor at Sealdah she learnt that it was a huge terminal station, the largest railway complex of the country connecting almost all parts of India by more than hundred long distance trains besides local suburban trains; its twenty-three platforms handled over six hundred trains and more than a million passengers daily. The junction had large car sheds that could house nearly two hundred locos, and must be more than two thousand station dwellers, she thought. The station offered a lot of opportunities for making money but also threats unknown to her. She needed support.

In one of her sessions with the present OC of GRP Sealdah she indicated her desire to establish a second base at Howrah station. Playing between her nipples he said that would be no problem as the previous OC of this station had moved to Howrah on promotion.

Next day she boarded a mini bus to Howrah. She stood before the monolithic building of Howrah station whose solemn architecture resembled an ageless tantric seer adorned in red unmindful of the constant clatter, varied shrills, high pitched horns and hoarse jostling of people going in and coming out. She stood motionless, bewitched and bewildered. But for a while only, as motions all around her pushed and pulled at her in different directions. When she was about to fall on the pavement she jostled back and straightened herself: she had a purpose on hand. She located an entry gate manned by a black-coat ticket checker, but she had no problem in gaining an entry: the broom stick peeping out from the bag now opened at the top was the passport and her curvature, the visa. She stepped into a sea of mankind; a big clock atop marking time in Roman digits, an arena where people sat waiting for arrival and departure of trains, gangways on all sides for passengers' entry and exit, police men moving by with watchful eyes, stalls selling tea, coffee, snacks and food, printed books—religious to thrillers—on one side, and on the other toilets for officers, men and women, railway cafeterias—vegetarian and non-vegetarian, and a staircase for upper storey, but she was unable to locate the police station. She flapped down the broom and asked a policeman in a matter-of-fact manner to take her to the OC, GRP who was expecting her. The constable looked at her from head to toe, thought for a second, and then asked her to follow. She entered a large hall-like room partitioned horizontally into two: at the front officers sat behind desks; some hearing complaints, taking FIRs et cetera, and one officer near the lockup sharing with a constable the thrashing of two urchins who were alternately holding the legs of the officer and the constable praying for mercy. She entered OC's cabin through an opening at the left hand corner of the partition. It was a spacious room in the middle of which sat the OC behind a large desk whom she recognised. On the right end corner a young man sat on a bench with a girl; an unaccompanied girl in adolescence was presently being questioned by the OC, a sub-inspector in attendance. Mashi took her seat on a bench on the left waiting for OC's attention. She heard him addressing the girl, 'So, you've nowhere to go, both parents dead, no relations; don't know anyone here too.'

The girl nodded.

'In that case we are presently sending you to an all-girls Home nearby who'll take care of you.' He turned to the SI and asked, 'What do you say?'

'Yes sir, that's the best we can do for the time being,' the SI replied.

'Then telephone Ranjit Babu to send someone to take her to his Home and also ask him to visit me in the afternoon.'

He now noticed Mashi. 'Ah-ha, you've come. I got the telephone; now wait for me till I dispose of the next case.'

He turned to the pair and called them. The young man and the girl stood on the opposite side of the desk. He scanned a paper laid on the table.

'So, you said you are a married couple.'

'Yes sir,' they replied in unison.

'I see; when were you married?'

The girl looked at the young man who quickly replied. 'Day before yesterday, sir; we are going to Digha for honeymoon.'

'I see; where were you married?'

'In our village, sir.'

'By whom?'

'A priest of the local temple, sir.'

'I see. Were your parents and relatives present?'

'No sir; they were against this marriage as we are of different casts; we married secretly.'

'I see, I see, all perfect; by the way what's the name of the priest?'

The young man was startled by the sudden question. He looked at his consort, dabbled something to her but she stood motionless. Turning to the OC he replied.

'Sir, in our village we all call him *purohit*, nobody knows his exact name.'

'I see, I see; in whose village temple were you married, yours or hers?'

'My village temple, sir,' the man replied quickly.

'You look nearly thirty; what's her age?'

'She is eighteen plus, sir; I've already submitted her eighth standard school certificate to the SI sir.'

'Yes, I've seen that.'

The OC rang the bell twice. A constable appeared.

'Take the girl to the back room,' he instructed.

When the constable left with the girl the OC called the man by his side, rose from the chair and slapped him so hard he reeled on the floor. Raising him from floor by the collar he slapped him again.

'*Sala harami*! Going for honeymoon, eh? I'll give you solid honeymoons here itself; now tell me at what price you've contracted to sell her and to whom?'

In response, the man quietly brought out a packet and placed it on the table. The OC sat down, looked inside the packet, put it inside the drawer and rang the bell. When the constable peeped in he asked him to send the SI.

'Is there any missing report?' the OC asked the SI as he entered.

'No sir. I've checked with all the police stations of the district.'

'Good. Take this sister fucker away and put him in the lockup."

The SI grabbed the man by the back of his collar and dragged him out amidst cries of 'Sir... sir... please release me... I shall make all of you happy...'

The OC now winked at Mashi to come forward.

'I understand you want to establish a second base here.'

'Yes sir, with your kind support.' She replied with a bewitching smile.

'Go ahead. I'll help you as I did in Sealdah.'

'Thank you sir, thank you very much. May I request for something now?'

'What's it?'

'When I entered I saw an officer chastising two urchins, possibly of this station. May I take them with me?'

'Oh, those two *bichhus*! We're fed up with them. If you take them we may get some respite. Let me call the ASI.'

He rang the bell; the constable's head peeped and vanished with the OC ordering, 'Send Bose Babu.'

When Bose Babu entered he asked. 'What you intend to do with the two *bichhus*?'

'Oh-ho. I've put them in lockup... don't know what to do with them... beating no longer scares them... they don't even weep... they've run away from all the three Homes we've placed them and landed back here. This morning they picked up two mobiles,' he put the mobiles on his table, 'But got caught red-handed when they attempted to pick the purse of a passenger, got solid beating by them and finally lapped on us... what to do?'

'Any written complaint?'

'No sir; it was office time, everyone's in a hurry.'

'Ok. Hand them over to this woman; I know her, she'll take care of them.'

The ASI Bose looked at her for a second and left. He now turned to Mashi and handed the two mobile phones to her.

'My gift to you; don't forget me,' he winked.

'Never sir; how can I?' She spread her bewitching smile again.

Mashi took the boys from the lockup after ASI Bose gave them a parting slap with a warning, 'If you get caught ever again and brought here, I'll kill you both.'

When they left the police station and walked toward a food stall one of the bichhus asked, 'Are you a police?'

'No. I'm like you, though older; the police are my friends.'

They sat on the floor near a food stall. She caressed their soft cheeks and asked, 'I'm feeling hungry, are you?'

'Yes, very much,' both of them said in unison.

She peeled out a few ten-rupee notes from her purse and said, 'Take this money and buy some food for all of us.'

They almost snatched the notes from her hand and ran for a food stall, not the one nearby but elsewhere. Observing their jump-running she thought to herself: children will always be children; let them remain children, not grow up like her, a wishful thinking though.

They brought food in three packets, passed one to Mashi and began eating immediately without waiting for Mashi to open hers; must be very hungry, she thought, probably have not eaten a morsel since morning, and nothing surely at the police station except beating. When they were half way through and the pace of eating had slowed down Mashi asked, 'Tell me how do I call you?'

'I'm Bichhu,' said one.

'And you?' Mashi asked the other.

'I'm also Bichhu.'

'But when I call for one Bichhu both will respond, that's problematic.'

'But we've been responding like this only, always together.'

'And that's the reason you always get caught together.'

'Yes, we want it that way only.'

'But think, if only one of you get caught the other may find ways to free him. Isn't that better?'

They consulted silently looking at each other's face for a while, and then one replied.

'Yes, you've a point; we agree, but one of us shall retain Bichhu.'

'Ok. You decide.'

One of them immediately pulled out a pack of playing cards from his pocket, shuffled them and dealt three cards each. They picked up the cards, brought them very close to their eyes and opened each card very slowly from the top like seasoned gamblers.

'Ace of hearts, king of spade and ten of diamonds,' one declared.

'You win. So you're Bichhu. But what'll be my name then?'

'You are Chikku. All right?' suggested Bichhu.

'So we are Bichhu and Chikku.' They raised their hands and clapped, Mashi also joined.

Bichhu said, 'Now that we are named separately, tell us are you an *Enjo* woman intending to put us back to another Home?' both looked anxious.

'No. I've already told you I'm like you, a station woman. But tell me why did you run away from all the three Homes?'

'In the first Home the food was awful'.

'And they gave us only a small quantity, no tea, no snacks, nothing. We were hungry all the time.'

'After a week, on a Sunday when there was only a few staff present we scaled the wall in the night and ran for the station.'

'And from the second one?' asked Mashi.

'We were assured by Kumar dada, an *Enjo* uncle, of good shelter, good food, lots of play and vocational training so we could earn good money in future. When we entered this Home the first things we noticed was that the walls were so high and smooth you can never scale them, a big thick man with a large moustache sat on a stool near the gate which was double locked, some men strolling the compound with *lathi* in their hands.

'We had to deposit our mobile phones and whatever money we had with the office. We were crammed into a dormitory of twenty boys, no space to move, one had to jump to reach one's bed, but there too one couldn't sleep well as it was full of bugs. We were roused up very early in the morning, given a cup of tea, two biscuits and a piece of bread. By nine thirty we had to clean the rooms, latrines, verandas and staircases, and then take our bath and be ready to board a covered van that would deposit us in small groups under the care of a security guard to various factories for what they claimed vocational training. Our job was to carry materials from one place to the other, stack finished products in *godowns* and do various odd jobs; we're never allowed to go near the machines. If we made a mistake, the factory supervisor would beat us mercilessly: beating by the police is a feather touch in comparison.' Chikku stopped and indicated Bichhu to continue.

Before Bichhu was to begin he asked Mashi, 'You have given us names but we don't know yours.'

'You may call me Mashi; everyone calls me by this name.'

'Even the OC here?' asked Chikku.

'Yes, he too. Now go ahead with the rest of your story.'

Bichhu picked up the trail left by Chikku. 'We decided to flee the place. The entire planning and execution took more than a month. With all the security guards around and high smooth walls we had no chance of escaping from within; it had to be between the to and fro journey, but we two alone wouldn't be able to do it. We needed a team. Most of the boys were scared;

we had to be selective to even talk about escape, it had to be done secretly. Finally we could organise a team of eight boys including us. Now the timing. We decided it couldn't be in the morning because all the four vans carrying us left the Home together, and in day time our escape could be noticed by other vans. But in the evening the vans returned Home at different times: ours not before seven thirty. On the appointed day we eight worked so diligently that the supervisor patted our backs. As before, we were herded in the canteen for a cup of tea and two biscuits, the security man and the driver also joined. After the tea the driver led us to the van and the security man went in to collect money from the manager. I positioned myself last in the queue, quickly picked up the kitchen knife and hid it at my back.

'When the van was half way we found the security man was already dozing. Chikku signalled by raising his little finger, moved silently to the side of the security man, closed his nostrils with the left hand and as soon as he opened his mouth gagged him by shoving a ball of jute into his mouth, and I moving quickly held the knife to his throat. Our third accomplice now shouted at the driver asking him to stop the van and come quickly as the security dada had fallen seriously ill, and convulsing, which he really was. He stopped the vehicle and came hurriedly inside the bus to meet the reception party ready with blows and kicks; all the twenty had now joined the game. Two boys now sat on his chest, two on his feet and one each on his two hands while I pulled out another jute ball from my pocket and gagged him. Keeping the rest on guard and Chikku holding the knife, I entered the driver's cabin to pull out two long ropes from under the driver's seat which they often used to bind the recalcitrant boys. Chikku first brought out a thick packet from the pocket of the security man and asked one to count the money; others began stripping them, soon they were only in underpants. We then tied their hands and legs with ropes and bound each one securely to the iron pole, one near the front and the other at the back, not visible from outside.

'We silently got down from the van but not before picking up their garments and every one giving a parting kick to them. We ran fast through the agriculture field. After running a mile or so we stopped under a banyan tree gasping for breath. Chikku said, "There's no time to lose, we must get out of the vicinity as soon as possible; how much money there?" A boy answered raising the packet, "Four thousand rupees, all in hundreds." Chikku asked, "Then distribute two hundred rupees each to all of us." It was done quickly. Looking at the notes in his hand Chikku remarked, "This is the first time in a month we've got at least a day's wage for our labuor. Now let's separate, not more than two in one group and walk casually to different directions. We may not meet again but let's celebrate our freedom by shouting "Hurrah".

"'Hurrah... hurrah... hurrah." The birds resting on the banyan tree flapped out, we looked up and clapped to their receding silhouettes. When we were about to leave two boys came forward and handed us the garments stripped from the two men. "Our gift to you; the pockets contain one hundred sixty rupees plus changes."

'We found our way to Mouri Gram station where we have some friends. The garments being much larger in size were of no use to us, we sold them for hundred rupees; so we had a total of six hundred sixty rupees now, and that was quite a lot for us. We stayed at Mouri Gram station for two months, didn't steal a thing, only begged. Soon we got bored and returned to Howrah station.'

Mashi clapped after Bichhu concluded the story of their adventure.

'I think it's time for tea,' Mashi said and gave them twenty rupees.

'Yes.' Two pairs of little feet ran for it.

Mashi suddenly realised she was just listening to stories, and enjoying too, without any emotional involvement as if these were being told by some other persons, not the boys who themselves suffered; she felt herself emotionally dry: nothing motherly or sisterly, no compassion, nothing. Even her claps were formal, not emotional. She had trained herself to this since she was left at Sealdah by her husband. She loosened herself only once with Jaggu but drew back though slowly after his arrest. These days she mixed with people, made friends, heard their stories to gather experience, but never got emotionally involved. She thanked herself for this achievement, but the weight of it often frightened her; a human being couldn't remain a robot all the time. But she knew she was no robot; she had learnt to enjoy life without getting attached to it and that was her strength, but how long could she hold herself like this?

Arranging the plastic cups and biscuits before them Bichhu said, 'There's still five rupees left.'

Finding no response from her he asked, 'Anything wrong, Mashi'.

'Oh, nothing', she replied. 'I feel so sorry for you; at such a young age you've been through so much.'

There is nothing wrong in pretensions though, she thought; it can white wash the dark walls of human mind. But Bichhu's reaction startled her.

'One request. Don't you ever feel sorry for us, we don't like it. We may cry as a tactical measure but we don't weep, not even pretend to do so. In a way we welcome adversities of life; they are pleasures in waiting: we enjoy the pleasure in planning, in executing and finally in celebrating when we get out of a jam. We know some day we may not be able to make it, we may be dead or doomed forever, but we don't care; so never feel sorry for us, not even pretend to do so.'

That's a good rebuff, Mashi thought; never play hide and seek with them. They were children with the mind of an adult; nay they were more adult than an adult. And what a resilience! She had seen many street children; always felt that they were more resilient, smarter than the home grown children. But this pair beats all!

She was roused by a tap on her leg.

'Hey Mashi, you angry with us, felt hurt for anything we said? Please don't be. We tell you all these things because we like you; we've never shared the story of our life with any one before.'

'No, I'm not angry with you; I like you too, and I feel fortunate to have met you. Now tell me how you escaped from the third prison.'

The boys looked at each other for a while, uncertain. Then Chikku broke in.

'Well... er... well... how do I put it, damn it... we're buggered,' the flow came in a torrent, 'buggered by the elders and other office staff, the manager in particular. We were still sore a little.'

Mashi looked aside for a moment pretending to be shy, then asked, 'How did you flee?'

'Oh, it was very simple but interesting,' Chikku was at ease now, 'this Home was like any other prison we lived before; they also took away our mobile phones and the money, we're not allowed to go out any time under any pretext. We came to know that the manager lived alone nearby at a rented house. We became cozy with him and told him that we wanted to be his exclusive, but not at the Home, at his residence only where it would be more private. He gave a big chimpanzee like smile and said, "We shall celebrate it tonight itself, and I promise henceforth none will disturb you."

'We left after dinner. We had no desire to go to his place but asked how long it'd take to reach his house. He replied with that chimpanzee smile, now broader. "Oh-ho, you're already feeling hot, me too; it's just about fifteen minutes." I smiled back. We were looking for a suitable ditch; there were quite a few on both sides of the road. Bichhu found a good one between two street lamps silhouetted by branches of big trees. He was walking by the side of the manager and me keeping a distance. He signalled by softly patting his bum. I cried out, "Sir" and stooped holding one of my legs pretending to be in great pain. The manager rushed backward and bent down to inspect my leg. Bichhu hit him on his neck and I kicked his balls hard. He fell flat on the ground holding his crotch. Bichhu quickly sat on his chest and gripped his throat to prevent any sound coming out. I stripped him naked—underwear and all, and Bichhu kicked him to the ditch. We fled with all his garments. Now imagine! The bastard couldn't even get up and shout for help. He was all naked. Hi... hi... ha... ha... ' The boys started giggling swaying their heads. Mashi put the edge of the cloth to her face to suppress her laughter.

After they were tired of giggling Mashi asked, 'Did you ever tell all these to the police?'

'No. They don't believe us, and we also don't trust them. Besides, we feel they know everything, perhaps... err... err... they might have a link with them.' Chikku looked directly at her face, so did Bichhu.

Mashi could guess it was a test-look; they were trying to understand the depth of her link with police. She decided to tell the truth.

'Yes, I know. I know many other things the police do. They also betrayed my trust when I was abandoned by my husband at Sealdah station and sought their help. But I've to survive, so I've made an arrangement with them; it's a mutual give and take, which you'll understand when you grow up.'

'We can understand, Mashi. We're no kids.'

Mashi could offer only a contrite smile which disturbed them.

'Mashi, please! Don't blame yourself and don't feel ashamed of it. Even god needs a survival strategy.'

Mashi now laughed. She wanted to know more of these two charming boys. She prodded deliberately.

'Why will God need a strategy? He is not like us human beings, He is omnipotent, can do anything.'

'Well, Bichhu has a theory which he expounded when I narrated him my experience of spending a whole night awake in a dilapidated temple of our village after I was kicked out of house by my drunken father. I invoked all the gods and goddesses to stave off advancing jackals with blue fluorescent eyes and ominous, grr... grrr... issuing from their throats. Whenever they came very near, their white teeth almost touching my flesh I hurled at them the names of gods—Rama-Laxman, Sita, Shiva-Durga, Krishna—over and over again and they'd back track. This went on till dawn when they left frustrated. And imagine Bichhu's reaction! He said coolly, "It is no god that saved you; it's your shouts that drove them away every time. Instead of gods' name if you'd shouted, *'sala harami, chutiya'* and all other abuses you know, the result would have been similar."

Mashi had a hearty laugh after which she asked, 'I think Bichhu has a point. But what's his theory?'

'He built up his theory through a question-answer drill. I'll mimic his questions first and then state my answers.'

"Why did you invoke gods the night before?"

"Well, I was afraid."

"Your father beats you every night after returning from the factory drunk, my father also does the same to me. But on that night he'd not only beaten you, also driven you out from the house. Now tell me why our fathers are drunk these days; they're not this type before. And why were you driven out?"

"You know, when our mothers died in the boat that capsized mid-river, they fell into grief and took to drinking. Added to that they were afraid the company might declare a lock-out soon and they'd be unemployed. They wanted us to do well in examination so we could stand on our feet and earn money to support our families of five, poor as we are. This time I'd come down to the eighth position in the class and you, the twelfth. My father had concluded I didn't study and had gone to dogs. He was outraged, beat me up and kicked me out of the house."

"Did you pray to god before the results were out?"

"Yes, every day and night, as I feared if I failed to hold my first position in the class he'd throw me out as he'd already warned."

"Does your father pray to God?"

"Yes, every day in the morning before going to the factory. He prays for himself, your father—his best friend, me and you too."

"I think that's enough. Now check the list. You invoke god when you are: poor, afraid, anxious and frustrated. Now suppose, there is no poverty, no fear, no anxiety and no frustration would you remember God?"

I thought for a while, delved into my mind and then replied, "Perhaps not."

"Ok. Now tell me how many times during the past six months you had invoked God without praying for a rescue from one or some of the negatives we've just listed?"

"I've always prayed for something."

"Now you'll agree the existence of god depends upon the existence of poverty, fear, anxiety, frustrations and similar other negatives. Simply put, if these were not there god is nowhere. And god would not like His creation to forget him. He created all these ills, so no one could forget Him. This is His survival strategy. And you know the kingpin of His scheme of things is the Devil, *Saitan* or *Mara* or *Asura* by whatever name you call him. He operates through him without his knowing about it. The poor fellow feels he is destroying the faith in God by his devilish activities but it's just the other way round, or may be the Devil is His own creation."

The discourse stopped, so also the mimicking of Bichhu who was following it with a curious smile.

Mashi was charmed at Bichhu's logical build up of arguments to support his conclusion. Howsoever faulty it might be it was coming from a boy of not more than 13-14 years; he could think beyond the conventional. She now spoke to him.

'You're an excellent polemic, but your premise is faulty, so also the conclusion which borders on oversimplification; it also goes against your life's philosophy. The debate on god is never ending. I'm not entering that debate. I only suggest why don't you look at it this way: god has created human beings not robots and thrown challenges before them to live a life. You say, you welcome adversity, means you love challenges. Imagine if all the adversaries listed by you were non-existent the fun of living would cease to exist. I don't think you'd want such a life. Adversity is the mother of all pleasures. You have also said adversities are pleasures in waiting.

So you should thank god for giving you such a life full of life. As for prayer it is an invention of mankind not of god; it's a confidence booster, for some it's necessary, for some not, that's all; there's no point in badgering it.'

Bichhu was taking in every word Mashi spoke with his head slightly bent. Observing this Chikku remarked, 'Now Bichhu is beaten in his own logic, look at him.'

Bichhu raised his head and said solemnly, 'I'm glad to have been beaten. I looked at the issue from a narrow perspective, didn't take a holistic view. Mashi has opened my eyes.'

'Okay, let's leave it at that. So, what I have before me: a polemic and a mimic. I must say, I'm amazed at his memory and mimicry; it must have happened some time back but he remembers every logical sequence.'

'You'll soon find Chikku mimicking you. He can also mimic animals' voices. You like to see for yourself?'

'I'd love to.' Mashi replied.

'Well, there are many cats here, distributed all over the place. When anyone's in trouble it gives an SOS call and all cats rush to its aid. Chikku would now give such an SOS call.'

Chikku put his palms on his mouth, lowered his torso and mewed a call sign several times. And lo! In about two minutes cats from all hideouts came running to the spot. Mashi got scared, so also the passers-by who scurried out, only Bichhu and Chikku were smiling impishly.

The cats circled them trying to locate the cat that had sent out the SOS call. After some time they left frustrated. Mashi gave a sigh of relief and exclaimed.

'My god! You also know call signs of different animals?'
Bichhu replied instead of Chikku.

'Yes. And this stupid boy was so scared as to forget it on that night in the temple when he was surrounded by black jackals.'

'Yes I did forget, which I realised only on the night we left our respective homes and stayed overnight in the same temple to catch the first train in the morning.'

'Were you also beaten by your father?' Mashi asked Bichhu.

'Ah, much more; my class performance had always been worse than Chikku's.'

'For him it was double beating.' Chikku added.

'Why?'

"Cause unlike my father his father remarried.'

'So you decided to leave together. By the way which class were you studying when you left home?'

'We just passed eighth class.'

'What was your escape strategy; by now I know you always have a strategy.'

Chikku recounted the story.

'We needed money for our journey to the unknown. We decided to steal the pay packets of our respective fathers which they brought home on the first of every month. That was also our D-night. As planned we left home after stealing money and taking whatever garments we had. It was past midnight, the village was asleep, no moon in the sky; we walked toward the temple in darkness. I was scared of jackals, so I carried a rod in my bag which Bichhu saw when we reached the temple and showed his taunting teeth. I was angry but didn't say a word. We sat silently for some time, then Bichhu laid himself down on the floor saying, "Call me when the jackals come." I couldn't sleep like him for fear of jackals. But there was no sign of them though an hour had passed. I thought, maybe they wouldn't come tonight, must've seen I wasn't alone as in the other night. I began dozing.

'I was roused by a hot breath on my face. I opened my eyes with a start and saw two fluorescent eyes and a set of canine teeth close to my throat. I picked up my rod and hit on its head while shouting for Bichhu. The animal fell but what I saw next took away my breath. Many... many fluorescent eyes were advancing toward us slowly. I heard Bichhu whispering, "Stupid! Call the hyenas; jackals are scared of them." I said, "But if hyenas come responding to my call?" He insisted, "Just call; there's no hyena in our village." At that moment I realised what a fool I was! I turned back quickly, lowered my head and mimicked the war call of hundred hyenas. I was amazed to find the entire pack of jackals began running for their life. We burst out laughing in such high-pitched laughter that all bats sleeping on the broken walls of the temple flew away fast as if chasing the jackals on the run. We had a nice sleep thereafter. We woke up with the whistle of the first approaching train. The railway station was very near the temple. We boarded the train and landed at Howrah station.'

Mashi said, 'I think some day Chikku would mimic every sound produced on the earth. Now let's break for lunch. Do you know a place here where we may get good food?'

'Yes, there's a place on the other side of the Howrah Bridge, about ten-fifteen minutes walk. It doesn't look good but the food is good and not pricey.'

'Then let's go there. You two walk ahead, I'll follow you.'

They walked along the pavement overlooking the river Ganges. Mashi observed the river flowing below the bridge, people standing with their hands on the railing observing the movements of boats and steamers while enjoying the cool breeze, continuous movement of automobiles of various sizes, shapes and sounds, the cacophony of screeching tyres, the loud voices of bus conductors announcing the arrival of Howrah station. But nothing touched her mind. She was thoughtful, her head slightly bent: the police who beat up boys like Bichhu and Chikku consider them nuisance, but abusable, send them to Homes for further abuse. But they are smarter than them, they escape. The abusers feel these boys are helpless children. But many are neither helpless nor children; help comes from their superactive brains, far superior to that of a society reared "normal adult" and they are children only in their natural behaviour, everything else is acquired, and that's why there is an unpredictable discontinuity in their behaviour.

Mashi's thought process was jarred by the shouts of Chikku, 'Not that way; it's on the other side'. He ran back and guided her to a shanty food joint. The eatery was nearly full. They found space on a bench that could accommodate three persons with some cramming.

'Today the food is on me, it's my *gurudakshina*,' Mashi said.

It was difficult to carry on a conversation where everybody was talking. So they ate silently. When they came back to the station they found the earlier place occupied and sat on the other side of the waiting hall.

Mashi said, 'I've some suggestions; you may accept or reject, I won't mind.'

The boys nodded and she continued.

'I understand you often get caught while pick pocketing. Let me tell you pick pocketing is no ordinary game; it's both an art and a science, requires training and organisation. If you want to pursue this vocation I can send you to a person who imparts such training. His organisation having nexus with the police can take care of your security; though you cannot escape public beating if caught but for you it's not a big threat. The problem is the uncertainty of income; many a days you may go dry but that is also not a big issue for moderate spenders.

'Second suggestion is you may find help from a good Home, oh-ho don't raise your hands. I know you've bad experience with Homes but there are a few which are good. I know one near Sealdah where you can pursue your studies further; with your intelligence you can go a long distance to become worthy citizens of the country.'

'But we don't want to become citizens and lose our freedom.' Chikku interrupted.

'Okay, you don't have to decide now. Keep it in your mind. Now the third and last suggestion: you may explore the money-making potential of Chikku's mimicries; it's preferable to perform them on a running train where passengers are more at ease than in a station where they are always in a hurry. So far Chikku has done it in private; he may have to reorient himself for a public show. You may deliberate on the suggestions and come to a decision by tomorrow when we meet next. In the meantime don't get caught by the police, behave like good boys and as a return of that promise I'll give you back the two mobiles which though stolen now belong to you.'

Their eyes sparkled as they took the phones in their hand.

'Not bad; one is Nokia, the other Samsung. Which one you want to take? Chikku asked Bichhu.'

'Let the cards decide.' Bichhu replied.

Bichhu won and picked up Nokia. Chikku threw away the SIMs of both the phones and asked Mashi, 'Can you give us two hundred rupees?'

'I know the reason,' said Mashi smiling and gave them the money.

They ran away with Chikku saying, 'Don't go, we're coming back in ten minutes.'

Mashi glanced at the running figures, amused: who could guess a few minutes back these two boys were giving her lessons on life, god and survival.

She thought: Bichhu is calm, confident, and courageous—a natural leader, but he also has a philosopher's bent of mind, he is generally aloof, a duck that shrugs away water from its body. Chikku is a follower, a very strong one but vulnerable too. They are bonded by love. If anything happens to Bichhu he will cry his heart out, might even commit suicide. But if a similar thing happens to Chikku, Bichhu would be very sorry, angry but not shattered, might retaliate but not kill himself.

The boys came back with a large bottle of coca-cola. 'We bargained hard to get this bottle along with the SIMs. Now let's enjoy,' Chikku said with all smiles.

While enjoying the fizzy drink Mashi spoke, 'I don't think you work under a Dada or a mashi, do you?'

Bichhu replied, 'When we came here first one of the Dadas picked us up—there are four Dadas here, no mashi, you could be the first—but he does not have much hold with the police. Being novice we got caught almost every day; the police chastised him so much he left us in frustration. The other Dadas didn't want to take us. I guess you want us to work under you. Let's see how it works.'

'No, I don't want you to work under me. I make business propositions for mutual benefit; any one of us can walk out any time, pursue any other activity outside the arrangement; you don't have to consult me for this. Even if you pursue a dangerous vocation, I won't stop you; neither would give you any advice even when you ask for it. Do you agree with this arrangement?'

'We do,' they replied after some consultation between them.'

Ok. Let's talk about the financials now. My share of the total income will be twenty five percent; the rest is yours.'

'You're being generous, Mashi,' Chikku said.

'No. It's my policy; I don't need much. Now I'll leave. Think about the three options I've suggested; the first two are not business propositions, the last one is. We shall meet here tomorrow morning.'

She rose to leave after exchanging telephone numbers. Chikku accompanied her to the station exit, waved his little hand, she also waved back; the mutual waving continued till they could see each other. 'Lovely boys,' she uttered silently.

'Oh-ho, stupid woman, not again!' Her tormenter VOICE slapped her as she boarded a running bus.

* * * *

Next morning Mashi found Bichhu and Chikku waiting at the same corner of the station where they sat first. Chikku waved, she acknowledged with a nod: It was already past 7 a.m., the first lot of trains must have left, whether they agree or not she had to work. She walked hurriedly to them. They sat together. Mashi looked at Bichhu.

'We've thought about you and your suggestions last night. The first two options we hold in abeyance, the last one is worth trying. Now tell us how to go about it. We've no experience working in a train.'

'I suggest for the present we limit ourselves to local suburban trains, with experience we may move to long distance trains. I'd board the last compartment with my broom a few minutes before the train takes off. If there is a direct competition it will be on my turf and I'll handle it by sharing a part of my collections. I don't think you'd face any competition directly; there may however be indirect competition, just settle or undo it in your own way.

'Initially Chikku might be nervous in facing the crowd. Bichhu should create appropriate ambience for Chikku to perform his tricks; think about ways of doing it.'

'What about earning?' Chikku asked.

'For the first two or three tricks you accept whatever passengers give. Then depending on the number of passengers in an enclosure, their profile and mood you may decide a price per trick. Like a magician Bichhu would present Chikku and each of his tricks by appropriate theatrics.'

'Oh, we're very good at theatrics, our first weapon for survival.'

'Oh, yes, I forgot. Now let's decide which train we target today.'

'Just wait here, we shall come back with all information,' Bichhu said as they ran off.

Nearly fifteen minutes had passed when they returned. Chikku announced, 'We shall board Bardhaman local which leaves in half hour, so we have time for a quick bite.'

'What makes you take so long a time; not just for gathering this little bit of information, I suppose?'

'That's a secret we won't reveal now.' Chikku grinned.

Must be a childish prank, Mashi thought, after all they are children. Aloud she said, 'Okay, I won't ask. Now, as Chikku said, let's have a bite.'

After food they boarded the train. Mashi saw them for the first time when she was half way through the train. She passed the enclosure without recognising them but stopped to hear Bichhu blaring away: Just for one rupee each, you'll visualise a tiger pursuing a flock of buffalos, catching one finally and making a lunch out of it. Just close your eyes for a while. I promise if the tiger didn't have a good lunch, we wouldn't take any money.

Mashi heard a guffaw issuing from the enclosure; the passengers standing on the floor between the two exits herded closer. What followed next was simply marvellous: They suddenly heard a tiger galloping after a running buffalo flock braying for life, jumping on one, pulling it down, tearing apart the throat, blood spilling out, gurgled at a good job done, then eating out the choicest portions of the carcass and finally a satisfied growl; all in about five minutes.

Mashi heard sounds of clapping when Chikku finished the mimicry. She peeped in to observe admiration in the eyes of the passengers. When Bichhu began collection only a few gave the promised one rupee: some gave two, some five, some tens. Satisfied, Mashi went her way and they theirs.

They met at Bardhaman junction station near a tea stall. The station was wide with a number of platforms. Besides suburban trains terminating here, most of the mail and express trains bound for the districts of West Bengal and also for other states of India had compulsory stoppage here.

Mashi had never been here but the boys came here frequently just for fun and to make new friends. After they had a stomach full of water to quench their thirst Mashi suggested they should catch a late afternoon return train: Chikku's vocal cord needed some rest. They agreed and went out for lunch.

The secret was not yet revealed, not even during lunch, might be because soon a gang of their friends arrived at the eatery. There was laughter, pleasantries and exchange of information. In between Bichhu introduced Mashi; a chorus followed with claps: 'If you are their Mashi you're also our Mashi... Mashi... Mashi... Mashi... '

Suddenly they heard someone shouting, 'Hey, the bunch of pigs, why so much *halla,* don't you know there are others who may feel disturbed?'

Mashi was stunned, so also the others. One of the boys spoke, 'It must be that bastard of a manager vituperating at us; today we shall give him a piece of our mind.' All eyes now turned toward the far end of the hall where the manager sat behind a counter. But they found him absorbed in preparing cash memos and making entries in the register. They looked at each other uncertainly. Then it dawned on them. One boy burst out laughing, 'It's Chikku, the Harbola, at his tricks again!' Full-throated guffaws followed the patting of Chikku who sat quietly with an impish smile on his face. This time the manager did look up, tried to guess what was happening, nodded his head in resignation and returned to what he was doing.

After lunch their friends dispersed one by one shaking hands with Bichhu and Chikku and saying *namaskar* to Mashi. The last one circled Chikku's neck and asked almost conspiratorially, 'Are you going to your auntie now?' 'Let's see', replied Chikku in a low voice. But Bichhu overheard the conversation and declared loudly 'Yes of course, we are going there; we still have three hours before the train leaves.'

Bichhu leading the way they entered the station, crossed several platforms and reached the other side of station. Mashi saw a woman at the far end of the platform sitting before a thatched outfit trying to ignite a *sigri* with pieces of firewood, a girl fanning its top with a palm-leaf fan, four other children moving about her, playing. As they sat before the woman she looked up and smiled, the girl too; others hopped in to shout, 'Bichhudada, Chikkudada... '

Bichhu quickly introduced Mashi, gave some money to the girl and said, 'Now off you go, and Chikku too; buy some tidbits for them, and play; I'll help auntie lighting the Sigri.' The girl placed the palm-leaf fan on Bichhu's lap, raised Chikku by the hand and ran off with other children. Mashi picked up the fan from Bichhu's lap and told him. 'You too go with them, don't show off like a big boy; I'll help her with the *sigri* and do chit-chatting.' Bichhu gave her a heavenly smile and ran for them.

The woman spoke first. 'These two boys are darlings of the children: good boys but my husband doesn't like them.'

'Why?' Mashi asked.

'He feels they are spoiling the children, but the actual reason is whenever they come they take away the children to play with and he has to raise himself from his drugged slumber and help me cooking these fries, carry the first lot to the *thana*, take orders from passengers sitting on the platform benches—that is running to and fro. All these are normally done by that girl and his brother.'

'They aren't your children?' Mashi was somewhat surprised.

'Oh-ho. No. They're bastards, must be children of some prostitute. To be frank, I don't want my children to mix with them, but they are useful in many ways, so I keep them. My nerves grate when they call me Ma, but I tolerate—one has to be tactful while running a family, which my husband doesn't understand.'

Mashi surmised the woman must be a village simpleton who loved talking, but she also had that cunning of a farmer who had seen life.

The oil in the pan began bubbling. Satisfied, she put one by one different types of vegetable balls covered with a paste of gram powder into the boiling oil. Soon the aroma of oil fries filled the platform, heads turned, someone asked, 'Hey auntie, send me two chops and one onion fry; where's your husband?' Similar demands followed. She raised her hand in assurance and called a passing boy, 'Hey Piku, get your uncle here quickly, he is sleeping at the end of this platform; I promise you a chop if you do.' As the woman began arranging the fries on a round *thali*, Mashi saw Piku almost dragging a man still wobbling.

'Why you got me dragged here? Where are the two bastards?' the man rasped.

'Shut up, sit here quietly and eat a potato chop.' The woman gave one chop each on a sal leaf to her husband and Piku, who went off dancing. The man took a bite of chop which was very hot and immediately cried out, 'Oohoo oohoo... oohoo... hot... very hot...,' his torso moved sideways, tongue out with saliva dripping like a dog.

'Rightly served. Now allow it to cool and eat slowly, don't guzzle like a *Rakshasa.*'

The heat-shock steadied the man. Mashi observed he was now taking each bite after feeling its heat content. After finishing the first one he asked for another but the woman refused:

'First *you* deliver this *thali* with all the ten pieces to *thanedars* then I'll give you another.' Utterly disappointed, he now looked at Mashi and asked his wife in a rough voice.

'Who's the woman you are gossiping with?'

'Don't talk like that about a woman; she has come with Bichhu and Chikku.'

'Oh! The bastards have come again, that's why I don't find the children here.'

'Shut up. Now do what I say before the constables come here to enquire.'

Reluctantly he got up with the *thali* and proceeded towards the thana, his wobbling nearly vanished.

The woman talked between frying and heaving the fries in cane baskets. The husband came back soon grumbling.

'There are only two *thanedars* present but they took all the fries, *sala, Rakshasas,* didn't return any.'

'What's that to you? It's their quota and they can keep them all. Now take these baskets one by one and sell the fries to the passengers who are already clamouring for it.'

When the man left the woman said, 'My husband doesn't understand. Can we live here without the support of police? They are very reasonable; charge only hundred rupees and ten fries per day. He doesn't understand, an idler, concerned only with his booze and inhalers.'

In about half hour six baskets of fries got sold at different platforms. The woman now slowed down the cooking and resumed talking.

'How do you know Chikku and Bichhu?'

'I work with them.'

'Your husband?'

'He left as I'm barren.'

'*Chook... chook!* That way I'm very fortunate. He is an idler and stupid but good at heart and virile too. But after the birth of the third baby I don't allow him without condom. He grumbles but I'm very strict, otherwise how can I manage? This is just a station platform, not our village home. But let me confide to you, I've saved good amount of money and I've a steady income from this fry business. Now I'm thinking of moving to a small flat nearby. I've already talked with the landlord; he wants a deposit of five thousand rupees which won't be a problem. I haven't revealed this to any one not even to my husband.'

'It's a very good idea but you'll miss your village environment.'

'That's true, but we've no way to go back to our village, though I always long for it. It is a beautiful village at Sundarban', her eyes turned dreamy, 'near the bank of the river. We're a poor share cropper but built a good home, though with mud and split bamboos; it had two large rooms, a kitchen and a large veranda. The Aila cyclone took everything away; half the village immersed in water. Suddenly we found ourselves down to the water, moved by a huge current, didn't know where we're going. In the vastness of the water we couldn't even locate the place where our house had been. Some time we swam with the two children, some time waded through it, some time we're just forced by the current. The rain storm above tried to drown us and the flood to tear us apart, but with god's grace we could hold together and found ourselves alive among hundreds of dead people and cattle floating by.

'When we reached a somewhat dry place we got help from government people, missionaries and NGOs. They dropped us at principal railway stations like Sealdah, Dumdum, Kharagpur, Bardhaman, et cetera. They promised to come back with more help but never showed up. We found ourselves at this station bewildered. Here we found Binni and Bisu sitting at a corner looking at us, the girl holding something in her palm. I felt sad. As I called them they rose and ran to me crying, Ma... Ma... Later I learnt I resembled their mother who got carried away by the flood, but before that she gave a thick gold chain to the girl saying, "Never lose, it may ultimately save you." The girl opened her palm and gave the gold chain to me. I weighed the chain for the price it might fetch, hugged them and said, "Yes, your mother was right, it'll save all of us, don't you worry, from today I'm your mother."

'I sold the gold chain for six thousand rupees, spent about thousand five hundred to build this outfit, buy utensils and other materials to start the fry business, rest I saved. From that day on they call me Ma. From the tit bit of information I gathered from them it became clear their mother was a prostitute entertaining a lot of men. What a shame—good she was dead!' she sneered.

'My husband wanted to throw them out, so ungrateful and idiot he is. Truly speaking I also cringe now when they call me Ma, but what to do, I tolerate, more so because they also bring in at least hundred rupees a day by begging in the morning hours. This my husband doesn't understand. He'll never be a man of the family; I've to take all the responsibilities.' She lamented with a tinge of pride in her voice.

Mashi heard the giggles of the children running back toward them, the man following a little behind.

'Give us our share of fries and also that of Chikku and Bichhu,' Binni demanded. Then seeing the man she said, 'Sorry Baba, you have to suffer all the labour today, but what to do, Chikku and Bichhu took us away.'

'Don't call me Baba, you bastards.' He burst out.

'Baba... Baba... Baba...' Binni and Bisu began chanting, soon others also joined the chorus.

Frustrated, he picked up the last basket, shouted, 'All bastards,' and left in a huff, the children following him with packets of fries chanting the same chorus. The woman gave out a suppressed laughter, Mashi also joined, and with that they became conspiratorial friends.

'Do you know Bichhu and Chikku want to take Binni and Bisu with them, possibly today itself?' The woman asked.

'No, I got no hint of it.'

'They might say it'll be for a few days only, but I know it is for good. Although I'll bargain a price for their release, deep in mind I want them to go. They're bad company, after all children of a prostitute. Besides, when we move to the rented house my husband wouldn't like to take them with us.'

Mashi nodded looking at the station clock over their head; the train was to leave in half hour, Bichhu and Chikku would come back any time.

With eight baskets sold the woman declared the sale closed, lifted the last pan full of fries from the *sigri* and toned down its heat. Arranging the fries on Sal-leaf plates she said, 'It's time for us to eat. Lo! My nincompoop husband is also coming; has perfect timing, never misses.'

The husband saw them eating and gossiping, took two handfuls of fries, put them in a packet and left without a word.

The woman said, 'He would now go to the other side of the platform where his friends are waiting with a bottle of country liquor.'

They had nearly finished eating when Bichhu and Chikku arrived. Picking up whatever remained on the plates Bichhu asked Mashi to proceed to platform number four and take a seat, the train was to leave in fifteen minutes; they would join her after finishing some business talks with the auntie.

Mashi gave an understanding smile to the woman, got up and walked out leisurely; there's enough time. A *paanwala* sat by the side of a tea stall. She stopped there and asked for a *paan* prepared with a certain *masala* paste. From there she saw Bichhu talking to the woman smilingly; Chikku was nowhere to be seen. Bichhu handed her some currency notes which she accepted with a smile.

As she took the *paan* and opened her bag to pay for it, she heard loud barking of street dogs from their direction. She saw the woman got up fast, turned and ran to opposite direction with a spatula in hand shouting, 'Again these pariah dogs! They'll spoil all my food stuff; this time I'd give them a lesson of life.' Mashi looked toward her direction but could not see any dog anywhere; Bichhu sat there as before. The boys must be up to some tricks! She placed a one rupee coin on *paanwalla's* palm and walked briskly to platform number four.

Mashi spotted the children standing on the platform by the side of a compartment. Binni was doing all the talking, her hands moving in all directions; Bisu stood by clinging to her skirt. They did not notice her standing behind so absorbed they were in talking. It was Bisu who noticed her and cried out, 'Oh, Mashi has come, but where are Bichhuda and Chikkuda?'

'They'll be here soon; now you two get into the compartment and reserve our seats,' Mashi replied.

'I've already done that. Look at the boy by the window seat, my friend, he is keeping a watch.'

Soon they saw Bichhu and Chikku walking toward them in hurried steps. 'Now you three get in fast; the train is about to leave.' Chikku hurried them inside. When the train gained speed the two leaped to the compartment catching the door handles.

'Bye bye... bye bye... bye bye...'

'Bye bye... bye bye... bye bye.'

The train was yet to be crowded. Chikku sat with the girl and his brother, and the three immediately began talking. Mashi and Bichhu moved to the other side of the aisle.

'What's the settlement cost?' Mashi asked.

'Not much, just one thousand.' Bichhu then turned to Chikku and asked. 'Hey Chikku, what's the take today?'

'Thousand sixty; not bad for a first time railway *Harbola*.'

'One thousand gone,' said Mashi.

'Not really.' Bichhu scratched his head.

'What? What's the trick?'

'Well let me put it like this. They had been exploiting the girl and her brother for long; they never considered them their children, just using them.'

'I've gathered as much.'

'They were earning not less than fifty rupees daily from begging and gave all the money to the auntie.'

'It's more than that,' Mashi said.

'Oh! I didn't know that. The girl never counted the money, I guess. I calculated their earnings at fifty rupees per day, thus they must've given around twenty thousand every year to auntie. If we'd asked her to give back a part of it, she'd invent hundred reasons for not giving it; so why bother? We just relieved her of their one year's income, just two packets of hundred-rupee notes; aren't we reasonable?' Bichhu grinned.

'I guess so. The dogs barked right in time,' Mashi suppressed laughter. 'May I make another guess?'

'Oh, no. You don't have to tell. I know you know Chikku loves Binni.'

'Now tell me, is this the secret you held back when we started off this morning?'

'Oh, no. That relates to our strategy. We wanted to surprise you if it worked. Now that it has worked I can tell you.'

'Please go ahead.'

'Well, we were a little nervous; this is an area we've never ventured. Chikku is an excellent *Harbola*, no problem there; we know theatrics too, but a theatrical presentation before a crowd is quite different. We've to experiment a strategy being in the environment itself. So we went to the platforms: trains arriving and leaving, passengers jostling, carts trotting, the *chaiwalas* hawking *chai... chai...* and all that, a cacophony of some sort. As we stood on a platform a train whistled to leave. I asked Chikku, "Can you copy that?" "Let me see," he said, and Wow! In the next second I found him totally absorbed, still, two hands up to ear level, nothing entered his ears except the sound of the train leaving the platform; a transformed entity, not that talkative, restless Chikku. Oh, what a concentration! When the train moved out of sight Chikku turned to me, "I've got to hear another train leaving." We spotted a train two platforms away readying to leave and rushed there. Chikku exhibited the same concentration. He told me after the train left, "I think I can do it. Let's test." We went to a platform where passengers were boarding a train scheduled to leave in ten minutes. He said, "You just stand here and observe," and then boarded a compartment to get down to the other side. Soon I heard the whistling and the sound of slow movement of a train issuing exactly from the waiting train. And lo, the passengers who were loitering near the train jumped into it, others began running toward it and a surprised ticket checker scratching his head vigorously advanced hurriedly. I was enjoying the scene profusely. I do not know how other *Harbolas* master the art, for him it was as natural as a child learning to talk.

'I was back from the virtual world with a nudge from Chikku. "Let's go somewhere less crowded." By that time I'd thought out a plan for our maiden presentation. I discussed it with him and finalised. We were no longer scared, a bit nervous, yes.

'We boarded our target train five minutes before takeoff. You couldn't see us as you were on the other extreme of the platform waiting to board only a minute before it started. Chikku mimicked all the sounds of the train leaving and the passengers reacted similarly.'

'Yeah, I also did the same. But when the train remained still the passengers of my compartment looked over the platform and at each other surprised. They began discussing what really had happened; various opinions were voiced, but between confusion and confabulation the train finally took off, they felt relieved and soon the episode was forgotten. Now I understand who were the perpetrators behind it.' Mashi smiled and asked. 'What happened next?'

'Then I took over. I assured the passengers with all the smiles of a charmer that it was just a demonstration of mimicry by my friend Chikku who has been trained by a great *Harbola* living in a forest. The Guru has asked me to report on his performance. "Now tell me does he get a pass mark?" While most of the passengers responded, "Yes, good... very good...," I found some angry for being tricked. I gave them no chance. The train was running full speed; the next station was far away. I declared, "Now you will feel the train slowing down and coming to a halt. Please close your eyes a minute." When Chikku finished there was hurray of laughter all around, the recalcitrant also joined. Rest of it was easy as you've already seen.

'If we had failed, we'd never have told you. So we kept it a secret. People like to hear the story of others' failed attempts for a chance to give advice, but we do not like to hear the chuckles followed by "try hard, next time you'll succeed" kind of hollow advices.'

Mashi said, 'You're right; the world is full of advisors not helpers; advice perhaps is the first social instinct of human beings and help the last. I'm thankful to you for not revealing it to me before; if you'd failed I might have ended up giving you some such advice.'

Bichhu said as he rose, 'Now that the secret is revealed permit us to earn some more money to compensate for the settlement money given to auntie. We can't touch the savings of Binni and Bisu. You keep their money in safe custody.'

He pulled out two packets from inside his shirt, handed them to Mashi and called out, 'Hey *Harbola,* enough of gossiping, now let's do it again.'

Chikku rose with a grin. The two left holding each other's hand, Mashi shifted to the seat vacated by Chikku.

It was late evening when they arrived at Howrah station. The return journey fetched three hundred twenty rupees; so the duo's total income for the day was one thousand three hundred eighty rupees.

'Fantastic'! Chikku exclaimed, 'much more than our three days' earnings at the station. Thank you Mashi for suggesting this line.'

'You're most welcome,' Mashi replied in mock acknowledgement.

'What's your take Mashi?' Bichhu asked.

'Not much, just four hundred eighty rupees.'

'Not bad either; you haven't worked during the return journey.'

'Yes. I was taking care of your wards,' Mashi said cradling Binni and Bisu, 'but it is still lower than my average take.'

'Ok. The total comes eighteen hundred sixty rupees; at twenty five percent your share is four hundred sixty five.' Bichhu gave the money to Mashi.

'But... but... that...' Mashi was about to say something but Bichhu stopped her.

'Accounts settled. No further talk on this subject. Let's discuss now our next strategy.'

The discussion continued for about half an hour. Mashi marvelled how Bichhu in a subtle way guided the whole discussion by organising stray thoughts, allowing others to evaluate various suggestions and options and finally arriving at concrete strategy formulations: There shall not be a repeat performance in one train before thirty days had elapsed.

Initially, they will target thirty trains divided between Bardhaman and Kharagpur lines.

It is preferable to board a train each day to alternate lines. Bichhu and Chikku will prepare the list of such trains.

Mashi shall always board a train different from that of Bichhu and Chikku combined. Binni and Bisu will work with Mashi. During Mashi's absence Binni and Bisu shall take over.

The group shall meet at Howrah station every day after completion of work to share earnings and experience.

There shall be no work on Sundays.

In case of any dispute, Mashi's decision shall be final.

Chapter 11

It was two months now Boomba and Toomba were working as drug couriers. Boomba got his weekly working days raised to five and number of packets per delivery day to four. Toomba stuck to his original schedule.

Minudi had promised to find a one room flat before his marriage with Chameli. He needed to earn more money now to pay for the landlord's deposit which might be between twenty and fifty thousand rupees and monthly rent of not less than three thousand.

Boomba saved his earnings with Mashi; Toomba spent the whole on food, booze, cinemas, hashish, inhalers and other merry-making activities with friends and non-friends: if he had excess money he'd lend, if there was a shortage he'd borrow. Although promises were made to return the money, no one really bothered; no duns among friends. In his spare days he would join his friends in loading and unloading activities at Koley Market. He loved the bargain with the *paikars,* the warmth and the sweat that smeared the whole body, the cheating and pilfering of fruits and vegetables and selling them later, and finally sharing the loot; this fun he never wanted to miss. But he never stayed with them for more than two-three days at a time lest he felt bored. This had always been his practice with every street group he made friendship with. His network now extended to Shyambazar in the north and Jadavpur in the south. Recently he had moved to Howrah district. Two urban areas, Bagnan and Santragachi he liked most. The boys there worked independently. Santragachi had special attraction for him. He would visit the place at least once every month, sit by the lake and lose himself among the cacophony of birds.

None of his friendship groups would ever know when he would surface except on emergencies, they could not plan any merry-making activities with him; over time they stopped making complaints and got used to his whims, but not Boomba. Being frustrated over his erratic appearance he asked him once, 'Do you know though you've perfect timing, you've no sense of time?'

'It's time's problem not mine; I don't buy time, time buys me,' Toomba replied but what that meant he did not explain.

Boomba met Raja more frequently than Toomba. They became buddies of sorts though Boomba still disliked his bragging. Raja would often treat them sumptuously with food and classy liquor at restaurants they had never visited before. Boomba could not savour the delicacies fully as he felt it as an expression of his ego. When he vented it before Toomba he replied, 'He has started liking us and us, him, which means we've touched a chord in each other's mind, and that's not bad. So why bother about his boastings? He may not be hollow as many boasters are or, maybe he is not boasting, just demonstrating a fact, though in a manner of showing off.'

'Don't try to cover him with your *gyani* talk; I know these kinds of people more than you do.'

Boomba had been insisting on visiting Raja's place unannounced which he often bragged as his kingdom.

'Why unannounced?' Toomba asked. 'If it were to give him a pleasant surprise I'd have readily agreed, but I know that is not your intention. When he invites us we go, not before that. I don't play games with friends.'

They did not have to wait long. One day after a grand dinner Raja wanted to know their evening programs.

'Boomba would go back to Gariahat and me to Sealdah, perhaps.'

'Can you skip?'

'I've no problem but Boomba may have.' Toomba smiled devilishly.

'Why do you ask?' Boomba queried.

'Well I've been thinking for quite some time to invite you to my place but couldn't wrest a day off my busy schedule. But I'm free tonight and tomorrow; I just thought why not spend time with you at my place?'

'We agree, let's go,' Boomba replied with alacrity.

They took a taxi and got down at a place in north Kolkata near the entry point of Maratha Ditch Lane, the last remnant of the great Maratha Ditch—a moat three mile long covering an area which later came to be known as Calcutta—dug up nearly two hundred seventy five years ago to prevent marauding Maratha "Bargis" from plundering the rich country side. The defeat of the "Bargis" took away the importance and glamour surrounding the Ditch, turned it to an abandoned canal for dumping all the filth of the growing civilisation of Calcutta, the smell of which forced the British government to order the ditch to be filled up that in turn created the Upper Circular Road and Lower Circular Road; the filth of the Ditch thus decentralised to hundreds of nooks, and to one such nook, a leftover of the Ditch, Raja led them through the Maratha Ditch Lane.

It was under a small overbridge, kind of a hamlet crammed with small huts built of bamboo splits and tarpaulin sheets similar to Mashi's at Gariahat. One hut between two pillars of the bridge was lighted by an electric bulb, some children playing before it, other huts partly lit by the ray of light coming from the road above and partly by kerosene lamp. People moved around like ghosts.

The place smelt of stench produced by a mixture of shits of all living creatures, carcasses of dead animals, bloodied sanitary napkins, medical and chemical wastes, dead flowers and leaves, all cooked with urine on a cauldron that was once a canal.

Raja guided them to the only fully lit hut. The children stopped playing and began chanting, 'Raja... Raja   Raja...' and a pack of dogs matched it with friendly barks. Raja smiled indulgently and tossed some packets of biscuits and lozenges to the children and dog biscuits to the dogs and said, 'Now go and send Mimi here.' He opened the door of his hut. It was rather spacious, well arranged with a mat on a raised wooden plank, a kettle, an electric cooker, a toaster, water jug, drinking glasses and also a large laughing dwarf with hands stretched out on two sides holding garments of daily wear. 'I bought it at a *mela* at Galiff Street.' He smiled pointing at the dwarf.

'But how come, you've electricity here while others don't have?' Boomba blurted out.

'I've hooked it from the overhead line, pay two hundred rupees a month to the line inspector; others can't afford it.'

A girl of their age quietly entered the hut, poured water in the kettle and placing it on the heater asked, 'Tea or coffee?'

'Get us coffee in china mugs, not glasses; they're my friends visiting first time, coffee must be good not the one prepared the other day for that inspector.'

The girl glanced at them for the first time and busied herself in preparing coffee.

As they talked, Raja's hand rested on the girl's bum caressing and pinching it often. The girl tried to shake him off but without much success. Gradually his hand moved to her breasts. The girl's body shook; she was finding it difficult to concentrate. At one point she burst out in exasperation. 'I can't prepare the coffee if you don't stop.' Raja was in a fit of rage. He slapped the girl hard, pulled her by the hair and kicked her out of the hut: *'Sali harami* bitch, dare raise your voice before Raja! I'll throw you and your family out of this place.' Something snapped out in Boomba's mind and he stood up to intervene but Toomba held him back. The girl raised herself from the ground and ran with tears soaking her small breasts.

Raja spat on the ground, dusted his hands and said in a frustrated voice, 'That bitch has spoilt the mood; I was just warming up, what's wrong in that, eh? I do it often, may be this time I overdid a little but one can't always have control on things like this. But just for that she'd raise her voice against me! This is my harem, I can do anything with them; you want to see?'

Raja shouted for one Kimi before they could prevent him. She came hurriedly munching a biscuit and holding two in her hands. Her face suggested she was younger than the first girl but filling up faster. She sat on Raja's lap without asking. Putting the second biscuit to her mouth she said, 'You must give me some lozenges, the boys wrested all from me.' 'Sure, I'll give you two packets of lozenges; I'll also punish the boys who did this.' Raja assured her as he put his hands inside her skirt. She giggled as Raja began caressing her breasts. 'See how obedient she is, not like that bitch. You know, I've named her Kimi Katkar, the movie heroin with huge breasts; some day she'd grow up like her. I've learnt from sex videos on my smart phone, which I use only for this, that if you knead breasts of a young girl regularly in a particular manner they grow faster, that's why I do it to hers regularly.'

Only Raja was talking, his listeners did not speak a single word since the frolics began. Suddenly Boomba stood up and went outside. No doubt he was angry with Raja; he was now angrier with himself: when Raja was doing all that he felt stirred up between his legs, and one could have seen it jutting out if he stayed longer. 'What a shame! What's the difference between him and Raja; nothing, pigs both of them.' He needed to cool his mind and body. He stood still to compose himself; the evening Easterly though full of stench helped.

Toomba was nonchalant but Raja felt something amiss. He put down Kimi from his lap, gave her a twenty-rupee note, and patted her back, 'Now go and buy your lozenges.'

He went outside and brought Boomba in.

'Arrey *yaar*, why look so grave? What happened?'

'Nothing.'

'Then let's have coffee first, I'll do it for you, then we shall have a tour of the place.'

They were sipping coffee silently. But Raja perhaps could never stand silence. He spoke out.

'You see, I take care of them, they take care of me, and my demand is not much: a little bit of frolics and an occasional fuck.'

'You also fuck?' Boomba asked.

'Yeah, when I'm very down or very high I do it with one of the girls, I also do it with boys, though very rarely. Why? You don't fuck?'

No answer.

'Any time you want to do it, just tell me.'

Coffee finished, Raja took them for, what he said, a tour of his kingdom. The first *jhopri* was near Raja's. He called out, 'Uncle... uncle...' An old man appeared with his wife and a sickly little boy in tow. He smiled and said, 'I've heard you've returned with two friends, I was expecting you.'

'Yes, they're my friends—Boomba and Toomba; they have come all the way from Gariahat, would stay with me tonight.'

'That's good,' the wife said, 'I'll send you some food for dinner.'

'That won't be necessary; we'd eat our dinner elsewhere, send some tea tomorrow in the morning. By the way, where's your elder son?'

'He hadn't returned yesterday; don't know whether he'd return tonight.'

'I know where Gullu is now, I'll send him back. Now tell me has he given you the money I gave him for buying milk for the boy?'

'Not at all.'

'Keep these three hundred rupees for buying milk; next time I'll give you money directly, just inform me when it is finished.'

When they resumed walking Raja said, 'That boy Gullu is a member of my gang. He is fearless, a dare devil but very restive, always looks for action; whenever there is no action he'd drink, take all kinds of substances, lie inside or near the *theck* and forget everything. But this time he'd crossed the limit; I'd given him three hundred rupees especially to buy milk for his sickly brother, he must've drunk them out; I don't like it.'

Boomba heard whispers from behind and turned to see a number of children following in tip-toe flanked by a pack of dogs. When he informed Raja he simply said, 'I know,' and continued walking. Perhaps the news of Raja taking a stroll had spread among all the dwellers. They observed people standing in welcome mode before every hut. Toomba thought: 'He is really walking like a Raja, surveying his kingdom, his gait has also changed to that of a king.' Raja waved to all, talked to some, heard their complaints, said something in response and moved on. Presently, Raja stopped for a while before a hut and shouted, 'Tell Mimi to behave properly, next time...'

They were nearing the end of the *bustee* when Raja stopped again before a hut and asked the man standing there to call Kimi. 'Anything wrong with her?' The man asked anxiously. 'No, nothing, just call her here.'

Kimi was still sucking a lozenge when she came out giggling. Raja now looked back and asked the children to stop there. Three of them began running. He asked the others to catch them. When they were brought before him he asked Kimi, 'Are these the rascals who snatched lozenges from you?' She nodded. He ordered the three to strip. One who hesitated got such a slap he rolled down a distance. Raja raised him by his ear and when he was about to deliver another slap the boy stripped himself fast.

'Oh-ho, your thing has grown big; don't want others to see it, feeling shy, eh?' He grabbed his penis and balls, caressed for a while and suddenly squeezed them so hard the boy wailed in pain. Raja released his hand and ordered.

'Now, all of you: hold your ears and do *uthak-baithaks* till I ask you to stop.'

When the boys looked exhausted from humiliation and physical exertion and tears began rolling down from their eyes, Kimi nudged Raja to stop it. 'Ok, now you may stop and go but remember next time you do it I'll...' The three boys quickly dressed up and scrammed.

Raja asked Kimi's mother, 'Auntie, get us some tea, we shall be sitting on the edge of the ditch for some time.'

They sat on the ground with their legs stretched out. Raja spoke.

'Well, look at the other side of this garbage canal, there's another *bustee* like ours, though somewhat smaller. A gang from there used to control both the *bustees*. I resisted when I came here but was beaten up. Then I raised my own gang and launched a surprise attack on them: they were eight and we were six but we were smarter than them. Four of them fled, we caught the rest and took them to the police station. After two days they were released from the lock up, maimed permanently. That was the end of their supremacy. They dare not raise their head again.'

'How come, the police did not arrest any of you?' Boomba asked.

'Why'd they arrest us? I pay them two thousand rupees every week.'

Tea came. After taking a few sips Raja pointed his finger once again to the other side of the canal and spoke.

'I don't like the people over there, they are mainly pickpockets; my people over here do hard-labour jobs; some pull rickshaws and vans, a good number peddle various things of daily use, some are even employed as security guards of large shops at Shyambazar and Baghbazar areas, almost all the women here work as maids or ayahs at households in the neighbourhoods. I and my gang protect them but no *tolas* taken. I pay my gang handsomely; they also have side business like working for a house owner to drive out tenants, acting as agent of a lender for collecting money from recalcitrant borrowers, selling hemps, et cetera. Though I do not demand any share from their earnings, for any big assignment they must get my approval.'

He now rose and said, 'Let's now go to our joint.'

They walked through lanes and bylanes to arrive at a dimly lit joint littered with people of various ages, some sprawled on the floor, a few on benches drowsing with a bottle in hand, some near the counter demanding additional bottles on promises to pay later while a lone individual doddering in the centre had begun a long lecture on the ills of society taking an occasional sip from the bottle whenever his throat went dry. 'Lovely place', Tommba murmured; he felt like joining. The spell was broken by Raja's high pitch voice, 'Where's Gullu?' A young man sprawled on the floor stirred, squinted at the place wherefrom the voice came, saw Raja and immediately rose to his feet and walked hurriedly toward him with remarkably steady steps and saluted , 'Yes, Boss.' Raja gave him a slap the sound of which echoed the four walls of the dungeon. Gullu fell but rose quickly, saluted again and said, 'Mistake Boss, mistake, but I'm not fully responsible; that bastard sitting behind the counter took away all the money to square my earlier debts. I didn't return home last night out of shame, how could I show my face to them?'

'Ok. Now go home; they're anxiously waiting for you.'

'Yes, Boss.' He hurried out.

Raja walked to the counter. The man behind it rose to meet him.

'Don't steal money from my boys; if the dues are heavy inform me, okay?'

When Raja turned to leave, Toomba said, 'I'll stay back and enjoy the night here.'

'Me too,' Boomba said.

Raja looked quizzically at them for a few seconds, then said, 'Ok, as you wish.' While walking out he addressed the counter man. 'They're my bosom friends, take care of them and don't charge for the bottles; it's on me.'

They drank and danced, soon others joined; even the man behind the counter began pounding the wooden plank rhythmically. The man who lectured on ills of the society now prostrated, also thumped the floor in resonance. The jocund night ended when all fell flat.

* * * *

Boomba and Toomba woke up early in the morning, used the latrine of the hooch shop and quietly left the place.

They leisurely walked southwards, saw a man lying face up on the pavement of the bridge, perhaps enjoying the warmth of morning sun rays having slept all night under falling dews; passed a family housed between two pillars of an abandoned lane, two small naked children playing before it, a man wearing a pant probably readying himself for going to work, a sickly woman with white conch shell bangles round her hands preparing tea or something.

They stopped for a while to observe a wrestler type man with thick large moustache. He had a very wide chest with a forest of black curled hairs that heaved up and down with his breaths. He was sleeping peacefully on the pavement, his left hand behind his head acting as a pillow, knees rolled up skyward. Both saluted him silently and passed by.

They had to walk by the side of the road; all the footpaths were strewn with people sleeping in different postures. They were amused observing a sleeping family; the child's left leg resting on the right leg of a man, the wife sleeping with her head turned to the other side, the first rays of rising sun falling tangentially on them. 'Beautiful.' Toomba remarked. At a little distance a cobbler just woke up and began spreading his instruments at a corner.

Municipal scavengers were out on the streets sweeping so also the morning walkers; a quarrelsome wife blaming her husband with brisk movement of her hands matching that of her legs for spoiling her life; another couple behind them walked slowly, the husband stopping intermittently to take photographs; a milk vendor pouring municipal tap water into a bucket of milk to increase its volume, two small children keeping a watch; a woman with dull white hair on her head sat on a footpath, a faraway look in her eyes, a small bundle held between her knees; fish sellers cycling fast with cloth-covered aluminium drums secured tightly to the back carrier, water spilling out to mark a trail to the nearby fish market; a heritage Phaeton drawn by two horses took a turn toward Dufferin Road; flocks of young boys and girls in school uniforms were crossing the streets chattering, newspaper hawkers flying past on cycles ogling at the girls; *bustee* children returning home with plastic water buckets suspended from their hands; a fat boy circling a roadside small park with 'Oohoo... oohoo' issuing from his navel, a stern looking man wearing a sweat shirt, probably a trainer, keeping a watch; close to the park a man sat on a low stool releasing mashed gram balls to the simmering oil of an oval pan.

A familiar stench drew them to the left of Rajabazar crossing. Following the smell they crossed a bridge over a canal that flowed from Raja's place. They turned right wading through muddy water, wet leaves and mounds of filth; saw Billy goats tied to railings munching leaves of jack fruit tree placed before them while prospective buyers engaged in bargaining with the sellers; they looked down to find men, women and children sitting by the shore of the canal defecating and conversing between strains of shit.

They came back by the same route to the main road and proceeded further to the south. They felt trees waking up with chirping of birds; flowers of different hues—red, white, yellow, blue—ornamenting the trees now shone with the rising sun signalling the birds: it's time to leave for finding food. They stood at a crossing to observe birds flying out.

'You know the names of these birds?' Boomba asked.

'Perhaps. But why ask for their names? Birds are as beautiful as they are without names. Just fill your eyes with their beauties.'

'Don't brag like Raja and don't give your philosophical *gyan* all the time. I want to know their names, as simple as that.' Boomba was angry.

'Ok, Baba, ok. Don't be so angry. Let me try.' Toomba concentrated on the flying birds.

'That must be a flock of mynas and that one of cuckoos; I've seen them in my village.'

'I'm sure that one is a dove. I often see them sitting on the parapets of the buildings at Gariahat,' Boomba added proudly.

'Those are papiyas—the Indian nightingales, the other should be magpie Robins and that's a flock of Bulbuls, but those yellow birds I can't name, I've never seen them before.'

Boomba stood still, eyes up savouring the beauty of the flying birds unmindful of the names being pronounced by Toomba.

In less than fifteen minutes all birds flew out of the tree. They resumed walking. Boomba spoke after a while.

'This Kolkata we haven't seen before—and it's only a small part, though we live in this city. We don't even know the names of streets and lanes that enmesh the city though we may have walked through them; we know the names of only a few major roads, stupid as we are.'

'The problem is we've seen them but didn't observe, didn't go beyond what we see. We've only seen the filth because we live in it, we didn't observe the beauty that lurks behind it.'

'Yes, you are right; here heaven and hell are entwined in a beautiful embrace.'

'Oh-ho, you have become a poet. I won't be surprised if some day you start composing poems'

'May be, but not before I bring Champi here.'

'Now I can very well understand the source of your poetic inspiration.' Toomba patted his back.'

They took a turn toward Liberty Cinema hall. They'd come here before—most of the street children knew this place—to buy and sell used garments. The bazaar was already crowded. Both the sellers and buyers were trying to bargain for the right price; the noise was so much one had to shout to make one heard which raised the decibel point even further. Boomba and Toomba jostling through the crowd visited almost all the hawkers, made bargains, smiled to some known faces: it had always been a pleasure to make a tour of the *mela* before selecting a hawker.

They bargained hard for a pant and shirt each and the exchange price of the ones they wore presently. The price settled they paid the net amount, entered the bathroom of the cinema hall, changed into new garments and handed over the old ones to the seller. As they were coming out, Boomba stopped before a stall where a woman with a child on her shoulder was scrutinising a small mosquito net stretching it on all sides. Satisfied, her face glowed as she nudged her husband to settle the price. But the glowing face turned gloomy when the hawker declared the final price; it was higher by thirty rupees the husband had; he counted the money twice but no miracle occurred. When they were about to leave Boomba winked at the seller who nodded and called back the couple, 'I'm reducing the price by thirty rupees only for your child,' he said and handed over the mosquito net in a newspaper packet. The face of the woman re-glowed and the husband thanked the hawker for doing this favour. As Boomba was paying thirty rupees to the hawker he saw the couple walking out, the wife showering kisses on the child and the husband chattering away proudly. Toomba saw Boomba's face also glowed though with a different hue.

They came out of the market and resumed walking.

'I'd known from the day we met that you're doomed. Myself and Minu tried to redeem you but I find all our endeavours have gone down the drains,' Toomba said looking at Boomba's face where the flush of emotion was still visible.

'None of you would ever understand this,' Boomba responded irritated.

'May be; now please come down to this small earth and find a place where we can have some breakfast; I'm hungry.'

Roadside food stalls were already open. They stopped before a stall and observed the activities there: a man was making *tandoori roti* inside a mud layered *tandoor*, another cooking meat on a large oval pan while a third was busy frying *parathas* on a flat pan, the mouth-watering aroma travelling a great distance. Toomba peeped through a narrow gateway and, Wow! They saw a well-organised restaurant inside. It was neat with sunmica top tables, comfortable chairs; waiters in apron were busy placing drinking glasses on tables. They entered and occupied a table for two.

Toomba ordered *tandoori roti* and Boomba, *parathas*; meat common for both. The food was delicious and they were hungry; the first serving soon finished and they ordered for a second. After taking a glass full of water Boomba asked suddenly, 'Don't you think Raja is a bully?'

Toomba jolted back to yesterday evening, thought for a while before answering.

'Yes, he is. But everyone's a bully of some sort.'
'Isn't he vain?'
'No, he knows what he is doing and why.'
'Hollow?'
'Not at all.'
'Proudy?'
'Showy, perhaps.'

The second helping came. They finished eating leisurely and silently.

Presently their destination was the drug factory to lift the day's quota. They walked leisurely. They stopped before a Majhar near Nilratan Sircar Medical College and Hospital opposite to a college of Homeopathic medicines and saw a small crowd sitting before a man—must be a Muslim Peer—with long white beard wearing a *lungi* and a half shirt. He listened to men and women of various religious and social groups complaining about some disease of theirs or of the children on their laps, and blew a puff of breath on some or strapped an amulet around the upper part of the hand of some others. Toomba peeped inside a hut at the back and saw a man sitting on his haunches praying for Allah's blessings, a woman wearing vermillion on her forehead and conch shell bangles on her wrists sat by his side: must be some special disease requiring special arrangement. They came out and walked thoughtfully to some distance when Toomba spoke.

'It is the disease that brings together all the religions, no other ills of the society can do that.'

'Long live all diseases! *Inquilab Zindabad!*' Boomba sloganeered raising his fist.

'Idiot!'

Chapter 12

Bichhu and Chikku were excited about their *Harbola* shows. In the past five months they had come up with newer presentation styles and a host of new mimicries. Binni quickly picked up scavenging the railway compartments with a small broom, often dishing out a bit of soft eroticism with an innocent smile. Bisu added brushing of shoes and helping older passengers in boarding and alighting. Average earnings of the group stabilised at rupees one thousand five hundred per day.

Bichhu and Chikku saved with Mashi at rupees two hundred per day, Binni and Bisu at one hundred fifty each.

Mashi had found that most of the street children did not save: there was no place to hide the money—always the fear of theft, no institution to take care of their savings; NGO workers often betrayed, so also the Dadas and mashis. So 'earn and spend' had become the norm, which also fit into their philosophy of 'living for the day only'. Mashi often wondered whether the economics of the street preceded the philosophy or was it the other way round. But the boys and girls who worked with her also saved with her, which might suggest that savings is innate in any individual; you provide a box they would save; but what if there is betrayal? Mashi once put this question to Bichhu.

'You are keeping money with me—it's now a lot of money. Don't you ever think I might someday vanish with your money?'

'We don't really care, betrayal is the norm of the street, faith transient; but still we need to keep faith on someone howsoever temporary it might be; it's more a convenience of mind.'

But Mashi resolved she could not betray despite herself having been betrayed, might be she still carried some old values the society professed though never cared. But the money could be looted; she lived in an open environment and it might happen any time. It was likely Bichhu and Chikku would forgive her but she could never forgive herself. She must have a bank account. But how could she open one; she had no official identity, no address!

In her fourth rendezvous with the OC, Howrah GRP she broached the subject when he lit a cigarette after a satisfying fuck. He squinted and chuckled.

'Oh, my chubby must be earning good amount of money these days, needs a bank account to keep her wealth, eh!'

'No wealth, sir, just about two thousand rupees. I'm saving a little bit every now and then for my future. If these are lost…'

'Ok, ok, my dear Apsara, tomorrow, be here by 9 a.m. I'll call a person who would take care of everything; I promise, your account would be opened as soon as the bank opens. Now give me a deep throat for a second journey.'

Next day her bank account was opened with a deposit of two thousand rupees. By 10:30 a.m. she left the bank with her escort, a pass book in her hand; the cheque book would be delivered the next day. She offered a fifty-rupee note to her escort. He stepped back and exclaimed.

'The OC sir will put me in lock up if I take money from you.'

'He'll never know; consider it a gift from your sister.'

'Ok… in that case…' He took the money hesitantly and left.

On returning to the station she bought a cup of tea and sat at a less crowded corner. Her comrades had already left. She decided to board a short distance train in the afternoon so as to meet them in time when they returned. That settled she began examining the pass book, a first in her life. Her name was written boldly on the first page, below it her address: What! She exclaimed, her hands trembled, the tea spilled on her dress; the OC had given her this address! A joke or convenience, a portent or merely a coincidence? She felt a tremor inside as the memory of her last night with Jaggu flashed in her mind. A few days back he had taken on rent a spacious two-room flat at that address just for two of them. He was in jail now serving seven years rigorous imprisonment. Last month she got a message from an associate of Jaggu that the syndicate would be paying the rent regularly till Jaggu returned from jail; they would not be using the flat for any other purpose if she decided to live there. She asked the messenger to convey her thanks to Jaggu but declined the offer. Now the OC had stamped it as her official address, very… very convenient; did he know? Must be, the police knew everything.

'I don't care.' Mashi shrugged her shoulders, gulped the tea, now cold and bitter, threw away the cup and walked with no-nonsense steps to board the scheduled train.

Mashi took about a month to deposit—always in odd amounts, her own savings and that of others in the bank account, and disclosed the fact to her associates only after the job was done. They were amazed, a bank account for a station dweller! None could even imagine having one. They took the pass book in their hands, caressed it with love and awe and looked at Mashi with renewed respect. But when she handed them each an account of their savings less custodial charges they returned the paper without even looking at them.

Mashi's base at Howrah station was well established. She now divided her time equally between Sealdah and Howrah. Bichhu and Chikku were yet to visit her at Sealdah though they desired to do 'soon'. That 'soon' happened one evening when she was taking rest after the day's work.

Chikku looked grave, Bichhu joyous. Mashi shouted for all the station children, some were still working, some loitering having earned their day's target. All rushed in. Mashi introduced the duo. They had already heard about Chikku's mimicries and Bichhu's theatrics. They all requested them to give some demonstration of their art. But Chikku was not responding. Looking at his glum face they asked Mashi to prevail upon them. She observed Chikku who sat still with head slightly bent... something serious, Mashi thought. She assured the children that she would definitely ask the duo to demonstrate their tricks but only after their business talk was over. 'In the meantime get us five fish fries from Chacha's with salad and all.' She gave one hundred rupee note to one of the boys with 'the rest is yours'. When they left Mashi asked, 'What's the matter? Why Chikku looks so dejected, anything to do with Binni?'

'Nothing related to Binni; he is angry with me.' Bichhu replied

'Why?'

'Ask him.'

'No, ask him.' Chikku spoke for the first time with anger in his eyes.

'Okay. Let me tell you: for the past few days I've been asking Chikku to resume his studies, and also to Binni who had to leave the school at standard four. You know Chikku is very focused to whatever he does; if he resumes studies he'd definitely excel; in our school also he was always ahead of me, but for my association he'd have been the darling of the school. I think he would be wasted if he lives with me. Besides, Binni nurtures a dream with him which cannot be fulfilled in the environment we live now. He loves her; he should respect her feeling. But he is adamant.'

'What does Binni say?'

'She agrees, had a fight with him the day before and stopped talking since then.'

Mashi gave an understanding smile and then asked.

'What happens to Bisu?'

'Well, he stays with me till he comes of age, and then he decides.'

'He agrees?'

'Yes. He is already feeling great that his sister would be resuming studies.'

The question-answer session came to a halt when the children came back with two packets. The boy who handed one packet to Mashi asked, 'Your business talks still continuing?'

'Yes. I'll call you when it's over,' she replied smiling.

Mashi placed two fish fries each on two plates with salads and passed them keeping one for her. When they began eating Mashi spoke, 'I can't be an arbitrator for resolving your disputes, but should Chikku agree I may talk to a girl who now works with a Residential Home run by a reputed NGO; she may be of help. It's not that kind of Home you stayed earlier; it has a learning environment with good facilities. Once you agree, let me know, I'll talk to her.'

There was no further talk; they finished eating silently. Mashi looked at the still glum face of Chikku and addressed him.

'Don't be so glum, no one's forcing you. Think over the issue again; if you don't feel like consulting any one, don't consult, take your own decision. I think everyone will respect your decision whatever it is. Now please smile and come back to yourself, the children over there are waiting for your show.'

Chikku looked back, saw the waiting children and smiled. He signalled them to come forward. What followed next was an evening soiree, with two performers holding the stage, mesmerising the audience now enlarged to more than half the waiting hall. When Bichhu saw Chikku getting tired he brought the show to a magnificent end. Amidst claps and hurrahs, cold drinks, tea and a variety of foods were brought in by station vendors. The feast ended at 10 p.m. The duo decided to walk to their station.

The telephone came a day later: Chikku decided to give it a try provided Bichhu stayed with him in the Home for a week to assess the environment; if he felt satisfied he would join. He had few other minor conditions which Bichhu could handle.

Next day Mashi asked Biltu to take her to the office of the NGO where the girl with whom he negotiated his release worked. Biltu agreed on one condition: he would not enter the Home.

Mashi located the girl in the lobby talking to a young man. She had not seen her for a long time as she was absent from meetings at her corner; her friends said she got a promotion and was getting married. She no longer looked sickly when she came forward to greet her.

'What a great moment! We're just discussing about you and Debanand or your Biltu; how good he was, how talented, but a perennial wanderer. Has he come with you?'

'No. He left me near the Home and fled lest you catch him again. I've come here to discuss the possibility of admitting two boys, more mature than their age, both brilliant, can do wonders under proper tutelage.'

'So many adjectives! Though I know you don't talk shop. What you say must be true. Let's go to his office,' she indicated at a young man, 'My husband, he is the Project Officer here with executive power.'

They went inside and entered a cubicle. After they sat the young man said, 'I've heard a lot about you from my wife; I've been following your discussion with interest. Apparently there is no problem in admitting them, rather we love to, but these boys are restless, unstable, may leave any time—you know what Debanand did.'

'I can assure you one will continue, I cannot vouch for both.'

'Any addiction they suffer from?'

'They don't take alcohols or drugs for sure, cigarettes may be.'

'Oh! Quite unusual for street boys. Did they attend any school before?'

Yes, both read up to standard eight; they are childhood friends.'

'Good. If you could get us their school-leaving certificates we can get them admitted directly to a school.'

'I don't think that would be a problem.'

'Then bring them here some day. Let them stay here, get familiarised with the environment. In the meantime procure the certificates; we shall also discuss it with some schools we have liaison.'

'I have another request.'

'Relating to these boys?'

'No. It's about a girl, presently working with me, may be two-three years younger than the boys. She also desires to be off the street. Do you know a Home good as yours which could admit her? I understand she had read up to fourth standard; she may be an orphan, I'm not sure.'

The young man thought for a while looking at her wife who nodded affirmatively.

'Yes, there is a girls Home and also an orphanage run by missionaries, well known for their good work, the facilities there are much better than ours. They have direct relationship with missionary schools all over India. If they have a vacancy they might take her. My wife had internship with them for a year before moving here; she knows them well.'

Mashi rose and thanked them profusely.

'Please don't thank us so much, the young man said smilingly; it's our mission and a livelihood too, and don't forget you are now a collaborator to our mission.'

The girl saw her to the gate. She was overjoyed as she walked savouring the feeling that comes from a good job done.

'Stupid! Why are you doing all these? Why getting entangled again?'

She was shaken by the chastising VOICE; stood for a while to cool her nerves, then thumped her feet on the ground and cried out defiantly, 'I'll do it, I shall do it; I don't care your admonition; now stop growling.' She walked to her station steadily.

Bichhu was happy to hear the results of her endeavours and requested her to come to Howrah station next morning though it was not her scheduled day.

All the four heads heard her with rapt attention.

'So we're going to that Home on trial basis,' Chikku said.

'And if the Home is found good you shall resume your studies,' Bichhu enjoined.

'There is one hitch. You must get your school-leaving certificates for admission to school,' Mashi said.

Binni asked them. 'Why don't you go to the school to procure your certificates; the school must still be there, not inundated like mine.'

They remained silent. Looking at their fallen face Mashi said, 'I could understand your unwillingness to revisit the village you left for good. Don't worry; I've a plan.'

They looked expectantly at her.

'I'd try to get the certificates through the OC here but I'll need your help. You must impress him with your *Harbola* skills.'

Bichhu smiled. 'No problem; just tell us when.'

'Right now; the OC remains in his office during the morning hours.'

Mashi asked the duo to write their original names, name of the school, the class they last studied, the village and the district. When they finished she asked Binni and Bisu to wait and proceeded to the police station with Bichhu and Chikku.

'Hey Bichhus, you've not visited my lock-up for a long time, what's happened, become *Sadhus*?' The OC quipped as soon as he saw them.

'No sir, they have left pick-pocketing altogether. They now showcase mimicries on the trains.' Mashi replied for them.

Ah-ha. I've heard about two *Harbolas* performing mimicries on trains. So you're that duo?'

'Yes sir,' replied Chikku.

'Good, very good. Now show me a few of your tricks.'

Bichhu elbowed Chikku. Soon a train whistled and began moving inside the police station. All the officers, constables and also complainants rushed to the cabin, puzzled. When the train left the platform the OC closed his mouth and asked for another, a chorus of demand followed.

'You won't beat us sir, if we mimic SI sir who we find is not here.'

'No, no, just go ahead'.

Then the beating started. '*Sala harami,* mother fucking pigs... thop... thap... thop... pickpocketing again... again... *sala* today I'll break your hands... ahin... ahin... promise sir... promise sir... oohhoo... ahhaa... ahin... we shall not do it again sir ...*sala chutiya*... *thap*... *thop*... *thep*... *thak*... the last time also you promised and before that also... *saraks*... *thop*... *saraks*... fucking *saitans*... aienh... aienh... .leave us sir... please... on god sir... we won't repeat... by god sir... *thop*... *thop*... eh Rambhajan see the bastards are crying but no tears in their eyes... put these swines in lock-up... enhe... enh... enhey.'

Chikku stopped but the remnant of the sounds reverberated walls of the cabin for some time, broken only by the laughter all around.

'Oh... ho... no.' The OC could not hold his laughter.

'Marvellous', he said, 'they'll never put you to lock-up again, I promise; if you face any problem on trains just inform me; I'll tell SI sahib also.'

'Sir, may we leave now?'

'Oh, yes, the grand *Harbolas.*'

The boys left the cabin with others but Mashi did not.

'Any other problem?' the OC asked.

Mashi told him the background of the two boys, reasons for them leaving their village, their desire to resume studies, the talk she had with the NGO, their readiness to accept them, the problem of getting their school-leaving certificates because of their unwillingness to visit the school, and here she got stuck. 'Sir, please help'. She concluded.

'So we're going to lose our *Harbolas*?'

Mashi just smiled.

'Since you've done so much for them I should also do my bit. Give me their details.' Mashi handed the piece of paper to him.

'Oh, it still smells your flowery skin.' He smiled coquettishly. 'Ok, you'll get the certificates in three days time.'

'Thank you, sir.'

Mashi came out with a feeling of triumph and walked toward the place they were waiting for her. When she was near them she heard the angry VOICE, 'Foolish woman, you'll never learn!' 'Chup, chup,' she retorted rather loudly.

'Who are you angry with, Mashi,' Binni asked.

'Oh, that's nothing; one of my bad habits.' She quickly passed on to the agenda. 'The OC said you'll get your certificates in three day's, time.'

'That's great!' Bichhu exclaimed.

'But what about Binni?' Chikku asked.

'I don't think there will be any problem; she can be admitted to an orphanage and from there to the school.'

'No. She isn't going to orphanage, she isn't an orphan; she'll go to the residential Home only.' Bichhu scourged.

'But... but.' All looked at him.

Bichhu said, 'You get us our certificates, I'll get hers.'

Three days later Mashi handed them two school-leaving certificates, and a week later Bichhu brought certificates for Binni and Bisu. The two papers passed from Chikku who gave an impish smile, then to Binni and Bisu who just kissed them, and finally to Mashi. Her eyes stuck at the column, 'Name of father'. She raised her eyes with a heavenly smile.

'Yes,' Bichhu said, 'they are my brother and sister.'

* * * *

Bichhu and Chikku went to residential Home. Bichhu returned after ten days and informed that Chikku had started going to the school; he had permission to come to the station twice a week; they were willing to take Bisu too but he was still adamant. When Mashi asked Bisu he simply said, 'I don't want to study, I'll be with Bichhuda only, never leave him in my life,' and walked away.

The girl working at the Residential Home took Binni to a Missionary Home. There was no vacancy right now though there would be one in about a month's time when one of the boarders moved to their Mumbai Home. The Father gave Binni a set of graded text books and asked her to prepare for an eligibility test; the admission to a particular class would depend on her performance in the test.

Binni would study in the day; in the evening she would show the completed tasks to Bichhu and ask him to explain things she did not understand. But she would always take half day off whenever Chikku came to the station. They would fly hand in hand, roam places in and beyond the station and dine outside. Binni would always return alone with a sullen face as Chikku had to go back Home before evening.

'Lovely pair,' Mashi smiled to herself.

'Damn you, idiot woman.' She heard the VOICE but did not respond.

Binni did well in the test; she was accepted by the missionary Home and admitted to class six.

The day she left for Home Bisu was nowhere to be seen.

After a week Mashi asked Bichhu. 'It's more than a month now; you didn't do a thing, busy as you were preparing Binni for the school test. Now that matters are settled, have you thought of a new vocation? I hear a new *Harbola* has appeared in the meantime and doing better than Chikku, which I don't believe; no one can better Chikku.'

'That *Harbola* is me and Bisu is my presenter,' Bichhu said with a cryptic smile.

'You... you?'

'Yes. When we were in the Home Chikku trained me in the craft.'

'And you're doing better than him!'

'Yes, because I've been trained by the master.'

Chapter 13

Raja called Boomba one day; he sounded happily excited, made four 'urgents' and that was a lot of money, wanted to give them a treat. Boomba replied he had no problem, would call Toomba to find out whether he could make it. Toomba had no problem either. They met at Shiraj and ordered Biryani. When they were settled Raja asked, 'How was your binge party at our den that night?'

'Oh, excellent! We danced and drank till midnight,' Boomba replied.

'I enquired about you in the morning, was told you'd left early.'

'Yes, we had an engagement.'

'May I ask you a question?' Raja asked Toomba.

Toomba nodded affirmatively.

'I've observed you don't talk much; I may say you hardly speak or you don't speak unless spoken to; you don't show much of emotion, don't react like Boomba. Any special reason? Or you're just like this?'

'I'm frugal at both.'

Food had come with all the beauty of saffron and aroma of screw pine flower. They began eating with their hands setting aside spoons and forks: '*Biriyani* is best enjoyed when eaten by hand,' Boomba spoke for all.

After the food Raja bought four nips of whisky, gave one each to them keeping two for him and hailed a taxi. He asked the driver to drop them at the crossing of Red Road and Park Street. They got down and walked to the trunk of one of the tall trees of the *Maidan* somewhat away from the main road; the rays of street lights had thrown a twilight shadow under the tree. They sat there and opened the bottles.

Raja took a sip and said, 'Whenever I feel very happy I come to this place, drink quietly and sometimes play games with me to contain the feeling of being happy.'

Boomba was about to say something but stopped; a police man in white stood before them. Raja smiled and handed him the fourth bottle. He returned the smile and left.

'I'm always scared of happiness; I don't belong to the world of happiness. You'll know when you hear the story of my life, will you?'

'It must be quite fascinating, we're eager to hear it,' Boomba replied.

Raja began narrating; his eyes were not on them but focused on the fast-moving vehicles on the road.

'I don't know who fucked whom to bring me to this world. I also don't know when and how I came to sense the world. But I can remember I was always hungry, and didn't know how to quench my hunger; I only felt I had to put something into my mouth and that's what I did. I was on my fours then, I picked up butts of cigarettes, *beedis,* dry leaves and sundry other things I don't recollect. My tongue threw away all except dry leaves, that took me to roadside plants, then to all grasses and then to a dustbin nearby. As I began standing on my legs my hunger increased. When I could walk I started searching for other dustbins and soon discovered quite a few of them in and around the locality. I soon noticed I had competition in dustbin exploration. The first set of competitors comprised dogs and crows but I won them over by sharing food with them, and we became friends; it was a pleasure to find them waiting for me. The other set of competitors comprised urchins senior to me, but I was smarter than them. I found out which dustbin got filled up when and I'd be there before others; I'd developed a perfect sense of timing. I still have that and that's a key point of my success. If you like I can demonstrate it here itself.'

They smiled encouragingly. Raja took a sip from the bottle, looked over the darkness of the sky and declared.

'It must be seven thirty plus minus two minutes.'

Boomba strained his eyes to read his wrist watch and exclaimed, 'Oh my god, it's just seven thirty two. Bravo!'

Raja smiled and asked. 'Do you want me to continue or you're already getting board. I don't know why but this is the first time I feel like sharing my life story with someone, may be deep in my mind I've began considering you my friends—my first friends, though I know you do not like some of the ways in which I conduct my life. Do I continue?'

'Oh, please continue,' Boomba responded quickly.

'Well, once I was late as I'd a stomach run the night before. I was very hungry when I reached the first dustbin but others were already there. They might have come to know that I was the boy who took away the best foods from the dustbin. They rushed toward me shouting, *'sala harami, chor'*—these were the first vocabularies I learnt which I'd be repeating many times later.

'I just stood there, didn't run because I didn't know about running. They slapped me, beat me all over with hands and sticks; I was feeling pain but studying at the same time their methods of torture. Someone burly didn't like me taking all the beatings standing; he lifted me by legs and threw me on the roadside; I fell with a thud, the pain unbearable; I felt something was tickling down my eyes, it was watery, tasted like salt in the food; I touched my nostrils, something flowed down from there too though of different colour but tasted the same. Right then I saw a boy stalking toward me with determined steps, a large stone in his hand. For the first time I sensed a real danger. I raised myself and sat on my haunch, hands on the road, all pains erased. As the boy came near me and raised the stone, I leaped to his legs and pulled them, he fell backward with a thud louder than mine, the stone rolled by. I picked it up with all my might and raised it over my head just like him but I didn't know where to hit, so I just hurled it at him; it must've hit the right place because he lay on the road, didn't get up. Other boys halted, surprised, though for moments only. They soon surged forward led by one with a stick in hand. But I was ready. I hadn't known fear then nor do I know now.

'So far the dogs were silent except for occasional barks, they didn't join me when I was being beaten but as soon as I snatched the stick from the advancing boy and hit him back the dogs howled and jumped on my adversaries, crows also began circling pecking their heads. I wasn't alone any longer. Suddenly I heard a canine call different from the normal barks and howls. Soon I found many other dogs running toward us. My own gang of dogs circled round me while others hurled themselves on them. The boys left the battle field and ran fast, the dogs driving them outside the locality. I felt exhausted and fell on the ground unconscious.'

'I find you had many firsts from your first fight; you've also learnt many things about dog's behaviour and you've not forgotten them, we observed it when we we're at your place,' Boomba said.

'Yes, I love them. The street dogs are slow to react but once they do they don't leave the arena, and they honour gratitude unlike the superior animals, the Homo sapiens,' Raja smiled.

'Have you realised,' Toomba asked, 'you always need help for survival?'

'Yes, but you don't get it unless you act. My next phase of life is a proof of that. When I woke up that day I found myself inside the roadside food stall by the side of the dustbin, a man who I later learnt was a doctor was examining me while three anxious faces watched. The doctor rose and declared, 'He will survive', the anxious faces turned hopeful. I tried to get up but the pain dragged me down. I felt something foreign on my body. I moved my hands slowly and found myself dressed like other boys I've seen before. I was fed and nursed by the two boys working there under the care of the owner. Later when I learnt language I was told by the boys that all of them saw me fighting, they wanted to help but the owner held them back saying, "It's his fight, let him fight, the dogs were already there to help; he'll survive."

'I stayed with them, learnt the language while helping the other boys serving food and tea to customers, understood, a-b-c-d... , 1-2-3-4-... , alphabets and numericals of Bengali language, I also learnt a little bit of Hindi from movies we used to see occasionally at night shows. But I didn't learn to write, I never needed it; now also it's the same. Those were blissful days. I grew up fast and strong.'

'What happened to the dogs?' Boomba asked.

'They remained with me till they were killed.'

'Killed?'

'One day two burly men came. We heard high-pitch altercations: they demanded some big money which the owner refused. They left after some time threatening to come back again. The owner engaged four young men from the locality for day and night vigil. For a week or so nothing happened. The owner felt they got scared, would not dare revisit the place and relieved the men. Two days later they arrived, now six in number, in the late afternoon when not a single customer was present and we were all busy preparing food for the dinnertime customers. There wasn't much altercation this time. One of them asked the owner if he'd pay. He remained adamant and replied, "No". Suddenly there was a burst of fire; the owner fell on the ground, his chest full of blood. The last word he said to us was, "Run". I ran to him while the other boys fled. He didn't move, his eyes still. I'd seen deaths in movies but this was the first time I saw a live death. They took away all the cash from the drawer and began ransacking the place. I fought but was overpowered soon. The dog now entered and attacked them, but it was short lived. They fired at them, all fell dead. I felt grief for the first time, but in that grief also I noticed keenly how the man was taking aim and pressing the trigger of the gun. That knowledge would come to my aid later.

'The dogs down, I thought they'd now fire at me. No, they dragged me and dragged me through the road to a corner of a street where I found some boys playing cards; a few others loitering around while two girls gossiping on the other side. The man with the gun threw me among them and ordered, "Hey, *chutiyas* keep a watch on him; if he flees, I'll kill all of you." Exhausted both physically and mentally I swooned on them.

'Next morning I woke up to find five boys and two girls looking at me, their eyes reflected a measure of curiosity and misery. I sat up with a start and looked around; the place seemed alien, so also the faces around me. Then I remembered all at once, my jaws clenched hard, palms turned to fists, though for moments only. I smiled at them, they smiled back and we became comrades. They heard my story and turned miserable again. One of the boys rose and said, "Don't waste time sharing one another's misery; let's get ready, Big Dada would come in an hour's time, if we aren't ready by that time he'll make our lives more miserable." He took me to the bank of a nearby pond for morning ablutions. Together we went to a roadside food stall. We each received two *kachoris* with gram *dal* and a small sweetmeat. I was very hungry, hadn't eaten anything since last night. I asked for two more *kachoris*. The man behind the counter replied harshly, "That's the order, I can't give you more." The boy who helped me in the morning walked to the counter, whispered something and brought two extra *kachoris* and *dal* for me.

'Big Dada arrived soon after we returned, a revolver tucked to his waist—must be the one who wiped out my blissful days once and for all. My teeth clenched but I immediately brought them to normal. This came naturally to me. I understood as much that there was no easy way to escape, I'd have to play the ball till an opportunity came. Big Dada noticed I was watching him. He rushed toward me and started beating me. *Sala harami ka bachha* how dare you look at me like that, want to fight me again, eh? The beating and abuses continued till he felt tired. He dragged me by the hair and sat on a makeshift brick and wood platform. As soon as he left my hair I fell at his feet begging forgiveness with repeated oaths, "I'll not do it again." He calmed down and raised me from his feet, this time by the back of my collar. I quickly raised my hands to my eyes to wipe out tears which weren't there. He observed me closely and said, "I find you've a lot of power inside, you don't cry like others; someday you might be a Dada like me if you follow my orders, will you?" I nodded my head fiercely. "Good. Now, let me see the source of your power, drop your pant." I did it quickly; I had no sense of shame and even today I don't suffer from any shame as gentlemen often pretend.'

He smiled cryptically. None of them responded; they were eager to hear the rest of the story. Raja looked at the sky, 'It must be eight forty now; you've problem staying late?'

'Oh, no,' Tommba replied. 'I'm thinking of spending the night here, what about you Boomba?'

'I also have no problem; it's such a quiet place despite the sound of the speeding cars.'

'You're right. I often sleep here. May I continue then?'

'Yes, you must; it's so cruelly interesting.'

'When I was undressing two other bullies came on two cycle vans. They stood there to enjoy the scene. Big Dada stroked my prick.

"Already so big! I'm sure it'd be bigger than mine when he grows to my age; I could guess this is the source of his power." He turned me around for a display. The boys giggled, the bullies too; the girls nonchalant, bored.

'So far I knew it was meant for pissing only, now I knew it was also a source of power, but what kind of power I'd no idea. The display over, I pulled up my pant.

'I followed others to assemble around the cycle vans. Big Dada brought out a note book from his pocket and read out three pairs of names and corresponding places. That done, he shouted, "Hey Gullu, come here." I saw a tough looking boy coming forward. "You shall pair with the new boy for next six months, be watchful; if he tries to play tricks destroy his balls, you understand?" Gullu nodded and took me by hand to a bully who was distributing five yellow paper packets and five white opaque pouches to each. Gullu took them for both of us. 'Remember, yellow for one hundred rupees and white for three hundred; don't make mistake,' the bully warned. Big Dada consulted his note book again and told us. "You two will be at the first crossing of G.T. Road, understand?"

'We boarded the vans: two pairs on a van. It was nearly an hour's journey from village to the town. Gullu was silent during the journey. He spoke first when we were dropped at our spot. "Inform me when the van takes the first turn and vanishes, look casual," Gullu said looking the other side. I nudged him when that happened. "Good. Now follow me." He asked. We crossed the road, walked some distance to enter a junkyard and sat at a hidden corner. Gullu smiled conspiratorially, "Keep a watch." He carefully opened the five yellow packets by peeling a part of cell tape, brought out from each an unsealed plastic pouch that contained finely cut dried green leaves, took out a small quantity from each packet and stored them in a new pouch of similar look and size he fished out from his pocket. Next he placed all the six packets side by side to examine its look-alike features. Satisfied, he took out a similar looking yellow paper and a small cell tape to seal it. The new packet thus ready he handed it to me, "Keep it in your breast pocket." He repeated the process for the other set.

'All done he brought out two *beedis,* gave one to me. Releasing the first smoke he explained the modus-operandi: we are supposed to beg; any money that comes from it is ours, but if a person places hundred rupees on your hand give him a yellow packet, if its three hundred give him a white one. Never make mistake. Also remember to deliver at the first instance the one in your breast pocket, that money is ours.

"How come you didn't do anything with the white packets, those are pricier?" I asked.

"Fool! Haven't you seen those are in opaque plastic pouches, machine sealed, can't be opened except by tearing."

"What these contain?" I asked.

"The yellow ones are finely clipped dry ganja leaves, the drug of Lord Shiva, the saviour of the world, and the white ones contain a small dark brown block which gets soft when opened."

'Later I'd learn from him more about drugs; presently he asked me to find out the exact time from a passer-by having a watch.

"It must be nine thirty."

"You sure?"

"Yes."

'He gave me a funny look but said,' "Then it's time to get ready. By the way, have you begged before?"

"No."

"Then follow me today to understand the theatrics; it's all very simple, from tomorrow you'll be on the other side of the road, otherwise Big Dada will beat both of us."

"After eating some snacks we started begging. It was really simple. I was soon on my own though not far from him. By five thirty in the afternoon all packets were sold."

"What to do now?"

"How much is your take from begging?", He asked.

"Sixty-five rupees."

"Then let's beg for some more time; when your collection reaches hundred rupees we shall retire for the day; the cycle van comes at eight to pick us up."

'I went to the other side of the road to practice my lesson with gusto. When I reached the target I signalled him and crossed the road.

"Let's eat some snacks now, after that we shall go to the junkyard; the van driver knows the place."

'We went to a roadside stall that sold oil-fried snacks. Before entering Gullu warned, "Don't talk anything here, they've people everywhere."

'The first things Gullu uttered after we entered the junkyard, "Big Dada is a real bastard and his two minions are swines. They'd find fault with anyone any day and give a beating. I don't know who are today's victims, may not be you as you got it in the morning. He says he is the headmaster who has to punish his wards regularly to keep them disciplined; he'd learnt it from his Guru."

"Who is his Guru?"

"I haven't seen him, they say he was killed in action; there are rumours however that Big Dada had a hand behind his killing. I hear that he has grown from a street boy like us to a very rich man. He controls the area, raises *tolas* from all traders, has close connection with the police and politicians, none can touch him. He has a three storey house nearby, lives in the second floor all by himself: the first floor is used to entertain the politicians and police men and the top floor for packing drugs. I've been there a number of times, so also others whenever there is shortage of hands. I steal yellow wrapping papers, plastic pouches and cell tape every time I go there."

'I told him I also raised myself in the street before a benevolent person took me in whom they killed and then dragged me here.'

'He said, "I've a family in a remote village off Canning Railway station. We were very poor, no land, nothing much to live on, but four mouths to feed. My father worked with a village money lender as a bonded labour because his father borrowed from him some money which remained unpaid. He'd often steal money from his drawer to feed us. Once he was caught red-handed, beaten up and jailed for two years. When he was released none in our village would employ him. Our only source of food was forest. All became sickly, my younger brother a pack of bones, father unable to stand on his feet, mother almost dying. I left my home voluntarily to find work in a town. I reached Barrackpore station but didn't know what to do next. I was noticed by one of Big Dada's men and brought here. It's really two years I'm in captivity, not allowed to go home. I tried to flee once but got caught and beaten mercilessly. But I've not lost hope; I've gained strength, no longer a sickly village boy. I can take on three-four persons alone; I may also get help from a man outside their network who claims to work for a large drug chain. He is looking for tough boys like me, the money is also big; he meets me often but as yet I haven't given much credence to what he says; he might just be a plant, but I'm keeping a watch on him; if he turns out okay I might seek his help to flee this place."

'I said, "You're telling me all these, I might as well betray you."

"No, you won't. Every one of us here wants to run away but is too scared even to think of it, but none would ever betray, and you couldn't be an exception; we're comrades with no arms."

"I think you've already concluded I'll collaborate with you."

"I know you'll; I've seen courage and conviction in your eyes and your craftiness too when you clung to Big Dada's legs." Gullu smiled meaningfully. I also smiled conjointly.'

'We heard repetitive honks.' "The sonofabitch has come, let's go; don't forget to give him ten rupees, otherwise he'll manufacture complaints like delaying him, quarrelling, fighting et cetera that'll increase our level of torture."

'We reached the street corner to find Big Dada caressing a girl on his lap;

at a little distance a boy was being beaten in the middle of the street while others were playing cards on the pavement.

'Big Dada released the girl who joined the card players. He lighted a cigarette and asked, "What's your take?"

"All twenty; he learnt the tricks quickly and sold his share all by himself." Gullu replied as he handed over the money to him. He counted the notes quickly.

"Good, very good." He chuckled looking at me, "When you're disciplined properly I might consider taking the two of you to my inner circle."

'We responded by grateful smiles. Soon all the Dadas left. "Let's go to a place," Gullu said holding my hand. One of the boys overheard it and asked Gullu, "Are you taking him to your Bhoot Bangla for a dinner with ghosts?"

"Why don't you come too? I've found a good looking witch for you to marry, not ugly like those two girls."

'There was a roar of laughter; the girls began throwing small pebbles at us as we left.'

'We walked through a forest to reach a dilapidated building. In the dark it looked like a spectre. Some nocturnal birds flew away with hoarse cries as we entered a room continuously wiping out cob webs from our faces. Gullu hit the cigarette lighter and picked up a wax candle from a corner to light the place.

'The room looked clean: a water jug at a corner, a rolled up mattress at another, a pack of *beedis* and a bundle of biscuits on a sill which once had a window.

"Wow! It's almost a home."

"Yes. I often spend my night here; it's so peaceful; the jungle, the bushes, the night birds, there's even a well full of water—never dries up. All these take me back to my village. No one comes near this place except some dogs who have become my friends. It was once a large mansion. There are rumours: all members of the family who lived here some hundred years ago were killed and their bodies thrown into that well; all the dead rise from the well every night and play family, though I haven't met any of them so far. Recent rumours are: people see lights during the night and hear sounds of water being lifted from the well, which of course are my doings.

"Let me show you now my savings bank; you could also have one for yourself if you like; you never know when these bastards snatch away your money."

'Gullu led the way to another room with the candle in his hand. Its condition was worse than the first one. He dug at a corner with a bamboo stick kept by its side and pulled out a plastic bag.

"I keep all my savings here. It must be quite a pile now, I've stopped counting. May I dig another hole for you?"

"No. You keep my savings also in the same hole."

'I gave him my hundred rupees which he kept inside another plastic bag, put the two bags into the hole and closed it. We slept the night there.

'For the next five months I engaged myself hatching a plan for escape; Gullu appeared to have left it to me, though became restive occasionally. I'd calm him by saying that for a foolproof plan I'd have to think of various alternatives: remember that he always carries a fully loaded gun; he might just kill us while escaping.

'Actually the gun was the stumbling block in all my plans. I'd also met the man two-three times—a young man four-five years older than us. He appeared trustworthy. One day he asked us. "Why don't you just kill your Big Dada and escape?"

'I replied. "He always carries a gun and his minions, daggers."

"Yeah, that's a problem; two against three armed toughies. Even if I give you a gun you won't be able to carry it, it'll show out; well, think of other ways."

'In the meantime the "torture for discipline" continued unabated: beating thrice a month, sucking and buggering of boys, and wanton sex with the girls four times a month, minor molestations of both boys and girls are not counted. I observed that willy-nilly they'd fallen into a pattern and a few norms like a boy buggered or a girl fucked today would be spared of beating and molestation the next day. I noted the days when both of us were free.

'Next time when the young man met us I asked him.

"Can you get me a dagger, small but lethal?"

'He gazed at me for almost a minute before replying, "You'll get it tomorrow here at this time."

'While handing me a package the next day he said, "When you do it I'll get the news fast; run toward this place, a jeep will pick you up."

'I opened the package at our forest retreat. It was a nice little thing I'd often seen in the movies, looked innocuous but lethal when it hits the right place. Gullu snatched the dagger from me and began piercing the air toward different directions.

'Give it to me; I'll kill the bastard in the bush when he buggers me tomorrow.'

'And get shot. In what position you'd then be? He has the gun by his side always even when fucking or buggering.'

'He handed back the dagger to me with a look of disdain.'

'I told him. "Look, don't be rash. I've devised a plan, listen attentively: We're free day after tomorrow; the minions would be busy molesting the girls.

Big Dada would not pick up his victim before he counted the money handed by us; you'll give yours first and move out gently behind the shorter toughie where you'd keep an innocuous looking but heavy stone on the morning of the target day. Same morning you'll also take out all our savings and hide them in the dustbin—it is emptied only once a day in the early morning. Now comes the action part. After you've handed the money and moved out I'd give him my part of the collections. Watch me carefully. I'll attack Big Dada during the middle of counting; soon after I pierce the dagger to his heart you'd hit the other guy with all your force on the back of his head and run. I'll follow you. And don't forget to pick up the bundle from the dustbin on the way. Remember, timing is very important. Have you understood the plan?"

"Yes." He nodded gravely.

"How good are you at running?"

"Much faster than those bastards."

"Good. Let's sleep now."

'On the target day Gullu did hit the other guy and ran like a sprinter but a little before I finished my job. The guy fell and the girls screamed. Big Dada stopped counting the notes, turned to the other side to see what was happening, the left side of his chest out of my view. As he went for his gun I slashed his throat, the gun fell to his side, I picked it up and ran like Milkha Singh. I could sense the other guy running behind; many others were also running in tandem. I knew they'd never be able to catch me. But I concentrated on my run unmindful of the road condition. I stumbled over a boulder on the middle of the road. Lying there I saw the guy advancing fast; I raised the gun, aimed and pressed the trigger, the way Big Dada fired at my dogs. The guy fell, other pursuers stopped. I got up quickly and resumed running. Gullu was not in sight. As I was approaching the main road a Jeep stopped by my side and two hands pulled me in; the vehicle speeded off.

'Gullu was inside the Jeep with the young man.

'He said apologetically, "Sorry Boss, I got so excited..."

"Stupid, a good friend though." I patted him on the back.

'None of us spoke further till the vehicle stopped at the approach road of Howrah Bridge. The young man got down and said, "The driver will take you to a secure place in Howrah. Take rest; I'll meet you tomorrow."

'The Jeep stopped behind a closed jute mill on the bank of the river Ganges. We walked inside a house which must have been the quarter of some officer, now abandoned. The driver beckoned a man, told him something and left. We could see quite a few innocent looking persons loitering around, the guns inside their trousers jutting out a little. We were ushered into a spacious room: a large bed near a window, a sofa set with a centre table, and bathrooms on both sides. We entered the bathrooms to freshen up. When we came out we found on the centre table plates-full of various snacks, tea and a bottle of whisky. We've never been to this kind of environment before; we were uneasy but hungry, and when you're hungry with foods before you, environment fizzles out together with uneasiness. We guzzled; the plates emptied in minutes and, then we opened the bottle. We took only a small measure as we never drank before. Taking a small sip Gullu spoke, "The house must be for some one big in their network."

"Or, it could just be transit point."

"May be, but it is such a luxurious place!"

"Don't get that into your head, we'd soon be leaving this place."

"You're such a bore."

'Dinner came at ten with meat and all that. We took another measure of whisky and retired to bed. It was soft and bumpy. Gullu took a few jumps lying.

"It's so soft, *yaar*. Sleep may elude me."

"Close your eyes; think of the cozy mud floor where you'd been sleeping so far, and would be sleeping for the rest of your life, sleep would come naturally."

'The young man who would later be my Guru came in the afternoon. He'd a smile of achievement on his face.

'Over tea he informed us that the Big Dada's network had been destroyed.

"What happened to our friends?" Gullu asked

"All fled and that's because of the courage you've shown."

"That's good news, I felt so selfish," Gullu said.

'I said, "All's selfish at some point in life. Their escape is collateral to our action and I don't take any credit for it."

'He looked intently at me before speaking.

"You may be right; we all love to give or take credit for something which is not due. Anyway, our people had taken over the market. My job's over, I'd soon be moving to Kolkata with you."

'I said, "You'd used us as your pawns, though I don't care."

"Partly yes." Guru had a curious look in his eyes. "Any way, I'll come back after three days for our journey to Kolkata; in the meantime enjoy your stay here."

'Next morning it dawned on me Gullu didn't have the bundle of our savings in his hand while we got down from the Jeep. When I mentioned this to him he was startled, realised for the first time that in his hurry he had forgotten to pick up the bundle from the dustbin. He was so remorseful his head fell, couldn't utter a single word. I was also dismayed; it was quite a pile, not less than a lakh of rupees. But nothing could be done now. I tried to cheer him up, assured him that we'd be earning much more than this within a very short time in our new vocation. After a lot of patting and persuasion he did look up, but I knew he'd never forgive himself for this, and would be punishing himself for the rest of his life.

'Next two days were uneventful except that Gullu started drinking more often; he'd also not go out with me in the afternoon for a stroll along the bank of the Ganges. In one such stroll I threw away the gun and the dagger into the Ganges.'

Boomba interjected the soliloquy.

'Dagger, I don't care much, one can buy it anywhere, but why the gun?'

'One cannot have any protection even with lots of weapons against a determined killer,' Raja said with that careless smile of his and continued.

'Gullu was still down when we boarded a seven-seater vehicle. Besides the three of us two more persons sat with their right hand inside the jacket which they never took out during the journey. We stopped before a multi-storeyed building somewhere at central Kolkata, walked by stairs to the first floor and stood before the door which opened as if by itself. It was a one room flat though not very small. "Get us some drinks," Guru addressed the air. We sat on a sofa. A middle aged man limped in, set drinks on the centre table and left without speaking a word.

'Guru said indicating the vanishing figure, "He was once like us, shot in the leg by the police, but escaped. Our organisation took care of him. After his recovery he has been placed here. He is invisible, but his visibility is great so also his sensory nerves; he can sense a danger from a mile and twenty four hours in advance."

'He poured drinks in glasses. Gullu picked up the bottle, poured another measure to his glass and swallowed the whole in one gulp.

'Guru asked. "Why Gullu looks so dejected even after doing such a heroic job?"

"Well, we've lost our lives' savings—Gullu's share the largest, during the run. He has a family in village, wanted to set them up here with all that money. Now he can't even go to the village; we are penniless."

'Guru thought for a while, went inside and talked for sometime over a land line before coming back.

"The network has a number of flats like this in Kolkata, all well protected. Gullu can stay in one with his family, and you at another; there's no cost."

"We'd prefer to live on our own," I said.'

"I guessed as much. The next alternative is, you find your own accommodation; if it is rented the network will reimburse the rent, if an acquisition and the cost is not more than two lakh fifty thousand per head you'll get the money as reward for helping us destroy Big Dada's organisation, if the cost is more than that you'll repay the incremental amount by easy instalments. When you finalise inform me; I'll visit the place as a matter of formality and arrange the money. Is the arrangement alright?" Guru asked turning to Gullu.

"Whatever my Boss decides." Gullu looked somewhat cheerful.

"Ok. Keep ten thousand rupees for your initial expenses." He handed a packet to Gullu and left.

'Next two days we plowed through the length and breadth of the city and finally zeroed in on the place we live now. It was sparsely populated then—only three-four huts; later I brought in other people.

'Major cost was the negotiation money that had to be paid to the local dada who would later join my gang and I'd be his boss. After the deal was finalised, he introduced us to a person good at constructing huts. Total cost was rupees three lakh fifty thousand including our expenses for one month. Guru visited the place, nodded affirmatively and handed us a thick packet that contained four lakh fifty thousand rupees.

"Additional one lakh is your reward; the organisation has great designs for you, some day you'll know about them," he said.

'In a month's time all the huts were ready. Gullu left for his village.

'We began working for the network under the tutelage of Guru. But Gullu was drinking too much, becoming unstable and problematic for the network. He was removed, and I made him the leader of my gang. When there is a war he is extremely courageous, fierce, somewhat rash may be but does his job to the finish. At such times he doesn't drink.

'This is the major part of my life's story, somewhat lengthy, though eventful, and at times you might have been bored also but I feel so good now after sharing it with you; I had not shared it even with my Guru.'

'What happened to your Guru?' Boomba asked.

'That's a different story I'll tell you later.'

'I find you've an excellent memory; you recount every event so meticulously as if all these had happened only yesterday,' Toomba said.

Raja replied. 'When you hold a story inside for long and recount it only with yourself you don't miss a thing; may be from tomorrow I'll start missing some. Besides, I really have a good memory. Guru was also surprised when I memorised and returned the delivery list in less than ten seconds.'

'That's your other strength,' Boomba said appreciably.

Toomba remarked. 'In the short term it's strength; in the long run painful.'

'Yes, you're right.' Raja had a different kind of appreciation in his eyes.

Chapter 14

Three months passed. Boomba's quota was increased to five packets per delivery day. He would often check his savings with Mashi to calculate how far away he was from the target.

Chameli did not know what Boomba was doing. She asked him once but Boomba replied, it was a big job, he would tell her about it later. That later never came. Chameli also did not pester him further: he might be engaged in some risky vocation, but in the street it was more of a norm than an exception, she consoled herself. She knew Boomba was working very hard with only one goal: their marriage and a settled life thereafter. In her dream she was already a housewife managing her family that must include at least two children like *baudi's*. She would often ask her this and that to increase her knowledge about managing a household. She had also stopped sulking when Boomba did not show up in time: after all he was working for the good of the family; she had observed *baudi* too not sulking much when her husband came home late.

One day Toomba received a call from Raja, he sounded somewhat frantic. 'It's a disaster, stop working immediately, throw away your mobile phone, take a taxi, proceed to our *Maidan* rendezvous and wait for me, also ask Boomba to do the same.'

Toomba informed Boomba and hailed a taxi.

Raja came a little late; he was working in the northern outskirts of Kolkata, had to come through lanes and bylanes, though he did not forget to bring some food and four nips of whisky. They were not hungry but a peg of whisky would do well to relieve the tension.

After all of them took two sips of whisky, Raja spoke.

'The drug factory had been raided by Anti-Narcotics squad. They arrested the man who organised deliveries and all other persons working there, and seized all the drugs.'

'In that case all deliveries stopped, income gone?' Boomba asked anxiously.

'Don't be upset, just lie low for some days; it'll resume in time.'

'How? The whole set up is destroyed now.' Boomba was unconvinced

'You're naive. We're part of a very powerful international organisation dealing in the costliest of drugs—heroin; its network spreads over all countries of the world. The squad here is just a chit. They will palm them off, politicians of top echelon will rush to their aid, the media will soon lose its steam and everyone will forget the matter. There'll of course be prosecution against persons arrested but charges against them would be diluted, some may be freed, a few sentenced for a year or so. The network would take care of them, though they wouldn't be reinstated in active service as their faces have become known.'

'How do you know all this?' Boomba asked.

'The way I learnt about the raid. Don't ask further questions. In this trade, the less you know the better. Let's talk about something else. How many *purias* are left with you?'

'Two.' Boomba.

'One.' Toomba.

'Three'. Raja.

'Good, it's quite a bonanza.'

'How?'

'Well, now the market is dry; there'll soon be a scramble, the price would sky rocket. During normal time it is twenty thousand rupees per *puria*. If I play it cool I could sell each at not less than thirty thousand rupees.'

'Wow! Sixty thousand rupees for me, a real bonanza as you said.'

'And close to a lakh for me,' Raja grinned.

Toomba was silent, not participating in the jubilation.

'What about you?' Raja asked quizzically.

'I'm not going to sell mine; I'll enjoy it myself.'

'Well, it's your choice, but my Guru warned me: never consume a drug you are dealing with; you'd soon become unfit for the trade.'

'But my Guru says: Beta, when a thing like this comes to you for free, just enjoy it,' Toomba replied.

'Who is your Guru, may I know?' Boomba asked.

'My Guru is His Celestial Excellency Shree, Shree, Shree Toomba the Great.'

Their laughter drove away the birds off the tree but attracted the police man. He didn't expect them so early. He took his bottle and went away. They opened the food packets.

Wow! It's *Biryani;* we also thought of eating *Biryani* this evening. How did you know that?' Boomba asked.

'Well, I didn't know about your wishes. While taking a turn to the main road I saw a restaurant; a boy was arranging packets on the counter, may be for home delivery. I was in a hurry, asked him what it contained, he said, *Biryani,* I asked the price and told him to give them to me. He was initially reluctant but an additional fifty-rupee note did the trick. So it just happened, may be a coincidence or I might have fore felt your wish. Raja suddenly stopped eating and turned remorseful.

He spoke after some time.

'I didn't know the discussion would take this turn reminding me of the most painful incident of my life.'

'Is it about your Guru?'

'Yes. I fore felt his disaster but didn't believe in it; I didn't act in time and I lost him.'

'Is it related to drug trade? A rash move in a drug war? An enemy from the past both of you underestimated?'

'None of that; if it were I'd not have been so remorseful. I don't know much about his past, he never told me, nor did he ask for mine. From his stray talks over drinks I could only guess he came from a rich aristocratic family of Delhi, dropped out of University for what reason I don't know, roamed the whole country before coming to Kolkata. I got no inkling how he came in contact with the network, but I could guess they held him in high regard. Probably on his recommendation I got higher daily quota, though he never told me.

'He taught me many things, not so much about drug trade but about life and death. When I was morose, he'd know I was thinking about the past, my painful childhood, the lovely time I spent at the food stall, its destruction, my first killing, and always that eternal cry—why all these had to happen to me. One day he sat closer to me, just where Toomba sits now and said. "I often observe you think about your past. None can ever forget one's past; I'm not also asking you do so, but you can smoothen its thorny edges by turning it to a story; share the story with someone you feel like sharing. Convert history into a story; it might lessen the weight."

'Twice he stayed at my place, may be inspection tours by a network man. He didn't comment on anything in particular. One morning before leaving he told me, "A kingdom should be run by violence and benevolence. Big Dada lost his kingdom because he practiced only violence."

'When I was selling drugs for Big Dada I didn't feel any prick of conscience—I was under compulsion, but I entered the present trade on my own volition. I could have walked out but I didn't. After some time I began feeling I was working against the conscience of the society; it often pricked me. I raised the question before him. He thought for a long time before replying.

"The driving force of civilisation is unethical practices. Ethics is an instrument of manipulation of one section of the mankind by the other. Old ethics change to new ethics which might just be the opposite of the old ones to suit the requirement of contemporary civilisation; there's nothing like eternal ethics. Who knows, some day drug might shed its unethical stigma. So why bother?"

'He always had a quizzical smile on his face and an askance look, conducted his life so dangerously and so casually I often got scared.'

'He'd say, "Don't get scared. You could enjoy your life the fullest only when you engage with death at every moment of your life. Death is my lover, I'm crazy about her, enjoy her beauty every moment of my life, never allow her to play tricks with me like an unfaithful consort."

'It was not easy to comprehend what he said; and I was also very young. But I did practice the first lesson to take on life and death with equanimity. I'd show you what it is.'

Raja looked at the sky.

'It must be six in the evening. Look at the road; it's peak hours, every second not less than ten cars are moving in high speed. I'll cross the road not when the cars stop at the red signal but when the signal turns green and the cars' speed reach its peak.'

Boomba looked alarmingly at him, Toomba nonchalant, but Raja didn't care to notice. He rose to move to the place of occurrence but stopped for a while to speak.

'A piece of advice for you: if I'm hit by a car, in all likelihood I'd be killed—no one can survive among a collision of multiple vehicles. Remain cool, rush to the place of the accident, take note of the car number first, create a ruckus; the police man over there will come to your aid, make sure the car owner takes my body to a nursing home, not to a government hospital, ask the police man to accompany you. I'd soon be declared dead; the policeman would take notes of the registration number of the vehicle, name, address, telephone number, et cetera of the owner and confiscate his driving license or that of the driver. Now starts the bargain. The minimum settlement amount should not be less than five lakh rupees, if the car is large and pricey you may raise the settlement amount, but don't go beyond ten lakhs. And don't forget to give the police man fifty thousand rupees; what he makes by the side is none of your business.'

'But why should we try to benefit ourselves from your death?' Boomba was exasperated.

'My Guru said: one's death is not a loss for everyone around; someone somewhere is always benefitted. You may consider my death benefit as an advance gift to Chameli on her marriage.'

He winked at Toomba and proceeded toward the road. He stood there waiting for the signal to turn green, Boomba and Toomba a little behind. When the cars began speeding, not ten in a second but twenty, Raja was down on the road. He began crossing it at uniform speed without raising his hands for once amidst blaring of horns, cacophony of abuses in different languages and screeching of tyres.

Boomba closed his eyes to the thought of impending disaster, but the possibility of getting lakhs also flashed through his mind, though for moments only, and he cursed himself for that under his breath when Toomba nudged him to open his eyes.

Raja was on the other side of the road waving and smiling.

They came back to their place. It was Boomba, not Raja who was perspiring. Raja patted Boomba on his back.

'Sorry Boss, it didn't happen this time; the cars were very careful.'

'Don't make joke of a thing like this.' Boomba was angry.

'Okay. Now tell me did you observe how I crossed the road?'

'No. I'd kept my eyes closed.'

Raja's voice suddenly lost its jocular tenor. He spoke slowly.

'I should also have closed my eyes on that fateful evening but that was not my wont. On that day I finished my game first. It was his turn. Guru's last advice before his journey to the road was: if I'm killed this evening don't fret, don't get emotional, follow the drill meticulously and don't grieve. Death is a beauty, never grime it with grief.

'Never before he exhorted me like this. I'd a forefeeling of what was coming, but I couldn't stop it. The cars ran over his body. When I reached him he was already dead; even in the pool of blood his enigmatic smile was visible.'

'And you did follow his instructions?'

'Yes, every step of it. I got six lakhs and put them on fixed deposits for Gullu.'

'But... but...'

'No, Boomba, no. It wasn't a lucre; he had purified it long before.'

* * * *

The Kolkata operation of the drug network was shifted behind a large provisions store in the south owned by the network. The store manager had no knowledge of who really owned the store and what really happened in the factory behind the store. He knew only that that it crushed spices in powder form for distribution among different retail stores in and around Kolkata including his store: the quality good, margin competitive.

Raja was busy during the setting up period. He told later, it was his idea to set up the new outfit behind the provision store and he was made in-charge of the entire operation.

On the day before inauguration of the new set up Raja invited Boomba and Toomba to a dinner at a hi-fi Park Street restaurant. Raja looked tired but radiant. They ate in near silence and went to their *Maidan* rendezvous after dinner.

The policeman left with his nip. After the first puff Raja answered their long-awaited question.

'You'll be glad to know I've been made the divisional head of Kolkata.'

'Wow! It's great news; we didn't expect this much, you're so young,' Boomba said.

'Yeah; I learnt later, that was the objection made by a few members of the Council which met yesterday in Kolkata. But the Chairman overruled them saying, "That's the advantage; you should also remember who'd recommended him for a higher position before he was killed in an unfortunate accident."

'Before that I was interviewed for an hour, queried about my past and present. One of them asked where I live. When I told them the Chairman said, "That's another advantage; just stay there."'

'You shall now be in a lot of money!' Boomba exclaimed.

'And very, very busy.' Raja's solemn look could not hide the underlying pride.

'Well, I've two offers for you; one, you may increase your daily quota to ten *purias,* the other is the bulk couriering: pick up a consignment—two feet by one foot weighing a kilogram, from border areas like Bongaon, Basirhat or Malda and deliver it to our new set up. You'll be paid thirty thousand rupees per consignment plus an allowance of one thousand rupees per day of your stay there; we have people over there who'll take care of every other thing. Present arrangement is two consignments a month.'

'I accept both,' Boomba said hastily.

'I accept none. I stick to my original quota.' Toomba replied. 'I'll never understand you.' Raja said resignedly.

'Me too,' Boomba joined him.

Raja rose and turned to Boomba, 'Meet me tomorrow at my office.' He was already a boss.

Chapter 15

Boomba's savings with Mashi began growing at a fast pace which astonished Mashi but she did not enquire as was her wont. But Chameli became anxious. She observed Boomba often vanished for a week or so without informing her, not reachable even by mobile phone. Frustrated, she once asked Toomba but all she got was silence from him.

She had more free time now as *baudi* was in the advanced stage of her third pregnancy and had gone to her parent's house with the children. So she and Boomba had planned a voyage together on the Ganges by boat. But on the appointed day Boomba vanished. Chameli was angry at first, then anxious: he has never done this before. What's the matter? Is he in some kind of secret deal which cannot be shared with any one, not even with his future wife? In the street it means only one thing, drug; so much money with so much secrecy could only come from drug. The conclusion increased her anxiety. She never bothered for legality or illegality of a vocation; it carries no meaning in the street. Consumption of drug and peddling of minor substances are open secrets like prostitution, stealing and pick pocketing, but dealing in drugs is something different, reserved only for those with high ambition of money and power—to become a leader. But Boomba is no leader, rather a follower; his only ambition is to marry her and raise a family. In contrast Toomba is a leader. But Boomba often says he never behaves like a leader; though he knows life more than any of us, he never cares for life, has no craze for money, no ambition, somewhat resembling Mashi. So, Toomba cannot be part of Boomba's new venture. Besides, he has been around even when Boomba is away. It must therefore be Boomba's own initiative driven by his desire to have a comfortable life after marriage; he wants to surprise her, to have a pat on the back from her after having done a good job, like when he could stand erect for the first time and, she had patted her. My god, the boy has not grown beyond childhood!

She smiled to herself, a motherly smile. But how could she protect him? She did not know the world of drug trade except that it was dangerous. The bullet that maimed Jaggudada could also kill. Oh! She could not think any further. She needed help. The stoic Toomba was of no help. She dialled

Minudi's number; it rang for a while then stopped. She dialled again. This time she picked it up. A distinct sound of boisterous kisses was followed by an animated voice, 'Hey Chameli, anything serious?'

'Yes, Paltu isn't home for seven days now.'

'Oh darling, we've no home, only streets; he must've gone to some other street for some childish merrymaking, don't worry he'd come back to you soon; he can't leave you.'

'But he's been doing it twice a month for the past three months, and every time he returns with thirty thousand rupees, doesn't tell wherefrom he is getting so much money.'

'Oh. That's quite serious. Ok, meet me at eight in the night, and bring Toomba with you.'

'Toomba, that silent man!'

'Yeah. I love silence.' Minu switched off the phone.

Chameli felt relieved, though she did not understand how Toomba could be of help.

She stared at the silent mobile phone at her hand and suddenly heard sound of a kiss. She was startled. Once again she looked at the phone; no, the screen was dark. No one's around in this hot summer noon except the cars moving by two sides of Gariahat Bridge. Then she realised it was coming from within her. She felt aroused and shy at the same time.

That day when Paltu ravished her she understood her body for the first time though through severe pain. Paltu's kisses conveyed something radically different from the ones she was used to, his throbbing manhood amazed her: so small then and so large now! Next three days she carried a pain between her legs, but also a different sensation that gave a different meaning to her body: only—only, if he had been a little considerate, little slower. She did not talk to her during those days whether out of anger or shyness she was still not clear, did not allow him to come near, nor even heard his mercy petition. Only after he got a thrashing from Minudi and she asking her to forgive him she resumed talking with him. Paltu had never touched her since, not even tried to come closer, always maintained a distance like a good boy. Deep in her mind she wanted him to be a little bolder but never expressed it.

She had met four girls of the Home Sick group, nicknamed as HS group in the street. Two of them married twice, now single looking for another husband, the other two had varied sexual experiences. She gathered that on the first encounter men behaved like animals if they never had sex before; the pain had to be tolerated, that was the fate of every girl. Next time onwards it'd be normal.

Chameli felt guilty of punishing Paltu for too long a time. She intended making it up: she would now allow him to come closer—some kissing, a little bit of petting but nothing more; sex only after marriage. But where was Paltu now? If he got hit by the police everything was over. Oh-ho, she could not think further. She decided to take a walk, but first she must dial Toomba for the scheduled appointment.

Toomba had more free time now. After Raja's taking over the Kolkata operation he got his delivery days reduced to twice a week. He had now expanded his network of friends to Maniktala on the north and Jadavpur railway station area on the south. He participated in all their activities that range from loading-unloading-carting-pilfering to begging. He would spend more than his share of earnings with them in fun and frolics. When he received the call from Chameli he was enjoying a puff of hashish with friends at Jadavpur. He agreed to be at Gariahat by seven in the evening.

Mashi observed Chameli's restlessness since noon; she was making telephone calls, talking to herself, pacing to and fro. It must be something to do with Boomba's disappearance, but she did not ask.

At six-thirty Chameli telephoned Toomba.

'I'm already here taking tea at the corner stall of Jashoda Bhawan.'

'I'm coming.'

Chameli walked briskly toward the tea stall.

'Come Chameli, have some tea.' He gave her a rare smile of his.

They sipped tea in silence. Chameli wanted to speak but stopped short of it; there was no point talking to a wall. They finished three cups of tea, some snacks in between brought by Toomba from a nearby stall. At seven thirty they rose and began walking toward Golpark. When they reached the site of the dilapidated building Chameli found it already grazed down, dug up here and there and construction equipments strewn around. She gave a surprise look at Toomba.

'She isn't here; follow me.'

They walked straight along Southern Avenue, turned left and entered from the crossing of Lansdowne Road to a grassy land surrounded by tall foliaged trees that shaded the light of the street lamps creating an environment of romantic mystery.

'Hey, Chameli'

They recognised the voice but took time to adjust their eyes to the fleeting light and shade. They saw Minu sitting against the trunk of a tree, her legs stretched before her as usual. She pulled them back and they sat facing her.

'Want to have a sip?' She handed the whisky bottle to Toomba with one hand and a bottle of cold drink to Chameli with the other.

'I'm sorry Chameli I had forgotten to inform you the change of venue; I was in a different mood then. Later I thought since Toomba knows this place you'd have no problem. I discovered this place when a friend of mine brought me to that white spectre-like building that houses a hundred years old boating club facing the lake. The cool breeze you're getting is coming from the lake, just about thousand meters from here. Members of the club are hi-fi people: top executives, bureaucrats, police officers, writers and other dignitaries. Boating helps them keep fit; some of them or their sons and daughters spend their illegitimate time here inside the car or on the grass; security guards of the club oversee the affairs for good money and the police never interfere. They know me through my friends, so, I've safe access to this field. This is a good place for our rendezvous but not as good as that *khandhar* of the Maharaja at Golpark.'

'I fully agree.' Chameli was short in response in the hope that she'd now address her problem. But Minu turned to Toomba.

'Hey, my silent man. I hear you already have a large following in the Gariahat area; a darling of girls, even of HS group. How could you do it in so short a time?'

No answer, not even a chuckle.

'C'mon, you should feel elated; now say something to us.'

'You're also a darling of streets among both boys and girls; though boys are a little scared of you.'

'But I talk, often garrulously, but you're almost silent except some occasional epithets. Then how?'

'It's better you ask them. By the way are you jealous?'

'Jealous, my foot! I just wanted to know the mystery, and presently to make you talk a little more,' Minu replied with an impish smile.

Chameli was not in a mood to hear the tittle-tattle. Before they strayed she blurted out.

'Minudi, please look at me.'

'Ok, ok. We're just warming up before discussing your problem which I think is serious. Would you mind enlighten us in detail?'

Chameli told them everything she had been thinking since noon and also her hunch that Paltu might be entangled in the drug trade. She felt relieved having shared it with them.

They heard in silence and remained silent for sometime thereafter. Then Minu turned to Toomba.

'Is he already in the drug trade?'

'It'll be better if you don't ask this question.'

'Why? You're his best friend.' Chameli was angry.

'The less you know the better.'

Minu said, 'I got the answer and also understand your anxiety point.'

Silence once again. Both Chameli and Minu looked helpless, didn't know what to say next. After some time Toomba spoke solemnly.

'I can only assure you, if Boomba ever gets into a serious jam I'll wrest him out.'

Chameli could only see Toomba's profile when he spoke, his face turned to the passing vehicles on the road. The breeze from the lake continuously stirred the branches of the trees making the petals of light open and close on Toomba's face making it more mysterious

She realised she could never understand this man, as Boomba often said: always casual, carefree, hardly expressed his feelings—if he had any, a granite wall surrounded by a magnetic field where no sound reverberated but drew people to it. Then who was this man who just made a flat statement that put her mind at peace as never before? Something welled up inside her, tears released the pent up emotion.

No one spoke.

Minu now knew what made her fall in love with Toomba on that day near Ladies Park when she intently looked at his eyes before he moved away silently throwing away the rod he wrested from her adversary. 'Silence is the greatest communicator,' she thought.

They walked back to Gariahat silently.

* * * *

Minu needed some unwinding. She turned toward Triangular Park when Toomba boarded a Sealdah-bound bus without even saying a bye-bye. Though by now she had become used to his nonchalance, this time she felt hurt.

She felt hungry when she saw the *panipuriwala* standing at his usual corner of the Park with an upside down cane basket full of tiny *puris*—round, hollow and crisp gleaming like large marbles in the street light. Four boys and girls each holding a tiny plate made of Sal leaf stood before him; the *Panipuriwalla* deftly piercing the hollow of a *puri* with his left thumb, putting a small amount of spicy potato paste inside, filling it up with equally spicy tamarind water before putting it on the leaf plate of a hand in the queue.

The *Panipuriwalla* nodded her in acknowledgement. She heard, 'Minu... Minudi...,' as eight girls of HS group thronged her and surrounded the *panipuri* stand. She welcomed them with a bright smile. After the fore comers paid for their consumption the *panipuriwalla* distributed the leaf-plates to them and began preparing the mixture. Mini noticed a girl among them with a sullen face.

'Hey Kajol, visiting your *maike (parents' house)?* Minu asked.

'Yes, I've returned for good. The bastard tried to sell me. This time I've taken a vow I'll never ever marry,' she blurted out after munching a *panipuri*.

'This is the third time she is making a vow to break it for the fourth time,' someone quipped from the opposite side. Everyone started laughing and surprisingly Kajol also joined.

A supra risible girl, never tired of getting married and breaking off. Minu often wondered how could she smile away all sorrows, all betrayals, cheating and intimidation: A daft smirking girl? No. She knew.

The giggles between gulping of *panipuri* got disturbed by someone calling attention.

'Hey Kajol, your Ma is coming to take you away for scrubbing utensils.'

A thick small dark woman with anger in her eyes was marching toward them. Kajol put her and of another's *panipuri* into her mouth and scurried off.

'Poor girl,' someone lamented.

Minu mused: 'No. She is richer than many of us—a heart full of gold. How many of us could continue to love without reciprocity, despite betrayals? She loves love; nothing else matters.'

HS was an all-girls group who pined for home. Other street children sniggered at them though that did not stop transactions among them, which included substances, cash loans, selling and buying of stolen mobiles, SIM cards, artificial jewellery, used garments and occasional sex.

They were often betrayed and intimidated but dared not fight back.

In an earlier visit Kajol narrated the story of HS group.

'You know, why we can't fight them because we all are timid by circumstances. We're in the street not by volition; we're thrown out from our homes for one reason or the other. For example, my step father had often been molesting me, I didn't so much care but one day he tried to have sex with me. I bit on his wrist and ran to my mother to complain. She didn't believe *me*, rather believed the concocted story told by *him*. I was beaten by both of them and thrown out for good. You know, we came to the street scared, not angry and we continue to be scared and timid.' Kajol had felt happy to open her heart before her.

Suddenly they heard a near insane laughter followed by a voice from behind the assemblage.

'Ooh-hooh. Kajol is a little more fortunate than me. My own father fucked me daily side by side with my mother: me more, she less. I was aborted twice at a town hospital. One day I couldn't tolerate any longer. I went to the police station, met the *thanedar* and told him everything. My father was arrested. On my return I found the entire village assembled before our house demanding of my mother to throw me out because I'd done as heinous a deed as to put my own father in jail with a complaint no one could imagine... bunch of *chutiyas*... all mother fuckers. But I didn't care. I pushed myself through the crowd and reached the door sill of the house. My mother stood there crying, but... but... she shut the door on my face. I heard her cry on the other side of the door but she didn't open it. I stood bewildered for a while, and then hurriedly made my way out through the howling crowd. I didn't know why and how I reached the railway station and boarded the first train that arrived there... I'm a fully fucked up girl from inside, outside... all sides.'

Although she was not crying hoarse but everyone felt her internal cry. A steeling silence stayed with them for some time.

Kajol whispered to Minu, 'She is Mahamaya, joined us a month back, yet to overcome the shocks.'

The silence was broken by a girl sitting by Minu's side.

'The funny thing about us is that despite all these harrowing experiences we still pine for our home; we reminiscence the good days spent there, feel happy in sharing our experiences and we all carry our original names unlike other street dwellers who change them frequently.'

'And we don't mind when others deride us as Home Sick group; we truly are home sick,' another girl had added.

'And since we know we cannot return to our family we recreate it here by establishing relationships with street families except Durga, Parvati and Lakshmi who did build up such a relationship when they came here first but now have severed all their connections,' Kajol said.

Lakshmi immediately became angry.

'Yes, I'd walked away from a roadside family I established relationship with. And why not? I did all domestic chores, gave them money, carried errands and shared with them any food I could gather. I sincerely called them Ma, Baba, Bhai—all familial names I used when I was with my family in the village. They also reciprocated and professed love. Slowly I realised they did not love me at all, they just pretended so as to take advantage; in fact they hate girls like us, wouldn't even allow their own children to mix with us except on purpose. When it came to taking money they'd smother me with love. What pretensions! How I hate those fucking families!' Lakshmi had been fuming.

'The experience is similar with all the girls here; you just check,' Durga said.

Kajol heard them with a distressed face. Then she spoke in a low voice.

'Well, what you say is all true. My street mother also does the same; she steals my money when I'm asleep but when she makes me wake up in the morning calling my name with many darling prefixes—may be pretensions, and when I still wouldn't get up her youngest son titillates me and does coo... coo... to my ears—may be for his daily quota of candy, or Baba admonishing me in a fatherly tone, "Enough of sleep, now get up, you're already late," though he often touches my breasts stealthily, I set aside the pretensions and enjoy those blissful moments full of affectionate blarneys. Our own parents often faked love, thrashed us for no reason, manipulated us for their own ends and finally drove us out. But have we stopped loving them? Don't we still cherish those moments of love at home? Yes, we do. Moments pass, subjects pass, only the object stays constant and that object is love. It's much more fulfilling to carry love in your mind than rancour.'

Amidst clapping they heard a voice.

'An incorrigible lover.'

'Diseased.' Another voice.

With stomach full of *panipuris* Minu decided to sleep the night in the park. She changed her societal dress-mask to street tunic and immediately felt at home with the girls. A few hurried to their street mothers, others slept with her.

Minu had met with the HS group after a fortnight. All members gathered around her except Kajol. When she enquired they suppressed a smile.

'C'mon, tell me what it's all about? Has she already found a new lover?'

'More or less; didn't you see her at Gariahat? One girl quipped.'

'No, I just passed by.'

'Well, she has gone to Gariahat to meet Toomba—this is the fourth time. She's developed a crush on him after she heard his story from us. She'll come back soon if she failed but if she succeeds this time, well…'

* * * *

Toomba's entry into HS group was not as easy as Minu's. When she first came here the street mothers came one by one to evaluate their level of threat but when they observed she was noninterfering they withdrew. But it was different for Toomba. He faced not the women but a group of five-six grownup boys some of whom belonged to the street families.

These girls were independent, not under a Dada or *Mashi,* but the boys exercised an informal control over them mostly by intimidation and occasionally by false love and affection. Toomba was male and powerful as street gossips went, could wrest control from them; a real threat.

Toomba saw the girls cringe as the boys approached. He asked the girls to move behind him and observed the boys keenly. Two of them had their hands clasped at their backs; must be armed with daggers or rods. He sat coolly without shifting his position.

A leader type came forward.

'What made you come to our territory?'

No reply.

'This is not Gariahat, it's better you leave this place.'

The answer came in a flash. Toomba scudded on the two armed boys hitting one on his ribs and the other between his legs; his two hands, now joined together, hit the leader on the back of his head. They fell like dead wood, daggers glistening on the grass, others fled.

'Fucking idiots! Domesticated animals can't fight street animals,' he muttered to himself.

He turned the leader upside and examined him, 'Not dead, just fainted. Sprinkle some water on his face, he'd soon come round.' A girl picked up a saucepan from a nearby stall and collected water from a municipal tap.

After five minutes of continuous sprinkling the boy opened his eyes and saw the girls looking at his face. He quickly sat up facing Toomba's countenance. Fully oriented now he wanted to get up and run but Toomba made him sit.

'Look, I'm not your enemy, could as well be your friend some day. Till that happens don't be around when I'm here. Understand?'

He nodded with his head down.

'Now collect your daggers and *daggerwallas* too, and scram.'

The other two boys now on their haunches heard the last sentence, gathered the daggers and ran before their leader could even begin staggering up.

The girls looked at Toomba with awe. He sat at the same place as before, somewhat bored.

Next half hour all the girls talked about various misdeeds of these young men: intimidation, beating, molestation, snatching of money and substances, running for various illegal errands, et cetera. Toomba heard them quietly. He spoke now.

'I don't think they'll disturb you again. If they demand something, refuse; if it's a prayer try to oblige; never forget all of us here including them are on the same feeble ground.'

The girls became thoughtful trying to understand what he had just said. Toomba broke the silence by giving some currency notes to the one near him asking her to get some snacks for all of them.

Two girls ran out saying, 'Yes, we shall celebrate your first visit. We also have two bottles of country liquor.'

When the food was brought Toomba placed his bottle on the grass, the two girls also did the same. After a couple of drinks and snacks one girl could not help voicing what was in the mind of all the girls.

'Please tell us how could you beat off those rogues; they are a terror in this area, always carried weapons. We feared you're finished but just the opposite happened and that too in a flash. Are you trained to fight like that?'

'Yes. I'd learnt the techniques from dogs and strategies from the street.'

'But... but... how could you do it?'

'When you're in a fatal jam drive away all anger from your mind, follow your instinct, don't think about consequences, fix your target, don't give him time to think and hit lethally. After it's over, don't carry any rancour in your mind; you'll feel happy.'

A couple of more drinks, the girls began falling asleep one by one. Toomba rose and walked the footpath, his head tipsy but legs firm.

Minu was not surprised when she heard from the HS girls the story of Toomba's fight; she had herself seen it and heard from Boomba a number of times. What she realised now was that he had a compassionate mind behind his steel frame, an empathy with street children, and he never carried any rancour against an adversary. Her first assessment about him was that he was a little insouciant sage, but such a person could never have so much compassion.

Her thought process was rattled by the stormy arrival of Kajol.

'I give up. You can worship a stone statue but cannot love it.'

Minu could not suppress a laugh.

Durga said, 'We all warned you; Toomba loves us all but he is not a lover; we aren't his type, he lives in a plain we can never reach.'

'Doesn't matter; I shall soon find one,' Kajol laughed with others.

* * * *

Next time Toomba came to Triangular Park the girls did come in one and two but with gloomy faces. He noticed one girl; Kali who hardly spoke but always smiled was absent. He had brought a lot of food articles for a night-picnic with them, but not sure now whether he would propose it. He asked instead.

'Why so much gloom? Have the boys again done some mischief?'

'No. The boys are very well behaved now.'

'Then?'

'Kali's dead.'

Silence.

All heads bent down expect Toomba's who seemed unperturbed. After a while some one spoke as if from a long distance.

'We were ten in the group, now eight; lights going off one by one.'

Silence again for a while then Durga spoke.

'Toomba, you must have seen Kali who always smiled. But you cannot imagine under that smile she suppressed an ever growing mountain of pain—the pain of hunger, pain due to hunger.'

Sita who was sitting by Toomba's side added, 'It's nothing particular of Kali; we all have a similar disposition, but we don't talk about it except to ourselves; no one's interested in hearing the others' sorrows, but we feel like sharing with you: we don't know why but it's a fact, may be perhaps we love you and you love us too. We know sharing doesn't reduce the physical pain but it helps tolerate it or may be, forget it for some time, and we smile as we do in the aftermath of inhaling.

'We can't afford to buy drugs, so we inhale Dendrite which comes cheap. I do the inhaling for fifteen minutes to feel sleepy, Kali required an hour, others between fifteen minutes and half hour. How long could we survive in this state? Kali's fate is the fate of all of us.'

Krishna said in a low voice, 'You know, we can't go beyond Dendrite; we peddle drugs but can hardly afford it except an occasional puff of cheap hashish. We don't earn more than one hundred rupees a day, sometimes it comes down to a mere fifty. Forget drugs we can't even buy good food at that income. We collect waste food from hotels, office canteens and marriage halls. We have tie up with the employees and sweepers of these places who sell these to us cheap; we clean or boil these foods and eat. Our stomach rebels: cramps first, then pain, then severe pain. For me the pain has travelled down; I feel terrible pain while defecating, so I avoid drinking water and now I feel a burning sensation while urinating. May be, I'm the next to follow Kali.'

'No, Krishna you won't die. I also had similar problems but was cured by a homeopath. Tomorrow we shall go there. He is good and not costly,' assured Parvati.

Krishna smiled weakly and continued.

'Poor us. We don't want to die, are scared of everything. We move in groups of twos or threes, never alone. Even when we do prostitution someone would always be nearby. One of us made a mistake once and she was dead the same day—the first one to die in our group. She was fed up scrubbing utensils for three hotels; hard labour, low payment, yes, but a steady income. But she wanted to earn a lot of money and went to Sealdah station alone to teach practical sex lessons to the station boys. She was found dead in a pool of blood, currency notes strewn around her.'

'I've seen it,' Toomba spoke after a long time.

'But we couldn't, we only heard.' Shyama spoke for the first time.

Unlike others Shyama wore sari, used lipstick, fake ornaments and cheap facials. She continued.

'Someone telephoned Kajol and we rushed to Sealdah station, heard that she was on the roof of the station morgue. We wanted to go there but saw police all around and left the place: we're very scared of the police.'

'Any idea what happened to her body? Shyama asked.

'No idea,' Toomba replied.

'No cremation, no dirge, always thrown out like garbage,' she lamented.

Radha who always sat beside Kajol was more of a listener, she preferred nodding than speaking. She thought it was time to articulate the basic need of the group.

'Our basic need is security—security of life, security of food. Love is a distant thing for us, lovey-dovey Kajol is an exception and we feel marriage is the only thing that could give us some security, may be fleeting, still. We try to dress nicely, apply cosmetics, wear glittering fake ornaments and smile coquettishly to attract boys. All our days are bridal days.'

'And we often end up in prostitution,' Parvati smirked.

'Yes, but what else can we do?'

No answer.

Radha spoke again and this time she smiled.

'I could guess the large bag of yours contains food items you wanted to share with us. Don't worry, we shall soon get over our gloom, more so because we could let off our steam, may be without any purpose, still, and more so because we know we could eat some good food whenever you or Minu visits us; we don't resent your sympathy, rather we look forward to it.' She smiled again.

Toomba also smiled when he spoke.

'I'm glad to hear that. We shall spend tonight in revel, not misery. The more time you give to misery, the more space it occupies. The truth is that we're like reeds, fleeting, momentary, always yearning to stay on earth but there's no earth beneath. Anyone who tries to beat this truth ends up in misery.'

'But... but... but we've got to live, can't kill ourselves,' Durga expressed her confusion.

'Yes, I also live but I refuse to grow up; I don't aspire to live beyond the street age: the longer one lives, dolorous the life.'

Kajol had not spoken at all. She was observing Toomba listening to them patiently sitting erect, he never shifted his position even when he smoked, and then spoke from far beyond. Now she realised what her friends said: he resides at a different plane unreachable for them.

'We've talked about life and death for long. Let's now open the bagful of delights and enjoy the fucking life,' Toomba declared as he unstrapped the food bag.

Chapter 16

Mashi had already heard the good news. Now she saw them coming: Chikku, Bichhu, Binni and the NGO girl who had become more beautiful though composed, now that she held an executive position; her husband having moved higher in the organisation was presently in Germany meeting a few donor organisations.

A celebration was in the offing: Chikku had stood third in the Higher Secondary examination this year. He had been in the news: in the television and newspapers which highlighted his humble beginning and the patronage he received from the Home and the school, and two individuals whom he did not name lest it embarrassed them.

The school and the Home were jointly organising an event to commemorate the achievement. They had come to invite Mashi.

Mashi had been observing Chikku and Binni. Their faces glowed with new confidence like the ones who had ultimately found an anchorage. Chikku was nearing youth but already looked like a man; he betrayed it only when he smiled. Binni had acquired the shyness of a girl in higher adolescence, no longer a fretting footle running through railway platforms; a young lady in the making, frail and graceful. She felt shy at Mashi's keen look and nudged Chikku.

'Mashi you're only looking at us, not saying anything.'

'And to her I don't exist,' Bichhu quipped.

'*Chup.* I'm looking at life, not at a rogue who had destroyed his own long back.'

'I've always been a rogue, ask Chikku he'll confirm.'

'I don't want a witness. I know it.'

'Then stop getting angry and favour me with at least half of your smile.'

All began laughing, Mashi too joined but not before calling him a *Shaitan*.

After the laughter subsided Mashi looked at the NGO girl and spoke.

'I'll definitely join the celebration but I'll sit on the last bench.'

'Me too. I'd always been a back bencher,' Bichhu added.

'And don't ask me to speak and please don't draw anyone's attention toward me.'

'This time I fully agree with you; these are my conditions too. I've already told them,' Bichhu said.

'*Badmash!*' Mashi's short retort.

The NGO girl thought for a while; she had other designs in mind, but she must respect their wishes.

'Agreed. But you two must come.'

'Of course we'll. But where is Bisu?'

'He is worse than me,' Bichhu replied.

The felicitation ceremony was held at a large prayer hall of the school where Binni studied. Residents of other Homes were also invited, particularly from a Home in north Kolkata who took care of HIV positive children.

Media persons took their position at a corner. All the children occupied the first rows, Binni among them. Next few rows were for donors and dignitaries, then the teachers and administrative staff of various schools and persons working at various Homes and then the social workers in that order. Mashi and Bichhu sat on the last bench though at least two rows were vacant before them. When the program started the NGO girl came and sat with them intermittently.

The chief executive of Chikku's Home explained various projects they had undertaken to bring street children to the main stream of society: their endeavours to give these children a future which they never had; Chikku was the brightest example of what one could do given an opportunity. He ended the lecture with a call to everyone to help them achieve their goal, to help them develop many more children like Chikku.

The school principal focused more on Chikku. He said Chikku always stood first in the class examinations, topping in almost all subjects; the school waived his fees, awarded him various scholarships to buy books and stationeries; at his request the school kept the library and laboratory open till 9 p.m.; like all students of the school he had open access to all teachers including himself but he made the best use of it. He was quiet, obedient and focused. They had been confident that Chikku would excel in the examination but that he would secure third position was something they did not imagine. Chikku had surpassed their expectation. He also informed the audience that Chikku was preparing for IIT entrance test. The school would continue to help him clear the test. He was also glad to know the Home had extended his stay there and he thanked the CEO of the Home for such a gesture.

When representatives from other Homes began speaking, the NGO girl came and sat with Mashi and Bichhu.

'You know, we've an intimate relationship with residents of other good Homes whose representatives have come tonight; we hold fests and conduct various games and cultural functions together; residents of one Home know their counterparts in other Homes closely; your Binni not only participates, she also is a good organiser of events particularly those relating to drawing and painting—you must be knowing she is a good painter.'

She now pointed to a boy in the third row with a smiling face and said, 'That boy stayed at a Jessore Road Home. He was picked up from the street when he was seven years old, doesn't know who his parents are, vaguely remembers his village but couldn't recall its correct name; he has also passed this time with seventy percent marks but he is more keen on playing football, already a player of the junior team of a well-known football club in Kolkata; his dream is to represent the state in all India league. And the girl by her side with long hair comes from another Home. Her father left her ailing mother when she was five years old. They had no means of livelihood, were driven out one day by their landlord and they came to Jessore Road suburban railway station. One social worker saw them and informed the Home which was willing to take the child but unable to provide her an accommodation. The mother requested them to take the daughter; she'd find something for herself, but as soon as the girl was out of sight with the Home people she jumped before a running train. The Home counselled the daughter out of depression and she picked up studies and dancing. She has cleared the Secondary Examination this year with seventy six percent marks, her interest is literature—she has already finished studying major Bengali writers and always pesters us for more books; she wants to pursue a career in Bengali literature and become a teacher. Her performance in the role of Radha in a dance drama pleasantly surprised everybody—she was so natural—and just imagine, who performed the role of Krishna, it's a girl from the HIV Home and none could imagine she was a girl till the names were declared by the director of the dance drama. She has also passed Higher Secondary examination this year. I must say this Home is doing an exemplary job. It's the first Home of this kind in Kolkata; presently they house seventy five children who are HIV positive and who are provided with full medical treatment besides all the educational and vocational training like any other Home. The other important thing the Home does is to continuously run public awareness programs in all the districts of West Bengal against the social stigma attached to HIV positives and the possibilities of a HIV positive to live a fulfilling long life under proper care.'

'I'm sure you people are doing exemplary things in converting bits of dirty pieces of clay thrown out by the society, and shaping them into human models and giving them back to society, but dirt heaves up every moment and you can't do anything about it; you're also not mandated to...'

Mashi interjected. '*Chup, chup.* Chikku's name is being announced.'

All three now focused their attention on the stage.

Chikku rose to speak but could not, he was weeping visibly. With a choked voice he uttered only, 'Thank you all,' and sat back. It was the last item of the agenda, the anchor was about to declare the ceremony closed when Mashi saw Bichhu leaving her side and running towards the dais. Before anyone could stop him Bichhu took the mike and raising a hand urged the audience to sit back.

'Probably you do not know that Chikku excels in entertainment too. He is a *Harbola* par excellence. He'd perform it before you right now, and I'll accompany him.'

While the audience returned to their seats clapping in anticipation, Bichhu moved to Chikku, 'C'mon Chikku, show them you aren't a study monger only, you can also make them laugh.'

Chikku looked at his long time friend with amazement, smiled for the first time and embraced him closely. When he released him Bichhu said, 'Let's start.'

The next half hour passed hilariously with laughter, shrieks, encores and 'one mores'.

When the show ended, there was a standing ovation with loud prolonged clapping.

Mashi did not hear anything, only observed the two. She forgot to join the ovation; she wanted to cry but held it back with tremendous effort which reddened her face.

Gradually the hall emptied but Mashi sat there still.

'Hey dear girl, you must be weeping,' Bichhu took her hand to raise her from the bench.

Mashi felt embarrassed, quickly composed herself and rose to join them.

'Bichhu, I've kept my promise to the letter but you revealed yourself,' The NGO girl gleamed.

'What can I do? I can't allow such a joyful event to end in tears. But Mashi is still weeping, though within, look at her face?'

'*Saitan.* Not me, look at Binni, she is still crying.'

All eyes turned to Binni. She ran behind Bichhu to hide herself. Bichhu drew her by his side.

'C'mon Binni. Don't cry like grownups here. Let's all cry like children; "Ha, ha, hi, hi," as we did in our station days.

'Ha-ha-hi-hi...' The NGO girl also joined the chorus.

After walking together for a while they parted ways: Chikku and the NGO girl walked to the Home, Bichhu accompanied Binni to her hostel and Mashi boarded a bus for Sealdah.

Although it was eight past in the night, the bus was full. She stood before a 'Ladies Seat'. The ups and downs of the bus did not disturb her talk with herself. She did not hear the VOICE as she was wont to in situations like this, but she questioned herself on her own: was she getting herself meshed in the web of emotions as ordinary people do? Despite her resolve to keep away from all emotional attachments she fell in love with Jaggu, and now this pair; was it a motherly craze that waited in her womb seeking an opportunity to come out? The VOICE had warned her many a times but she did not care; it must be tired now, gasping; she herself had choked the VOICE.

A girl rose from a seat to get down. Mashi sat in her place. She looked vacantly at the passing habitats and tried to banish all the conflicting thoughts; she needed some peace of mind.

Bichhu was gradually coming out of Harbola shows and concentrating on station activities. Mashi found him frequently talking to porters, cart pushers, loaders-unloaders of goods trains, vendors selling tea and snacks inside and outside the platforms and on the trains, and sundry other people engaged in sundry other vocations in the station area. Bisu was always by his side listening and learning.

The station trade was controlled by a gang of four. They also controlled the flesh trade in and out of the station. It was a big money racket; daily collections in the station area averaged around thirty thousand rupees, part of it went to the police—a fixed sum per week, and some to the hirelings who worked at their biddings.

All members of the gang came from outside, had established their authority by intimidation with the tacit approval of the police. They did not live in the station but elsewhere luxuriously.

It was not difficult for the gangs to guess the ultimate objective of Bichhu but it was not easy to put him off. They offered a compromise, a partnership with them. He refused and met the OC of the police station with whom he already had a rapport, and offered a straight twenty five percent rise in their weekly take. On the other side, he offered a thirty percent reduction to station traders in their daily *tola* or protection money, and creation of a loan fund by setting aside five percent of daily collections: any member of the trade could get a loan of up to five thousand rupees repayable in twelve months at an interest of one percent per month. Bichhu calculated, with all the hikes and reductions he and Bisu would have more than ten thousand rupees daily, a manifold increase from their present earning from *Harbola* shows.

The offers were irresistible both for the police and the station trade, but a big threat to the gangs and the money lenders who charged an interest rate varying between twenty and thirty percent per month. The gang of four now joined hands with the money lenders. First they spread rumours against Bichhu and Bisu labelling them as charlatans; when that failed and members of the trade began refusing to pay *tolas* to them, and take loans from the money lenders they approached the police who looked the other way. They decided to act directly.

The attack came when Bichhu and Bisu were returning from dinner through the twilight area near the goods sheds which they were using for about a week now, abandoning their normal route via the waiting hall.

Three men attacked Bichhu, one concentrated on Bisu while four circled round them. Bichhu was a fighter; he still had that edge though living in peace for quite some time. He put out two of his adversaries quickly. For Bisu it was a first time challenge but he knew it was a fight for survival. While he was fighting his attacker the other four circled around Bichhu, their daggers shone even in the twilight. Bichhu ducked them to seek an opportunity to snatch a dagger. He approached a target that he thought was a weakling, but before he could snatch the dagger he was knifed by another. He fell but not before throwing a hard kick below his rib cage which made him roll down with the dagger flying out. By that time Bisu had his adversary flat on the ground. He saw what had happened to Bichhu. With a hoarse cry he administered a final kick to the nose of his attacker and rushed to Bichhu's aid. The cry was also heard by the loaders who turned to see what was happening. They picked up rods, crowbars, and shovels and rushed to the place with a war cry. Seeing them coming, the attackers fled except the two who were on the ground. Bichhu was bleeding but conscious. As the loaders were about to put him in a taxi for taking him to a hospital he asked Bisu to go to the police station and inform them.

The wound was deep that caused loss of blood but no vital organ was affected. The attacker targeted his rib cage but missed it by six inches.

The police arrested two of the gang members who waited on a platform close to the goods sheds to hear the good news from the hoodlums. A look out was issued for the other two; they never showed up. Four hirelings were also arrested, others fled. The money lenders went underground.

The hospital was full of visitors, all belonging to the station trade, keeping a vigil day and night. Bisu left Bichhu's cabin only when the OC of the police station visited him on the fourth day to record Bichhu's statement.

The OC remarked after recording his statement.

'You are quite a leader, a cunning one I must say, already a great following among the station trades. Any idea of joining politics as Amitabh Bachhan did in his movie, *Coolie*? That's the next step if you play the ball well.'

Bichhu replied with a weak smile. 'I've seen that movie, sir. I'm no messiah like the character played by Amitabh. Mine is a simple trade competition; this time I've won over them, next time I may lose out to some other.'

'A good political statement. Anyway, if you join politics, remember me.' The OC left with a cryptic smile.

Mashi visited Bichhu two days before he was to be released from the hospital.

'Hey Mashi, I never thought you'd visit me.'

'Why?'

''Cause you're angry with me.'

'I'm no longer angry with anyone except myself. I've come here to ask you a question.'

'Fire away.'

'Did you premeditate the attack?'

'Yes. I know I can't hide it from you, you're smarter than all of us,' Bichhu grinned.

* * * *

A good news.

Chikku had secured thirty-fourth position in the merit list of IIT entrance test. He had received calls from all the major IITs but had chosen IIT Kanpur. It was likely he would get a scholarship for waiver of academic fees; otherwise he would take a loan from a bank which was easily obtainable.

Before his departure a small house party was organised by the Home. The principal and all teachers of the school attended. Mashi could not attend and Bisu did not.

After about a month Bichhu and Binni came to Sealdah station to meet Mashi. These days she operated mostly from Sealdah adding more and more stations to her itinerary. After Bichhu moved to the new venture she visited Howrah station once a week only to meet with them.

After eating the fish fries, Bichhu informed that Chikku got a fee waiver but he would have to pay hostel and mess charges which would be nearly three lakhs during his entire stay at IIT. Right now he had to deposit six months charges. It was unlikely he would get a bank loan for this.

'So you want me to remit his savings to him?' Mashi asked.

Binni said, 'Send him my savings too; Bisu also wants to send his.'

'*Chup, chup*', Bichhu stopped them and asked Mashi to tell the amount of total savings of his and Chikku.

Mashi responded after consulting her note book.

'It's one lakh five thousand rupees for Chikku and eighty two thousand for you, so the total comes to one lakh eighty seven thousand.'

'Send him this money; I'll remit the balance in three months time. Let him concentrate on studies without worrying about money.'

Chapter 17

Chintu vanished. Mashi's core team in the station area now consisted of five boys including Biltu who was their natural leader. But Biltu had not been seen around for the last three days. Mashi was used to Biltu's taking a day off in a week for movies, small gambling and drinking but never for three days at a stretch. Mashi never questioned nor enquired about the whereabouts of the boys working with her, but this time she was anxious: had he gone Chintu's way? Should she stop him? Could she stop the inevitable? No. Damn it! Just keep off. Mashi returned to peace.

Biltu returned after six days and met Mashi when she was leaving for work, his face flush with excitement. He implored.

'Mashi, please cancel your trip for the day and sit down to hear me first.'

Mashi was glad to see him back. She thought the boy had something in mind to share with her. Why not hear him? She sat back.

Biltu's eyes looked like round marbles when he spoke.

'Imagine how much I've earned the last five days: six thousand rupees net of all commissions and expenses; food free.'

'Drug?'

'No Mashi, it's not drug, though people come here somewhat drugged by something more powerful than drug.'

'Don't be enigmatic; just tell me what kind of heaven you've found on this poor earth.'

'You're close. It's really heaven for professional beggars and also for touts, brokers, astrologers, *tantrics* and priests who help one negotiate with God; money's just floating.'

'Are you talking about Kalighat?'

'Oh, yes. You know the place?'

'I'd been there once in my earlier life; I saw these people but was too dazed to observe much. Now I recall I also fell prey to some such people.'

'Imagine! If now you play the ball from the other side of the court all of us can make thousands a day.'

Mashi felt the boy must be over-reacting in his enthusiasm. She probed further.

'If business is so good in God's market, you can't enter it so easily... '

'You're right. It isn't easy to enter the racket, a lot of resistance one has to break. Fortunately I've a friend there; he has a small group which he wants to strengthen by inducting some of his trusted friends. And he called me in, which was not liked by other groups. There were quarrels, skirmishes, fights and brick battings; daggers also came out, but we didn't relent. Police didn't intervene initially but as the business of all groups were getting hampered which in turn affected their commission, they asked all the leaders to settle the issue amicably.

'All groups held a meeting at beggars joint by the side of the Milkmen's Park. It was decided that our group being small could raise its membership by a maximum of four. We agreed and peace returned to the place.'

'So you've done a lot of ground work before coming to me.'

'Yes, it's all peaceful now; you'll have no problem. I'm sure you would do wonders there with your intelligence and police connection.'

'Well, I've no desire to live in thousands, am happy the way I'm, but I'll visit the place to find out whether it's suitable for shifting my base there; plans are afoot to reconstruct and expand Sealdah station, I'd be thrown out from my place in two years time, so I'm on the lookout for an alternative place.'

The business was in full swing when Mashi and Biltu arrived.

Now that Mashi observed the place from a different perspective she was amazed to find the congregation of beggars far outnumbered the worshippers and god's agents. She had never seen such a large number of beggars assembled at one place: greater the god, larger the assemblage, she mused.

A worshipper upon arrival at the courtyard of Goddess Kali has to pass through various payment gateways of god's agents starting with paying for a basketful of worship articles, the go-between who has picked up the prey first deciding which basket and which articles to buy. He then carries him through the channel making him stop and pay at different other gateways controlled by other agents named *pandas* and priests to the image of the goddess, and makes him stand there to have the cherished *Darshan* of the image of Mother Kali. The *purohit* in charge of the day now takes over. By looking at him he would make an estimate of paying capacity of the worshipper and match it with the intensity of the prayer to decide the monetary value of the prayer payable to the priest for remittance to the Goddess.

All agents work relentlessly towards relieving the worshipper of the burden of earthly wealth except perhaps the amount of return fare so that when he finally emerges from the circuit he is as light as a child just born, free of all sins.

Mashi experienced this side of the market when she came here with her husband in earlier life and made a costly vow for a child who never came, and she was abandoned at Sealdah station. She also recalled a brush with the other side of the market when she gave alms to at least ten beggars while going in and coming out of the temple.

Biltu introduced Mashi to members of the group. She learnt that many of the beggars did not stay at the temple courtyard or places adjacent to it; they came from other parts of Kolkata and adjoining districts like North and South 24-Parganas, Howrah and Hooghly. Many belonged to families: they came in the early morning by the first trains or vegetable trucks wearing smart garments like jeans, shorts, salwar kameez, leggings, et cetera. They changed to beggar's uniforms before entering the arena.

Mashi was fascinated by observing the working discipline of the beggars: to a casual observer—most worshippers are—they might appear an unruly crowd but a keen observation would reveal their discipline, alacrity to catch a prey, and their ethics—if one is on a prey, others would move away—and finally the acting ability: pretentions of crying and weeping—almost natural—and grasping the legs of the victim, similar to that of Bichhu and Chikku.

It was noon time. Mashi heard a commotion among beggars; all were rushing to the centre of the courtyard where a mini truck had just stopped followed by a large car. Boys and girls chorused in joy, '*Laddu Babu* has come....' as a bulky man wearing a white cap on the head alighted from the car; two women in their mid-thirties already standing by the car touched his feet with as broad smiles as their mouths permitted. With a nod from him the women positioned themselves by two sides of the truck, picked up *laddu* boxes from the truck hold and began distributing the sweetmeats to the beggars already queued up.

The *topiwala* stood there till the distribution was over, hands folded before the chest which occasionally touched the forehead, face solemn though with a touch of smile at the corners of the mouth calculating perhaps how many kilograms of sins had been shed by distributing fifty kilograms of *laddus* among the gods-in-poor.

Mashi did not know at that time that someday she would similarly dole out charities though not at Kalighat, elsewhere; her arguments then would of course be different.

The distribution over, the two women left after picking up their share of *laddus* from driver's cabin and a thousand-rupee note each from *topiwala's* hand.

Mashi learnt there were four such *mashis* who managed distribution of various items of food stuffs such as *kachuri,* orange, local sweetmeats, and clothing brought in by *Babus:* they are also nicknamed by the items they are known to bring regularly. At the minimum four such trucks arrived daily, the number increasing from six to eight during Saturdays and on important lunar days.

Mashi calculated; these *mashis* must be earning not less than three thousand rupees per day. That was a lot of money. Biltu perhaps wanted her to occupy one such position. When she broke the subject before him he spoke enthusiastically.

'Yes. Though the *mashis* are elected by the beggars' council from among the female beggars having not less than ten years experience in begging, you can tilt the scale in your favour by exercising your influence with the police—people here are scared of police.'

'No. I won't do that.' Mashi was firm.

She could now understand why the *mashis* here avoided her whenever she wanted to be friendly with them: word must have spread; they regarded her as an intruder.

With her 'no' to Bichhu she felt light. Slowly she walked toward the *mashis.* They were resting on an open porch of one of the buildings lining the courtyard waiting for arrival of the next truck. Their stiff countenances were relaxed when she told them that she had no intention to join the trade here; she had just come to see the place, would be leaving that evening itself. They relaxed and soon became friends. They shared with her their food and life stories: none of their husbands worked, they lived on their income; though always drunk they no longer beat them lest they walked out; now they were independent and had some position in society; their children went to good schools, some had even joined colleges.

That evening when Mashi was leaving, Biltu was nowhere to be seen but two of the *Kalighat mashis* saw her off to the bus.

This time Mashi did not hear the VOICE. She felt happy to have made the right decision: it was not a question of ethics; in the street ethics was as volatile as flowing liquor, and personally she no longer believed it ever existed among the mankind. Her decision was based on two things: first, she did not need so much money—she had no family to support—and second, she did not really know how to beg though she had beggars working under her goodwill and support.

* * * *

Mashi's income from the station area came down with Biltu's departure with two of her boys. Paltu now worked with the remaining three boys; their average income ranged between Rs. 250 and 300 per day which was just about one fifth of what the group earned under Biltu's leadership. Paltu was no leader; Chameli was but Mashi did not want to bring her back to the station. She had virtually immersed herself in the household she was working with. Whenever she was alone with her and not talking about Paltu she would talk incessantly about the family—the wife, husband and the child.

One alternative was to recruit more boys and train them up. About ten children came to Sealdah station every day to join the street. They were grabbed by competing agencies like NGOs, Dadas and other *mashis*. She could pitch in to get a few of them, but she never competed, preferred voluntary association and never exercised any force or persuasion even when they decided to leave. She did not want to revise her basic principles.

Another issue was whether she would reduce her network activities which now covered a good number of major stations of Sealdah division. Every week she spent a day with a station family to unwind. It had become a habit; she felt bad if she could not make it in a week. She did not want to curtail this.

She thought it was necessary to review her financials which she had not done for quite some time. The last review she had made when Bichhu drew away his and Chikku's savings to finance Chikku's hostel charges.

She now worked in almost all suburban trains originating from Sealdah, which had increased her income substantially besides the pleasure she received from mixing with station families; the loss of income due to Biltu's departure was just a small fraction of it. She realised she was no longer dependent on station area income.

She consulted her bank pass book and the note book where she recorded the savings of others associated with her. She found she had a cash balance of seven lakh rupees, sixty percent of which was her own savings. Even if she did not do a thing, the savings would carry her at least ten years, and for a station dweller ten years was a very long period.

Free from financial worries Mashi began expanding her network to cover more stations except Dumdum junction to avoid meeting with Banku and her family, but deep in her mind she knew some day it would happen.

She would just take a day off unannounced even to herself and come to a station family in the morning with a bagful of vegetables, fish or meat and packets of snacks for the children. She would help the wife in cooking and managing children, eat together and scrub the utensils thereafter. All the time they would be talking incessantly which would turn to gossiping when they rested side by side on the platform near the makeshift *jhopri*.

She found that although the origin of these families and the reason for their coming to station were different, the problems they face were similar; most pressing among them was perennial shortage of money for which they had to borrow money from the money lenders operating in the station area at an interest rate of thirty percent per month. She also learnt, besides these families, food stall owners and hawkers of the station were also regular borrowers: amount of loan varied from rupees five hundred to five thousand. Most of them ended up paying the interest amount only, the principal remained unpaid, and the lenders also never pressed for it, unpaid interest was just added to the existing debt: they were in the cobweb of rising amount of debt.

It occurred to Mashi that she could as well enter the money lending business by creating a loan fund transferring, say an amount to rupees three lakh to another account. She did not expect major withdrawals by her associates; in fact their withdrawals were never more than one thousand rupees at a time and that too only occasionally. So why not make use of a part of this idle money for this profitable venture. In fact, to start with she need not touch the savings of others; she could do it with her own savings; later if the business became successful she might.

Thus resolved, Mashi recalled, Bichhu also did a similar thing for station traders, but he had a socio-political objective; she had no such thing in mind. For her it would be a commercial venture though she would neither be as sucker as the existing money lenders nor as generous as Bichhu.

An interest rate of ten percent per month in place of thirty they were paying now would be welcomed by the station borrowers, but she would insist on a repayment period as Bichhu did. She anticipated the existing lenders would gang up against her as happened to Bichhu but she could not do what Bichhu did to wipe out competition. She needed police support. But she would not neutralise them by paying substantially more than what station lenders paid now; she would make them take an interest in her lending operations.

She found out, in all stations of Sealdah division existing lenders paid the local GRP an aggregate amount of rupees three thousand per month pooled amongst themselves. She thought of sharing with the police forty percent of interest income which calculated on a loan fund of rupees three lakh would be rupees twelve thousand leaving rupees eighteen thousand per month to her, a major part of which would go toward expanding the capital base.

She would inform the local GRP every time she made a loan. It had twin objectives: one, the police could easily calculate their monthly receipt; second, if there was a recalcitrant borrower she would request the police to pull him up, though she would resort to this remedy only for a wilful defaulter.

It was now time to meet the OC, GRP of Sealdah station. One night after returning from work she sat at her corner with pen and pencil to finalise the plan before meeting the OC when Paltu came running to inform that the OC sahib was urgently looking for her. 'Dog in the heat', she muttered to herself and began readying herself for the night's orgy.

He had a quickie to start with. Mashi knew he would be taking quite some time for the second round. She revealed her scheme during this interval. He heard it patiently while smoking, asked a few questions here and there to understand it fully and then spoke.

'I think your Bichhu had introduced some such scheme at Howrah station which, I gather, is working fine even today.'

'Yes sir, I took several cues from his scheme, not the whole; mine is a commercial venture.'

'I could see that. I think it'll work. Now tell me what kind of help you seek from me.' He was quick to understand the reason behind Mashi discussing the scheme with him.

'I intend to work at various stations of Sealdah division. I've shortlisted ten stations. I'd be grateful if you could recommend me to the OCs of these stations.

'Oh, just this. Give me the list tomorrow morning.'

'Thank you, sir.'

She wrapped her mouth around his manhood which began growing fast. Before entering her the second time he advised, 'Why not make a start from Sealdah station itself?'

Mashi was amazed, how could she have missed the obvious! She wanted to thank him again but could not; her mouth got locked with his.

She began discussing the scheme with the station families, station traders, stall owners and hawkers—there were so many, she could not imagine, and most of them borrowed from money lenders, all unhappy with the exorbitant interest rate, would welcome a rate of ten percent, but were skeptic about her capacity to deliver loans at such a low rate—a cock and bull story, voiced some.

Mashi selected the first set of borrowers from among the station families she knew closely. The second set comprised stall owners, traders and hawkers. She took down their requirements that included outright repayment of the existing loan; any additional amount which should not be more than twenty five percent of the existing loan must be paid off by instalments. Repayment period for station families was a maximum of one year, two years for stall owners, one year for traders and six months for hawkers—she was more careful in choosing borrowers from the last group. Once finalised the loan was delivered the next day.

She soon found her initial loan fund of rupees three lakh was fully absorbed by the borrowers of the three wings of Sealdah station—main, north and south; how wise the OC had been! But she resisted the temptation of expanding the loan fund now. She also decided to postpone her overtures to other stations for six months. She needed to gain overall experience of the station loan market, to learn the financial behaviour of the borrowers, locate any loophole in the scheme that needed to be plugged before opening loan books in other stations.

Local lenders resisted, first by spreading rumours, then by threatening and finally by complaining to the OC, GRP who simply asked them to match her offers if they wanted to do business within his jurisdiction; no violence would be tolerated. Sealdah station lenders were not as big and as powerful as Howrah lenders, and they could not find any ally among other traders. They receded to concentrate on the borrowers rejected by Mashi.

Mashi had a good grip of lending operations in less than six months: after all it is a small market, not much complex, the groups of borrowers exhibited almost uniform behaviour. She had decided to add two lakhs of rupees more to the loan fund—half of which would come from plough back of profits and repayment—and expand the business to ten stations originally selected by her. She had already briefed the in-charges of GRPs of these stations and talked with the prospective borrowers.

It was now time to launch, she thought reclining against the wall of the station lobby when sharp retorts came from within her: Why was she doing all these? To get out of boredom of earning a livelihood by showing her brooms and boobs? Bichhu might have also become bored by playing *Harbola* every day and decided to change the vocation. But so much money just to get out of boredom! Her net income per month would soon cross thirty thousand mark, then... forty... fifty... one lakh..., the money she would never need. Why amass so much wealth? For power? Probably. During the past six months she had tasted the power of money for the first time, and she enjoyed it. The passion for power, she realised, was greater than the passion for love. In love heart takes over, mind recedes; in power heart stops, mind rules. Nothing is immoral for a power seeker, no book of ethics, only book of accounts. Otherwise how could she charge an interest of ten percent per month—annualised to hundred twenty percent—from the hapless borrowers? Yes, she had reduced the rate to one third of what was being charged by the money lenders, but it was more to eliminate the competition than altruism.

These questions had nagged her often during the past six months but she had set them aside, busy as she was in implementing the scheme. Now that she had seen success and was getting ready to venture into new markets these questions hurled themselves on her like angry black cats. She always knew the answers and because she knew, she avoided dealing with them.

Yes, she never needed so much money and on this ground she had earlier rejected Biltu's offer of doing business at Kalighat. Her life had been an epitome of frugality; she just needed a maximum of five thousand rupees per month for livelihood including the luxury of station picnics—she was earning more than that from her original vocation, yet she had been squeezing so much money from the poor borrowers! She knew she had been immoral, unethical from the day she devised the scheme; yes, she had been devious and calculative all through, a blood sucker, no different from the money lenders she had weeded out.

The black cats scratched her, beat her, and bloodied her from inside, the pain unbearable, values crashing down. The street despite its turmoil and everyday uncertainty had given her a piece of mind which she would lose if she pursued the lending activity further, the immorality embedded it would haunt her for the rest of life.

'Hey knucklehead! The VOICE roared, who do you think you are? A fucking moralist, a cross bearer of superficial values of a superficial society that had fucked you high and dry and thrown you on the street to be fucked further!'

'But... but... despite everything there are some eternal values which you can't deny in whatever station of life you belong.'

'An incorrigible dumbass! How could I make you understand, values are vomited on gullible people like you by the top echelon of the society so they could amass wealth without any prick of conscience. Don't think they need all the wealth for livelihood as you also don't; they enjoy the process of making money and the power that comes with it. You've also enjoyed both during the past six months. So why bother, just enjoy.'

Mashi was restive, thoughtful and silent. But the VOICE would not let her be. It roared again.

'What are you thinking? Why creating unnecessary turmoil in your mind? The turmoil of the middle class to which you no longer belong but still carry its values. Were you born on the street or had come there at an early age you'd not have the baggage of rotten values. Look at the street children; they aren't bothered about these values. What matters to them are opportunities to make money, no matter how, and to thrive at any cost. They are a restless lot, always mobile, seeking newer opportunities on newer turfs. It's the same at the top layer of society. No values at the top nothing at the bottom, only people like you are caught in the middle. Shed the values as they do and enjoy the power, the luxury and the social status. You're already called Mother Lakshmi by the station dwellers; one day they'd worship you; you'll go places…'

'No, no… no, I don't want to give up all my values for all the allurements you're dishing out before me. Let the riches do it and become richer and richer, I've no such wishes. I live in the street and I don't want to be rich. That's all.' Mashi was angry this time.

The VOICE was conciliatory now.

'Please don't take a rash decision. I know it's not easy to shed the load of beliefs heaped on you over ages. Take your time; review the whole thing from different angles before taking a decision.'

* * * *

After fighting the VOICE for two days Mashi finally conceded that financing was an addiction like doing drugs; she had tasted it and she could no longer live without it, but she could limit the dose lest it destroyed her and others too.

It was one year now, she had not increased her loan fund. She often held long discussions with Bichhu about the management of the lending business. She had already adopted two of his suggestions: one, not to increase the loan fund beyond rupees ten lakh, otherwise it would become unmanageable—the borrowers being located not at one place but at different and distant locations; she could however increase the loan book but only out of repayments. Second, amount of loan to a borrower must be based on the ability to repay: 'Don't falter under any circumstances,' he warned, 'if one is a real destitute make a charity payment, not a loan,' he added. His third suggestion was to engage a dependable boy to help her manage the routines of the business. She decided to increase her loan fund to seven lakh rupees but only after she found such a boy. Paltu was dependable but too young, other boy's working with her might leave any time. She began searching among the grown up children of station families.

She had given up her original vocation of scavenging railway compartments and no longer travelled for free but by monthly tickets: she had several of them for different stations. But she had not changed her dress and she continued to be as friendly with the station families as before. She found that she was being regarded more as a friend-in-need, a wealthy but benevolent woman who was always there to help. She often observed a look of awe in their eyes, a pride to be a friend of her.

She had not abandoned her station picnics, rather did it more lavishly now. Taking Bichhu's advice she had created a charity fund by setting aside five percent of monthly profit. Besides picnics and helping the destitute, she had extended her charitable activities to include distributing new garments to station children once a year, and helping the studying children of the borrowers with school fees and books.

In her search for a suitable boy to assist her she went to the Bandel station with her usual picnic things. In earlier visits she observed two adolescent boys belonging to two families actively making arrangements for the picnic, managing other children and were always at her biddings. This time she wanted to observe them closely; one of them might fit her requirement. After the picnic she took them for a stroll to various platforms of the station. She learnt both of them had primary education in a nearby school run by an NGO affiliated to Bandel church: Fathers in the church loved them, often engaged them to run errands, clean window panes, dust and wash floors; the activities increased manifold during festive seasons like Christmas and New Years Eve. They were paid for every job done. The caretaker's eldest son, a guitarist with a sweet voice supervised their work; payments were made through him, but he never cheated. No, they had never stolen a thing from the church. Fathers told them they would rot in hell if they did; their parents also warned them against stealing: besides rotting in hell they would be thrown out of the church and lose their earnings.

Mashi saw a train leaving the platform. It was gaining speed. She ran toward it, 'Come, just jump in, we'll have a nice ride together,' she asked them as she caught the handle of the passing train. But she saw them standing on the platform stupefied. Mashi could only smile and bid good bye to them: 'Nice boys, domesticated and churched; still children, not toughened and aged by the street, no use to her.' She concluded as she dropped herself on a seat.

She decided to ask Bichhu in her next visit to Howrah station. Of course she would not be asking for Bisu though he was the best; Bisu would never leave Bichhu even for God, she smiled to herself.

'Hey Mashi.'

She was startled by the call, and more startled to see the caller.

Banku approached her with a weak smile, a small girl in tow. Her initial stiffness loosened when she observed him closely: a spectre of a boy famished and tired, eyes drooping; all youthful exuberance blotted out—a good portrait though for a beggar, she could not help musing. But what had happened? The girl must be Chumki equally famished tagging along like a sleep walker.

Mashi squeezed herself for some space, made Banku sit by her side and took Chumki on her lap. She searched out some snacks from her basket and gave them; she could see they were hungry.

'Any idea which is the next station? I haven't gone beyond Bandel.'

'It's Bansberia; you've boarded a train of Bandel-Katwa branch line, we shall be there in two minutes.'

'We shall get down there to have some food; I'm hungry.'

As she turned her face to the passing sceneries of countryside to control her emotion she could not see Banku becoming equally emotional: the quivering lips and wet eyes betrayed his attempt to suppress the emotion.

Mashi ordered equal amount of food for both of them and milk and rice for Chumki. They did not talk while eating, Mashi only nibbled at the food. When Banku finished eating he looked at Mashi's almost untouched plate and asked, 'I find you've not eaten much, can I take them with me?'

'Of course you can, ask them to pack it for you,' Mashi smiled.

They walked back to the station. Chumki was already feeling sleepy; Banku carried her on his shoulder. Mashi located a less crowded corner of the platform. Chumki was fully asleep when Mashi laid her on her lap. She observed Banku was not looking at her but somewhere beyond.

'Where's your mother?'

Banku was startled back to the present and answered quietly.

'She is dead.'

Mashi was not surprised; she'd already guessed.

'How? She was very healthy and stout when I met her. What happened?'

'She committed suicide.'

Mashi was stunned; she did not expect this. She fell silent; all her memories rushed back at once: a loving wife, doting mother, an undaunted spirited woman determined to rebuild her family.

Suicide!

Banku broke the silence; for the first time he wanted to share the travail of his life.

'We couldn't imagine mother would take this extreme step though we had been noticing for some time a behavioural change between our parents. They'd either fight or not talk at all; mother began loving us more than before, becoming more anxious when we two brothers were late returning home while our father was distancing himself from us except when thrashing for no apparent reason. He was particularly cruel on Chumki. We couldn't understand the reason behind such a drastic change in his behaviour as we were always out for the whole day.

'Father was nearly cured of leg injury and began walking on the road without crutches. He'd often return home very late in the night, fully drunk. Those days there'd invariably be loud recriminations and mother would sleep outside the hut.

'Two nights before she died the worst happened. For the first time father beat my mother: he was feral, furious; we thought he'd kill her, but we were so stupefied we couldn't move to her aid, but Chumki ran to stand between them clutching her sari; he caught her by the neck and threw her violently; hadn't I caught her she'd been dead. She began wailing at high pitch that drew the neighbours to our place. They railed him to stop beating her. When he wouldn't relent one of the station uncles slapped him so hard he reeled down. This uncle was a rickshaw puller; he loved us very much, protected us from other urchins of the station area, took father to the hospital, and always refused to take fare despite mother's urging. He looked down at the prostrated figure of father and said, "Next time I see you raising a hand on my *Didi,* I'll break both your legs and you'll be permanently lame, understand?" Father murmured something with folded hands. Uncle uttered, "Bloody ungrateful man," and left. The women moved forward to comfort mother and tend to her bruises.

'That night I couldn't sleep. When others inside the hut fell asleep I went out to lie beside my mother. She was fully awake looking at stars. She wrapped me close and said, "Should anything happen to me, you three must leave the place." I didn't quite understand what she really meant. I said, "You don't worry, father wouldn't dare do this again, he is scared of rickshaw-uncle." Mother didn't respond and I soon fell asleep in her warmth.

'Nothing happened the next day though they didn't talk to each other. She prepared a dinner of fish and rice and we went to sleep peacefully thinking all was over, nothing to worry now. She however slept outside; we thought it was normal, as before, after a big fight.

'Next morning when I woke up I found mother still sleeping. That was unusual. She used to rise very early in the morning, take a bath, finish all the morning chores and prepare food in time for us to leave for work. But that morning the *sigri* was not lighted, no sound of the movement of utensils, nothing. There was an eerie silence. I moved closer and observed bubbling saliva oozing out from her mouth. I touched her body; it was very cold; I put my finger below her nose, no sign of breath. I cried out in despair and ran out to find the rickshaw-uncle.

'When I returned with the uncle I saw a gathering round her body. Krishna was crying hoarse, Chumki urging mother to wake up, and father standing among others, head bent to his chest.

'I didn't know what to do. I clasped the hand of the uncle. He came out of the crowd and holding my hand went hurriedly to the GRP. He told something to an officer who rose from the chair, asked a constable to inform the railway doctor and accompanied us to the spot. The crowd receded back. I raised Chumki to my shoulder and pulled Krishna by my side. The officer looked at my mother's face; her whitish colour now turned black, saliva still tickled down from her mouth. He asked the crowd to pull back further and inspected the ground. Soon he located a bottle which was not visible earlier because of crowd. He tried to read the label of the bottle without touching it.

'The doctor came with a constable. He put a stethoscope on her chest, held her wrist for a few seconds before declaring her dead. The officer showed him the bottle. He picked it up, read the label, smelt it and told the officer, "It's Folidol, must've drunk the whole bottle, a probable case of suicide, send the body for post-mortem," and then he left hurriedly.

'While such arrangement was being made we were asked by the officer to follow him to the police station. My mind was vacant; I was just following the motion. Chumki had fallen asleep on my shoulder. Uncle prodded us along, father and a part of the crowd following. We're interrogated separately: father first, uncle next, then me and Krishna, and a few of our neighbours last.

'We got delivery of mother's body in the evening and cremated her in a local crematorium; uncle made all the arrangements.

'Next day father was arrested. Also arrested was Sabitri auntie. She worked as an ayah in the hospital where father was undergoing treatment. She was very friendly with us, came to our place a few times; mother regarded her as a friend of the family and often gossiped with her for a long time. She also promised her an ayah's job in the hospital. So I didn't quite understand what made the police arrest her. I also had no time to inquire further as I was busy making preparation for leaving the place.

'We reached Naihati station. I started working; thought Krishna would soon find some work at the railway colony. But he was morose and unmindful, would sit on the platform most of the time with a vacant look. I felt he needed some time to recover, so let him be. In the morning after breakfast I'd give him some money for lunch and left for work taking Chumki with me. That was a mistake; I should have taken him with me. He began taking drugs with the money I gave him for food, which I learnt only from the doctor attending to him after he was hit by a train while changing platform and taken to hospital by some station traders. He had a severe concussion on the head, was in the hospital for six months. No bed charge, but I had to buy very costly medicines and take food to him twice a day; that cost me money and time. My earnings reduced substantially, I couldn't buy enough milk for Chumki that made her sickly day by day.

'Krishna was released after six months, but still incoherent, had to be taken to hospital once a week. I made arrangements with a stall owner of the station to feed him and take care of him during my absence at a cost of sixty rupees per day. This continued for another six-seven months. He has now recovered substantially though not fully cured. The doctor said it would take another three months for complete recovery.'

Banku now fully looked at Mashi and concluded, 'I'm tired but not frustrated. Whenever I'm in despair I recall my mother; wherever she is now she'd be happy to see me trying my best for the confidence she reposed on me to rebuild her family. I haven't given up.' Banku's smile was brighter now.

Mashi heard Banku's long story without any interruption allowing him to release his pent up emotion. She was fascinated by his recall of every bit of detail: when you are hurt deeply it occupies a permanent space in your mind, and when you are in crisis only an ideology can help you overcome it. 'But what a boy... is he a boy any longer?'

'We shall get down at Naihati,' Mashi declared.

They reached Sealdah station from Naihati late in the evening. Chameli and Paltu were eating and gossiping at a corner, other boys scattered here and there after the day's work. Mashi called Chameli and Paltu. They came slowly with the half-eaten food in their hands. As soon as Chameli saw Chumki, she chortled, 'Ah-ha, what a beautiful little girl!'

She placed her food plate on Paltu's hand, 'you eat them,' and ran to the water tap to wash her hands before picking up Chumki who was still asleep on Mashi's lap. 'She must've learnt at her work place the need to wash hands before touching a child,' Mashi smiled to herself.

'What's her name?' Chameli asked.

'Close to yours; Chumki,' Mashi replied.

'That's good: Chameli-Chumki.'

Other boys guessed something was happening. They came running. Chameli raised her forefinger and addressed all.

'Look, this is Chumki, my little sister; you must take care of her when I'm away.'

In the meantime with all the cradling and kissing Chumki woke up and began crying.

'She is hungry; feed her some milk and bread, slowly, okay,' Mashi told Chameli.

'I know.'

She ran out to buy milk and bread, all the boys followed her.

Mashi turned to Banku and Krishna, 'You don't have to worry about Chumki any longer; Chameli'll take care.'

They had been observing with amazement as if a drama was unfolding before them; Krishna was trying to get into his weak brain all things happening around Chumki, though with a glint in his eyes; Banku was crying, tears rolling down his eyes.

'Cry as much as you can,' Mashi said; 'Memories suffocate, tears help wash out memories though the scar remains.'

After Banku became peaceful Mashi told him, 'Don't think I've brought you here as a gesture of kindness only, I also have a purpose behind it. I'm no longer scavenging the trains, I'm in lending business and I want you to assist me in that.'

Then she explained to him the operations of the lending business and the job he was to perform.

'You'll be paid a fixed sum of one thousand five hundred rupees per month and a commission of two percent of all collections you make. Together it won't be less than four thousand rupees a month.'

'What happens to Krishna who still requires care and medication?'

'I've thought about it. I'll place him at a good Home which would take care of him and his medication too free of charge. After he recovers fully he may continue staying there for studies or any vocational training. Is the arrangement all right? Can you join me?'

'You're so kind.' Banku was about to cry again. Mashi admonished him.

'*Chup, chup.* Don't cry; the crying prelude is over. I'm not kind; I find you suitable, so I engage you, that's all.'

When Mashi moved to Gariahat, Krishna was in school; Chumki grew up fast under the tutelage of Chameli and was admitted to a Girls Home, Banku continued to work with her.

Chapter 18

Toomba received a call on his mobile phone when he began walking toward Gariahat after making his last delivery. An unknown number. He switched it off.

Boomba was not in town; even if he were he would never call him except from the number recorded with him. He had shared his number only with four persons: Mashi, Boomba, Chameli and Raja. It was unlikely they would re-share his number with any other person. Then? Was it Anti-Narcotics trying to guess his location? Were they close? He was half way between Jadavpur and Gariahat. He became cautious and looked around; found nothing suspicious in the neighbourhoods of the road he was walking. The mobile rang, the same number, again he switched off.

He hid himself at the corner of a bylane. The mobile rang again. By that time he had decided to throw away the phone in the open drain running beside the lane and catch a running bus, but before doing so he wanted to know who the caller was—come what may. He pushed the 'Answer' button and uttered 'Hello' cautiously.

'Hey silent man, is your mobile as silent as you?'

Relief, anger, joy.

Toomba smiled into the phone and asked, 'How could you get my number?'

'A silly question, stupid boy. Aren't you happy hearing my sonorous voice?'

Silence.

'Alright, you don't have to admit the truth. Now tell me what are you doing tomorrow?'

'Nothing but everything.'

'Then meet me tomorrow, eight thirty in the morning at Raja's rendezvous. We shall be doing many things together starting with breakfast.' Toomba smiled at the silent phone.

Toomba spent the night with his friends at Park Street-Free School Street crossing, a walking distance to the meeting place. He reached early.

He had not been here in the morning. It looked so different now; sun rays replaced the neon lights, the birds of the trees flocking out instead of coming in, the sound of their chatter also different from the ones in the evening, only few cars moved at leisurely pace. The place looked so serene now though in an hour's time it would be lost to the progress of civilisation.

'Hey Lord Buddha, enjoying the peace of the place?'

Minu approached with a large bag hanging from her shoulder. Toomba looked at her with appreciating eyes. She wore street dresses, not the ones she wore when they met before, no smell of perfume either; so natural, so close!

'Hey, you're looking at my dress or me?'

'Both.'

'Ah-ha, that's quite romantic coming from a marble man. Now unload this heavy bag from my shoulder.'

Toomba lifted the bag from her shoulder and placing it on the dew-wet grasses of the field asked, 'How many names I've acquired from you since we met first?'

'Quite a few; more will be coming gradually.'

They looked at each other, smiled. Heaven passed between them.

'I've brought all breakfast items from Flury's. Let's eat.'

She pulled out a thick polyethylene sheet from her hand bag, spread it on the ground between them and arranged the food items. When it was done Toomba could not help exclaim.

'Are all these foods for breakfast only or lunch and dinner taken together?'

'Could be, but the reason is different. It was rush hours at Flury's; all Calcuttans seemed to have thronged there for breakfast, all tables occupied and a large queue before the take-out counter. I stood in the queue, no one liked my dress and the smell I exuded, but didn't mind pushing me and touching my body; the one behind me became a little more courageous and placed his cuff-linked hand on my shoulder; quietly I put the heel of my shoe on his instep and crunched real hard. I heard an "Onk" and he retraced fast. After that he maintained, as they say, an honourable distance from me all through to the counter. The reaction of the counter man was no different. "What you want?" he asked haughtily with a wrinkled nose. I put ten five-hundred rupee notes on the counter and asked as haughtily as he was, "Get me all the items you've here, two pieces each." He was flabbergasted; you should have looked at his face. Before leaving the counter I turned back to see the face of my pusher. He looked a standard gentleman with a creamy well-shaved face wearing suit and tie. I advanced my leg a little toward him and asked, "Should I thank you for waiting behind me for so long?" He quickly retraced his steps and uttered, "No, no, please go." And now there all the Flury's right before you.'

They burst out laughing.

After they overfilled their stomachs Minu began repacking the remaining items into the bag. While helping her doing it Toomba asked, 'Have you ever been to Flury's before or was it the first time?'

'I know what you're hinting. I've been there many times before with my friends. Over there people are regarded by the garments they wear, not by the person within.'

'What's the program for the day?' Toomba asked.

'Just wandering... and a little bit of philandering,' Minu replied with a glint in her eyes.

'You lead the way,' Toomba smiled.

'Oh, my god, a leader asking me to lead!'

'I'm no leader.'

'But people in the street regard you as a leader.'

'They're wrong. A leader acts, I don't. Occasionally, I react to a situation or execute a job at someone's bidding, but that's only a reaction. A reactionary leadership is mistaken by people as true leadership.'

'Okay, you're not a leader but a male no doubt, and all males all over the world and ages always exhibit their power to lead and show the way to impress the female of the species.'

'And destroy them afterwards,' Toomba said coolly.

The cool words pierced through Minu's heart. She stopped to regain her composure and noticed for the first time that they had walked quite a distance through the long untamed grass of the field opposite Victoria Memorial Hall. They did not enter the Memorial, which was already crowded by visitors coming from all over the country. They sat on the grass.

'At least as a human male you could have carried the food bag which is still quite heavy,' Minu tried to lighten up the gloom.

'Next time I'll do that, promise,' Toomba smiled.

'Do you know how many times you've smiled since we came here?'

'I haven't kept the count.'

'Neither did I, but I must say many times; quite unusual of you, as they say.'

'Whatever comes naturally to me I do, I don't pretend.'

'Have you ever noticed you have a lot of "I" in you?'

'Yes. In the street it's only "I" that protects you.'

"*Chai... .. ... chai...,*" a *chaiwala* manifested before them from nowhere holding a kettle-full of tea, and clay pots inside a make-shift cloth bag hanging from his shoulder. Minu asked the *chaiwala* to first serve tea in one small pot: if it was hot and good they would take four large pots.

The man poured tea in a small pot and waited. Minu took a sip: except for the tinge of saccharin it was ok. With a nod from her he filled two large pots and left saying, 'Enjoy the first serving, I'll come back after ten minutes.'

'I think you're sitting on the grass with a girl for the first time.'

Toomba nodded.

'You must've noticed the *chaiwala* didn't ask for money for the first round of tea. That's the rule, no cheating here. Anyone breaking the rule would never find a place here any time next. They've photographic memory. I know a few of them. They live in the street, get up early in the morning, buy prepared tea from the road side tea stalls at a discount and sell here at a standard price, none overcharge. The business is brisk in the evening, the place is full, a couple at every meter. These *chaiwalas* also provide ancillary services ranging from giving advance warning of a police raid to touting a companion for you if you're sitting alone counting stars. Want to venture, eh? Come in the evening someday.'

No response from Toomba, not even a smile.

'You're simply a bore. I don't know why people love you. I see the *chaiwala* returning. Let's take the final round and liquefy the crystals of our mind.'

When Toomba was paying for the tea, Minu asked him to give two rupees extra. The *chaiwala* counted the money and left.

'I must say,' Minu said, 'The services don't vary with the amount of *bakshis*; its uniform, still one feels like giving.'

It was a flat statement, no brief for the *chaiwala* but its coolness touched a familiar chord in Toomba's mind. He looked queerly at Minu who was quietly sipping the tea.

Toomba said, 'The crystals aren't getting liquefied. Let's move.'

They rose. This time Toomba carried the food bag.

'Any desire to visit the Museum, its close by?' Toomba asked.

'None.'

'I guessed as much; you hate history.'

'How do you know?'

'A silly question, stupid girl.'

The smile turned into a guffaw. Toomba hailed a passing taxi.

'Where now?' Minu asked.

'Don't ask.'

'That's a man!' Minu smiled mischievously.

When the taxi reached Esplanade crossing, Toomba instructed the driver to proceed to Howrah station.

'Wow! We're on a country tour; that's interesting. I haven't been to country side since I left my village.'

Toomba bought two tickets for Santragachi station. The train left in five minutes. It was heavily crowded, no chance to find a seat.

Overcrowding was not a problem for them. They were used to travelling by overcrowded buses, swaying off and on between pot holes of city roads, jerking and de-fattening the passengers free of charge. The train as compared had a steady run on the rails whatever might be packed inside its belly. But the problem for Toomba was to protect the foods inside the bag from being converted into paste of multiple tastes. He first tried to hold the bag above his head, but some passengers were taller than him, and whenever it hit them they raised their objections not always in civil words. Ultimately he put the bag on his head despite giggles from Minu now pushed to a corner by the crowd.

The train reached Santragachi, a junction station with a five minutes stoppage, but everyone was in a hurry, all wanted to get down first, might be to get fresh air and relax their muscles. Toomba waited for other passengers to leave, so was Minu who now took the bag from him.

'Just giving time to the strained muscles of your arms to relax.' Minu smiled coyly.

'A real naughty girl,' Toomba patted her on the back softly.

That small touch made a shiver run through her entire being. Not that it was the first time she was touched by a male. Her body had been handled, mishandled, malhandled, violently and softly many times before, but this was different. It triggered an implosion inside her more violent than the violence she knew of. To hide and control the surging emotion she lowered her head to the chest, but of no help; she wanted to sit somewhere and cry, but that would be too foolish. She was saved by a loud voice.

'Hey, Tiger!' A group of boys walked towards them.

'Hey, Petka.' Toomba moved forward and shook hands with him and three others of the group.

'Nice chick, well stuffed, where from you got her?' asked a boy winking at Minu.

Toomba saw Minu stiffening, jaws clinched. He tried to save the situation.

'Oh-no, Patka. Never wink at her, little bit of eyeing ok, but always maintain a distance of at least six feet, otherwise even before you start thinking of hurling *patakhas* you'll find yourself in the sky judging the weather above, and she quietly waiting for the next adventurist.'

'Oh, my god!' Patka really retraced measuring the distance.

All others burst into laughter. Minu also joined, which not only dissolved the discord, also calmed the tremor inside her.

Toomba introduced his friends to Minu.

'This is Petka, a guzzler of food; his stomach must be a mile long; that's Patka who made you stiff, he's good at making *patakhas* or indigenous bombs and has never missed a target, and those two standing at the back: the left one is Gaanda, though he handles guns very well he always sings, even between two shots and that's why we call him Gaanda; just notice now also he is singing, and the one by his side is Paanda, always chewing pan and planning devious schemes; these two are always together.'

'A nice pack,' Minu laughed heartily.

'And do you know why we call your friend Tiger?' Petka quipped.

Minu replied. 'Yes I know. He scuds like a tiger but its better you call him Cheetah, he is more like it.'

'And how do we call you?'

'Singhee, the lioness,' Patka said coming a little forward.

'Enough of name giving, now let's have some tea, I'm thirsty,' Toomba declared.

They sat at a corner of the platform. Minu brought out a fifty-rupee note but Petka objected.

'You're our guest; we can't take money from you.'

'Consider me your host and do as I say,' Minu exhorted.

When tea came Minu took the bag from Toomba and spread on the mat the snacks, all intact, no mashing. She smiled at Toomba with thanks in her eyes.

'Wow! So much and so many varieties.' It was Petka.

'Divide them among yourselves, we had enough,' Minu said.

Patka raised one hand with a tea cup and another with a pastry and toasted.

'Welcome Singhee among our midst. Let our friendship last as long as we last.'

The high decibel clapping made many a commuter look back.

Petka asked Toomba between guzzling of food, 'I'm sure you have come to take her around the *Jheel*. This is late February, some species of birds have already migrated but still there are many; Singhee will love the scenery.'

Minu said, 'He hasn't given me any hint of it, a surprise he kept to himself; still a child this Tiger or Cheetah of yours.'

Toomba really smiled, a child caught unaware.

Petka said, 'You know he really loves the *Jheel* and the birds. He comes here at least twice a month and also whenever we are in a jam. He is known to all our adversary groups operating here, his very appearance scares them. You can't imagine the amount of risk he takes. We're all armed in a fight but he is bare handed; he catches a live bomb in the air and throws it back in split second, hits back adversaries with their own knives and guns.'

'I've seen a bit of it and heard a lot about it,' Minu said looking at Toomba but it seemed he was not with them but somewhere unknown.

'Don't bother. He is like this always, hardly joins in any of our talks. After a fight was over—with him it was only a few minutes—he'd quietly leave us, go to the *Jheel* side and spend the night there. Though he never liked it we kept a vigil on him.'

Patka said, 'All serious talks now over; you two come with me, I'll take you round the *Jheel* and acquaint you with the birds playing on its water.'

Petka tried to suppress a smile but ultimately burst out laughing, so also Gaanda and Paanda. It was Petka who responded to the surprised look of Minu.

'Well it's like this. During the season a number of visitors come here; we often act as their guides. Most enthusiastic among us is Patka; he'd often surprise his clients by naming every species of migratory birds and also places they come from. He learnt all these two years back from a birdwatcher with whom we became friendly; Patka was his self-appointed assistant. He'd name the birds, the places of their origin and their habits. He left after a week and Patka immediately began heaving his new found knowledge on his unfortunate clients, but with his elephantine memory he'd often name a Sarus crane as northern Shoveller and switch its place of origin from the Himalayas to North America, or name a Gadwall couple as Mr and Mrs America though they belonged to northern Himalayas. And for the next client all these might change. So, be ready for bursts of bird names which even the birds wouldn't dare imagine'.

Patka rushed to beat Petka but Minu raised her hand to stop him and spoke in his defence.

'I don't think there is anything wrong in Patka's ascribing different names to same species of birds; he may be out of the text book but it doesn't matter. Aren't we doing the same thing; your Tiger is now Cheetah, elsewhere he has a different name. I'm Singhee for you; I also have different names at different stages of my life. This, I suppose applies to all of you. Birds are unaware of their names. They remain birds with all their features and beauties, and don't care for your naming game. So why bother about names, just enjoy the company as I'm enjoying yours.'

They heard her attentively. When she finished Paanda exclaimed.

'Oh, my god! You speak like Cheetah. Are you with him for long?'

Toomba returned to their world some time back. Minu's lecture fascinated him. He smiled at her while addressing others.

'She must've been like this much before we met. I got my first thrashing of life from her in our second meeting. Let's now move to *Jheel* side, and Patka don't suffocate us with your knowledge of birds.'

When they reached the lake Patka and others dispersed to catch clients. Minu and Toomba chose a place on the northern side of the lake. The chirping and chattering of birds filled the air. The sounds were different and distinct, but if one heard them quietly for some time with eyes closed one would hear a well-orchestrated symphony. Minu asked Toomba.

'Are you hearing music beyond the cacophony?'

Yes. I always hear it whenever I'm here.'

Minu's hand moved unknowingly on to Toomba's hand resting on the grass. Again that sweet shock, more profound now. She removed her hand hastily.

'Why, feeling shy, eh? Ok, let me hold your hand,' Toomba smiled taking her hand into his.

The tremor returned. Efforts to control it made her perspire, palm becoming moist, but despite her present state of mind Minu could not help being surprised that Toomba's palm was as soft as a girl's, no sign of toughness there.

They saw a man leisurely walking by their side, head turned to Jheel water, a fluffy poodle following him. Minu uttered, *'chuk, chuk* and spread her hands. The dog came hurriedly and began smelling her first and then licking her hands with amused '*kuin... kuin'* sounds coming from its throat. Minu quickly searched the bag for some crumbs but found instead two patties inside—must have been deliberately put there by Patka—broke one into halves and placed one half before the poodle which immediately began eating it in small bites. The man having walked a distance suddenly felt the dog was not following him. He turned back and saw it eating something from Minu's palm. He came running, stood akimbo before them and blasted.

'You dirty beggars! How dare you feed my dog with your rotten food and dirty hands?'

It was so sudden and full of so much asperity that Minu shuddered and the patty fell from her hand but she quickly picked it up. The dog unmindful of its master's anger continued eating.

'I think your dog likes dirty people and dirty food,' Toomba said coolly.

'How dare you?'

The man was trembling in rage, or perhaps pretending to, Toomba thought as he noticed that though the man was talking to him his eyes were on the torso of Minu. He turned and saw the upper button of her ill-fitting top had loosened exposing a part of her breast.

He replied the man with a wicked smile, 'Our garments may be dirty but your eyes are full of filth; why don't you look at me rather than ogling her?'

Minu looked down at her chest, re-buttoned the blouse quickly and addressed the man with a taunting smile.

'Respected sir, I don't so much mind you ogling through my torn garments; I'm used to your kind of creature, but a small advice to you free of charge; when you're walking with your wife—if she hadn't already left you—be a little more discreet.'

'Hey Cheetah, any problem?'

The man suddenly found himself surrounded by four boys and began fumbling, but Toomba was jocularly merciless. He told the man, 'My dear clean man, I doubt the dog may not be yours, otherwise how could it still eat the patty from her hand despite your protestations?'

Minu suppressed a smile but what Paanda did none could imagine.

'Oh, this poodle! Oh, my dear Fulu-Fulu, I've been searching the whole area for you and you are here? Come now darling; let's have a bath to cleanse your dirt.'

In seconds Paanda picked up the poodle with the half-eaten patty still between its teeth, jumped into the lake and began swimming to the other side.

'Hey... hey...,' the man ran around the lake following his dog at Paanda's hands. Hilarious laughter and clapping made him run faster.

'A real mischief monger, this Paanda. Now go and attend to your clients.' Toomba told the rest.

The place had a natural serenity, Minu thought: It is very close to Santragachi railway station but away from it within its natural enclosure. The number of birds resting on trees bending on the water body, and those creating ripples on its surface while hunting fish or just sporting, and those sitting on the bank of the lake far outnumbered the crowd, their cacophonic symphony absorbing the rumbles of the rambling crowd. One could just sit here and not know how hours passed by. One would be poetic here without being a poet, and philosophic without being a philosopher. And that's why Toomba loved to come to this place.

For the first time Minu felt herself in tune with Toomba. She looked at his serene face and took his hand, not much tremor this time; her entire being enveloped with a unique feeling she could not comprehend.

She wanted to savour the flavour of her new feeling but that was not to be. Paanda after crossing the lake three-four times making the man run around the bank of the lake was finally swimming back towards them.

He rose from the water holding the poodle to his bosom, water dipping on all sides. They saw the man coming with uncertain steps; his heavy breathing very much audible as he stood before them. Paanda thrust the dog at the man and complained.

'The dog is very naughty like you, must be yours only.'

He could not speak but the anger in his eyes could have dried up Paanda's dripping garments. He left hurriedly with a grunt.

'Well served; the swine won't ever come within hundred miles of the lake.' Minu clapped.

Toomba feigned a serious look before speaking to Paanda.

'I know, you'd never admit to having a fever ever, but no client would come to a man with wet garments, better you change them.'

Paanda pulled out two *paans* from a plastic packet, put them together inside his mouth and saluted in obeisance.

'Yes Boss,' he uttered between munches and left.

They returned to their quietude.

Minu came to a sudden realisation that these migratory birds were like them, moving from one place to the other without nesting anywhere. She shared this thought with Toomba. He considered it a while before speaking.

'Your emotional simile is partly true. These birds get kicked out from their original homes by adverse changes in weather condition. But the similarity ends there. They do return to their nests every year with a favourable change in weather. For us there is no return journey.'

'You may be right but how could you be so flat, so insipid to an emotional expression of mine?' Minu mocked anger.

Suddenly Toomba was nowhere though he sat by her side. Minu thought she would never comprehend this off-on behaviour of Toomba. He might have something deep in him where he often dipped switching off everything around him: an incisive wound of a hurtful rejection or an unconfessed sin gone so deep in the depth of his mind it could not find ways to surface? She did not know but felt only a deep love could reach the bottom of his mind. Or, all these were her imagination stemming from her love for him. It might simply be, he read a lot of wrong type of philosophical books. Whatever it is she wanted to resume her conversation with Toomba. She nudged him.

'Hey caterpillar, will you kindly emerge from your cocoon like a butterfly and pay a little attention to the girl sitting by your side?'

'What's that? Any new idea?'

'Yes. Do you read a lot of useless philosophical books?'

'I don't even read a newspaper.'

'One down,' Minu murmured.

'What's that?'

'Nothing. Just answer, do you love me?'

Silence.

'Okay, you don't have to answer that; I was not expecting one either. Tell me what made you save me on that day near Ladies Park when I was fighting the lumpens. We'd just made a small acquaintance a few days back and that too among many others. Boomba and I are known to each other for quite some time. It was usual for him to come to my aid but you flew in gallantly. Wasn't it an exhibition of male chauvinism, an attempt to impress a girl as a prelude to wooing?' Minu tried desperately to keep the conversation going.

'None of that. I just saved myself from committing a sin. The man was in a killing mode. Boomba wanted to rush to your aid but I restrained him; he is a weakling type and he wasn't armed. If I hadn't stopped him either you or Boomba or both would've been dead. So I did what I could and should do. It would have been a sin if I hadn't acted in time, I'd have carried the sin all my life: great sins are committed between should have and shouldn't have, between acting and non-acting.' Toomba went silent.

So it was a sin. But Minu did not dare probe further; she must have touched a raw nerve unknowingly.

It was late afternoon when they rose to leave. After a lot of 'come again' they boarded a down train. Not much crowd now. They sat side by side but did not talk; none wanted to break their individual spell. That continued in the taxi also. When they reached Park Street crossing, Minu asked the driver to stop. The street was coming to lights. They walked on the pavement and stopped before a large book stall below a well-known hotel. Minu hesitated a moment before entering the store. The attendants smiled at her knowingly though with a surprised look at her dress. She examined the new arrivals meticulously, read the first page of some and finally bought two novels.

'I guess you read fictions only, not serious books; I observed you didn't even look at them,' Toomba said as they began walking.

'Yes. I'm no scholar.'

'That's why you live in a fictitious world bereft of facts,' Toomba teased her.

'You're wrong. A good fiction brings out the truth behind the insipid facts.'

'I surrender.'

When they were about to leave the hotel area Minu asked him to mark a beggar woman with a child sitting by the side of a wall-fitted *paan*-cigarette shop.

Minu narrated the story.

'It was last Christmas. I was with a friend of mine. After a couple of drinks we danced till midnight. When we came out he wanted to have a *paan* from that shop. It was a chilling winter night though I was warm due to drinks and dances. I saw that woman sitting there trying to cover the child with a part of her torn sari but it didn't help much. The child was shivering and whimpering in the biting cold. I felt sad and gave her the shawl I wore that night. After five days, on the night of New Years Eve I again saw the same woman with the child behaving in the same manner, but the shawl wasn't there. I felt so cheated I didn't even ask her about it. I know you often do begging, must know a number of beggars. Do they always cheat like this?'

'Beggars don't cheat, they simply fake.'

'What's the meaning of that statement? Minu asked haughtily.

'I'll tell you when I know.'

Their small laughter dissolved the anger.

Minu took a left turn toward the Free School Street and after walking a distance entered a hotel. It was not the kind of seedy hotels his friends often went to; much better, though not a starred one. The girl behind the counter recognised her despite the dress. She handed her a key with a professional smile.

They entered a room, moderately spacious and well furnished. She put the key quietly on the dressing table and stood at a distance from him with a nervous diva like smile on her face. She was taking time, did not want to destroy the moment. For the first time in her life she felt moist without physical manipulation. The unusual thing happened in the morning when Toomba looked amazingly at her and, for the whole day oozing between her legs never stopped, and now it was dripping wild.

She now advanced with a mild tremor in her body, wrapped him with both arms and gave a long kiss. Toomba was cool initially but began responding soon. She felt his hands on her breasts; the nipples of her swelled-up breasts strained to burst out of the linens, a wild rush of hormones filled all pores of her body. She undressed herself and Toomba as fast as the tremor in her fingers allowed. But what's this!

He was flaccid!

Minu raised Toomba's bent head and looked inquiringly at his eyes.

'What's the problem? You can't be impotent... then what... a guilt perhaps, isn't it?'

She put her arms around his shoulders, kissed him softly and spoke assuredly.

'There's nothing to be ashamed of. It happens. Now let's lie on the bed and hear your story.'

Toomba lay on his back looking at the ceiling with narrow eyes as though trying to read something there. Minu waited for some time, then moved closer and placed a hand on his chest.

He shivered a little, gave a constricted smile and began re-telling the story holding her hand firmly on his chest, eyes still on the ceiling. When the story ended Toomba turned to Minu and spoke in a choked voice.

'You now understand why I said sins are committed between should've and shouldn't have. That evening I should've immediately turned back and left but I didn't, I should have killed the man but I didn't. I stood there observing the man making love to my mother and I found myself aroused. I also desired to make love to her the way the man did, and later when I masturbated I imagined I was doing it to my mother. I did what I shouldn't have done. From that day I never masturbated, never tried to get close to a girl.'

Minu heard him silently. When he concluded she kissed him on his forehead with a sweet smile and spoke.

'Stupid boy. All things aren't learnt in the street. If you'd continued reading after leaving the school, you would've known all boys desire to make love to their mothers and girls their fathers. With time this fixation gets diluted though not gone completely. A man searches for the mother in his mate and a girl the father. What happened to you is natural. And anything natural is not a sin.'

Minu's hand had already moved down to wrap his penis within her palm. It began growing and soon stood perpendicular to the base. 'What a majestic spear!' She kissed its tip softly.

'Now shove that inside your mother.'

Minu had never seen a first timer to go on such a long time. She was ready for a premature ejaculation but he went on and on. His endurance amazed her. Later, she surmised he was probably redeeming that fateful night replacing the man by himself or it might be his natural coolness and controlled mind. But right then she was losing a bit of her world around her with every orgasm, and after half an hour it was completely lost to her. And when he came crashing on her it was like a Himalaya inundating the Ganga; she nearly fainted.

Deep in her mind she wanted to hold him longer but her limbs were numb to prevent him from dismounting. How long she lay in this state she could not remember. She came to her senses when she felt Toomba stroking her cheeks calling, 'Hey dreamer, time to wake up now.'

'Why you shattered my reverie?'

'I'm hungry.'

'Disgusting. What a flat statement from such a romantic rogue!' She sat on the bed facing him.

'You'll never change. Now tell me what you prefer, Chinese or Mughlai?'

'I'm no expert.'

'Let's get some light Chinese,' She winked at him and lifted the telephone from its cradle.

'It's time we wear our garments.'

'And be civilised before the room service boy enters,' Toomba added.

When removing the plates after they finished eating Toomba asked, 'I find you eat little. In the morning also you didn't eat much. How could you be so strong eating so little?'

'Strength is like love; it's in the mind, not in the organs of the body.' Minu modified a "quotable quote" of Toomba, which he guessed and smiled.

Minu spoke after being silent for a while.

'Do you know, in contrast to your body your palms are very soft which signifies a sensitive mind.'

'So what?'

'Not much. The only problem is that a highly sensitive person is prone to developing a wrong notion from an empirical observation, expand it by logical steps to formulate a general theory and be guided by it. For example you mistook the deep love of your mother for her husband as a horrible attachment. Some exceptional women do carry the love long after the physical disconnect with the man they loved. They die with this love and become legends of folklore. It's like love of God at its highest level: the two become one, and that's no attachment, it's pure love. For ordinary mortals, love moves to a new abode.'

'But how could you explain her making love to that man while she was attached to her husband so much? Are the two different? I'm confused then, more confused now,' Toomba retorted.

'How am I to value-judge her? She might as well belong to the second category, have fallen in love with the man you wanted to kill or it may be purely out of necessity. But in none of the situations attachment could be presupposed. But you misjudged the whole episode, became scared of attachment from what you observed and concluded that since its love that brings attachment you must maintain a safe distance from love situations.'

'I could guess you're in a destruction mode tonight, shattering all the guiding principles of my life. Now Goddess Kali, just tell me in simple language: attachment is good or bad.'

'That's a good name you've given me though I'm much fairer than the Goddess. As to your question I'd say attachment is a disease. Love doesn't demand attachment; it's independent in its own beauty. When attachment tries to subjugate love it moves elsewhere.' Minu stopped for a while then said, 'I might add that love is the only cure for attachment.'

'Have you learnt all these from the novels you read?'

'To an extent, yes.'

'Are you suggesting I start reading books again?'

'No. You can write one, but later; now let's make love,' and she drew him close to her.

They made love four times that night; it was wilder and more wanton each time.

Toomba lay exhausted and was asleep soon. But Minu wanted to remain awake to celebrate with herself the most beautiful day of her life. She knew it could never be repeated. What a pleasure it would be if she died tonight. Even otherwise she would be stepping into the dying age of the street soon. So why not tonight?

She went on fighting the approaching sleep repeating, 'Let me die tonight, let me die.'

Toomba woke up late in the morning; no sign of Minu anywhere in the room except a note on the pillow:

I want to reminisce *alone* all the beautiful things that happened to me yesterday, nay from the day I met you. You'll be there but your presence is *not* necessary.

Don't feel shy of asking for breakfast, its waiting there.

Chapter 19

Six years had passed since Mashi moved to Gariahat.

Chikku had cleared his B.Tech from IIT, Kanpur with a high rank in computer engineering, got a job at a multinational company based in Pennsylvania. He could not come to Kolkata before leaving for United States as he was busy arranging for travel documents. He had promised to come to India in a year or two. He wrote Binni regularly.

In the meantime it was becoming increasingly difficult for Mashi to continue staying at Gariahat. Besides routine raids by the police to fill up quotas, pressure was on them to clear important areas like Gariahat of street vagrants due to rising threat of terrorist activities. Last August, a day before the Independence Day, the local police swooped on the street dwellers and *lathi-charged* them to vacate the area. As she was known to the OC, Gariahat—one of her old paramours—she was not thrown out but pushed to a small nook among stacks of construction articles abandoned by Public Works Department. The situation had not changed much since then. The OC told her he had order from top to keep the area off the vagrants. He asked her to look for some alternative places; he would also be on the lookout. Meanwhile he asked her to open a tea-snacks stall at her place; he would try to get her enrolled as a member of Hawkers Association, the police did not touch them as they enjoyed political patronage. If that did not happen she would have to move to another place.

Mashi called Minu one day and told her the problem; there was no point in discussing the issue with Boomba—he was useless—and Toomba did not care, but as Minu moved to places she thought she might help find a place where she could move in case she was driven out; she did not care where it was except that it must be a street dwelling place.

Mashi seeking help to find a dwelling! Minu wondered: the richest woman of the street, who could easily live off the street any time, was anxious to find an alternative accommodation!

But Minu also knew, she was like her, would never leave the street; both of them hated society, were scared of re-entering. And Mashi never sought help from anyone except perhaps from the police. Was she getting old? The shine of her youth was receding but sparkles were still very much there to move men. The OC would definitely do something for her. But at the same time she wanted to assure her.

'Mashi, don't worry. We exist in filth. The society can only move the filth from one place to the other, can't erase it. So we always find a new mound. I'll definitely keep my eyes open.'

At this point they heard Kajol's ever cheerful voice.

'Hi Minu, hey Mashi, are you discussing something serious?'

'Not very serious; you may as well sit here,' said Minu.

'Then meet my boy friend, Rahim.' Kajol brought forth a young man by hand and introduced him.

'I've heard a lot about you from Kajol,' Rahim addressed Mashi.

'Must've, Kajol is an incessant talker,' Mashi quipped.

Rahim was tall, well built with a groomed moustache, a well-trimmed beard and always had a smile on his face. A good choice this time, Minu thought.

Kajol said enthusiastically, 'You know, he lives in his own hut at Narkeldanga, earns good money, and also knows cooking; not like me.'

'Which part of Narkeldanga?' Mashi asked.

'It's below the northern part of the bridge; you know the place?' Rahim asked

'A little bit… once upon a time… forget it. Have some tea and snacks with us.'

'Where are your toddlers?' Kajol asked.

'They no longer toddle, they walk. Chameli takes care of them. I only keep an eye during the day when she is away for the household job. She comes back in the noon for a while to feed them with foods she brings from her present *baudi* who is as good as the earlier one. They've also learnt to stand and walk under her tutelage. She has also named them, Google and Googlee. Look, they are coming towards us; the one with a round vermilion mark on the forehead is Googlee.'

Kajol put down her tea cup and ran toward the children. She carried both to her shoulders kissing them all over and made them sit between her and Rahim, broke a chocolate bar into two and gave one each to them carefully peeling off the outer cover.

'Rahim presented it to me; he doesn't understand, I'm no child; now it has gone to proper mouths.' Kajol smiled affectionately observing the children munching the chocolate.

Rahim rose; he had to make an urgent delivery. Minu also rose; no point discussing Mashi's problem before her. Kajol followed her after trying to give a kiss to the children but they shoved her away busy as they were in eating the delicious bar.

They entered a roadside food joint. Kajol ordered two plates of Chow Mein. 'It's on me; Rahim has given me hundred rupees; isn't he good?' she asked.

'Must be,' Minu concurred.

'You know, we shall marry soon; his second, mine you know.'

'I could guess.'

'He says he'd come to a lot of money in a month's time from a big deal. Then we'll have a gala marriage in some hotel. I'm inviting you in advance, you must come.'

'Of course I will.'

Kajol now whispered to her.

'Let me confide to you; I already have sex with him. He is very good, did it for a long time unlike my previous one-minuter husbands. But the sad part is I won't be able to give him a child; I'm barren. He loves children so much, but says don't worry, we'll adopt one, and then it will be a lovely family: me, my husband and a child. You understand, its private between you and me, don't tell others.'

'Of course I'll not,' Minu assured though she knew by tomorrow everyone in the HS group would know about it.

'Incorruptible lover!' Minu murmured to herself as they bade good bye.

* * * *

Mashi had not moved from Gariahat, rather she consolidated her position.

She used some construction materials stacked there like wooden planks, drums and tarpaulin sheets to build the tea stall complete with counter, racks and storage. It no longer looked like a nook, rather a spacious stall. One day a junior police officer came with a constable while the construction work was going on; they took two thousand rupees offered by Mashi and left.

She however did not abandon the 'ownership' of her original space, though open now on all sides, which she used to meet people relating to her other vocations.

The OC, Gariahat helped her secure a membership of the Hawkers Association. She had to pay ten thousand rupees as entry fee. In addition she would pay fifty rupees per day as membership fee. The leadership of the

Association maintained relationships with all important political parties. So whichever comes to power their position remained unassailable.

Mashi bought another tea stall close by for thirty thousand rupees, the old owner leaving for his village permanently.

She herself looked after the first stall, a young boy picked up from a street family helped her generally and distributed the tea and snacks to employees of various trade establishments twice a day, the money paid by the owners on monthly basis. For the days she was away she would ask a woman from a street family to run the stall. For the other stall she chose a woman from another family, two boys from two different families acted as her helpers. Six percent of sales were paid as commission to the woman and two percent each to the helpers.

Presently an amount of rupees ten lakh circulated in her lending business. The additional capital had come from accumulated profits; she had not touched her savings or that of others. Of late she had been thinking to limit the loan fund to its present level, the profits she would invest in bank fixed deposits. Bichhu had long warned her against further expansion as it would be unwieldy. She was already feeling it.

Banku would come every evening with the counter foils of bank deposits and an account of day's collections. She had opened accounts with four different banks at strategic places where Banku would deposit collection amount whenever it exceeded rupees two thousand. Now that bank operations were computerised the amount could be deposited at any branch of the same bank. When the accounts were settled Banku would leave with the next day's collection list. He would often bring new loan proposals from existing or new borrowers. She would invariably visit the borrower whether existing or new; assess the requirement and repayment capacity before taking a decision. She would also meet the OC of the concerned stations to personally hand over the packet.

Now that his brother and sister were well settled, Banku had much less to worry, his health had improved, signs of approaching youth visible. He had learnt the basic dos and don'ts of lending business. His net savings with Mashi was nearing a lakh of rupees. She encouraged him to employ a part of it in lending business. Initially he began funding request for additional loans from existing borrowers. It remained in her name but the accounts were kept separately. She had in mind to hand over the entire lending business to him some day when he was mature enough to handle it independently.

Mashi continued her charitable activities and station picnics, but restricted them to stations within her area of operation.

She would visit Howrah station every fortnight to spend time with Bichhu, Bisu and Binni who was now a teacher of the school where Chikku had studied. The school had provided her a campus accommodation. She majored in Philosophy and obtained a first class in B.A. (Hons.). Her M.A. final examination was due in three months for which she was studying hard to get a first class. Chikku had told her if she did well in M.A. she might get a scholarship for doing Ph. D. in an Ivy League University of United States.

Binni had been coming to Howrah station every evening since Chikku left Kolkata. She preferred studying here rather than in the hostel; she had special permission from the school authority. She would dine with them and Bisu would accompany her to the hostel. Mashi never missed her whenever she came to Howrah station. Even if Bichhu and Bisu were not around she would see her studying quietly in the dins of the station occupying a space between platform number five and six—must have been 'reserved' for her by Bichhu—a boy would come every half hour and place tea and snacks before her. She always carried her painting articles and a small easel which she would place by her side and turn to painting whenever she felt bored reading.

Bichhu had gifted Binni a laptop on her graduation. Instead of writing long letters and waiting for weeks to receive a reply she now corresponded with Chikku by email, though he could not always send a prompt reply as he was a busy man now. Besides talking over mobile telephone they could now see and talk to each other through Skype. On appointed date and time all of them including Mashi joined together to talk to Chikku 'face to face'. They also had a fair idea of his apartment as Chikku walked through different places of the apartment while talking.

Chikku was now a manager of a newly set up department of innovation and it was unlikely he would get leave before one year. Binni was sullen for some days, did not talk to anyone, nor replied to the mails sent by Chikku. After a lot of consolation and coaxing by Bichhu and Mashi, she showed signs of relenting. Finally Bisu declared, 'If that learned idiot couldn't come now ask him to send us an American pre-marriage dinner by overseas mail'. Binni beat him for this but that melted the ice which though was already breaking up.

Chameli had stopped fighting Boomba for his long absence—at least five-six days every fortnight—did not also question him about the big money he brought on return. She now knew why he was doing all these and she had the 'assurance' of Toomba. She had also shed her 'untouchability', allowed Boomba to hold her hands, permitted occasional kisses and did not mind his accidental brushing of her breasts.

Of the two kids Googlee had been running a high fever for last ten days. Mashi took her to a doctor near Triangular Park as suggested by Kajol who also accompanied her on the first visit. After the second visit and some changes in the medicines her body temperature began receding, and now it was slightly above normal. The date of the third appointment with the doctor coincided with the date of ceremonial distribution of garments Mashi had planned for the station children; the OC, GRP of the station was to preside over the function. The appointment with the doctor was fixed at ten in the morning and the distribution ceremony to begin at 11 a.m. It would take about an hour to reach the station venue even if she took a taxi from Gariahat to Sealdah station. The doctor would take at least fifteen minutes to examine Googlee if he called her at the appointed time which he hardly did. She could request Chameli's *baudi* to release her for an hour for taking Googlee to the doctor but she would be highly displeased as it was her busy hours. The OC, GRP would also be displeased, and the station children disappointed if she failed to reach the station in time.

When she was in deep thought to find a way out of the impasse she heard, 'Hey Mashi, how is Googlee today?' Kajol had already picked up the child to her bosom, Rahim standing by her side smiling.

Mashi felt they were godsend. She smiled at Kajol and asked, 'Would you do me a favour? I've to take Googlee to the doctor at ten but I've an urgent appointment elsewhere at about the same time which I can't avoid. Can you take her to the doctor?'

'Oh, that's not a problem at all,' Kajol said loking at Rahim who nodded.

'Thank you very much.' Mashi gave her five hundred-rupee notes, three for doctor's visit and two for any medicines he prescribed. She advised Kajol to hand over the child to the care of the woman who was running the tea stall for her today on return from the doctor.

The ceremonial function was over at quarter to one. After she had tea with the OC during which time she also handed him the monthly packet, Mashi boarded a down train leaving at 2:15 p.m.

She felt happy, always so after such a function. The glittering eyes of the station children when they received colourful garments gave her a feeling of fulfilment. As the train speeded off she began exploring other avenues where her charity could flow; the fund was growing in size every month.

Her mobile phone rang. It was Chameli. She sounded frantic: when she came to feed the children at 1 p.m. Googlee was not there. The *Didi* at the tea stall said, Kajol didi and Rahim bhai took her to the doctor at quarter to ten and never returned. She tried to contact Kajol didi several times but her mobile phone remained switched off.

'Contact Boomba and Toomba immediately,' Mashi advised.

'I've already telephoned them they would be here within an hour.'

Don't panic, sit quietly, I'll be there soon.'

Mashi was thinking hard, weighing various possibilities: What could it be? An accident? Kidnapping? Or anything worse? Whatever it is must be very serious. By the time the train reached Sealdah station she knew the answer.

'It was my mistake,' Mashi murmured after boarding a taxi.

Boomba had already arrived before Mashi reached Gariahat. Toomba would arrive in five minutes, Chameli informed.

Boomba and Chameli had already met the doctor who said that all of them left at ten thirty. Mashi's face turned stony, jaws clenched visibly.

Toomba got down from a taxi, walked without any haste and sat before Mashi.

Mashi looked straight at Toomba's eyes and spoke crisply with a steely voice emphasising every word.

'Rahim—Narkeldanga—Ilabu's godown.'

'What about Jaggudada?' Toomba was as calm as Mashi.

'I don't care. I want the girl and the child back alive and intact at any cost,' her voice did not waver.

Toomba rose without any further question. He moved aside and began telephoning. When Boomba went by his side he asked him between calls, 'Do you have a dagger or something?'

'Yes. It's with Mashi.'

'Get that but keep it hidden.'

When Boomba came back Toomba was still talking. He indicated him to stop a flying taxi. It was already evening when they boarded the taxi. Toomba told the driver, 'Narkeldanga Bridge, fast.'

They took a left turn from the other side of the bridge and walked a few minutes to arrive before a large dilapidated godown, small rays of light seeped through various cracks of its tin roof; except that it was pitch dark everywhere, no street lights, nothing to illuminate the place.

A boy manifested before them from the darkness. They walked some distance from the godown and stopped under a tree. Toomba asked quietly.

'Is that Jeetu?'

'Yes.'

'How many have come?'

'All the twenty five you asked for.'

'How many exit doors?'

'Two. One in the front and the other at the back both bolted from within.'

'Any sound from inside?'

'None, perhaps they had taped their mouth.'

'How many bombs?' 'Ten.'

'Guns?' 'Five; all others have daggers.'

'We can't break open the door; they'll kill the girl and the child first if we do. We've to find other ways.'

Toomba looked around and saw a gleam of light coming perhaps from a lantern.

'That must be a tea stall, let's go there.'

It was. A young boy with a glum face was tending to the boiling water in an aluminium saucepan. He put a handful of dust-tea in the boiling water and looked up.

'Where's your father?' Toomba asked him softly.

'He has gone to the market… I can't give you tea… don't waste my time.' He replied angrily without a pause.

'But you're already preparing tea…'

'Yes, but it's for those *goondas* of the godown, not for you. I'll deliver a kettle of tea to them, close down the stall and go home.'

'Okay. But you may give us at least a biscuit each.' Tommba proffered a fifty-rupee note.

'I don't have change.'

'It's alright, keep the note for you.'

'All of it!' The boy smiled for the first time.

'Yes, all of it,' Toomba smiled back.

As they were munching biscuits the boy gave them some tea from a mug kept by his side. Toomba took a few sips of tea and then spoke casually.

'You're a very good boy. Do you take the tea inside the godown?'

'No. they never allow me inside; I just knock the main gate twice and shout, *chai, chai; a chutiya* would open the gate partially, take the kettle from my hand and close the gate but not before slapping my face shouting, *'Pille,* you're late again!' but you know I'm never late, but that motherfucker wouldn't hear me: *Sala harami,* can't even stand properly on both legs, must be lame; god must've punished him for being such a rouge.' The boy fumed.

Toomba said, 'You're absolutely right, he is a real *chutiya* and *harami* too. He'd taken from me three thousand rupees a year back, and when the time came to return the money he just vanished. Now I got information he is hiding in that godown with his double *chutiya* friends. If you could help me a little I may recover my money and also give him a lesson of life for beating such an innocent boy.'

'Will you beat him good? I also want to but my father will be very angry if I join you fighting them.'

'No, no. You don't have to fight; we'll do that for you. When the tea is ready you just carry the kettle there, knock the gate as usual and shout your *chai... chai*, and when that *chutiya* opens the gate hand over the kettle to me and run. I'll deliver the tea for you and beat him up solid. Now keep this hundred rupee note, it's all yours, hide it somewhere safely, your father shouldn't know.'

He took the note and said smilingly, 'That's all I've to do? No problem at all. The tea will be ready in two minutes, another three-four minutes to close down the stall. You wait for me there; I'll arrive in ten minutes time. But promise me you'll at least break his right hand with which he slaps me every day.'

'I promise.' Tommba replied as he rose with others and briskly walked back towards the godown.

They sat under the same tree and Toomba began explaining the plan to Jeetu.

'We must get the child and the girl unhurt. There will be five groups of three each; one of them must have a gun, the rest daggers. The remaining ten boys will form two groups of five each; they shall guard the two gates and kill anyone who tries to escape.

'When Jaggu opens the gate I'll hold him by the neck, your group will push open the gate and enter, all others shall rush in simultaneously. Four groups shall take positions at four corners. Your group will cover the captives. There shall be no indiscriminate firing—one shot one down. Don't spare anyone. No bombing now, I shall tell you when to. Entire operation must be finished in ten minutes. You understand the plan?'

'Yes.'

'Now go and organise the groups; they should be ready before the tea boy comes.'

Boomba heard Toomba silently so far with wide eyes, though not visible in the darkness. It was a war plan and Toomba, the General, was a real leader though he abhorred the term. In the darkness also he could see the familiar solemn face of Toomba, calm before the launch of war.

Now he asked, 'What is my role?'

'You'll escort Kajol and Googlee back to Gariahat after it's over.'

The operation was over in less than ten minutes. They were just six; an unequal fight, six against twenty seven. Toomba had information that Ilabu gang had about thirty dangerous merciless men; might be he had shifted his maiming factory elsewhere—no sign of maiming activity here—and used this facility for some special business. What's that?

Jeetu fired his first shot; it was Rahim who was running toward the girl with a gun, down now.

Ilabu did not run; he aimed at the girls with a shining revolver

Toomba told him with a level voice, 'Hey *basta*. If you harm them this one goes first, then you,'

For a moment Ilabu's attention got diverted toward Jaggu whose tongue flapped out of his mouth. Toomba tightened his grip further.

Jeetu fired.

Other three fell almost simultaneously with Ilabu. The boys now gathered near Toomba. Someone said, 'All down except the one you're holding. What to do with him?'

'Not much; he is already dead.' Toomba released his hand and Jaggu fell with a thud.

Toomba now turned to Boomba who stood by his side with dagger in hand. Toomba now turned to the corner where Kajol and Googlee lay bounded and asked Boomba.

'Cut the threads with your dagger; remove the tape from Kajol's mouth only. Let it remain on Googlee's mouth, you shall remove it only when you approach the Narkeldanga Bridge.'

Toomba went out the front gate and told the five boys, 'It's over, but you continue to keep the vigil for anyone approaching the godown.'

He returned inside through the back gate after instructing the boys there similarly. Kajol stood there wrapping Googlee to her chest. Boomba stood by her dagger in hand.

'Give the dagger to me; take Googlee from her, Kajol is rather weak now.'

He now chose two boys and told them to follow the departing party from a distance. 'Kind of stalking, you understand? When you observe them boarding a taxi, just vanish.'

Kajol stood before Toomba, her lips quivering.

'Don't cry. Leave the place fast. And hold your tongue till I ask you otherwise,' Toomba smiled.

After they left Toomba asked the boys to search the place.

'There must be money here,' he said as the boys began searching, 'When I was holding Jaggu I noticed two brief cases near Ilabu. One must contain the traffic money they'd already received; else we wouldn't have found them unharmed. The other might be drug money. All yours now.'

One briefcase contained six lakhs in six bundles of thousand-rupee notes; the other had five lakhs in ten bundles of five-hundred rupee notes. They also found some bottles of whisky, a box-full of drugs in small blocks covered by thick polyethylene sheet. Jeetu tore open a block and smelled the drug.

'It's pressed hashish blocks of 1.5 gram each, good quality,' He declared.

Toomba now called in the other boys from outside and advised.

'Collect the revolvers, hide the notes and drugs under your garments but don't take the whisky bottles, rather pour their contents on all the six bodies. Now leave the place in one and two after throwing all the bombs inside the godown. Meet tonight itself at some place and share the loot equally among yourselves. After it's over just vanish and remain so for about a week. As for me I'm taking my share now.'

He picked up seven blocks of drug and left.

* * * *

Toomba reached Sealdah station after the last suburban train left. He switched off the mobile phone, hid it under an abandoned railway carriage in the yard and slept on the roof of the morgue.

Construction activities were still going on though it was more than three years now that the authorities had embarked on expansion and reconstruction of Sealdah station. It was unlikely the morgue would be shifted as it was already far outside the platform areas of the station under the new plan.

The contractors were always in short supply of labourers. Toomba had no problem in joining them. He found that these labourers were mostly farmers coming from different districts of West Bengal and neighbouring states like Bihar and Orissa after the harvesting season was over. Some commuted daily, others went to their village every week end and those from other states, once or twice a month. While their departures were known their return to work was very uncertain.

The labourers and the masons who stayed in the tent spent their evenings in small groups scattered all over the workplace; some sang village folklore accompanied by a *dhol* or an aluminium pan which would be used later to cook food, some played cards with small stakes, others just gossiped mostly about their village and family, and occasionally vented their anger against the contractors with choicest abuses. The *chaiwallas* moved from one group to the other with kettle-full of hot tea and plastic cups in their hands and locally brewed hooch in polyethylene pouches inside the side bag. Merry-making would be over by about nine in the night. Some would go out of the station area for dinner while others prepared theirs inside the tent or under some shed. By ten, the yard was asleep.

Toomba mixed with all the groups. They began liking him partly because he spoke very little, listened more with occasional nods and partly because he spent lavishly on foods and drinks. When they went to sleep he walked out quietly and slept on the roof of the morgue after taking a block of hashish.

One evening he went to Raja's place to inform that he would not be available for delivery job for a fortnight. Raja did not ask the reason as he knew he would not get it, but he was very glad to see him coming unannounced. He immediately proposed a gala party where all the subjects of his kingdom were invited. He walked to the middle of the canal stretch, called all and declared his intention. All came out to receive the good news including Gullu who looked much sober now. Toomba saw that belligerent girl among them now blossomed to youth and exhibited girlish shyness when Raja asked her specifically to join the party. He learnt the girl would be married soon to a boy from another *bustee*; Raja did the matchmaking, and was presently overseeing all the arrangement for the ensuing marriage. 'The marriage ceremony would be grander than this party, you and Boomba must attend,' he declared, and then called Gullu and some others to discuss the arrangement for tonight's party.

Toomba felt, although Raja was egoist and epideictic, he had a benevolent mind; those who were the recipients of his benevolence did not really care about his occasional misdemeanour like that girl and Gullu and many other families in his kingdom. But there was also another group who resented his ego privately, but did not mind accepting his largess; deep in their mind they wanted to be like him but did not have his capabilities. This type would be the first to betray him when the endowment flow dried up or he became weak due to some changes in his material environment. But the first category of people would stand by him in such situations. Boomba belonged to the second category, perhaps.

Raja nudged Toomba and proceeded toward his hut. Along the way he asked a boy to get them some chips and nuts.

The hut looked the same, no change in inside arrangements either. Raja opened a bottle of whisky and spoke between pouring drinks into glasses.

'You must've heard Ilabu's outfit had been burnt down; it was a big fire the newspapers say.'

'I don't read any newspaper.'

'Oh, I see. Any way, they say six charred bodies were found inside, though there was in fact no inside because the entire structure gutted down to the ground. The fire brigade appeared after one hour and the police after two hours. The police believed it was an intra-gang affair. The underground grapevine also subscribed to this view as in-fighting has intensified to take control of the gang which doubly confirms Ilabu's death. The police had put their hands off: "Let them kill each other" kind of attitude.'

Raja took a sip of whisky after putting some peanuts inside his mouth and continued.

'It's a good thing the bastard is dead; he maimed children, an evil man. Of late he began trafficking and also entered into drugs, though not the one we deal in: the inferior cannabis varieties where competition is stiff; it could be one such competing gang that destroyed him.'

'Hey Boss, all's ready,' Gullu shouted from outside.

The party continued late in the night. Good food, bottles of drinks, dancing and singing— a grand binging event. Every one turned blotto, fell one after another and passed out.

Toomba woke up late and by the time he reached Sealdah station it was noon. He missed the day's work, climbed to the roof of the morgue and slept the whole day.

A week had passed. Toomba took out the hibernated mobile phone and put it to a station outlet for recharge. The first call he received after he switched on the phone was from Minu.

'Hey Colonel, now you're over ground I suppose. I've been telephoning you three times daily for past two days. I've not been able to get anything out of them including Kajol, our great talker. I employed all my tricks but failed miserably. This time you've gagged them fully. Ultimately I could not help but settle for the director of the drama. I'm throwing a party at 7:30 p.m. today to commemorate the grand success of the drama, the same guest house at Lansdowne I took you once. I'm informing others. No excuse is welcome.' The phone went dead.

Toomba came to Gariahat at 6 p.m. and went straight to Mashi. She smiled and indicated a stool to sit on. She was frying a huge quantity of *pakoras*. 'All these go to my customers with afternoon tea, but you'd get a few, just wait,' Mashi said with a motherly smile which he observed when he met her first, though that time the smile was directed at Boomba, not him. That evening also she was frying *pakoras* though of lesser quantity.

'I've retained Kajol to run the tea stall since that incident; look there, the kids are also with her—these days they always move about her. Now eat some *pakoras* before they come to collect them for distribution,' Mashi handed him a plateful.

Toomba did not bite into the *pakora*, he looked at her eyes. Mashi felt uncomfortable. To brush it aside she came straight.

'I know Jaggu is dead. No, they haven't told me, I also didn't ask but I know. I shouldn't have stopped Paltu and his gang to do it when he first tried to snatch babies from our stretch. It was my fault. But womenfolk are that way. Now I don't care, womenfolk are this way too. Mashi's eyes wetted; she turned to hold back the droplets.

She still loved Jaggu: womenfolk are this way also, Toomba thought; Minu was right: love goes beyond attachment.

Kajol came to collect the *pakoras* the toddlers clinging to her and saw Toomba. She exclaimed with her eyes only but Googlee blurted out, 'O... O... O...' and jumped into Toomba's lap.

'See how some incident gets stamped on a child's fragile memory. If she had all the vocabulary she would have described the event, as you say, blow by blow. You can gag a grown up but not a child.' Mashi smiled sweetly at them. Googlee's chortles helped her recover quickly.

Kajol said, 'I'm coming soon after making arrangements for distribution of *pakoras*. Chameli would be here by seven.' She left with Google; Googlee continued to sit on Toomba's lap sharing some bits of his *pakora*.

Mashi said, 'I understand Minu is giving a party tonight. She has invited me also but I won't be able to make it because Banku would come with account books during that time.' She paused a little then added, 'Minu is a nice girl with a mind of her own, isn't she?' She smiled at Toomba with a twinkle in her eyes.

Toomba did not respond.

'I know. You don't have to tell me. Girls in the street dote on you but she is special.'

Boomba startled them with his sudden appearance.

'Hey Mashi, any *pakoras* left for me? Or you've given all to Toomba.'

'*Badmash!* Toomba isn't a guzzler like you, take your share,' Mashi handed him a plate with a benign smile.

'Googlee is more *Badmash* than me. See, she already knows whom to humour. But where's Champi?'

'Don't get mad; she won't be able to come before seven, has to prepare dinner for *baudi's* husband.' Mashi admonished Boomba and turning to Toomba said, 'Chameli's *baudi* has gone to her father's place, would be back after a month or so when her delivery is due. She has also taken her two children, so Chameil has more time now as that of last year when the wife's second baby was due. But this Paltu is nowhere to give her company; it was the same last year also. What would she do? She spends her free time playing with the toddlers and helping Kajol in the tea stall. And now he misses her by the eyes, *Badmash!*'

Chameli came at 7:15 p.m. and they immediately started off. When they entered the party hall Minu was arranging a table at the centre with the help of a steward of the guest house. She put two plates of assorted snacks in the middle flanked by two bottles of red wine and just one bottle of whisky. Foods were arranged on a table near the back wall waiting to be warmed up.

Minu dismissed the steward saying, 'I'll press the buzzer when it's time for dinner; you aren't needed before that.'

She now placed two vases of white flowers on two ends of the table. Her face looked tired but jubilant when she declared, 'It's a gag-off party, not a binging one. Two bottles of wine are for ladies and only one bottle of whisky for the lads. Now please take your seat.' She bowed like a well-groomed hostess. They burst out laughing.

Minu poured wine in three glasses and only a small measure of whisky into the other two. After they took their respective glasses, Minu raised her glass to a toast.

'For Kajol, Googlee and our beloved Mashi.'

The glasses clinked and they took the first sip. Now Minu declared, 'All grandiose formalities over, now let's hear the gory tale.'

All eyes except Minu's focused on Toomba but Minu nodded her head negatively.

'No, no, not Toomba; he is a one liner except when he makes statements on life and living; he'll finish the story in one sentence like: we went there; found Kajol and Googlee tied to a pole, neutralised the adversaries, and sent back the girls to Gariahat. I don't want that, so Toomba is out.'

The high pitch of laughter with thumping rattled everything on the table and the chandelier above. Even Toomba could not help joining them. When the laughter subsided Minu looked at Boomba.

'Your gag's off. Tell us the story in every detail.'

Boomba recounted every bit of the preliminaries beginning with Mashi's stern overture, Toomba making phone calls, planning the operation, storming Ilabu's godown, destroying all of them ending with freeing Kajol and Googlee, and Toomba's gag on Kajol. 'I think I haven't missed much,' Boomba rested.

Chameli and Minu heard the story with awe. Even Kajol also had the same look; she had no idea of what kind of preparation went behind the rescue operation, the scale of risk Toomba had undertaken, and all that just to rescue two street girls! Kajol felt like crying but Toomba would not like that. She spoke instead, 'Toomba, we all know you're our leader but…'

She could not finish as Toomba raised her hand to respond, but Minu interjected.

'I know his answer. It's like this: I'm no leader. A leader acts, I don't. I only react and execute a job, it's only a reaction and a reactionary leadership is mistaken by people as true leadership.

'Have I correctly rephrased your answer?' Minu winked at Toomba.

'Are you pulling my leg?'

'A little bit. Now my dear Marshall would you please tell us in more than one sentence what you did after you sent them off to Gariahat.'

Toomba smiled, others suppressed laughter.

'Actually there's not much to add. We searched the place, found some money and a box of drugs. They took them away and bombed the place before leaving.'

'Some improvement over one liners. Now spare another line; what's the amount?'

'Eleven lakhs.'

'Wow, so much money! What for, any idea?'

'Part might be traffic money, part drugs.'

'Which means they were already sold out!' exclaimed Chameli.

'I suppose so.'

Minu noticed a shudder in Kajol's frame.

'What happened to all the money?' Boomba asked.

'I told them to share the money equally among them.'

'And your share, how much?' Boomba again.

'What my share? They did the operation, they must take the loot. I'm grateful to them for helping me rescue the girls. They however didn't mind my taking seven blocks of hashish which helped me spend my days in exile,' Toomba smiled widely.

'Okay, Lord Shiva, the interrogation's over; you're acquitted,' Minu said.

'How many names I've earned today?' Toomba quipped.

'Only three if you consider the morning call; for a street boy it's nothing,' Minu grinned. The discussion was about to end when Toomba noticed some restlessness in Boomba.

'I think you've something in mind.'

'Yes. You always say you're not a leader but how could you organise so many boys with guns and daggers at such a short notice.'

'Stupid! An organiser is not necessarily a leader. Mashi is the leader here, not me. As for the guns, these are available on hire any time at five thousand rupees a day with six cartridges. I made a mistake in over estimating their numbers and they underestimated our ability to offer a gun battle. Ilabu knew the street boys are not used to fighting with guns and they had six six-shooters which could wipe out thirty persons in seconds. So I'd asked Jeetu to help me; he controls a *tola* racket in Rajabazar-Maniktala area, close to Narkeldanga; he himself owns a gun and the rest he hires. They were the best marks-men in his protection squad.'

'What a devoted company of friends you have who would come to your aid with all their might at such a short notice,' Kajol exclaimed.

'Oh, my dear ever devoted girl, by now you should realise your version of devotion doesn't exist in the street. Here faith, trust, devotion, belief and things like that are highly volatile, they change from one moment to another, even the definition of friendship changes to suit one's immediate needs. Jeetu may not come to my aid next time. We fight amongst ourselves for small things, beat up each other to prove who is the boss, change sides without notice; we betray all the faith-trust-devotion combine without batting an eye lid. And we don't mind. That's the beauty of the street.'

'But, then...' Boomba was about to say something but Minu cut in.

'I know what you've got in mind. Despite everything what Toomba has just said, if there comes a threat on a street dweller from outside the street system—remember Ilabu no longer belonged to the street—friends combine with all their might to prevent the onslaught. I've experienced this twice. And that's another beauty of the street. Am I correct Guruji?' She again winked at Toomba.

'That's another addition to my nomenclature,' Toomba smiled. 'Yes, Minu is right, and she could say that. She has a wide network of friends possibly wider than mine and that includes people from the society as well. In fact she herself could have executed the rescue operation, may be in a different way. And if it comes to that she is faster and fiercer than me. Am I correct Madam Lakshmibai?' Toomba returned the wink.

'That's a good one,' Minu replied.

'Which one?'

'The naming one; you're a fast learner.'

All clapped and chortled like children in play.

Boomba raised his hand amidst laughter. 'I've a complaint. Toomba didn't allow me to participate in the operation, except cutting the ropes tied around the girls and bringing them back to Gariahat. He also took away my dagger, hasn't as yet returned it to me.'

'Well it's like this: you aren't toughened like other street children, if it were Chameli I might have allowed. Besides, you live inside a glittering cocoon with Mashi and Chameli. I don't want to rupture that. As for the dagger, I've thrown it into the canal while crossing the bridge. Sorry, you would've to buy a new one,' Toomba nudged Boomba with an expansive smile.

'Ok. You're forgiven. But you must thank me for abiding by your command like a disciplined soldier; I didn't fret. And now I'd join others to thank you for wiping out all those evil men.'

They raised their hands to clap but stopped observing a constricted smile on Toomba's face. An uncomfortable silence loomed on the table. It was Toomba who broke the silence.

'This is the second time I've heard the term, evil, and I'm pained. Everyone is evil in one way or the other, so why label Ilabu and his gang particularly? This is a vague religious term thrust upon us by the society. We won't survive a moment in the street if we allow the pseudo value system of the society to interfere in our daily struggle for survival. Besides, who are these Ilabus? They have risen from the street. So why carry a rancour against them? I wouldn't have destroyed them if they had surrendered and let the girls go. I was more pained to kill Jaggu. When I was giving the final twist to his neck Mashi's face flashed through my mind. Although I had a clear mandate from her, I knew deep in her mind she would have been happy if I'd spared Jaggu, though at the same time she knew I could not and I did not.'

A pale of gloom was about to fall but Minu would not allow that. She quipped, 'Many quotable quotes of the evening, and we shall begin using them from tomorrow morning. Presently I'm very hungry, you must also be so; I'm calling the steward for warming up the food. Let someone unlatch the door.' She pressed the buzzer.

They ate in near silence, partly because they were very hungry, partly because the steward was there and partly because..., but Kajol could not help a quibble.

'Minu, you're a great liar! You said you're very hungry but you've taken the least food among us.'

'Oh, that one was just to break the spell. In fact I tasted all the foods to find out whether they were as good as I wanted them to be, and this one or two spoonfuls per item filled up my stomach,' Minu said casually.

'A smart liar is always superior to a truth teller,' Toomba remarked blandly.

At last the dinner ended with a happy note. When they rose to leave Minu spoke with mock seriousness, 'I find none of you except Toomba is tipsy; you may walk the street easily. I'm holding back Toomba; he needs some straightening up.'

'Yes I know, only you can straighten him. Bye, have a busy night,' Kajol was out on the street before Minu could catch her.

They took time walking up the stairs, Minu resting her head on Toomba's shoulder, he holding her by the waist. He unlocked the door, kicked it open, she back kicked it to close.

Four walls of the room reverberated with sounds of their smacking lips.

Chapter 20

Mashi had more free time now.

Kajol had proved to be dependable, efficient and innovative. Besides adding a variety of tea preparations like black tea, lemon tea, *masala* tea, diabetic tea, double milk tea and the premium priced Darjeeling and *malai* tea, she had also introduced a selected range of coffee preparations. The range of snacks had also increased to include cookies and patties.

Mashi was amazed to discover her ability to make intricate cost calculations for every item and fix a competitive price after making a survey of the market. Initially she sought her approval but now she had left everything to her discretion.

Kajal had also coordinated with the woman of the other stall in introducing similar items there and exchanging inventories between the stalls to minimise inventory level and wastage.

Sales of the two stalls more than doubled and profit trebled. The woman of the other stall and also the helper boys were happy because their commission income had also doubled. Mashi had increased the wage of Kajol to five hundred rupees per day of which two hundred for keeping accounts and overseeing the other stall.

The girls of the HS group would often visit Kajol and Mashi to gossip about happenings of the street and share their lives' worries. All their talks ultimately ended with some quotes of Toomba.

For some time now Kajol had been asking Mashi to acquire another stall nearby where besides tea and coffee they could also sell ready-to-eat foods. She found out that profit in the food business was not less than thirty percent of sales net of all expenses. Mashi could guess her prime motive behind the project: to find employment for some of her friends in the HS group. Good girl, she thought and decided to fulfil her desire. She requested the secretary of the Hawkers Association to look for a suitable space.

Kajol had perhaps come out of love mania and seemed to be diverting all her energies to managing the stalls. But you never know, Mashi smiled to herself. She only hoped Kajol to be more careful this time, though she knew it was wishful thinking.

Mashi had extended her twice-a-week station family picnics to a feast for all the station dwellers. She would be away for the whole day on such occasions but would invariably return to Gariahat by 7:30 p.m. except on the days of her fortnightly visit to Howrah station when the time might get extended by another hour. On such days Mashi allowed herself the luxury of travelling by taxi.

On one such return journey, inside the peaceful space of the taxi Mashi began reminiscing her long journey from the day she was abandoned at Sealdah station. She was thrown out of her family by the person she loved most. Her concept of love shattered and she took a vow never to fall in love again. But what happened? She fell in love with Jaggu, a love she still carried in her heart despite his misdemeanours and her ordering his destruction.

She avoided being caught in a family situation, always maintained a formal working relationship with all her associates: a give and take policy, no obligation from either side, any one could leave any time or withdraw money kept in deposit with her—no questions asked, she never exercised any authority over anyone.

The policy worked fine and kept her in good stead. But with all these self-imposed restraints had she been really able to avoid creating a family? No. Despite warnings by the VOICE she went ahead to create a conglomeration of disparate families.

She ran out of Banku's family lest she fell enchanted to a familial picture, always avoided situations where she might meet him, but could she look the other way when she saw him in distress? Yes, she made it clear to him that it was simply a give and take proposition, nothing beyond, but was it just like that? Unconsciously she took the position of his mother. Otherwise why was she thinking to pass over her lending business to him—her heir apparent?

Then this Chameli and Paltu, now Boomba. She procured them and brought them up for a selfish purpose. But over time the relationship had gone beyond that. Although she never enquired what Boomba was doing, but hadn't she become anxious when she learnt he had entered the drug trade?

Google and Googlee were under her care similar to Boomba and Chameli and she would be treating them similarly as they grow up.

And who was this Toomba who hardly spoke but exuded confidence of the eldest brother of the family whom she could task to perform so risky a job, and which he did without questioning. Wouldn't all these converge to anything but a family? She was enjoying all the pleasures and concerns like any other family person.

Otherwise why would she never miss her fortnightly visit to Howrah station? She no longer worked there, nor did she have any financial relation with them, except Binni and Bisu whose original deposits she still carried. Then why she yearned to go there and why she felt so shocked and perturbed seeing Bisu bandaged round his head and his left arm resting on a sling?

She felt agitated when she learnt that their enemies whom they thought to have neutralised fully had reorganised to regain their lost position. Some mercenaries engaged by them waylaid Bisu when he was returning after dropping Binni to her hostel. A repeat scenario: he was overpowered but saved in time by some coolies. He was in hospital for a week, would take another week to fully recover. She knew Bichhu would take good care of him and indeed he did; he also identified the persons behind the attack, informed the police who swung into action and put them behind bars under such sections of the Indian Penal Code as to put them off for at least seven years; not that the police had suddenly become very humanist, they were indeed protecting their thick weekly packets. Bichhu handled the matter competently, then why did she feel so concerned?

And why did she feel so overwhelmingly happy when Bichhu gave the news of Chikku's coming to India in a fortnight's time and joined Bisu in teasing Binni who showed a glum face because Chikku would be staying in Kolkata only for three days.

And now Kajol, a new addition to her ever-expanding family for whose satisfaction she was on the lookout for a space to launch a ready-to-eat food joint, though she never had in mind to own a chain of stalls.

She had many more boys and girls working with her in streets and railways; there were also the station families and station dwellers, some of whom were very close to her but none belonged to her family. Unconsciously she had created different independent units of families which rotated around her, bound to her only by empathy, not by any blood relation. Was it a family at all or just a fanciful imagination of her traditional mind?

'Incorrigible woman! Do you know what you've created is far superior to a conventional family because it is boundless. And in the process you've betrayed the basic ethos of the street: it's only survival that matters here, nothing else.'

Mashi had heard the VOICE after a long time. She thought she'd buried it forever, but no, it was very much there, and it prowled on her at a time she felt fulfilled. She reprimanded the VOICE quietly.

'You've a narrow outlook. I live in the street and I've never betrayed the ethos of the street. Survival is not simply physical survival, a mental survival as well and I'm trying to achieve both. What's wrong in that?'

'Your sufferings will manifold,' The VOICE vanished.

Mashi knew what the VOICE had indicated. Whenever she felt fulfilled something would happen to test her resilience, but she never bothered. This was also part of living.

* * * *

It did happen one after the other.

It could not be said Toomba did not except this to happen someday or that he was not warned; he simply did not care. Jeetu asked him to take one of the six revolvers they collected from Ilabu's godown but he refused.

One day after finishing his day's delivery he walked through various by lanes of Bowbazar Street to reach Sealdah. As he was passing through a construction site to make a short cut he received a call from Jeetu on his mobile inviting him to a party to celebrate their victory. But instead of hearing a 'yes or no' in response Jeetu heard:

'Ah-ha, Gattu! So you're now the leader. Congratulations! But why aim four revolvers at me, you want to catch me or kill me; but why? You should rather thank me for killing Ilabu to make way for you to become the leader of the gang,' Toomba smiled from ear to ear.

He was thinking fast: they would not kill him, at least not now, must have other things in mind. What's that? He must continue talking.

'Where's the money?' Gattu asked in a hoarse voice.

'What money?' Toomba mocked surprise.

'The forty lakhs you've stolen from Ilabu's place.'

So, that's the reason. But either they had wrong information or Ilabu must have siphoned off twenty nine lakhs without their knowledge. Toomba laughed out so loudly the revolvers shook in their hands.

'Look, you people can't even hold the revolvers properly and you've come to kill me? What a pity! Besides, you're a big fool. Do you think if I had all forty lakhs I'd have been here? I'd have fled the city the same night to Mumbai or Chennai and enjoyed a good life there. Let me tell you, I'd not seen any money. Ilabu must have hidden the money somewhere else to cheat you. Search his other nooks, you might recover the money.'

Even in the dim one-bulb light of the construction site Toomba could observe Gattu being uncertain.

'Who else was with you?'

'A stupid question. Jaggu and Rahim must've told you earlier I don't require collaborators for a small operation like that,' Toomba again smiled.

'Boss, he is lying. Let's take him to our factory, I'll take out his balls one by one with my tong and before I begin sharpening his pencil he'll retch out everything.' The tallest among them implored.

Gattu nodded and addressed Toomba.

'Lamboo is right. You must be an inveterate liar. Just tell the truth and we won't harm you, else I'll hand you over to our canal side experts, and I promise you'd start parroting in less than two minutes, but by that time you'd have lost one or two limbs, say your balls as Lamboo desires.' He smiled menacingly.

Toomba lowered his head as though considering their proposal. He was thinking hard: all information passed over through the mobile, it was now time to act. They had one weakness: they would avoid killing him here itself; he could play on that advantage; but could he take on all the four, doubtful as they were all armed, but he could make an attempt. Also the phone must be destroyed as it contained classified phone numbers.

'Hey Lamboo, take this.'

The mobile phone sped like a flying saucer and hit Lamboo on the throat. Toomba jumped at the same time, kicked Gattu on the rib and snatched his revolver, fired at the mobile phone to destroy it and then pressed it to the ear of the next man. But suddenly he was hit on the back of his head and fell unconscious. He could not guess there could be someone watching his back.

Toomba opened his eyes inside the cabin of a Nursing Home. He was soon fully awake and smiled at Jeetu sitting by the bed.

'You're out of danger now and okay on all parameters. The doctors said your nerves are extremely strong and that probably saved you. He's advised a few more days rest to come out of your bodily weakness.'

'How many guns do you possess now?' Toomba smiled.

'You're just incorrigible! It was the first question that came to your mind! Ok, let me calculate: one plus six plus nine equal to sixteen.'

'Oh! You are an army now.'

'You won't hear how we did it?' Jeetu was somewhat offended.

'I knew you'd be coming and that's all for me, but I won't mind hearing your gallantry,' Toomba grinned. Jeetu now pulled a chair by his bed, sat comfortably and began retailing.

'We more or less followed your strategy. All the twenty five who participated in the last raid stormed into Gattu's canal side maiming factory. This time we carried ten guns, seven own and three hired. We gave them no chance. The first group of five having two guns covered you and the rest killed all the fifteen in about five minutes. I asked two of us to rush you to the Nursing Home.

'When we're about to search the place we're startled by a chorus of mixed sounds coming from the other side of the godown. We noticed about thirty-forty people huddled together, some clapping, some crying, some just shouting hoarsely, a high pitch, hi... hi... hee... hee... ha... ha piercing intermittently through all other sounds. Then they began moving toward the bodies lying in a semi circle. Some of them moved on threes, some on fours, some tottered like hunchbacks, the one-legged hopped, two-legged either had one eye or none but hurried nonetheless following the sounds of others' movements, two one-eyed ones carried on their shoulder a girl each whose legs were severed from the waist. It was a ghastly sight. We stood stupefied. But they didn't so much notice us. I could only hear someone shouting amidst din, "Well served, the bastards." They began kicking the prostrated bodies, turned them up, again kicked, the two-legged helping the one-legged do it, those who could, began dancing on the bodies, others crawled up and smeared their faces with the blood oozing out from their bodies crying, hi... hi... hee... hee... ha... ha.

'Leaving them to their workings we began searching the place; there was not much money—about a lakh only, probably the day's collection from the begging business and some third-class chandu type drugs. We didn't take the money, decided instead to give it back to them. I tapped the back of a girl sitting astride a body to tell that we were leaving the money for them to share. She turned to me, her face smeared with blood, locks of hair undulated over it revealing a socket where there once was an eye; she looked at me with the other eye and a hee... hee... haa... haa... issued from her toothless mouth. I back tracked, felt as though all witches of Goddess Kali were let loose on the corpses in the battle field. One might say we just ran out of the place.'

Toomba noticed Jeetu still had that horrified look in his eyes. He said, 'Your simile is good but the sight was pleasant.'

'Oh my god, you find pleasance in it! It was horrible.'

'For you it was horrid, for them it was pleasant.'

Jeetu renewed his invitation for the big party, bigger this time for two victories and his recovery. Toomba requested him to postpone it for a few days; he had to catch up with things.

A day before Toomba's release from the Nursing Home, Jeetu gifted him a mobile phone loaded with a SIM card.

'Purchased or stolen?' Toomba asked.

'Pilfered. I can't show disrespect to you by buying one; this is the last piece left from the contingent we unloaded from a truck,' Jeetu broke into a wide smile, so also Toomba. They shook hands with cryptic understanding.

Toomba made the first call to Minu; phone switched off. The next call was to Mashi. She responded, 'Come quickly.'

* * * *

Mashi was holding a discussion with four girls of HS group when Toomba reached Gariahat, a length of medicated tape still covered the back of his head. She looked up and asked him to sit and dismissed the girls who rose to proceed to Kajol's tea stall. One of them asked.
'What happened, anything serious?'
'Not much, some small skirmishes.'
Mashi looked fully at Toomba's face; the remnant of illness still visible, also somewhat emaciated but his eyes still carried that impassive look.
'How long in the hospital?'
'About a fortnight.'
'Must be Ilabu's friends and for the money you stole,' Mashi concluded quietly.

Toomba was always surprised by her sudden bursts of intelligence, her ability to tie up things quickly and arrive at a conclusion. Her smiling face betrayed a cool analytical mind, and on top of all she exuded a warmth that drew people to her. He looked around to find Chameli or Boomba.

'Chameli is in a Nursing Home', Mashi said as if following his thought, 'and Boomba hasn't yet returned from his fortnightly disappearance.'

Toomba waited for Mashi to elaborate.

'You know Chameli's *baudi* has gone to her father's place. That morning when she had gone there to prepare breakfast for her husband he informed that he had invited three of his friends to a small party. He asked her to buy some chicken legs, pomfret fish, nuts and snacks. He gave her the money and the door key and asked her to come at five in the afternoon for roasting the chicken, frying the fish and arranging the dining table with polished glasses and cutleries: his friends would be coming around seven in the evening by which time everything should be ready. Earlier when *baudi* was here she helped arrange such small parties. She knew the cooking and had seen before the arrangement of the table. She welcomed these kind of parties because plenty of leftovers would be there which she would carry here to share with us. But this time she was a little nervous as she was to do everything alone. I encouraged her saying someday she'd have to do everything alone and this could be her testing ground. Chameli left for *baudi's* place at 4:30 p.m. and I for Howrah station at 5 p.m.'

Mashi stopped for a while and asked Kajol to bring some tea for them. 'I'm coming in a second with *malai* tea,' Kajol replied raising her hand.

Mashi said, 'You must be thirsty, I should've offered you tea at the first instance, but the delay would be more than compensated when you taste Kajol's *malai* tea, her own innovation.'

Kajol requested her friends to take care of the stall and carried the tea and some patties on a tray. When she was handing the tea Mashi said, 'This girl has saved Chameli's life in more ways than one. It's better she tells you about the incident.'

Kajol sat by Mashi's side and said, 'Good news first. Durga has just come back from the Nursing Home and informed that Chameli's bleeding stopped in the morning, and for the rest of the day she remained dry. The attending doctor said she's out of danger now though it would take a few more days for her to recover from the shock. Once that is taken care of her physical recovery will be faster and she would be completely cured in about 3-4 weeks. He has already given a call to a psychologist for counselling; he would be meeting her tomorrow morning. But Toomba, now that you've come I'd request you to visit her; you can restore her confidence much faster than the psychologist.'

'I'll definitely do that. But tell me first what had happened to her?'

'Oh yes. On that night I had two friends with me at the stall. When we're closing we saw Chameli running, no, wobbling across the road. I felt something wrong. Mashi had returned a few minutes back. Before I could tell her anything Chameli reached Mashi and fell on her lap repeating one sentence, "I fought but they were four..." I looked at her; she was bleeding profusely down the waist. I could immediately guess what had happened. I'd this experience twice before. I told Mashi. She gave me twenty thousand rupees and asked us to carry her to the Nursing Home at Dover Road. While we're about to pick up Chameli Mashi asked me to tell the hospital people that she is the niece of Shankar Roychoudhuri, and get her admitted as Chameli Roychoudhuri, also to tell them that Shankar Babu would telephone them soon.

'She was admitted quickly. The doctor said she needed blood transfusion immediately but the Nursing Home did not have her group of blood and asked whether we were willing to donate blood if it matched with hers. We said, yes and they tested our blood, only my blood matched. I gave blood once that night and another the following morning. After that there wasn't much problem. She began recovering and today she is out of danger.' Kajol ended with a fulfilling smile.

Mashi spoke after Kajol left to attend the stall.

'I went to Roychoudhuri's house and knocked the door. He opened it and before he could do anything I pushed him hard and entered the drawing room. He knows me, saw me more than once: first when I accompanied Chameli to his house and later, on quite a few occasions when I bought and delivered vegetable and fish at *baudi's* request.

'I sat myself on a sofa and asked him to sit on another opposite me. I saw his right hand bloodied, he hadn't found time to tend to his injury, but I didn't care. I told him, "Chameli has been admitted to the Nursing Home at Dover Road as your niece with your surname. I know you've good relations with them; your two children were born there and probably the third one would also. 'You shall telephone the Nursing Home now confirming it, so that she receives the best treatment and tell them you'd pick up the bill."

'Observing his hesitancy I assured him, "You shall do it in your own interest. If Chameli dies, you are destroyed."

'He understood and picked up the telephone. After he finished talking to the Nursing Home I spoke.

'Good. Now give me a lakh of rupees as compensation; I'm being moderate, my friends will be angry when they hear I let you go with such a small amount. Also give me the addresses and phone numbers of your other three friends, I might need their help."

'He had his head bent, didn't answer immediately. I felt, for the first time, he had begun to realise the magnitude of the crime he and his friends had committed.

"You promise, you shall not go to the police, and keep the affair a secret?"

'He went inside, brought the money and wrote the addresses and contact numbers on a paper. I counted the money, scrutinised the paper and left.'

When Mashi finished Toomba asked, 'How much savings Chameli and Boomba have now?'

Mashi was surprised to hear such a disjointed question, but Toomba had always been like that. She consulted her books before replying.

'Three lakh eight thousand plus the new addition, say four lakh. I haven't visited the other three; I might get another three lakh from them.'

'I'll visit them, give me that paper.'

Toomba read the addresses and commented, 'I find one lives close by—three or four blocks from Roychoudhuri's, one at Shyambazar and the third in the Deshpriya Park area.'

He turned to Mashi, 'Does this Roychoudhuri own a car?'

Mashi had decided not to be surprised any longer. She answered, 'Yes, he has a car.'

'Large, medium, small?'

'Very large.'

'Hey Kajol, will you give us two more cups of your *malai* tea, bring one for you too?'

'I'm coming in a second,' Kajol replied jubilantly.

When Kajol brought the tea and sat with them Toomba asked, 'How is this *malai* tea of yours selling?'

'Quantity-wise much below the *chalu* teas but profit-wise it's on top. You know why this tea tastes so good; I prepare this with condensed milk.'

'Yes, it's very good; I haven't tasted this type before. Now read the name of this man and his address, any idea about him?' Toomba tore out the last portion of the paper and gave it to her.

Kajol studied it thoughtfully before replying.

'No. I don't know this man but I can find out. Is he one of those *badmashes*?'

'Yes. Now listen carefully. I want some information about him like whether he owns the place he lives in, does he have a family, if he has a car, the size of the car and if possible, the company he works with. Have you understood?'

'Yes. You'll get all the information in two days' time.'

'Good, and thank you for the tea.'

Kajol collected the cups and left. Toomba made a call to a friend at Shyambazar, spoke the name and address of the third person and the information he required. He switched off the mobile and asked Mashi, 'How far have you progressed with your ready-to-eat food venture?'

'The Association secretary has located a space, rather large, near Lake Market but the price asked for is rupees two lakh and the rent per month two thousand because it has a permanent structure. Both appear high for me; I haven't yet told him yes or no.'

'Have you seen the place?'

'Not yet.'

'May I request you to visit the place with Kajol. And if you two feel it has prospects, finalise the deal.'

Mashi smiled at Toomba's solemn face: she could now see the pattern. Good boy and an intelligent one. Goodness and intelligence do not always go together but he combined the two.

'I'll do it.' She gave him an understanding smile.

Toomba met Chameli the following morning. Her eyes glittered despite the black lines under her eyes. She tried to get up to see if Boomba had also come but fell back on the bed.

'Don't strain yourself; Boomba will be back in a day or two.'

Chameli was silent. Toomba observed her body shaking, tears gathering round her closed eyes. He pulled the visitor's chair by the bedside and sat observing her. She was not crying, which would have eased the pain, but weeping made the pain more painful. She was trying to suppress the emotion, but that also indicated her resolve to fight.

Toomba waited. Slowly the shakes in her body receded, so also the weeping, her body rested on the bed. Toomba touched the mass of hair on her head. She spoke after a long time.

'I've realised one thing, I've lost the spirit of a street girl, become domesticated, also forgotten the ethos of the street. I followed Mashi in trusting them; I treated them as my elder brothers, also called them as such. So when the attack came I got puzzled, I reacted late. If it were that girl roaming at Sealdah, the outcome would've been different. I've also lost that fierceness which scared the boys there. Instead of biting the wrist of *baudi's* husband and scratching others I could've bitten their throats. I was in a defending mode; not that aggressive girl who fought to finish, but I promise when I recover I'm going to take on all of them and give them a lesson of life.'

Toomba now took her hand which no longer shook and said, 'I'm glad you don't think yourself a rape victim but a courageous girl who could review and analyze the reasons for her failure to win a battle. But you must promise not to weep any longer.'

'I promise.'

Toomba rose and said, 'I shall not be able to meet you for the next four-five days; I've some urgent business.'

'I know'. She beamed at Toomba.

'What?'

'You're going to award advance punishment to them.'

'That's a smart girl.' He joined her smile.

Toomba knocked the door of Roychoudhuri. He opened it with a glass of whisky in his hand. Toomba glided past him and sat on a sofa opposite the whisky bottle.

'Let me tell you before you ask. I'm Chameli's friend, was in a hospital when you did it to her. In a meeting of the Street Dwellers Association of which I'm the president it has been decided to request all the four of you to contribute two lakh each toward rehabilitation of the girl. She was to be married soon which got delayed because of your misdemeanour. Her betrothed is on a business trip now, otherwise he'd have come with me. You've already paid one lakh to Mashi. You need to pay now another one lakh. I hope you'll cooperate. By the way, the good news is that Chameli is recovering fast and expected to be released in about 3-4 weeks which would lighten your expenses on her treatment, and the bad news is that the Nursing Home has preserved her smear and all that as per rule in the event of this turning out to be a police case. You may now take a sip of whisky from the glass you're holding for a long time.'

The man looked at the glass he was holding in his hand since Toomba came in. He now took a gulp and put it down on the table with a clunk. This appeared to be serial blackmailing. He regretted his weakness by succumbing to the pressure-tactics of that woman; it was a mistake to give her a lakh of rupees. And now this! It must be put to a stop once for all. He had anger and banter in his eyes when he spoke.

'Hey, an urchin of the street what do you think you are, the president of street dwellers association that no one knows of? How old are you, just a boy? I am much older than you and I know how the world works. I shall get over it soon and you and your damned association can't do anything. But I must appreciate your dare to come here and blackmail me. Now be satisfied with the one lakh I'd given to that filthy woman and get out of my place right now before I call the police!'

Toomba showed no inclination to go out. He spoke with a chilling softness in his voice.

'I find you have no idea of street children. One year in the street is equal to four years in the society and by that count I'm your age. We're kind of gods in heaven. So let's talk one to one. You know you can't call the police because if you do the whole thing would be out in the open and that wouldn't be nice for your families. Besides, the police may ultimately arrest all three of you. I have taken good care of preserving the smear of the girl. They wouldn't dare destroy it whatever money you give them. As for blackmail let me tell you, you did a black deed to an unsuspecting girl who regarded you as her elder brother; I'm just trying to whiten it up a little. Don't you agree?'

The man looked at Toomba with amazement and fear in his eyes. He'd really misjudged the boy; the bastard had thought of everything and taken all the precautions like a mature person! His head fell, two hands gathered on his lap. After a while he spoke.

'But I don't have so much cash at home; can you come tomorrow?'

'No. Give me a cheque instead.'

He went inside, brought his cheque book and began writing.

'What name shall I put?'

Toomba told Mashi's name. He handed the cheque to Toomba. After examining the cheque he warned the man.

'Should the cheque bounce a crowd of hundred street children will *gherao* your house shouting slogans; the issue will be public: the NGOs, media and police will converge on you.'

Toomba rose to leave but sat back.

'I've a small request. Will you kindly advise your other three friends to get the money ready so as to avoid unnecessary waste of time? Please also tell them that my friends are keeping a watch on them, they won't be able to escape. I shall be personally visiting then in a day or two.'

Toomba rose to leave but again sat back, this time at his request.

He said, 'Look, all my three friends are family men like me, some have grown up children; they'll guess something if you visit them. Could you avoid meeting them?'

'How? I need the money.'

'I've an idea. May I talk to them?'

'Of course you can.'

The man picked up his mobile and went inside. Toomba picked up his whisky glass.

He came back to the drawing room and saw Toomba drinking from his glass.

'Sorry, no other glass here, so I used your glass; you may've to get another glass.'

'It's okay,' he said with distaste in his voice, 'Now listen, I'll give you another cheque of six lakh from my account. They'll deposit their share in my account by the first hour tomorrow morning. You just wait a day before placing this cheque for encashment. Is that okay with you?'

'Sure it is, saves a lot of time.'

While receiving the cheque from him Toomba said, 'It seems you're much concerned about your friends; if you'd shown such concern for the girl this situation wouldn't have arisen.'

He did not wait to see his reaction.

Boomba came to Gariahat after three days. Toomba saw him talking agitatedly to Mashi.

As he approached he heard Boomba say, 'You sold my ulcer when I was a child and now you sold Chameli's rape. And on top of that you've added the surname of that bastard to Chameli's name! What for?'

'For you and her, said Toomba as he sat by his side.

Boomba did not even hear what he said. He flared up.

'And you, the hero of the street, you could've killed those salacious bastards, Mashi could've gone to the police with whom she has such a thick and thin relationship. Instead, what you did, just bargained some money for such a heinous crime.'

Toomba saw Mashi chuckling, but he could not help a loud laughter. Boomba was confused, the tea spoon slipped from Kajol's hand at the stall; she'd never heard Toomba laughing so loudly.

'Hey Kajol, please give us some cold drinks, the situation here is very hot,' Toomba said amidst continuing laughter.

Boomba did not touch the cold drink; he looked alternately at Mashi and Toomba who were quietly drinking the cola.

He retorted heatedly, 'What's all this laughing and smiling?'

'Nothing. Let's talk seriously. Suppose, that day you were present, not Mashi when Chameli came tottering here and fell unconscious smeared with blood, what you would've done?'

Boomba replied, 'Well of course, I'd have immediately taken her to a nearby Nursing Home and then…'

We'll talk about the "then" later. Now just tell us which Nursing Home in Kolkata would admit a street girl and that too without a surname and an address, no matter how serious the injury was. Even if it were a public hospital she'd have to wait in queue before the Emergency, unconscious and bleeding, and by the time her turn came she'd have been dead unless of course you'd had recommendation of an MLA, MP or some such influential person. Do you know any such person?'

Boomba tried to think resolutely with tight jaws. Slowly his jaws relaxed, face fell. Toomba spoke.

'Now about Mashi's going to the police or…'

Boomba raised his hand.

'Please. You don't have to explain further. I understand.'

'That's like a good boy. Now have your cold drink, though it has lost its coolness long back.'

* * * *

Mashi had not moved from Gariahat for nearly three months now.

About two months back, Bichhu informed her over phone the good news of Chikku's arrival at Kolkata and Binni being with him for all the three days. Bisu was angry why Chikku could not even find a little time to visit them at the station. How tall he had become he wanted to measure when he came next. Mashi laughed with Bichhu over the phone.

Chameli was released from Nursing Home after three weeks but was still weak, unable to sit and stand without aid. Mashi met the doctor on the day of her release who advised her about care to be taken during recuperation:

she still had some difficulty in urinating for which there must be adequate intake of water, next to timely administration of medicines and application of ointments; cleanliness and hygiene were of utmost importance to prevent any infection. 'You must bring her every Thursday in the morning for next one month and fortnightly thereafter. I hope she'd be fully fit in two months,' he advised.

Mashi took over the nursing. Chameli had to re-learn many things. Mashi would say, 'Recall those days how you learnt sitting, standing, walking and then running... hold my back and try to stand up slowly... now try to stand up on your own... now let's go for a walk, hold my hand, we'll have a cup of tea at Kajol's stall...'

On the day of her fourth visit to the doctor, Chameli walked all the way to the Nursing Home. She was tired but radiant. The doctor examined her for about ten minutes. He had a look of satisfaction when he said, 'She'd improved fast. You don't have to visit me any longer unless some new complication arises, which though is unlikely; just continue the medicines for another fortnight, that's all.'

For a long time they had not been so happy together. While returning Chameli walked on her own, did not hold Mashi's hand even once, prattled all the time about their new venture.

She was the first to notice Binni sitting on a stool at Kajol's stall sipping tea and talking with her.

'Hai Binni, waiting for a long time?' Chameli beamed at her.

'Not much, just about ten minutes, learning things about your new venture. Chameli stayed with Kajol as Binni went to meet Mashi.

'Have you come alone?' Mashi asked.

'C'mon Mashi, I'm no longer a child that I need someone to accompany me.'

'Oh, yes. I'd forgotten you're a school mistress now teaching children.' Mashi smiled.

'Mashi, I need the money lying in deposit with you.'

'You want it right now?'

'If you can.'

Mashi went inside Kajol's stall and brought out the trunk concealed at a corner among provisions. Only this morning she'd withdrawn two lakhs from the bank to defray expenses for the new venture.

She consulted the register, counted the money, packed them securely in an opaque plastic bag and handed it to Binni.

Binni thanked Mashi, wished good luck to Chameli and Kajol for the new venture and left.

****

Negotiations with the landlord of the stall near Lake Market had reached the final stage. The *salami* was brought down to one and half lakh rupees and the rent to one thousand two hundred per month. After some childish fights between Boomba and Chameli it was decided to buy the space in Chameli's name but she did not relent on naming the stall as Boomba Foods.

They decided to give the stall a modern look with glass counters, teak ply racks, luminous lighting and modern cooking gadgets. There would be three counters: (1) the ready-to- eat foods, (2) cold drinks and lassi, (3) Kajol's range of tea, coffee and snacks.

They had hired one experienced cook at rupees six thousand per month—one thousand more than what he was getting from his earlier engagement. He'd come with an assistant at rupees two thousand per month. Kajol and Chameli had tasted the foods prepared by him at the stall he was working before. Satisfied, they had made the offer.

Kajol had estimated the cost of furnishing and buying various gadgets to be one and half lakh rupees and another fifty thousand for working capital. Costing and pricing of various products would be decided by Kajol in consultation with the cook. They engaged three girls from HS who were presently working with Kajol as understudy.

The stall would open on the first of *Baisakh*, the Bengali New Year's Day, which corresponded with 15th April according to the Gregorian calendar. They had about a month's time.

Boomba was morose as he was unable to participate much in the discussions due to his preoccupation with drug peddling. One day Toomba took him aside and assured that he'd get him out of drugs.

'But that's impossible and you know that.'

'I'll talk to Raja, a big boss now; he'll definitely find a way out.'

Toomba met Raja at his kingdom.

They sat outside Raja's hut. He'd always been a good host. Drinks were arranged on a low table with nuts and fries, a boy in attendance. It was retreating spring time. Southerlies carrying the stench of the canal passed by them ruffling their hairs and cooling their bodies.

'Don't you think this smell of stench is spoiling the pleasance of spring air?' Raja asked.

'When all's smell, there's no smell. The moment you begin sensing the smell you're changing.' Toomba replied with an enigmatic smile.

Raja fell silent, thoughtful.

After a couple of drinks Toomba presented the problems Boomba presently faced and his desire to get out of drugs.

'But that's very, very difficult, you may say, nearly impossible, more so because he now knows many more things of the trade.'

'That's what Boomba has said. But you've overcome much impossibility in your life; your present position is a proof of that. I'm sure you'd find a way out.'

Raja was in deep thought, possibly weighing the pros and cons of various alternatives. He spoke after sometime.

'You know at this juncture I miss the person who was behind Boomba's recruitment; no he didn't recruit him directly, just sent a feeler; the funny thing is that Boomba pick pocketed him when he was travelling by a bus and he liked him. He was much closer to the top bosses, may be of equal rank with my Guru, but he was killed in a police encounter last year in Bengaluru where he was transferred as chief organiser. He could have got Boomba's release with much more ease. I know he did it for one operator whose wife was suffering from cancer. But let me tell you I'm also Raja and you're my best friend who had never asked anything before for himself and this time also it is for someone whom he loves; if I fail you what for I call myself Raja? Don't worry, I'll find a way. I might even go to the length of talking to the Chairman of the Council personally when he comes to India in about two months time. By the way, if it comes to that will you stand guarantee for the fidelity of Boomba post release?'

'Of course, I'll.'

'That's settled. Right now I'm putting Boomba on two months' leave. I promise, within that period I'll get him released. Let's have another drink on that.' Raja raised his glass.

Toomba's mobile rang. He saw the number and pressed the button.

'Hey Lord *Mahadev*, if you're free from your godly duties could you come to Dalhousie Square?'

'At this hour of the night?'

'Night's beautiful there. Wait for me near St. Andrew's church; you may play footpath carom under the church light with the boys there, if you know how to, till I come.' Toomba raised his eyes from the silent mobile phone to Raja who was smiling.

'I could guess: the voice oozed out from the phone. Ok, go ahead; a night call is always promising.'

Toomba reached Brabourne Road crossing at 9 p.m. and walked to the footpath fencing St. Andrew's church, originally known as Scottish Kirk and locally as Lat Sahib *ka girja*. On the right stood the monolithic Writers' Building, the seat of state administration and also the final destination of all political rallies; its crimson colour now looked dark brown due to artificial lighting, only the whites of the columns and arches were visible. He heard the administration would soon move to a building in Howrah to make way for undertaking massive inside repair and reconstruction of this two hundred thirty years old Heritage Building.

He had visited Dalhousie Square several times before but during day time; number of visits increased when he entered drug peddling: some clients preferred taking delivery during office hours at pre-designated places which could be a restaurant, at a shop inside Burra Bazaar that could be reached by carefully traversing the snake lines adorning over-filled shops on both sides, gliding past the rickshaws, cycles, wheelbarrows, cycle vans, coolies and Matador vans and the flow of mankind always in a hurry; near or at a shop in Poddar Court, at some of the electronic shops of Chandi Chowk or cycle whole sellers on crowded Benthic Street opposite the headquarters of Kolkata police, or to a particular counter of General Post Office, a wall-fitted fruit juice stall opposite Calcutta Stock exchange, at the Strand Road entrance of the Floatel Hotel and Restaurant on the river Ganges; inside the cafeteria of *Akashbani*, the zonal headquarters of All India Radio, at a particular spot on the Council House street footpath adjoining Raj Bhawan, the residence and office of the Governor of the state, or directly at the cabin of the client at any of the innumerable offices of the Square.

Every time Toomba visited the Square he was fascinated by the flow of people to and from this place: people come here from all over the state and outside, of different stations of life wearing varied garments—some wearing suit and tie, some pant and shirt, some dhoti and *kurta* with or without a cap and a large number with shorts and T-shirts who crowd the footpaths selling garments, household things and food items ranging from fruits to parched rice—you name a food and you get it here, that's how the saying goes.

Population in Dalhousie Square and adjoining areas would be more than a lakh during day time, but now it looked almost vacant; the crowd had taken back all the dins with themselves while returning home; the ear shattering sounds of buses, minibuses, taxis and private vehicles were now replaced by an occasional horn of a lonely vehicle that could not submerge the sounds of gravels hitting each other on the carom board near which Toomba stood now.

Back from reminiscences of Dalhousie Square he concentrated on the carom board. He did not know how to play carom but liked the movement of two sets of gravels—white and black, and a single red; each team trying to put the gravels of the other into any of the four corner holes of the board by a striker gravel of a larger size, but both attempting to do the same to the red one, kind of winning a beautiful girl by force.

Minu had not yet arrived. With nothing else to do he tried to discover the rules of the carom game. It dawned on him that the objective of the rules was to provide a level playing field for the two opposite parties to win the game only by excellence. This also meant that the game came first, the rules evolved as it was played, which were later firmed up by a different set of persons to minimise the chaos and conflict that emerged when the game was being played by a large number of people. The inventor of the game living in the pleasure of invention was unable to see beyond the invention. He did not bother about its impact on the players, the chaos it might create among people who played the game. That way the inventors of the game of carom and of atom bomb were no different. He had himself seen the pleasure of invention in the eyes of a local smith who had invented a six-shooter revolver far more lethal than the ones imported from abroad. When he explained to him the killing power of the machine: its ability to hit a person from a certain distance—almost one and a half time the distance of an imported one—and its recoiling power to fire all six bullets in less than a minute, his eyes shone like a village boy who had just crafted a sling-shot from a perfect Y-shaped branch of a tree and strong elastic bands that could shoot a stone pellet to a great distance. The six-shooter invented by the *dhoti-clad* man soon captured the fancy of the underground market; his son raised the scale of operation and now dominated the market with a lot of clout. Toomba remembered when he read the history of Second World War and how it ended in his school text book he hated the scientists who invented the atom bomb, but when he met the local gun maker he stopped hating them. He realised that an inventor thinks beyond the value system of the society, rules were later framed to contain the effect of his invention.

Toomba was so absorbed in his thoughts that he did not feel a tap on the back of his shoulder. Only when there was a second tap fallowed by a little push he turned and saw Minu.

'Were you on the carom board or elsewhere?'

'Well, it is like this. Your Royal Highness ordered her subject to wait here for her royal appearance but she took a lot of time to emerge; meanwhile the devil noticing her loyal subject standing here with an idle brain took him to his workshop to plant some of his thoughts. Now that Your Highness has finally appeared, the devil retreated.'

'A good one.'

'Hi Minudi, seeing you after a long time,' someone cried from the small crowd.

'What's a long time? I came here just about two months back.'

'But that's a long time, isn't it? You normally come here at least once every month.'

'What to do? An ass of a doctor interned me to a Nursing Home for about a month, subjected me to a battery of tests, found nothing but gave me some stupid medicines and asked to come back after a month for some further tests.'

'That explains; you look tired.'

'Don't talk like a glum-faced doctor, always a precocious boy! Now tell me did you have a chance to talk to this silent man.

'No. We saw him intently observing the game; thought he might be waiting for someone but couldn't guess it was you,' replied the precocious boy.

Okay, now meet Toomba, my friendly enemy and let me tell you he was not observing much of this stupid game, his mind went to a workshop which you haven't seen. Now give me your striker; I'll play a match against Jhantu—best of three, eh.'

Minu lost all the three games and threw the striker on the board.

'Arrey, you play like a champion. I shouldn't have chosen you to play against.'

'He is already a champion of Dalhousie after defeating the three times champion Neel of Council House Street last month,' said another boy.

'You should've told me before. I would've chosen Kittu to play against. Anyway, congratulations Jhantu! Now take these *Biryani* packets and celebrate the win.'

Minu brought out several *Biryani* packets from her bag, placed them on the carom board, said 'Bye, see you,' and left with Toomba splashing smiles all over them.

While walking Minu asked, 'Have you seen the night Dalhousie before?'

'No. It's so different. It appears the day Dalhousie and night Dalhousie are two different entities.'

'And the population too. After the migratory *babus* clear the area latest by eight the locals take over. You want to have a walk through the village?'

They first walked in the direction of Writers' Building. As they neared, gangs of dogs from all sides came rushing toward them barking ferociously. Toomba soon found themselves in the middle of a circle surrounded by barking dogs. It seemed to him the dogs were trying to scare them away, not attacking and their barking mostly directed at him, not at Minu. Might be they wanted him to leave her alone to square up some past misdemeanours. He would have to find a way out. He turned and gripped her hand but found her smiling as though enjoying the spectacle.

'For the first time I find a tiger scared of *billies*, though the hand holding is great it could break my wrist if held longer.'

With an impish smile she pulled out packets of biscuits from her bag and threw them to the dogs. They retreated though a few of them came closer and began smelling him.

'Next time they won't disturb you.'

A policeman with a rifle hanging from his shoulder, his palms busy in mixing raw tobacco with lime walked to them and told Toomba, 'I was observing your harassment; they know the Miss but not you, so they barracked you. They wouldn't allow any intruder to come near the Building during the night; self-appointed guard squads of the place, probably much better than the men squads around the Building.'

He examined the state of tobacco paste in his palm, satisfied put the small lump between his lower lip and teeth, gave them a quarter of his smile and walked back to his station of duty.

Toomba continued to hold Minu's hand though the grip slackened now as they wandered along the roads of the Square.

'I wonder why I haven't seen these dogs during day time,' Toomba asked.

Minu replied. 'They're part of the locale, incognito during the day, emerge after the *babus* vacate this place and take up the onerous duty of guarding the buildings and the footpath inhabitants: every roadside family here is protected by a family of dogs.'

Keeping back side of the Writers' Building on the left and Calcutta Stock Exchange—once the seat of Indian capital market, now struggling to maintain at least a regional status—on the right they walked involuntarily toward Netaji Subhas Road. Footpaths of both sides of the roads presented a familiar sight: some already in deep sleep, some readying, married couples fixing mosquito net and covering it with thin rags for some privacy—not much different from other city footpaths in the night.

'There is one difference,' Minu said following Toomba's appraising look, 'unlike other footpaths and unlike us many of the dwellers here have their families living in some distant villages, they work here to earn for them, though some are living here for more than one generation.'

Toomba said, 'Another difference which strikes me is that the buildings here look deader in the night than the buildings adjoining other city footpaths.'

"Cause they look more alive during the day.'

Toomba was following the heels of Minu. They now stood on the right end of Netaji Subhas Road overseen by the tall Gillander House, though one could now only feel its gothic tallness, not see it, the street lights lighting the road not the buildings.

'I think I should be feeling hungry; I've already crossed the dinner timetable by one hour as prescribed by the doctor who is bent upon curing me from all imagined illness,' Minu said.

Toomba suppressed a smile. Footpaths being all full they sat on a footpath-side road on the left of Gillander House where it was taking an angular turn. Minu placed two *Biryani* packets on a plastic mat and another two by her side, a bottle of mineral water, a bottle of liquor and polyethylene cups completed the arrangement.

Three dogs appeared from nowhere and sat on their haunches quietly.

'Hey my darling wolves. You got my scent or the *biryani's*?' They could have answered 'Both,' but simply barked and wagged their tails.

Minu gave them the two packets of *Biryani* she had kept aside and opened theirs.

Between eating and sharing the bottle Minu said, 'This is the place where my street life began, and these three dogs—much younger then—who protected me and taught me how to survive in the street.'

'I also learnt from dogs.' Toomba remarked.

'Yes, but you only learnt the techniques from them from a distance like *Eklavya* practicing archery of *Dronacharya* School without the knowledge of his Guru, *Drona*. Both you and *Eklavya* perfected the techniques but none of you learnt the guiding principles of life and war. I got both.'

Toomba finished eating his *biryani,* but Minu ate only half of it. She took a sip of liquor and said, 'So much for honouring the promises made to the doctor and my friend who took me to him. But they must know I can't eat much.' She gave the rest of the *biryani* to the dogs.

Minu observed the dogs quietly eating the food, the swaying of their tails displayed happiness. She had a motherly smile on her face which turned reflective when she spoke next.

'I'm an ordinary mortal packed with emotions, can't detach myself from me like you do. I can never forget these three dogs *who* saved me from distress that night. I've developed bondage with them. When I give them food they know it is an expression of love, not a return gift or pity. Many a times I had no food with me to offer them but they'd come invariably, sit here quietly and when I'd get up to leave they'd accompany me and leave only when they'd feel I was safe.' Minu fell silent.

After some time Toomba said, 'I'm waiting to hear the story, and I promise there shall be no value judgment.'

Minu smiled at Toomba before she spoke.

'I've already told you that after I was released by the Juvenile Board I came to Howrah station. I had with me with all the gifts the media persons gave me, namely food packets, dresses and other articles. Among these was also a spring-operated dagger encased within a beautiful box, which I discovered later.

I collected my money hidden in the station latrine, put it inside the large bag given by them and boarded a minibus, the name Dalhousie Square and within bracket B.B.D. Bag painted on its side as the last destination. I'd heard about the place but didn't know where it was. In about ten minutes the bus reached its final destination and I got down with others. I saw the Writers' Building of which I'd read, passed through various roads like Brabourne Road, now B.T.M. Sarani, Ezra Street, Lalbazar Street, India Exchange Place and Netaji Subhas Road, lined by office buildings and trading houses but did not quite notice Dalhousie Square written anywhere. Not that I cared much still I asked a girl carrying some files whether this place is called Dalhousie Square. She gave me a funny look and said, "Of course it is," and passed hurriedly.

'It was afternoon and I was hungry. I sat on the footpath at the back of Writers' Building, opened the bag and saw for the first time the dagger; must've been gifted by a well-meaning media person—might be a woman who knew what I did with the kitchen knife, and wished next time I do it with a real thing. I smiled to myself and thanked the unknown fire-wisher. I found the food would last me another two days.

'I felt sleepy after taking food but didn't venture to sleep. I was in the open for the first time, not sure what lay ahead and undecided about future course of action. I rose and began exploring the area further. I reached Strand Road and was immediately welcomed by a cool breeze. I crossed the road and saw a beautiful park alongside the bank of river Ganges: The Millennium Park. The evening was descending and soon the place was lit by an aesthetic arrangement of lights—a fantastic view! I could never imagine such a beautiful place existed alongside the humdrums of Dalhousie Square. I saw people entering and exiting the place through a number of gates. The place was yet to be crowded. I entered and saw several benches on the river bank vacant. I bought a large coffee in a Styrofoam glass and sat on one such bench. My intention was to think about my future and chalk out a plan but I did nothing. I was overwhelmed by the rippling sounds of small waves, the cool breeze, the passing of boats and steamers under the Howrah Bridge and all things beautiful. Gone were my woes, my future plan; I just sat there relishing the present. I didn't even notice people sitting by my side and leaving intermittently. How long I sat there I can't recall except that it was a long time as I heard someone striking the side of the bench with a *lathi* and declaring in a guttural voice, "It's time to leave". I rose to find a heavy-built moustached man wearing security uniform. The park was now nearly empty, several persons were at the exit gates, others hurrying toward them; I also joined the line and came out on the footpath. I thought for a while about the next destination and decided finally to return to Dalhousie Square. I was similarly surprised as you were tonight—the landscape changed with the nightfall, the inhabitants different. I wandered aimlessly.'

'And reached in front of the Gillander House,' Toomba finished her sentence with a smile.

'You're right,' Minu smiled back.

'I may also add that you sat exactly at the same place where we're sitting now.'

'How do you know this part?' Minu asked.

'Madam, you're reliving that night with all its pleasures and horrors.'

'How intelligent of you,' Minu retorted mockingly.

'Some time I feel like displaying my intelligence, now please proceed.'

'Are you getting bored?'

'How foolish of you,' Toomba mocked Minu's earlier tone.

They laughed out loudly, none of the footpath sleepers bothered. Minu continued.

'Yes, when I reached Gillander House, I observed all the footpaths full, no vacancy, like tonight. I chose this place. I felt like eating something. I opened the bag and brought out several packets to choose from. I observed some six-eight dogs walking silently toward me. I got scared, but they did not surround me, neither did they snatch the food packets, they just sat in a line with these three dogs in the middle—I found later that they are the leaders of the dog squad in this area. My fear dissolved, I threw them several packets which they began eating quietly with occasional looks of satisfaction at me. After they finished eating they retraced back to their corner.

'I ate two pastries, gulped some bottled water and dozed off unconsciously.

'A volley of hot, smelly breath jarred me to consciousness. I saw a man very close to me advancing his hands toward my breasts. My first reaction was to find my bag; it was on my lap. I picked it up and securely fastened it to my neck and stood to run. But another man standing behind held me clutching my breasts. I bit his wrist to loosen the grip, kicked at the face of the squat and ran. With a hoarse cry they ran after me uttering loud invectives. Soon I heard snarling of a pack of dogs, must be their pets I thought; I could ditch my pursuers but how would I save myself from the dogs. I was thinking as fast as I was running: first enemy first, then next. When I felt they're about to catch me, I stopped suddenly for a second and took a right turn to hit the wall of a building. The pursuers lost momentum and fell one upon the other. Then I saw the dogs leaped with a feral cry, not towards me but on my pursuers. They pinned them on the ground, tore away their garments; two rode on their chests snarling at their horrified faces, others surrounded. But they didn't kill them. Later I realised the street dogs like street children don't have killer instinct, though there are exceptions like the one presently sitting by my side,' Minu smiled at Toomba.

'You don't have to stop intermittently to check my level of boredom. Just continue; if you're thirsty take a gulp of water.'

'What a bore, worse than *Yudhisthir* of Mahabharata... can't help... let me continue.

'I was exhausted both physically and mentally. I slowly lowered myself on the pavement. Three dogs—in fact these three—came to me with small gallops waggling their tails, smelled me, mewed assuredly and sat before me on their haunches just the way they're sitting now. I embraced them by their necks and showered unending kisses on them. After some time they rose with small barks and walked forward. I didn't know what to do, I just sat there. They stopped on their path, looked back and barked like before. I felt instinctively they wanted me to follow them. I did.

'We passed through a few streets and lanes, reached the back side of Lalbazar police building and stood before a woman cleaning large utensils. The dogs barked. The woman replied without raising her head, 'Okay, now go to meet your kin, I'm busy'. The dogs barked again. 'What's that for? No food left,' she said raising her head and then she saw me standing by the dogs. She gazed at me intently, then exclaimed, "Hey come here, all of you and see my Minu has come back, reincarnated."'

'By now the dogs disappeared to meet their in-naturales. An elderly man emerged from behind accompanied by few others. They all gazed at me, stood stupefied. Then a woman in her thirties came forward and held my hands, "Yes, you do look like Minu whom we lost five years ago." I couldn't keep standing any longer, I collapsed on her.

'I woke up late next morning inside a shack. I saw a girl of my age watching me with a book in her hand and a child on her lap. I sat on the mat, looked around but found none else. "Where're others?" I asked.

"Ma has gone out to buy provisions; father and brother-in-law had left early in the morning with their cycle vans, *Didi* has just gone to that restaurant to wash utensils."

'So now I'm under your charge.' I smiled at her, she smiled back and we became friends. She took me out for morning ablutions and then gave a glass of warm milk and two *rotis*.

'You do look like *Mejdi*, even the way you tear a *roti* in four pieces and dip each piece in milk before putting it in your mouth. You do resemble her... she loved me very much... killed in a road accident five years back while returning from school.'

'The child on her lap was looking wistfully at my *dudh-roti*. I wanted to give him something and suddenly I remembered my bag. It was lying by the side of the mat. I opened it, found two patties and gave them one each.

'And guess, what else did I find in the bag?'

'The dagger again, which you forgot to make use of,' Toomba replied.

'Yes, and I realised its uselessness. I gave it to auntie but she wouldn't accept it, "What am I to do with it? I'm living in the street for three generations now, passed through many crises but never needed a weapon," she replied. I said, "No auntie, I'm not asking you to keep it; it's a pricey thing, just sell it and buy some books for your youngest daughter; she is preparing for secondary examination and she needs more books".

'I stayed with them for a week. After the lunch I joined auntie in preparing basic materials for a variety of oil fries. She has a huge following of customers who throng near her open pavement stall after office hours. She is assisted by the eldest daughter, the youngest one would join after returning from school and finishing the cleaning and dusting job at a doctor's clinic nearby. All fries would be sold out by seven thirty in the evening. At eight I'd leave to explore the environment of night Dalhousie.

'On the second night I went back to Gillander House pavement to seek out my pursuers. As I was searching for them I heard someone said, "They've fled, well-served the bastards." I felt a tug at my dress; one of the three dogs. When I looked back the dog left the dress and the three walked ahead. I followed. The dogs stopped before two persons sleeping side by side on the portico of the GPO building. I recognised.

'I kicked one on the ribs and at the exposed throat of another with my pointed shoes. Even before he could utter anything I pulled up the first by his long hair and began hurling choicest invectives: *sala chutiya... harami...* rotten prick... corpse eater... mother fucker... dirty slink of a bitch... fucking gutter worm... sister fucker... daughter fucker... rotten placenta of a whore...

bastard of a miscarriage... bloody swine... You want to fuck me, eh? Come *sala*. I boxed him between his legs and gave him a flying kick again at his ribs. He fell on the other sleepers who now fully awake sat on their haunches observing the spectacle. They didn't join against me, rather pushed the man forward. I pulled him up. He stood before me crying in pain, hands folded to his chest. I looked at his eyes and said, "*Saala chutiya*, if I see you again anywhere near Dalhousie I'll tear the balls out of you; leave the place right now." As he turned to leave, I gave him a parting kick on his back. He fell but rose immediately and ran.

"Now, you!" I turned to the other. He might have tried to flee earlier but my dogs didn't allow that. He already had his hands folded to his chest, eyes pleading. But I was merciless, though I didn't abuse him additionally—the earlier ones were meant for both, I kicked him left and right, at and on every part of his body, pulled him up, kicked him down and did all things ferocious. When I felt tired I pulled him up and with a final kick and ordered, "*Sala harami ka bachha*, get out of this area, now! Never show your bloody face here again." He fled and I left with my dogs.

'That was my first tryst with the street. You like it?' She asked Toomba.

'Gallant, choice of invectives great except that "swine" is rather weak among the high-octane abuses,' Toomba sounded a school teacher.

Minu raised her fist to hit him but he had already moved away. They laughed instead. Minu drank some water and spoke, 'I learnt several things during the initial days of my stay here: one, the instinct to fight and the instinct of fear are inherent in human beings. I was overcome by the instinct of fear on the first night; to survive one has to pass on the fear on to the opponent and bring forth the fighting instinct to oneself. Two, surprise attack is the best policy.'

'And it must be preceded by a high pitch volley of choicest abuses,' Toomba added.

'And when it comes from a girl the impact is very high. In all the wars from the days of Mahabharata to the present this is used to shatter the nerves of the opponents, to force them to make a wrong move.'

'But wherefrom you learnt all those grand abuses?' Toomba asked.

'Some at the police stations—the largest abuse producing conglomerate of the world, and some others my own improvisation. May I proceed further with your permission?'

'Oh, yes'.

'I've also realised that weapons don't win a fight, a fearless determined mind does it; weapons are servants of the mind and these can always be snatched. When one is fearful the brain triggers appropriate neurons to make mind more fearful, opposite happens to a fearless mind. And as for the physics of the physicals…'

'Your legs move faster than your hands. I've seen that before,' Toomba completed the statement.

'What a damp squid, didn't give me a chance to glorify. May I progress further?

'Every night I roamed the area—from Esplanade on the south to the approach bridge of Howrah station on the north—made friendship with hundred of dogs, almost every dweller of the streets. I had two similar fights at Curzon Park on the Esplanade for similar reasons. I honed my skills on them and drove them out. I created my first network of friends.

'I also met my first paramour here at Millennium Park, and shredded the invisible but weighty girdle of chastity which I'd been carrying from ages despite being raped multiple times. With him I understood the distinction between sexual violence and violent sex, though I'd had to wait more than two years to feel the difference between sex and love making.' She stopped for a while to smile at Toomba and continued.

'I come here every month to nurture my network as I do with my other network friends.'

'But I wonder why we've not met before,' Toomba remarked.

'It's because you network in the South, Central and Northern parts of Kolkata and I on the Western part.'

Minu turned to the three dogs sitting patiently before them and spoke with a particular gesture of her hand.

'My dear wolves, it's time for you to go back to your kin', and rose with them.

'I think you intend to tag me along to spend the night at your auntie's place.'

'How intelligent of you,' Minu quipped.

'I've never doubted my intelligence.'

'What a proudy!'

'A la Raja.'

Next morning they woke up on the pavement adjoining auntie's shack. They were already late: the dogs and other urchins who slept by them had left. Minu peeped inside the shack. The girl came out hurriedly with the child.

'Finish your ablutions. Your milk and *rotis* will be ready by the time you come back,' the girl said with a sweet smile.

'That won't be necessary, we're already late, will have it somewhere on the way,' Minu said kissing and patting both.

They began walking toward Esplanade. The Square was waking up fast; the overcrowded buses retching out flustered citizens who began walking fast immediately after getting down from buses; cars, taxis and sundry other vehicles had started jamming the roads, the hum gaining strength with every passing moment.

They entered Dacres Lane between Esplanade Row and Waterloo Street, the roadside food paradise of office goers through generations. It had already woken up and welcomed Minu and Toomba with offerings coming from a variety of stalls ranging from South Indian *Idli-Dosa* to simple toast and omelette. The lane was not crowded at this hour. They sat on a bench opposite a stall and ordered for toast-omelette-tea.

Minu ate silently and spoke only when the tea came.

'I'm going incognito for a month or so. I often do it, you know. It's unlikely I'd be able to attend the opening ceremony of Boomba Foods or the marriage of Chameli-Boomba which Mashi had planned soon after opening of the food stall. So I've decided to give my gift to them in advance.'

Minu handed an envelope to Toomba and said, 'It contains a cheque, give it to Mashi for their deposit account.'

She rode a taxi to the South and he for a bus to the North.

Chapter 21

Toomba slept the whole day on the roof of Sealdah station morgue. He rose in the late evening feeling bored, uneasy. He went to the bus stop and boarded the first bus that came. He bought a ticket to terminus not knowing where it was, didn't even ask the conductor. The bus was over crowded; he stood by the gate enjoying the cool air. The crowd swelled up as the bus crossed Shyambazar. Soon he found himself on the stair holding the handle of the gate. He liked the occasional bursts of air fluttering his shirt and unravelling his hairs. The bus ascended the semi dark Belgachia over bridge with a jerk—most of the street lights were either stolen or broken—and while screeching down toward the bus stop hit a person who fell by the way side. The bus did not stop; it sped away with increased speed. Toomba jumped out from the bus, ran forward a few seconds along the moving bus to steady himself and then rushed to the fallen man. He was unconscious. Toomba noticed in the dim light huge spots of blood on his face. He looked around to find someone who could be of help. There was none at that hour of the night. He turned to the fallen man and thought he might die if left like that. He was frail, could be carried by him, but where to? He saw, at some distance on his left down from the road level, series of dim lights by two sides of railway tracks. He picked the injured man up, carefully placing one hand under his neck and proceeded towards those lights.

As he descended a young man stopped him, his eyes reflected both surprise and doubt.

Toomba slowly laid the man on the ground and said, 'I found him on the roadside, unconscious, hit by a speeding bus.'

The young man exclaimed as he saw the face of the man, *'Arrey,* he is our Hekim Chacha!' and immediately roused the neighbourhood. Soon a lot of people came rushing in. They observed the bloodied face of the man and began lamenting in varied languages and gestures.

'Toomba said quietly, "May I ask you to stop lamenting; he isn't dead yet but will be if not taken to hospital immediately.'

Now they realised the gravity of the situation. A burly man now moved in and said, 'Yes, you're right. We'll take him to R. G. Kar Hospital which is not far away.'

He asked a young man.

'Get some four-five van-rickshaws immediately; no taxi will be available at this hour of the night.'

Five van-rickshaws materialised in a minute. Toomba rose to the largest one and advised them, 'Now lift him carefully: one must keep hands under his head to keep his neck straight and two others should raise him perpendicularly on the van resting his head on my lap.'

This done the burly man boarded the van, sat by Toomba's side and shouted others to follow. When the van began to move the man pressed buttons of his mobile phone.

'Hey Nantuda, this is Ismail. Hekim Chacha has been hit by a speeding bus, unconscious; we're taking him to R. G. Kar Hospital. Please ask the doctors there to take proper care of him... no, no, the bus didn't stop... that we shall take care tomorrow... right now, tell the hospital people not to do any hanky-panky. If anything bad happens to Hekim Chacha we'll burn the hospital.'

He switched off the mobile and told Toomba almost apologetically, 'That pig, Nantu Ghosh is the municipal councillor of our Ward. He doesn't do a thing unless you're on his head. He purloins seventy five percent of every rupee allocated for development of this ward. He knows we know. But we really don't care as long as we're left to ourselves. We constitute more than twenty five percent of his voters, and we've voted for him in all the last three elections despite him changing party three times. He's an opportunist, so are we. He gets us released when any of us is arrested, takes care when someone suffers an injury or falls seriously ill beyond Hekim Chacha's ability.'

He stopped as he heard, 'ooh... aah' issuing from Chacha's throat. Toomba looked at his face and said, 'I think he'll survive.'

The van carrying Hekim Chacha entered the compound of the hospital and stopped before the Emergency. Others left their vans and walked in.

Two doctors, a nurse and two attendants were already standing on the portico of the Emergency. One doctor and the nurse carried Hekim Chacha quickly inside with the help of the attendants. The other doctor asked to know what had happened to the patient. Toomba described the incident. He went inside and soon they began appropriate protocols. Ismail indicated Toomba to sit by him on a chair placed on the portico, others loitered near the closed doors of the treatment room.

Ismail switched on his mobile phone and instructed someone on the other side.

'Organise a crowd of hundred people to block all approach roads of Belgachia over bridge from six tomorrow morning, another hundred on the railway lines to stop all the trains; not a single vehicle or train be allowed to pass.'

Ismail realised for the first time that he had not thanked Toomba, nor even asked his name or wherefrom he came. He tried to mend it.

'We must thank you very much for what you've done. Hekim Chacha is regarded as father to all of us; a great soul, Allah's gift to us. By the way what's your name?'

'Toomba.'

'That's a funny name.'

'I'm a funny person.'

'Yes, funny you must be, otherwise who would've bothered to save the life of an unknown person hit by a speeding bus which never stopped to look back; passengers also didn't force the bus to stop, none but you jumped out off the bus to save him, funny you must be.'

Toomba did not respond. Ismail continued.

'Our Hekim Chacha is a great man, not like us rouges. You may like to know why at that hour of the night he was on the road. It's for our well being only. He was going far off to collect certain herbs from a *bagicha* owned by Noorjahan Bibi, an eighty-year old widow. She planted these herbs only for him, which have to be picked up after the first dew on a particular lunar day—a meticulous *hekim* par excellence. We often joke about his nocturnal journey—Chacha going to meet his old flame. He was a great flute player in his young days, but stopped playing it and threw away all instruments after his wife died at a very young age—just about a year after their marriage. He mourned for a week, then all of a sudden locked his hut and vanished. He returned after three years as a trained *hekim* and immersed himself looking after the health of the entire *bustee*. He never asks a fee, takes whatever one gives and that could range from small money to one or two pumpkins or a bagful of cucumbers that our women grow on the tiled roofs. Whenever he needs money he'd ask one of us; we know it is for our benefit only and we never deny it. He is Allah's man among us...' His voice trailed off in a pensive note.

'I didn't know at that time I was helping out so great a man—a rare human being, I must say,' Toomba said.

'Yes, he is. Now imagine, how our people would react if anything serious happens to Hekim Chacha. They'll burn the buses, uproot the railway lines, ransack the municipal office, arson and all that which even I won't be able to control.'

'I have a feeling he'll survive.'

'Let me pray for that,' said Ismail and sat on the floor in a prayer posture; others loitering around followed him.

A doctor emerged at dawn to inform them that Chacha was out of danger now; they were removing him to the intensive therapeutic unit; he will be all right in a week's time. Toomba saw Ismail weeping like a child holding the doctor's hand. So much child living inside that burly frame!

Except three boys who were to keep a vigil at the hospital others proceeded toward the *bustee*. Ismail took Toomba in the same van they came.

'You want to see the *tamasha*; it would be quite a thing to experience,' Ismail asked Toomba.

'I don't mind, I'll stay by your side.'

'Good. By the way where do you live?'

'In the street.'

'Oh. We've provided shelters to quite a few street children of our locality. You want any?'

'No. Thank you.' Toomba replied modestly.

'In that case please live with us for a few days, say till *Chacha* returns; you may stay at *Chacha's* hut, it's a spacious one.'

Toomba thought for a while. He was free from drug delivery for next ten days; there was a supply shortage, Raja had informed him over phone. So he may as well stay here which will also help him get away from the boredom. He said yes to Ismail.

On reaching the bridge they found all its approach roads were full of people: boys and girls in their teens, young and old men, and women with children on their shoulders filled up the place; some were having breakfast there; lines of buses, lorries, taxis, cars and even hand carts stood still on all sides. Toomba looked down the bridge, the same scene there too: two down trains and three up trains stranded on their tracks.

'Good job,' Ismail remarked after surveying the build-up.

Soon a contingent of police men arrived followed by Nantu Ghosh, the councillor who looked around to locate Ismail.

'Now the real *tamasha* begins,' Ismail remarked as he saw the councillor coming towards him. He addressed Ismail with a broad smile on his face.

'I'd telephoned the hospital this morning. They said Hekim Chacha was out of danger, but I asked them to keep him in the hospital till he could walk out on his own, fully recovered. I've asked them not to charge anything for his treatment. This morning I also had a talk with the Mayor-in Council, about the lighting before I came here; he assured me that all the old light stands of the streets would be replaced by Tridents with L.E.D. lights.'

'Thank you,' Ismail responded casually.

'But what's all this?'

'Do you think we'll let go of the erring bus so easily?'

'But the driver and both the conductors have fled, though the police would soon apprehend them. I've asked the Superintendent of Police to arrest them within twenty four hours.'

'We don't care what police do with them. We want the bus owner here, right now.'

The councillor took him aside. Ismail winked at Toomba to follow. He gave a questioning look at him. Ismail told him. 'He is a friend of mine and he is the person who saved Hekim Chacha's life yesterday night.'

'I see,' the councillor gave Toomba a cursory look and turned to Ismail, 'Now tell me what you want?'

'A compensation of ten lakh rupees for Hekim Chacha.'

'That's too much, Ismail, be reasonable.'

'Tell me then what's in your mind?'

'Settle at five lakh, I'll personally donate fifty thousand—after all he is my *Chacha* too, that makes it five lakh fifty thousand rupees. If you agree I'll call the bus owner right now.'

'Make it six lakh full.'

'Ok, as you say.'

The councillor walked a distance and talked over his mobile phone. The bus owner arrived in ten minutes—must've been waiting at the councillor's house—and handed a brief case to him. The councillor opened the brief case to show the money: eleven bundles of five hundred-rupee notes; he now put his own of fifty thousand in the brief case and handed it to Ismail. They shook hands with Ismail and left in a huff.

The message had been passed over to the crowd and the blockade withdrawn.

While returning to the *bustee* Ismail asked Toomba, 'Do you think that piglet has given fifty thousand from his pocket?'

'Not even in my wildest imagination. He'd already taken it from the bus owner and probably another fifty thousand too for himself.'

'Oh-ho, you're absolutely right. But I don't care. The money goes to Hekim Chacha, none of us will even touch it. In fact by giving the money to him we're giving it to ourselves; he'll spend it all for our well being only.'

'That's very good, but if I were you I'd have taken another fifty thousand on the by line for the revelry of the boys who worked so hard since last night.'

'Allah Meherban! You're a real *Saitan.*'

'People often call me by that name.'

They shook hands amidst laughter.

Toomba stayed at Hekim Chacha's hut.

The overwhelming love and respect showered on him by the inhabitants of this largest *bustee* of Kolkata touched even an insouciant like him. It indicated the space Hekim Chacha occupied in the minds of these people. Toomba had no problem for food: one family would bring breakfast of *roti*, vegetable curry and tea in the morning, another, lunch of rice, *roti*, some vegetable fry, *dal*, meat or fish and a third family would bring dinner of *roti*, meat and curd. The family set would change the next day. Toomba understood they were repeating the same routine they followed when *Chacha* was here.

During the day he moved around the *bustee* meeting households, making friendship with them and helping them in their day to day activities which range anything from weaving to tinkerings. He enjoyed oral fights breaking up almost every hour between households full of all imaginable abuses. When both the families got tired and the solution was not in sight it would invariably end with one family declaring, 'Let Hekim Chacha come, he will judge,' and the other family agreeing to the proposal quickly, which meant, Toomba thought, Hekim Chacha was not only a *hekim*—a medicine man—but a *hakim* too—judging and arbitrating between quarrelling families.

It was a good place to live under the care of such a godly person respected by all except the mosquitoes who showed no respect to any, attacked every living being in the ratio of one to hundred, but over time one got used to them.

During the evenings after dinner Toomba would go to the Milk Colony area near the *bustee* with a group of boys and revel the night there in booze and drugs inside the shell of one of the innumerable abandoned buses lined up for ages by the side of the lanes, their engines and tires long removed.

Hekim Chacha returned from hospital after a week ahead of a procession wearing a large flower garland round his neck put over by the councillor when he left the hospital. It was afternoon; Toomba waited for him outside his hut.

Ismail introduced him to Chacha who raised his hands skyward and murmured something in prayer.

'*Allah Meherban*! He sent His man in time to save this unworthy servant of Him.'

'You're wrong Chacha, you're the God's man not me; I'm just a heathen.'

'*Tauba, tauba*! *Allah-ho-Akbar*, you'll never know in which form He will send His man.'

He took Toomba inside his hut, made him sit on a mat and said, 'Beta, this is your home, stay here as long as you want.'

'Thank you Hekim Chacha. I'll remember your kind gesture all my life. I've enjoyed living here among so many good people, but I'll leave now; I'm a roaming street boy.'

'Hekim Chacha said with a smile, 'I know Beta, Ismail told me; wanderers prefer wandering. But whenever you feel like, come here, our doors will remain open for you.'

All who gathered near the hut joined Chacha, 'Yes, yes, please come any time.'

Ismail said as he shook hands with Toomba and exchanged telephone numbers, 'Any time you need help, just give me a tinkle.'

255

Chapter 22

Preparatory work for opening *Boomba Foods* on first of *Baishak* was in full swing.
Boomba now free from drug peddling had joined the activities full time. They distributed the work among themselves: Kajol would be responsible for costing and pricing each product, and designing a menu card at least a week before the opening date. Mashi had relieved her from the Gariahat tea stall which was now being managed by the street woman who earlier did it when Mashi was away on trips.

Boomba would look after the furnishing of the stall which must be completed with all lighting arrangement and glow sign board three days before the inauguration; he would also be responsible for sourcing raw materials—decide on the quality and cost and enter into long-term arrangement wherever necessary. Kajol had given him a list of names from whom she was getting supplies for the existing tea stalls; he would start with that.

Chameli would organise publicity and campaign. A pamphlet announcing the date of opening should soon be finalised in a joint meeting of all participants. It must be attractive, colourful and printed on good quality paper, not the run-off-the-mill kind of leaflets. The first lot should be distributed a fortnight before the opening date at all the road crossings—from Rasbehari Avenue to Ballygunge railway station—at the letter boxes of the households and offices—all during the afternoon when people returned to their homes. It would be repeated the following week. Chameli had three local boys to assist her in distribution.

During the last three days all would participate in distributing the last lot of pamphlets along with menu-cum-price list to the households and offices, talk to them personally and invite them on the inauguration. For this they had divided the marketing area in three zones; Boomba, Chameli and Kajol would divide the zones among themselves.

Every day at 8:30 p.m. they met at Mashi's place to review the progress. Although Mashi was regarded as the head of the project she hardly spoke. In fact she was so impressed by their planning and organisation she thought it better not to suggest anything; she only wondered how these teens could be so meticulous.

Boomba often brought Toomba to their meetings. But he never talked, even when someone sought his opinion on an issue and others waited for his response his face remained as impassive as ever, not even a smile could be elicited from him, though on such occasions a cryptic smile appeared on Mashi's face. But none could afford getting angry with him; frustrated, yes but not angry. Once out of desperation Boomba spoke, 'You're the most intelligent person among us, we value your opinion, that's why we ask, but you never respond.'

For the first time and last time Toomba spoke.

'It's precisely for such a belief of yours I don't speak. I don't understand a thing about business, you're far better in it than I am. But if I express my opinion you'd follow blindly, and that might lead to a disaster; I don't want that to happen to you.'

Mashi's cryptic smile turned to a look of admiration.

* * * *

It was now time to finalise the list of special invitees as the date of opening was just a week ahead. It was a small list. Mashi would invite the secretary of the Hawkers Association, Officers in-charge of Gariahat and Lake Police stations; Chameli would invite other family units of Mashi.

Chameli made her first call to Bichhu. Instead of saying 'yes or no' he asked her to tell Mashi he would be coming to meet her tonight at 8:30. When Chameli conveyed the message to Mashi she asked her to shift the review meeting to stall premises.

Bichhu and Bisu came together when Banku was discussing with Mashi about a few difficult borrowers who were habitually defaulting on repayments. She dismissed Banku saying, 'Leave the matter to me, I'll take care of them.' Banku rose to leave when she added, 'They're holding the meeting at the stall premises; you may go there.' Of late Banku was taking interest in the project, might be he wanted to get some relief from the drudgery of his day to day work.

Mashi turned her eyes to Bichhu and Bisu. Their ever joyful faces looked ashen. What could it be that Bichhu could not handle? Anything gone wrong with Binni or Chikku; must be.

'Where's Binni?' Mashi asked.

'That's what we've come to discuss with you. Have you met her recently?'

'Oh yes. She came about a month back, withdrew all her savings and left.'

'You didn't ask why she needed all the money.'

'You know, I never do that.'

'Yes, she also knows it,' Bichhu said in desperation.

'She'd also withdrawn all the money from her salary account with the bank,' Bisu added.

'You're yet to tell me what had really happened,' Mashi said.

'Well yes, I didn't tell you before as you were already in great trouble: she had just vanished leaving a resignation letter on the school principal's desk which said she was leaving for a pilgrimage. The principal said he was confused: she never displayed any religious inclination before, then what's this pilgrimage suddenly.'

Bisu unable to suppress his anxiety any longer spoke, 'I haven't thought it earlier. I feel she must've been kidnapped by our enemies at the station. They had failed to uproot us, now they turned to her, an easy target. All our searches have failed. A person can't just vanish like this unless kidnapped. Let's get hold of some of them, beat them thoroughly; I'm sure they'll belch out everything.'

'No Bisu it's not a kidnapping; it's a planned disappearance, that's why we are unable to find her. She left behind her laptop and mobile phone in her hostel room which we discovered when we searched her room with the principal of the school—the entire memory of both the instruments was destroyed beyond retrieval; "A very intelligent workmanship," the forensic expert of the police remarked. All her books were stacked at the hostel room, but no letters, no notes that could give a clue except a painting on the easel, probably unfinished, full of X marks in different colours.'

'What do the police say?' Mashi asked.

'They've done all they could, sent information to all police stations with her photos including the village she originally came from, made phone calls to emphasise the importance of the case, but no information so far. They're of the same opinion as mine: it's a deliberate act.'

'Have you informed Chikku?'

'There comes the saddest part. I made calls to his mobile several times but a machine-fed voice repeated: this number does not exist. I sent him emails but all returned: mail could not be delivered to the addressee, which denotes he has changed his email ID. I sent a mail to his office and received a one line reply: he no longer works here. Frustrated, I turned to OC, GRP for help. He thought for a while, and then gave me a letter addressed to a lady at US consulate office in Kolkata. I met the woman to know the whereabouts of Chikku.

Even at his distress Bichhu could not help mimicking the entire conversation that followed.

'She was a little surprised. "Wow!" she exclaimed, "Some time back a girl also came to enquire about this gentleman. I told her he had moved to Brazil; we've no further information about him." I went back to the OC, procured a similar letter from him addressed to the Brazilian consulate. When I met the consulate officer she said, "This is the second enquiry. About a month back a girl came to know the whereabouts of this man... she was such a sweet girl I couldn't deny her request, thought she must be his lover. I procured all information about him in a week's time: he is a big shot at the largest IT company of Brazil, has married his Brazilian colleague and settled at our capital city, Brasilia,... sad... very sad... but I had to pass over the information to her... what to do? By the way, are you related to him?"

"Yes, he is my close friend and the girl, my sister and his betrothed."

Sad... very sad... Do you want to know the company he works with, their telephone number, the email ID?"

"Not now, I'll come back to you if I need them, in the meantime thank you very much."

'That was yesterday,' Bichhu concluded.

'Bastard!' Bichhu rose throwing up his hands and proceeded to the tea stall.

'So that's it,' Mashi said, 'I can understand Binni's reaction; it's a double shock for her; a woman would rather give her man to Death than to another woman.'

'But... but... I couldn't imagine Chikku... '

Mashi raised her hand and said, 'Don't convert your disdain to rancour, such things happen.'

Bichhu looked at Mashi and said, 'I understand; you know these things better than I, but what I should do now? Stop searching her?'

'Precisely. Let her be. She is an intelligent girl, planned everything before leaving. Respect her resolve to live incognito.'

* * * *

Mashi met OC Gariahat and invited him for the inauguration of *Boomba Foods*. At her request he telephoned OC Lake Police station who also agreed to be there; she had also met her personally to extend the invitation. The secretary of the Hawkers Association would not be able to make it because of his other engagements on this auspicious day, but the assistant secretary would definitely be there he assured.

The response to their publicity campaign was encouraging. At the review meeting, a day before the opening ceremony they considered the inputs from Chameli who led the publicity campaign, and estimated the sales of the inaugural evening to be around five thousand rupees.

But to be on the safe side they decided to keep a reserve of another two thousand rupees worth of foods across different varieties.

On first of Baisakh, Mashi came to the stall at 5 p.m. She had not visited the place after finalising the deal. She now had some difficulty recognising the stall; it had changed so much, now it really looked like a modern food stall—remarkably different from the road side cranny food joints in the neighbourhood. Inside, the three departments were perfectly compartmentalised, the moving areas neatly planned, the upper and bottom storages not visible from outside, neither the gas cylinders. A small sitting area for four persons had also been carved out, every inch of the space properly utilised. And all these had been done by a few boys and girls of the street! A professional interior designer would not have done better.

When the lights were on, the stall gave an impressive look that could be seen from a distance; the inside lights and the glow sign—*Boomba Foods*—illuminated the pavement and a part of the road.

People had started coming in. Boomba soon found himself busy taking orders and passing them to the counter. Delivery would be made according to the serial number of the cash memo after the stall was formally opened. At one point it became difficult for Boomba to handle the rush. Mashi took charge of the cash counter and relieved Chameli to join Boomba; Kajol followed soon.

A large crowd gathered in front of the stall when the OC, Gariahat P.S. alighted from the jeep accompanied by the OC, Lake P.S. They were seemingly overwhelmed by the look of *Boomba Foods* and the size of the crowd which now parted to provide them a passage.

Order taking now stopped. Chameli went inside and hastily taped a long red ribbon across the frontage of the stall and readied a brass candle stick with a matching oil-filled lamp, the wick soaking in it. Kajol was ready with a box of long match sticks and a scissor on a copper plate. The OC, Lake P.S. kindled the candle. The OC, Gariahat cut the ribbon amidst clapping and entered the stall with his colleague. Addressing the crowd he said he was overwhelmed by the entrepreneurship of a group of hitherto street dwellers attempting to rehabilitate themselves, he wanted others to follow their example; he also implored upon the crowd to support the enterprise. Kajol blew a conch shell which was followed by clapping from the crowd.

Mashi took the guests to the sitting area and entertained them with *lassi* and assorted foods. The assistant secretary of the Association came at 8 p.m. when crowds were at their peak. He congratulated Mashi for her enterprise and was similarly entertained.

They stopped taking orders at 11 p.m. The stall was finally closed at midnight. The cash tally was seven thousand six hundred rupees. All were exhausted but jubilant. They missed Toomba and Minu. Boomba specially requested Toomba to attend the opening ceremony with Minudi. He said he would but not sure about Minu as she was out of reach presently.

Toomba did try to attend the opening ceremony of Boomba Foods. When he got down from the bus near Rash Behari Avenue crossing at 6 p.m. and began walking toward Lake Market his mobile phone rang. It was from Minu, but instead of hearing the familiar nasal bantering tone he heard solemn voice of a lady: 'Speaking from Sky View Nursing Home. Miss Minu desires you meet her very urgently. She is in a critical condition; Cabin number 303.'

Toomba took a taxi and reached the Nursing Home at 6:15 p.m. Boomba had seen this Nursing Home many times before from bus window, also entered once to deliver a *puriah* stealthily to the cabin of a well-known industrialist. From outside it looked like a palace and inside it was more a hotel than a nursing home. Kolkata's best doctors were associated with it: best place of recuperation for the wealthiest of the city.

Toomba walked to the reception counter and enquired about Minu from the lone woman sitting there; she looked a matron by uniform, might be doubling for someone junior. She called him inside and told in a sympathetic tone, 'You might be knowing she has leukaemia... last stage... sweet girl... at such a young age!... has gifted me her mobile phone... the doctor said she might not survive the night... She insisted on a blood transfusion two days back... the doctor warned it might be fatal... she said I don't care... I can't die before I meet my Panditji. ... said the same thing time and again to the attending nurse... I don't know who is this Panditji. ... she asked me to make the last call to you from this mobile ... but you don't look like a Panditji. Are you?'

He left her, entered the lift and pressed the button for third floor.

He knocked the cabin door; a nurse opened it but was hesitant in admitting him when she heard Minu saying, 'It is okay, allow him in,' she moved aside and Toomba walked toward the bed placed in the middle of a spacious room overlooking a large water body lined by symmetrically planted trees. The nurse still had an uncertain look in her eyes. Minu told her, 'Don't worry Karunadi, he has come from my Solicitor's office. I've a will to make. Please don't disturb us. I shall press the buzzer if I need you.' Satisfied, the girl left.

'Hey, Panditji,' Minu gleamed at him.

Toomba observed her. She was lean but her face and smile were radiant as ever, even the voice had not lost that ting.

'Don't look at me like that; come here and lie by my side.'

Toomba climbed the bed and kissed her on the forehead.

'Not that childish one, kiss me deep,' she pressed his lips to hers.

They kissed a long time; Minu placed his hands on her hot breasts and Toomba began responding.

They made love, recreating every moment of their first night together. When it was finished Minu smiled that cryptic smile of hers.

'You know, I saved money all my life to die luxuriously, that way I may have a better communion with God because He also lives in luxury... And I wanted to make love to you before passing away... I'm fulfilled...'

Toomba saw Minu turning sleepy. He rose and tip-toed to the door. As he touched the door handle he heard Minu, 'Hey, Lord Vishnu.'

Toomba turned.

'Don't cry when I die. If you do, I'll be dead, twice.'

She fell asleep with a smile on her face.

* * * *

The sales graph of *Boomba Foods* was on the rise; seemed it would soon cross ten thousand rupees per day but Kajol warned against over enthusiasm and consequent overreach.

She said, 'It happens when something new comes up. It's likely that after a month average sales will taper down to say, five-six thousand rupees per day and rise only slowly thereafter. Let's not over-react but wait for a month to see at which level sales settle down, otherwise we might get saddled with unsold inventory. Of course that does not mean we shall refuse orders, but at the same time we must concentrate on developing a stable sales base, and that comes from home-deliveries and party orders.'

'Splendid! A beautiful analysis, but how could you have so much insights to a business we've just started,' Boomba spoke.

'Stupid!' Chameli admonished Boomba. 'Don't you know she had been managing two tea-cum-coffee-cum-snacks-cum-food stalls at Gariahat for more than a year? We must pay due attention to all her suggestions in matters of food business, but she must follow our advice on other matters like say, conducting her love affair with Banku.'

Kajol raised a spatula to beat her but she was already out on the street.

They campaigned for home-deliveries and party orders. A discount of ten percent was offered on orders of three thousand rupees and above. Home-deliveries picked up quickly. Party orders also trickled in—one or two per week.

One day soon after the stall opened in the morning a large white car stopped before it. Boomba came out of the stall and walked quickly to the car expecting a large order. It was. A man from the back seat asked him to bring the menu which he did. The man began placing orders. By the time he finished the total value of the order exceeded four thousand rupees. The man asked how much time they would require to deliver the order. Boomba replied: not more than an hour.

'Ok. Let me inform my office.' He put his left hand inside his pocket to find the mobile phone but it was not there.

'I must have left it at my office. May I use yours?'

Boomba hastily handed him his mobile phone. While pressing the button of his mobile he asked, 'Do you need some advance, say two thousand rupees?'

'That would be very nice.'

'Then take it.'

Boomba went closer to the man.

'Blob, blob.'

As the car sped away Boomba fell with a thud, his brains splattered on the road.

* * * *

After leaving the Sky View Nursing Home, Toomba wandered aimlessly for some time, and then boarded a bus for Belgachia. The bus screeched to a halt after it crossed Belgachia overbridge.

There was no change in the behaviour of the bus driver but the lighting arrangement of the street had improved considerably, though no Trident lamps were visible.

Toomba heard a clink-clink sound on his mobile phone announcing the arrival of a short message; might be from the Nursing Home, he thought. He pulled out the phone from his pocket. It was from Raja: supplies still irregular, consider yourself on leave for another fortnight. Delete the message after you've read it.

'Good for me,' Toomba murmured to himself and walked toward Chacha's hut.

Chacha had just finished with the the last patient when Toomba appeared before his door.

'Arrey Beta, come in; it's so good to see you again.'

Chacha called back the last patient and asked her to send dinner for two.

They ate dinner quietly. Chacha observed Toomba's somber face intently and said, 'Beta you look tired. Go to sleep now, you'll feel better tomorrow morning.'

Next day, while helping Hekim Chacha preparing herbal medicines Toomba asked, 'Chacha, is there any cure for leukaemia?'

'No Beta. If one has it, take it one has already become Allah's favourite. It's just a matter of time before His call comes. God willing, we can prolong it for some time, but cannot hold back.'

Toomba fell silent. Hekim Chacha observed him closely for some time, then spoke, 'Beta, I guess you must've lost some one very dear to you. I'd also lost my wife the same way ...may god give her peace. After her death I left everything, studied medicine to seek out a cure for this ailment, but there was none; no one can fight Allah's will.'

One night Toomba left Chacha's hut and reached Milk Colony. How many days and nights he spent there he had no recall. He revelled the night and slept during the day. His friends would wake him up when they returned from their work.

One day he rose before noon and thought it was time to go elsewhere. He finished his morning ablutions at an abandoned bus at the far end of the line, dressed up and walked toward the crossing of Raja Manindra Road and Jessore Road.

As he waited for a bus his mobile rang. It was Chameli. He pressed the answer button. At that moment a small Maruti-800 car screeched before him.

Three bullets were fired: one entered his head, second pierced through his heart. He fell, the mobile screaming 'Toomba... Toomba...' slipped from his hand; a third bullet silenced it.

Chapter 23

A year had passed in three successive deaths. The pains and pangs that accompanied these deaths had also passed, except for a few.

The street has a unique death support system, Mashi thought, which provides opportunities to die at an early age. The system also liquefies the pangs of death faster, except for those who have descended on the street from the society like her, and those who are ascending toward it like Chameli.

For Chameli it was treble mourning. For three days she did not talk to anyone, did not cry, followed the daily chores mechanically, only her eyes shone.

On the fourth day she woke up early, ate breakfast, dressed and walked towards *Boomba Foods* taking Google and Googlee with her.

She took charge of the stall as though nothing had happened. Many thought she was behaving abnormally normal, but not Kajol who felt she had resolved to keep *Boomba Foods* alive and growing. She asked Google and Googlee to participate in the activities of the stall, familiarising them with the routines of running the business.

A few days later she announced she was taking Kajol as a twenty five percent partner. Mashi did not say anything. She was watching Chameli for the last few days. She had matured fast: now a business woman with a determined look. Mashi could understand she was doing everything for Boomba—to keep him alive. And that's problematic: love turning to attachment, which bereft of consummation, would make her consumptive from within. Maybe, some day she would find a man who would sway her off to a new valley of love. But it should not be too early—let the ulcer turn a scar, but early enough before consumption took hold of her.

Mashi now spent more than half her waking time in station picnics and charitable activities. She had no imperative to return to Gariahat every day by seven thirty in the evening now that Google and Googlee came under the care of Chameli, and Kajol overseeing her two tea stalls. Taking a cue from Chameli she had made Banku a twenty five percent partner. Now he was to show her accounts only once a fortnight. But he came here almost every day, took a cup of tea at the stall, talked to Mashi a few minutes if she was there and went to *Boomba Foods*.

Mashi guessed Banku and Kajol loved each other. Perhaps Chameli knew it long before, perhaps her decision to make Kajol a twenty five percent partner was partly motivated by her desire to give her some stability in life.

She had stopped visiting Howrah station to avoid the pain of not seeing Binni sitting at her corner.

Bichhu telephoned her every week. He got back his jocular self, also revived his *harbola* skills. He would often start with a new one over phone. Last week she picked up the telephone and was startled by the loud cacophony of two warring cats.

'How was it Mashi?' he asked amidst laughter.

'*Badmash!* I got scared.' Then she also joined the laughter.

These days she yearned for his call.

One morning when she was readying herself for a trip, Bichhu telephoned.

'Mashi, please cancel your morning engagements. I'm coming.' 'But... but...' the telephone on the other side turned silent.

These days only Bichhu could order her like this, she smiled to herself.

In less than an hour Bichhu came by a taxi. He walked slowly toward Mashi holding a bundle to his chest.

He laid it softly on her lap. She looked at it and exclaimed, 'But... but... I can't take another... no.'

Two tiny eyes smiled at her. Soon a smile also appeared on her face.

'Looks like...'

'Yes. She came early this morning, dropped the child on my lap, said, "Take care of him and don't search for me," mixed herself quickly in the morning crowd of the station and vanished.'

The street always renews itself.

•••

Acknowledgements

I convey my regards to Surinder Kumar Ghai, Managing Director of Sterling Publishers (P) Limited for taking personal interest in publishing the book.

I thank Sonia Saini for editing the manuscript meticulously. She made many useful suggestions which improved presentation of several paragraphs of the book. She volunteered to write the back cover of the book that synopsised its contents. My special thanks to her for this kindness.

Proloy Mallick administered and coordinated the publishing processes of the book with patience, intelligence and kindness. I thank him for a good job done.

Number of people and institutions associated themselves in more than one way to bring the work to fruition; particular mention must be made of Research Institute for Human and Agricultural Development (RIHAD), an organisation registered with State Child Protection Society, West Bengal. I have been associated with them for more than 5 years now. My heartfelt thanks to all of them.

My wife, Gouri first noticed my going back to my first love — literature, away from my professional writings. She just smiled. My son, Saraswat and his wife, Sridevi read the first draft of the manuscript and made valuable suggestions. Daughter Orphi was, as usual, always ready to bring out a particular book from my horribly organised library: It is only she who knows where I have kept a particular book. I am sure they will all be happy when they see this book.

I admit, I might not have written the book if not due to the continuous prodding of my brother-in-law, Manik Lal Das. His insistence often angered me but he was relentless. It would be my immense pleasure to hand him a copy of The Street.